CLOSE MATCH

TRACEY JERALD

CLOSE MATCH

Editor: One Love Editing (http://oneloveediting.com)

Proof Edits: Holly Malgieri (https://www.facebook.com/HollysRedHotReviews/)

Cover Design: Madhat Studios (https://madhatbooks.com/)

Photography: Wandar Aguiar Photography, LLC

Models: Andrew Biernat and Ivenise Ruidiaz

For the nights with Arbor Mist, Diet Pepsi, and conversations on porches while covered in blankets.

For never ending support, ceaseless laughter, and courage under fire.

And finally, for butterflies, birds, and dragonflies. For the way they seamlessly entwine and the circle of miracles they wrought that I give thanks for every day of my life.

So, with that in mind, this book is dedicated to James and Mady. May every star you wish upon give you what you need. It may not be perfect, but it will be close.

WHAT IS IT ABOUT STARS?

Stars represent the most beautiful and impactful objects in the night sky. Their brilliance on the dark sky has been documented as far back as Ovid, their legends further than that. Their glow has been used to trace the history, dynamics, and evolution of man.

We are fascinated by the stars. We spend hours watching those overhead as well as those that link above the social norms to form their own kind of constellation—celebrities.

But what makes them more omnipresent? Greek mythology lures us with tales that say stars were tossed into the sky at the whims of the gods and goddesses. Is it because stars appear to shine brighter and have the force to overpower anything, even when in reality they are made of the same particles of dust we all are?

Within our chaotic lives, we look to the stars—all kinds—to present a reassuring order to our lives. But do we rely on them too often for the emotional power history has given to them, a power that has not been verified through science?

Do we rely on them to save our wishes, hopes, and dreams much like the way we do our gods, our celebrities, and our heroes?

PROLOGUE

Prologue - Evangeline

P

"AND THE WINNER of the Tony Award for Best Leading Actress in a Musical is Evangeline Brogan for Thea in *The Dream Sequence!*"

Stunned, shaking, I push myself to my feet. Hugs and kisses are being laid on me by my cast members, my mother, but I don't even know if I'm smiling.

Dreams should be harder to attain than just wishing for them in my heart late at night.

Numbly, I make my way up the stage. It seems to take forever, but the reality is it's only a few seconds. Hardy Martin, last year's winner for Best Leading Actor, comes down the few steps to take my hand. Carefully, I lift the edge of my siren red dress so I don't trip on the fluted edge. My hand is tucked protectively in the crook of

Hardy's arm as I climb up the four short steps. "Smile, Evangeline. Be proud of what you've done."

And that's when it hits me. I won the Tony. My knees almost buckle at the exact moment the presenter hands me the squatty little statue. I grip it tightly as I turn to face the audience, who are sitting cheek and jowl to the rafters at Radio City Music Hall.

"I left my purse with something resembling a speech back at my seat," I blurt out. A reassuring titter floats through the room. My eyes seek out and find my mother's in the crowd. She's never let me down. Not once.

And I know at the most crucial moment of my life she's not about to start.

"I guess this is why they recommended an improv class during my senior year at NYU," I joke. "So, first, thank you to my alma mater, the Tisch School of Performing Arts at New York University." A smatter of cheers from other NYU grads as well as generous applause. Taking a deep breath, I go on. "*The Dream Sequence* would not have been possible without our amazing director, Pasquale Beecher—." Raucous cheering from the cast of *The Dream Sequence* ensues. I let it die down before I lean back in toward the mic. "—and the brilliant cast, crew, and orchestra, who are simply flawless every single night." My eyes fill with tears as I see my theater family give me an impromptu standing ovation in the middle of my acceptance speech. "But above all, I have to thank my actual family. Dad, I..." My voice chokes up. I hold the statue aloft. "I wish you were here sitting next to Mom and Bris to see this. I hope you're proud. Mom, Bris, you are my anchors in this crazy storm called life. I don't know what I would do without you. This is for you. Thank you for supporting my dreams, for making sure that while I chased them, I'm still grounded, and for loving me through it all. And to the theater community as a whole, you have my heartfelt gratitude. Again, thank you."

I step back and hear the combined pounding of seats slapping against their chairs as people rise to clap.

It's humbling.
It's enormous.
It's only the beginning.

ACT 1 - ARE YOU SURE?

ONE

EVANGELINE

MAY

The Fallen Curtain - All About Evangeline Brogan
Evangeline Katherine Brogan is more than just a star on Broadway;
she's the sun it orbits around.
Although she's been singing and dancing since a very young age, she's
been quoted as saying it wasn't until she was first in a production of
The Wizard of Oz *playing the role of Auntie Em that she felt her*
calling. Early in her career, she acted in small roles Off Broadway
under an alias until she graduated from New York University's Tisch
School of the Arts with a Bachelor of Fine Arts in Drama.
Her first breakthrough role happened at twenty-four when she
auditioned for the role of Lisa Rhodes in Best Thing *at the City*
Theater Workshop. The show was so popular, the entire cast was
moved to Broadway. That year she was nominated for the Tony Award
as Best Featured Actress in a Musical against her mother, Brielle
Brogan, making them the second mother/daughter in history behind
Jennifer Ehle and Rosemary Harris to earn that distinction. Including
Lynne Redgrave and Natasha Richardson as well as Richard Rodgers
and his daughter Mary Rodgers (for composing), they were one of only

four families in history with the distinction of competing against one of their relatives for the same category.

Following her success of Best Thing, *Evangeline's been seen in revivals of* Anything Goes, *where she said, "It's a production near and dear to my heart as Mom named me for the character she portrayed while she was pregnant with me." She's been cast in* Chicago, *where she gave new meaning to sultry in her revival of Velma Kelly's character. She even did a short stint with the New York City Ballet saying, "I can't let my skills get rusty," when questioned why she'd join the corps versus going for another Broadway spotlight appearance. Brogan jumped at the chance to sing on the cast album of* Best Thing. *Her solo of "Anywhere, Anything" garnered her a Grammy nomination and win. Her humbling speech thanked her fellow castmates and her family was much like the woman herself: emotional and authentic.*

Although she was going to take some time off to travel, it's reported the director of The Dream Sequence *begged her to read for the part of Thea. Rumor has it she jumped onto the stage partway through, stealing the role from the actress who became her understudy. It was the right move as her performance won her the 2014 Tony Award for Best Leading Actress in a Musical.*

Taking a break to watch her younger sister graduate with honors from Wharton Business School, Brogan decided to spread her wings across the pond, accepting the part of Laurey to Simon Houde's portrayal of Curly. The two's revival of the Rodgers and Hammerstein classic brought down the house night after night in the Royal Albert Hall production of Oklahoma!. *Their chemistry onstage was outrageous, and Broadway was fortunate when it returned with them to the US when they both came back to star in* She *where Evangeline lost out on the Tony to her mother, who won for her role in* Powerhouse *that same year.*

Finally, Broadway—and the musical brilliance of four-time Tony Award composer John Thomas Michaels—put these two brilliant actresses together. In 2018, Evangeline and Brielle took the stage

together in the sold-out Miss Me, *with Evangeline in the starring role*
as Kate Hynes. This all-star cast also includes Simon Houde as her
love interest, Michael Kirby.
This musical—about a falling-out between a mother and her daughter
—is expected to sweep the 2019 Tony Awards. Nominations will be
announced on April 30 with the live broadcast from Radio City Music
Hall on CBS June 7.

"**D**id you see this?" Bristol slides her iPad across the table
to me.

"You know I don't read that stuff, Bris." I shove it back
at her. "Why are you showing it to me?"

"Because this one's a halfway decent article on you. They're not
gossiping about you beating out Michelle for the role in *The Dream
Sequence.* They're not saying you and Mom are scratching each
other's eyes out onstage. And best yet, they're not saying you're
having a flaming affair with Simon." She rolls her eyes.

I grin at her. "That's your favorite part." Ever since I treated
Bristol to a trip to England to see me act in *Oklahoma!*, she and
Simon have been inseparable. America should consider itself lucky
that Simon tumbled head over feet over my baby sister, or juicy role
or not, he'd still be in London. Gossips assume it was because of our
"magnetic stage presence." I chortle every time I think about it.

We both must be better actors than we let on. After all, when you
individually eat onion- and cilantro-riddled food before going onstage
for your big romance scene, it's all you can do to not laugh at each
other. Or deliberately burp in each other's faces. Yet, night after
night, our "sexual tension" keeps receiving rave reviews and amusing
Bristol to no end. Since she's long dealt with our onstage romance,
she delights in slapping a cup of mouthwash in Simon's hand before
she'll even come near him after a show.

Especially now.

"How are you feeling?" I ask her. Bristol is about six weeks pregnant. Neither Simon, she, nor I have said anything knowing the gossip rags—much like the one she is trying to make me read—are going to go insane when they realize who the father is.

"Fantastic so long as Simon doesn't come near me until he's brushed his teeth about eight times," she mutters in disgust.

I heft my water glass in the air. "To morning sickness."

She clinks hers back. "To everything sickness, when it comes to cilantro." We both burst out laughing.

"It must be from Dad. Mom loves that stuff." I'm laughing as I peruse a menu I should have memorized already. We're at Wolf's Delicatessen at least once a month. Their pastrami on rye is one of the few luxuries I'll allow myself while I'm onstage.

"Mom loves it, but nothing like Simon does. I swear, he'd make it another food group if he could," Bristol agrees. "I know it's just a stage kiss, but how you don't vomit in his mouth night after night..."

"That's why they call it acting, darling." We both turn. Even at sixty-three, our mother turns heads everywhere she goes. "Scoot over, Bris. And tell me why your iPad is on the table. Didn't I teach you better manners than that?"

I shoot my sister an amused sneer before I answer for her. "She wants me to read some piece of garbage that was written about me this morning."

My mother sighs. "It appalls me you never read your own press."

"Probably because most of the time I'm reading about the fact we all hate each other?" I arch a perfectly groomed eyebrow.

"Linnie, that's half the fun." I shake my head at my mother in amusement.

"Mom, you just like having gossip to spread on set," I retort.

She shrugs. Guilty. "Only when I can substantiate it, darling. And besides, I know which one of my daughters is pregnant."

Bristol and I exchange horrified looks. "Tell me someone's not..." I whisper, leaning forward.

"Darling, if you didn't want the rumor mill to start, you should have let me go with your sister to her first appointment."

"She'd have had to have delayed it, Mom! You were flying in from Paris," I snap.

Mom shrugs. She's still pissed I got to see her first grandchild before she did. Not that she didn't march Bristol back to the OBGYN the next day to make her do to it again, but did the paparazzi follow her? No, of course not. They wouldn't dare follow Brielle Brogan.

It's just me.

I grab my oversized Louis Vuitton, stick my head into it, and scream. Since it's New York, no one pays me any attention, not even Mom or Bristol, who are chattering away. I catch the tail end of their conversation even as I manage to get something caught in my hair as I remove my head from my purse.

"...swear this one is actually a good article."

"Let me see it." My mother holds out her hands. Bristol unlocks her iPad.

"Are we still talking about that damn article?" I demand as I untangle my Mont Blanc from the end of my hair.

My mother hushes me. "Let me read this." Knowing there is no choice, I toss the pen back in my bag and do what my mother tells me. "This is a decent article, Linnie."

Crap, when Mom sounds impressed, I know I'll have to read it. "Give it to me." I hold out my hand. Scrolling to the top, I scan it. Scrolling down, I frown. "What the...who is this person? Courtney Jackson? This is the most legit article I've read about myself since I was twenty-four and was actually in *Best Thing*," I admit.

"I don't know, but I'd pass this along to your agent. This is the kind of person you want in your corner," Mom advises me.

She's not wrong. One of the things they don't teach you at school is how to deal with fame. Likely because they don't think you're going to get very far, I surmise. But the problems that can occur when you're young and trying to deal with the media can be outrageous. If I didn't have my mother providing me guidance along the way, I'd be in much worse shape than I am.

Just as I'm about to thank both her and Bristol, Mom mutters, "I need to tell them to drop the heat in here. I understand it's still cool out, but still. This is ridiculous."

Bristol and I exchange worried looks. "Mom, it's not that hot in here," I contradict her.

"It's really not."

"Do you see us old people sitting around with hats and sweaters on?" she snaps. "That means it's too hot in here."

"First off, you're not old. And second..." I don't get to number two before my mother—ever the diva—stops a passing waiter.

"Excuse me, young man," He blinks at her a few times before his eyes light in recognition.

"Wow, you're Brielle Brogan." He's practically genuflecting. I roll my eyes at Bristol and reach for my coat. We're about to be frozen out of the restaurant.

"Indeed, I am." Mom shoots him the dazzling smile I inherited. "I'm a touch warm. Would it be possible to turn down the heat?"

"Of course, Ms. Brogan. Would it..." He looks away before squaring his shoulders.

Here we go, I think to myself.

"Would it be possible to ask for a quick photo? I took my mother to see *Powerhouse*. She said it was the best gift I ever gave her. She'll never believe you come in here like regular folks."

My mother jumps up. "It's no trouble at all..."

"Lance."

"Lance. In fact, if you give me your name and a good day, I'll make sure you have tickets to my new show waiting for you and your mother waiting at the box office."

He's stunned. Truly. "But *Miss Me* is sold out for months."

"I think my daughter—" She nods at me. Lance's eyes flash over and widen even further. He doesn't scream or cause a scene, which I give him credit for. "—and I can pull a few strings."

And then for the second time in one day, the unexpected happens.

"Ms. Brogan, you're tremendous, but I couldn't take those seats away from someone who's waited months to see you. It'd be an honor just to get a quick picture with you. I promise I won't post it online or anything. But let me get that air adjusted first." Lance is about to scurry off when I stop him.

"Lance." He stops at the sound of my husky voice. "Mom and I have a box that we can give away tickets to. If we don't, they sell at the last minute. You're not taking the seats away from anyone. Let her do this for you."

My mom smiles at me in approval.

Damn, when did I become so jaded by life that I forgot about the humanity of the people beyond the stage lights?

"I...I..." Lance is staring at me now like I just worked a miracle.

"How about that air? And maybe some fresh water? Then swing by with your schedule for Mom," I encourage him.

It's like I'm releasing him from a trance. He dashes off, weaving around busy waitstaff who are carrying sandwiches the size of my forearm. Once he's out of earshot, I lean in and ask, "Should we shock him by leaving backstage passes with his tickets at will call?"

Mom, who's still fanning herself, falls into Bristol laughing. "That's my girl," she roars.

Bristol just grins at both of us.

God, I love my family even as they drive me crazy.

I don't know what I would do without them.

TWO

EVANGELINE

Hours later, we're standing in Saks so Mom can find a new Judith Leiber clutch. Mom has an obsession with the crystal clutches and builds her look for the Tony Awards around them. I've already convinced her that the one that looks like a ball and chain isn't quite the look she's going for. Bristol had to make a run for the ladies' room when they pulled one that looked like an enormous tomato out from the case. When she came back, I didn't even have to ask. "It reminds me of salsa. And that reminds me of..."

"Cilantro," we both say together before laughing hysterically. Our mother rolls her eyes before turning her attention back to the saleswoman.

"Okay, girls, I'm down to three," she announces. Laid out on velvet are a crystal ice cream cone, a red-and-white-striped popcorn holder—with the popcorn, of course—and a teddy bear that—I narrow my eyes—has the face of a gummy bear.

"Not the ice cream," Bristol says immediately. I agree, but I want to hear her reason with my temperamental mother. Then again, as an investment banker for UBS, she is calm, brilliant, and logical. It's one of the many reasons Simon, Mom, and I trust her with our investments.

"Why?" Mom's pouting. Of course, the most flamboyant of the bunch was her favorite.

"Because the jewels on the bottom don't scream elegance to me. If anything, Mom, it looks a bit"—she lowers her voice—"juvenile." Mom's appalled. She immediately pushes the superfluous bling of the ice cream sundae purse to the side. The salesperson calmly puts it back in the case, knowing someone will buy it.

Bristol is smooth. Mentally, I give her a high five. Mom embraces her age and wisdom. She lords it over us. She thinks the silver streaks left artfully in her hair make her look regal. There is no greater insult than to tell her she looks like a teeny-bopper.

Down to two.

I step in. "Mom, I think the popcorn is cliché," I say bluntly. "You're going to a theater awards show. You don't want them to write that about you in the press."

She shudders. Using a nail, she pushes the velvet with the popcorn clutch away. "This one was actually the one I liked the least." Her voice has a bit of a whine to it.

Bristol and I exchange looks. "Just think, by the time you carry this, everyone's going to know you're going to be a grandmother," I whisper.

Mom turns her head, and her blue eyes meet my green ones. They have tears forming. "I never thought of that."

My lips tip up. "You'll be the talk of the red carpet carrying that bag in a dark purple gown, making everyone wonder boy or girl," I murmur.

"I raised such smart girls," she declares. And she did raise us on our own after our father died of lung cancer when we were young. It was horrible because there were practically no symptoms. As far back as I can remember, he was coughing and wheezing, but we attributed it to his asthma. No one knew until it was too late and his illness was too far advanced. In some ways, it was merciful; in so many others, it led to years of guilt.

For all of us.

Leaning over, I kiss her on the cheek. "Now, can we get out of here? We have a show to get ready for."

Turning back to the salesperson, she announces, "This is it, young man."

"Will that be on a Saks account?"

Bristol steps in. "No, American Express." Muttering to herself, she adds on, "Like I'd let her get a Saks account with what they charge for interest."

I grin. What can you do?

Prepare for the show to go on. That's what.

"UGH, what did you put in your mouth tonight?" I mutter in disgust as Simon and I make our way off stage right.

He throws a dazzling smile at me, and his noxious breath almost knocks me into the red velvet curtain when he says, "Cilantro and ginger hummus. It was del—"

I slap my hand over his mouth. "Stop talking. Right now. Until you get a breath mint, I swear, you can't speak."

"We eth ogo un eery ecs, aril," he mumbles behind my hand. I have no idea what the hell he said. Nor do I particularly care.

"I thought I told you not to—" He licks my hand. Ew, gross. Now my fingers are going to smell like that soapy crap for the rest of the night.

"We go on in less than thirty seconds, darling." Stopping a stagehand, he calmly asks for a breath mint. Our antics are legendary by now to the stagehands. We're both unsurprised when he's handed both a mint and a breath strip for his tongue. He begins chomping down on the mint in my ear.

Gah! That sound is like nails being run down a chalkboard. I loathe the sound of food being eaten so vocally. It drives me insane.

"I hate you," I declare, in this moment genuinely meaning it.

"No, you don't," he says confidently. His arm slips around my waist as we wait for our cue.

No, I don't. Simon is like a brother to me. He's been my friend for forever in a business where there are too few of them. When we met in London, our only goal was to see how hard we could push the other to laugh on stage. Our genuine enjoyment for each other and the show translated to our characters. Together, we've become theater gold.

When Bristol came over to visit me, I almost fell over myself watching him try to charm my baby sister. He went from being this giant goofball I joked around about over FaceTime to this pompous peacock strutting around, trying to get noticed. It wasn't until I downed a sandwich made of tomato, mozzarella, and onion—accidentally forgetting to brush my teeth—that Simon dropped the act backstage. What he didn't realize was Bristol was standing there for his little tantrum.

"You did that on purpose," he'd accused me.

"I swear I didn't," But I couldn't keep the laughter out of my voice.

"All week I've been trying to impress your sister. Tonight, she's here, and it was all I could do to prevent barfing in your mouth."

I snickered right in his enraged face. "Trust me. You haven't impressed her much."

"You're just mean." He sniffed the air before groaning. "For the love of all that's holy, someone get her a breath mint!"

I was sure my laughter could be heard in the front row. "You don't like onions?"

"Not when you must have eaten the whole damn thing like an apple."

"Hmm, too bad. I don't think Bris brushed before the show either, did you, darling?" I looked around Simon's shoulder at my sister, who was doing all she could to contain her laughter.

Simon's face paled right before he spun on his heel. Before he could get his mouth open, Bris slid her hands up against his chest and kissed him lightly on the lips. I know for damn certain she ate exactly what I did, but did Simon utter a word? Nope.

"Maybe they don't taste quite that bad" was what he whispered.

It was the first and last time he ever missed a cue.

While Bristol overlooked their auspicious beginning, it was the declaration of our halitosis war anytime we have a scene onstage where our lips are forced to meet. Since we're often cast as romantic leads, that can be every damn night. I vow I'm going to find the most grotesque onion-laced cheese I can find for tomorrow's performance.

As we take our bows later, I realize it's been two fabulous years of working with a man who's become my closest friend outside of my blood family. I wouldn't trade a second for the world.

As he escorts me from the stage, he grins. "I knew that combo would get you."

Elbowing him in the ribs, I grumble, "It's going to be my luck your kid's going to come out farting cilantro."

Simon laughs. "Are you going out tonight?"

I shake my head.

"You're passing up a night at Redemption? Marco will be devastated," he teases me. Simon's older brother owns a nightclub located on the edges of Manhattan in an area called Fort Washington. Luxurious doesn't begin to describe it. The minute you step inside, you're sucked into seductive temptation. Between the crushed velvet, the spotlights glancing off the exquisite crystal chandeliers, and a sound system that makes music pulsate through your blood when you take to the floor, it's a playground for the bored and beautiful.

I dismiss Simon's not-so-veiled attempt to hook me up—again—with his brother. He'd love nothing better than to see two of his favorite people happy together. It's just not there. Don't get me wrong. Marco Houde is devastatingly handsome, and he's not faking the refined smoothness Simon tried to use to win Bristol's heart. He just is that way. But it does nothing for me. Marco gave it a half-hearted shot, not that I'll ever admit that to Simon. We quickly decided we were better great friends who would eventually become family.

"*C'est la vie,*" I say, dismissing Simon's overly dramatic eye roll. "He probably just needs some quality time with his brother."

"You never gave him a chance." He raises his voice dramatically. Several people stop.

Pulling away from him, I raise the back of my hand to my forehead. "But darling, somewhere out there is a love just for me. A man who will see only me when he looks at me..." I frown as if I've forgotten my line.

He slaps his hand over his mouth to cover his laugh. When he's able to speak, he dons a British accent and snootily decrees, "Sixth toe?"

"Yes! My sixth toe. You couldn't deal with it, you roué! You left me for my sister, damn you!" I go stomping off toward my dressing room to a round of applause from the backstage crew. When I reach the door, my mother has sidled up to Simon. She's flushed but grinning like a lunatic. "Bravo, darling!" she calls out.

I bow with a flourish before sweeping into the room to cream off the heavy stage makeup. It isn't until the door closes behind me that I collapse in a fit of giggles. It's nice to see that the crazy is genetic in this family. Bristol and Simon's baby doesn't stand a chance.

THREE

MONTAGUE

"That was a brilliant show," my mother says to my stepfather, Everett.

"I can't believe you managed to score tickets, son." Ev thumps me on the shoulder. "That's one hell of an anniversary gift."

"You guys deserve it," I say gruffly. It's true. Ev and my mother have been married twenty-five years this weekend. My father—better known as my sperm donor—has been out of our lives since long before I was even born. With everything that's been going on in Mom and Ev's lives, I didn't want to miss the opportunity to take them to New York City where they first met when Ev came to town for a work conference. He was the brains behind an internet startup giant; my mother worked for the hotel the conference was being held at. They'd had an instant connection which my mother assumed would end when the software mogul realized she had a child.

She was wrong.

Everett Parrish turned the same intensity he used to build one of the world's biggest internet companies toward Charlotte Sanderson and her twelve-year-old son. Within months of dating, he convinced my mother to move to Northern Virginia. Within a year, they were engaged. Six months later, they were married. And fourteen months after meeting him, at the age of fourteen, Ev asked me if I wanted him to find my biological father, to find out if there was a man there worth knowing. I told him I didn't care about him; he was only a bunch of cells that formed half my DNA. The only reason to find the cell donor would be if Ev planned on making him give up his rights to my real dad—the only time I've called Ev that.

And he did.

I was sixteen when my name legally changed to Montague Parrish. I owe everything to my mother, a woman with a love of Shakespearean theater who gave up her dreams of the stage when she realized she was pregnant with me. Instead, she saddled me with the need to be able to defend myself at an early age with a name like Montague, despite my insistence at shortening it to Monty. So, in the end, she did what she needed to do to give me everything.

I'm just grateful she found her soul mate in the man walking along the street with us. Taking them to New York to celebrate their wedding anniversary was nothing.

I'd give them anything if I thought it would bring this kind of joy to their faces.

We walk companionably, the petite half-Italian woman, the tall Irishman she fell in love with, and me—the man who could pass for their biological son even if I'm not. I inherited my mother's dark hair and hazel-colored eyes. And most people, unless they know I was adopted by Ev in my teenage years, assume I inherited his height. I can only guess that's from the cell donor's DNA, but I really don't care. I have no desire to find out anything about him. Frankly, between my Mom and Ev, I've never missed his presence in my life.

It's not like anything he's given me has ever impacted the way I live. And it's not the money or influence Ev brought into our lives; it's the stability and the support. The love he showered on Mom and me.

Which is why, deep down, I wanted to give them this memory. I'm terrified of all the ones we're facing.

"The redhead on stage was amazing. I think I'm going to steal her away just so she can sing to me every day," my father deadpans. Mom elbows him in the ribs.

"No comment," I say drolly. But my mind drifts back to "Kate." Her long red hair curled down her back as she sang and danced all night. Even from our seats, you could tell she was flirty, shy, and passionate. But her voice...wow. Her voice blew the doors off the place. To get tickets, I had to be seated apart from my parents, something I was grateful for as listening to her husky tones immediately made me hard. When she started singing, I thought my legs might cramp trying to hide my reaction in the tight theater seats.

Nothing has ever affected me quite the way that voice did. And since I gave my small binoculars to my parents—which Ev said my mother hogged all night—I never saw her face. I even, stupidly, passed up one of the Playbills they offer when you walk in the door. I whimsically think about looking her up when we get home. But suddenly, Ev wobbles, Mom starts to lose her balance in the heels she's wearing, and I forget everything but what's happening in front of me. "Geez, old man. Did you drink too much during the intermission?" I joke.

"You know how I get with soda, Monty. Can't hold my caffeine." His voice is laced with humor. But his eyes are tired. It's a good thing we're only a few blocks from The Monkey Bar where we're having a late dinner otherwise I'd have insisted on hailing a cab.

I'll be sure to on our way back to the hotel.

"Come on, Ev." Mom sidles up on the other side of him. "I hear this place will give you an entire bowl of fresh whipped cream with your cappuccino."

He wiggles his brow at her. "Think we can get one to go?"

"Seriously? Gross." I shake my head. Ev barks out a laugh that can be heard over the traffic that's like white noise to city-goers. Ev's and my eyes collide briefly before we both grin. I pretend to back away before declaring, "I'm putting an official ban on sex talk. Do you both hear me? If you want to have a night out, I'll go back to the hotel."

Ev reaches out and snags Mom around the waist. Leaning down, he murmurs into her ear. Her face softens. Laying her hands on his biceps, she rolls to the balls of her feet. Brushing a kiss on his lips, she says, "I love you too. But let's stop torturing the poor boy. Right now, let's eat. If I were that redhead, I'd be ready for a steak right now. So, on her behalf, I'm going to eat one."

And with that perfectly woman logic, we make our way down the street to get my mom her steak.

And her bowl of whipped cream.

THE NEXT MORNING, I've just helped my mother and Ev into a horse-drawn carriage near Central Park. As dorky as it may seem, they wanted the romantic clop around the famous Manhattan landscape. And I wanted time alone with my thoughts.

Ev's not getting any better. All the money he has and ultimately, nothing will save him.

I'm not paying any attention, so I'm startled when a warm body brushes by a bit too close. I'm about to blast out something to warn the runner when I get a good look at her. I can't help but notice her sleek legs as she runs by, oblivious to the stares she's earning from more than just me. Her dark hair dances almost down to a perfectly shaped ass. The skin that's not covered by her T-shirt is like the palest porcelain. My body immediately begins to tighten in interest. Then I shake my head ruefully. What is it about the women in this city? Is there something magical about them? Maybe you can't see the stars in the night sky over the cityscape because it's being poured onto the women who inhabit the city below it. I wish I had the time to find out.

Unfortunately, today's our last full day in the city. The sooner we get back home, the better. Ev will be more comfortable. Mom can get back to her routine. And me? I can finish moving out of my apartment in DC back to the farm where I can be closer to my family.

Leaving my job to move back to the farm was an easy decision for several reasons, one that I'm glad was ultimately taken out of my hands. Now I can be there for more than just the occasional days off. It will be good to be able to give Mom and Ev the support they need.

Checking my watch, I lament the fact it's only eight in the morning. It's way too early for a drink. Then I remember our hotel serves mimosas with breakfast, and I perk up a bit. If I'm going to suffer a day of sightseeing with my family, I'm going to need something to sustain me. Leaning against the stone pillar, I pull out my phone. It seems like just moments, but between debating between the breakfast buffet or eggs Benedict at the Palm Court and answering a few emails for the team keeping things together back home, it's closer to a half-hour before I realize the carriage containing the two most important people in the world has come to a stop in front of me. Mom and Ev step out looking as in love now as they did when they first met. I hope the memory of this gives them enough strength to carry them through what I know is to come.

If not, they're welcome to whatever of mine is left.

FOUR

EVANGELINE

After I finish my lap around Central Park, I dash past my doorman, waving. Punching the PH button and typing in my code, I pull out my phone. I have about an hour until my first class at the Broadway Dance Center. That leaves me just enough time to grab a quick shower, get a bite, and make my way there.

There are some habits that I can't break, no matter how successful I've become. If I want to keep the pack of eager young actresses at bay, I have to be at the top of my game not only vocally but physically. It's why I'll leave the nights out clubbing to the younger cast members. Me? Even during performances, I keep up a steady routine of running three times a week, and every Monday I spend all day in the studio fine-tuning my moves.

Without fail.

Dropping my running gear on the way to my en suite bathroom, I'm startled when the phone in my hand rings. It's my agent, Sepi. "Hey, what's up?" Sepi's represented me since I was in college.

"How do you feel about London again after the run of *Miss Me?*"

Laughing, I turn on the knobs to heat the water. "Not happening. Bris's pregnant."

"Really? Oh my God! I'll have to send her something." Sepi is one of the few members of our inner circle we trust, so I know Bristol won't care that I shared her news.

"Not yet. She refuses to let us buy her anything until the twelve-week mark."

"When's that?"

"In about six more weeks."

"Then she should start expecting regular deliveries after that," Sepi continues smoothly.

"Can I put you on speaker? I'm going to be late for class if I don't shower." Pressing a few buttons, I step in and sigh in happiness. Sepi chuckles.

"It amazes me and appalls me how regimented you are."

"Why? Because you're not?" Sepi gave up her regimented work-outs after her third child was born.

"No, because you still look like you did when you graduated college, and I look close to our age," she retorts.

I grin and am rewarded with a mouthful of water. Sputtering, I ask, "Was that the only offer?"

"There's a record deal on the table."

"Cast recording?"

"Actually, no." I pause in the act of soaping my body to stare at the phone.

"Seriously?"

"They weren't sure what. The record company pitched Christmas music, but that's so trite..."

"Lullabies," I murmur. "And children's music. What about something like that?"

There's silence on the other end of the line, which is always a good sign. "I'll get back to them and let you know. Great idea, Evangeline."

"I have a pretty great inspiration these days." There's a thousand-watt smile that can be heard in my voice.

"I completely understand that. I'll let you go for now. We'll talk soon." Sepi hangs up while I'm already thinking of songs I could record. I think of all the music my mother sang to Bristol and me as kids and just smile.

This is going to work out beautifully.

FOUR HOURS LATER, I'm gasping to catch my breath. I may not ever get to record the album because I might be dead, I think ruefully. I feel like that character in *Monty Python and the Holy Grail* whose arms and legs have been cut off. It was supposed to be an advanced class in stiletto heels—it wasn't supposed to feel like I'd just run the Marine Corp Marathon in Louboutins.

My calves feel like they're on fire. My ankles are so shaky they're about to give out at any moment. I'm seriously debating whether or not I want to call an Uber to get me the mile back to my home and on the way, call my personal masseuse and demand he meet me at my condo in the two hours I imagine it will take the car to navigate the city's traffic at this time of the day.

I let out a small whimper and pray no one hears as I slide down the wall. My ass lands on my heels before I can reach my hand down far enough to touch the oak floors. If I could find the strength and an object sharp enough, I'd gladly slide it into Madame Veronica Solomone's heartless body on behalf of the other students heaped in a similar fashion around the room.

"You all are woefully out of shape," she declares, twirling around on the ball of her foot. I wait for some brave soul to stick out their leg and trip her. They'd have fifteen witnesses swearing it was an accident.

Some naive woman speaks up. I think she's in *The Lion King*, but right now, I'm not even sure of my name. I may have to look at my driver's license for my address. "I am in excellent shape. You, Madame, have unrealistic expectations."

Well, that was a mistake. Never, *never* challenge Madame on her routines.

Madame Solomone strides around the room on heels so high I feel amateurish in the four-and-a half-inch shoes I'm wearing. Contorting my body left and right, I begin loosening the joints in my hips and knees. I tune out the angry words. It isn't until I hear a snapped "Brogan!" that I straighten. Madame is standing in front of me, impatiently. Sliding my sore legs back under me, I stand up wordlessly.

"Front and center. Start at the beginning." She bites off the words. "Stefano, you will partner her." She nods at her assistant, who begins the music from the beginning as her male choreographer joins me on the dance floor to my back left.

The rest of the class scrambles on tired, aching legs to get a seat for the show. Selena Gomez starts playing. Slow hip roll, knee lift into a ball change. Stefano's hands slide between mine as I go up on the balls of my feet in first position, then plié, and his hands hold my thighs out wide. Shoving him back, I spin out, one hand sliding between my sweat-soaked sports bra, the other covering my face coquettishly. With a toss of my hair and a devilish smile that hides the aches, I sway my hips back and forth, grand plié, and jump all while in heels about as high as I wear to the Tony's. Twisting, Stefano comes up behind me as I thrust my hips backward, the hipsters I'm wearing accenting the way he grabs my hips before dragging my body upward until my arms circle around his neck. My back is to his front, adding additional force when he spins me out for a series of chaines turns. They're made even harder in the stilettos I'm wearing. I have to rise even higher on the balls of my feet to give the impression of lift and to prevent twisting my ankle.

Stefano strides to meet me at the end of my turns, wrapping me in his strong arms. I want to shove his gross sweaty body away, and I think, *Why not? As long as I sell it...* With a smirk, I push a hand into his chest. His eyes narrow down at me as I turn what's supposed to be a duet into a solo. Double pumping my arms as I drop into another grand plié, I lunge left and drag my fingers up my leg before I spin in a full circle to the hoots and hollers of my classmates. My arm flies into the air as I step back—ball change—and come face-to-face with an angry choreographer. Mentally shrugging, I throw myself back into the routine, two full body waves before dragging my thumb up down between my breasts, over my bared stomach, and across my center, before grabbing Stefano's hand.

"Think you can manage the fouettés?" he hisses. "You were off before."

Bastard. He lifts me, letting me slide against his muscled body. Hitting the note right on, I begin to pirouette. The class cheers as Stefano assumes an arrogant pose near me. My leg flies out. I'm grateful I wore the shoes with the ankle straps so my shoes don't take out a random gawking passerby. One, two, three, four, I tuck my leg in and twirl on both feet to get my bearings right before I stop and pose.

I did it. I have no idea if it looked good or not, but I managed to get through that sadistic routine without breaking something.

Stefano gets in my face. "If you change my routine again, I will have you barred from this class."

I sneer, "The way I danced it is what I felt. This isn't the stage."

He puffs up. "It's my stage."

I roll my eyes. He goes to open his mouth when Madame interrupts him. "It is good, is it not, when the students become passionate about what we do, my pet?" She smooths a hand down his sweaty shoulder. "Isn't that true?"

I must be a better actress than I thought because my face doesn't move a muscle knowing Veronica and Stefano are lovers. I still stand there waiting.

"Dancing isn't your true passion, Evangeline." I acknowledge her truth with a nod, because why deny it. Dancing is simply another way of expressing myself on the stage. "But that was a joy to watch, nonetheless."

"Thank you, Madame."

The barest smile crosses her mouth. "Now you may go collapse against the wall. The rest of you..." Her voice pitches higher. "Rise. Until you can dance, you will at least stand."

The combined groans and muffled sounds of pain soften my own as I slide down against the wall. I'm slipping the strap from around my ankle when I feel something cold tap against my shoulder. The plastic water bottle touching my overly warm skin feels wonderful. I follow the line of it to meet Stefano's dark eyes. "She's overly critical. While I was right"—arrogant ass, I think with humor—"you danced perfectly. You could dance anywhere, Evangeline. Even now. They"—he nods out to the dance floor—"don't have the heart you do. Don't lose it."

Reaching up, I tug the water from his hands. "Thanks, Stef." Knowing the pride he takes in his craft, I offer up my version of an apology. "The music just took me over."

He grins before tousling my hair. "You were out to shove the dance down our throats for making you move from your comfy wall."

Too true. "Did it work?" I bat my long eyelashes at him. He laughs before offering me a hand to my feet.

"Go home and soak. Otherwise, Wagner will call and yell that you are useless tomorrow night." Wagner is the choreographer for *Miss Me.*

"Trust me, that's one direction you don't have to give me twice," I grumble. Lifting my other foot, I quickly slip out of the heel before padding barefoot toward the door leading to the women's locker room.

"See you next week?" Veronica calls out.

"If you're teaching it, I'll be there," I call back. And it's true. Whether she's teaching a conditioning class, Theater Jazz, or this psychotic stiletto dance, I wouldn't miss the chance to work with my godmother. Or, apparently, her newest love interest.

Grinning, I wonder what my mother will think of this little tidbit of gossip considering Veronica has been her best friend for the last forty years. And considering Stefano is younger than me, I want to give her a standing O. Then again, she might be getting enough of those.

Cackling, I slip into a pair of slides and make my way out the door. I'm already pulling up the Uber app. There's no way I'm making it back home without some assistance.

Ten minutes later, I'm settled in my Uber on the way back to the Upper West Side. With some amazement, it hits me my mother has to be some kind of genetic freak to be thirty years older than me and still able to maintain this pace.

FIVE

EVANGELINE

Mom and I have the audience in the palm of our hands. Our voices are in perfect harmony even as we sing opposite one another through a standing mirror without glass about how much we miss the other. We're pouring our souls into the final lyrics about how our hearts don't work right without the other's, how a man shouldn't come between our love, when I catch the tears glistening in her eyes. Her face is slightly flushed.

My eyes narrow, but she shakes her wigged head, setting the curls dancing. My eyes dart upward at the hot stage lights.

We step around the mirror to wrap up the final song. "My heart was filled with pain," my voice projects.

Mom's voice sings, "I'll be with you wherever you go."

"I'll be with you wherever."

Mom sings, "Forgive me," before I cut in and we sing together, "Our love is forever. Miss me no more." We hold the last note as we step around the mirror, our fingers touching. The sheer curtain envelops us as the audience jumps to its feet as Kate and her mother reunite in the final scene.

And my mother collapses in my arms, completely unscripted.

The red velvet curtain which had begun to descend hides her weight almost entirely knocking me off my feet. The noise of the crowd masks my cries. "Help! Help!" I sink forward, still clutching my mother to me. Her eyes are wide and frightened on me, her breath heavily labored. She tries to talk, but I lean down. "Hush, Mom. I'm trying to get... Oh, Pas. Thank God. We need help! Something's wrong with Mom!" Tears are streaming down my face as I face our director.

"9-1-1 has already been called. We have to move her off the stage, Evangeline. You have to take your bows," he says grimly.

"Are you mad? I'm going with my mother to the hospital!" I snap.

He grabs me by my shoulders. "If we don't keep the theater seated, it's going to be a madhouse trying to get your mother out of here. We have to do the curtain call without your mother. We're going to make an announcement she twisted her ankle backstage."

Right. Think, Linnie. "I'm not leaving her until the EMTs get here." I slide the wig off my mother's head. Pulling the stocking cap off, her natural gray-streaked hair falls around her shoulders. My fingers glide through it.

"I'll have the announcement made now. I'll let people know we'll be starting in five..."

"There's no need for that," Simon joins us. "Give me the mic." His face is strained with anguish as he takes in my mother. "I'll go on stage and tell a story about what happens after."

"But...nothing happens after! John Thomas is going to freak." Pasquale sputters.

"Let him," Simon says harshly. "Where's the damn mic?"

Within seconds, Simon is entering the side stage and weaving a soft tale about how mother and daughter reunited in time for Michael to ask for her hand in marriage. Even as the EMTs roll their stretcher urgently toward my mother, I hear him say, "The most important thing is to remove all the obstacles preventing you from finding love."

The audience gives him another standing ovation.

When he's done, Simon comes straight to us. My mother has an oxygen mask over her face. They're ready to wheel her out. Simon kisses her cheek and murmurs, "We'll be there as soon as we can."

She blinks her eyes at him before darting them over to me. Her mouth tries to move underneath the mask. I hush her. "Shh, Mom. Whatever it is can wait. I love you. I'll be with you soon." Squeezing her hand, I ask the EMTs, "Which hospital is she going to?"

"NYU," one tells me.

"We'll be there in less than thirty minutes. Keep her safe," I order. Simon slips his arm around me as the EMTs wheel my mother to the waiting ambulance.

"She'll be okay," Simon's whispers.

"She has to be." But I'm so worried. How on earth did she go from singing her soul out one minute to collapsing the next?

"Come on, Linnie. Let's get this over with so we can get to her. Bris is going to be a wreck by the time we get there."

Knowing that's the truth, I exit stage left, still shaking. When it's time for my mother to come out, the calm announcement about my mother's fall backstage is met with a standing ovation.

She'd love it, I think with a teary smile.

Simon and I meet in the middle. I sink into a deep curtsy while he regally bows. We do this four more times; the waves of applause keep coming. Usually, I'd be overwhelmed with the audience's response.

But it's all I can do to stop myself from running offstage to get to my mother.

The minute the curtain closes, I dash off, with Simon hot on my heels. "There's a car waiting for you," Pasquale calls out. "Blue BMW out the back door."

Fluttering my hand at him, I only stop in my dressing room long enough to grab my purse. Knowing our costume designer will likely have a meltdown over us leaving with show property, I mutter, "Like I give a shit," to myself.

Simon utters a distracted, "Hmm?"

"Asia's reaction to us taking the costumes off set."

"I agree."

Twenty of the most hellish minutes of my life later, we're jumping out of the car and racing into the crowded hospital emergency room. Simon texted Bristol when we were close, so she's waiting for us. She races into Simon's arms the minute she sees him before reaching an arm over for me. We're in a tight little huddle before she whispers, "I'm so scared."

We're buzzed through the door. Simon and I quickly get a wristband attached so we can move into and out of the ER. "What are they saying?"

"They're running tests. They think it might be a stroke or a heart attack."

I stop in the middle of the hallway. "Mom? The woman eats like a damn rabbit and is in terrific shape. Are they crazy?" This is completely unbelievable.

"That's what the cardiologist said, Linnie. They just took her for testing."

"So, we have to wait?"

Reaching for the pins placed around my head to hold the red curls in place, I begin plucking them out. I need to be me, Linnie, not the actress Evangeline Brogan, when I face what's going to happen. "How long did they say it's going to take?"

Bristol checks the clock on the wall. "A few hours."

"Let me text Pasquale and see if he can drop off some clothes for us. He can take these back because there's no way I'm making it to tomorrow's performance."

"Me either," Simon declares, wrapping Bristol in his arms.

Pasquale assures me he'll have both Simon's and my street clothes here in half an hour. He also wants an update on Mom, which I can't give him.

I wish someone would come in and give it to me.

"HELLO. I'm Dr. Pilcher. I'm the head of Cardiology here at NYU. Are you the family of Brielle Brogan?"

We all jump up from where we've been sitting uncomfortably in the cramped cubicle where Mom's supposed to be returned. "Yes. Can someone please tell me where my mother is?" I demand.

"Come with me and I'll take you to her." His voice is brisk, and he turns out the door. Bristol scrambles off Simon's legs to take my waiting hand. Simon grabs our bags and quickly follows.

"Ms. Brogan," the doctor begins, but I snap. My patience is at an end. It's been hours of waiting with no answers.

"My sister is here too." I nod at Bristol. He looks abashed and checks his chart.

"Of course. I'm sorry. Ms. Brogan, Ms. Todd, You both were aware of your mother's previous drinking issues?" We've reached a set of elevator banks. After the doctor pushes the button, he catches Bristol's and my unsurprised faces. Although my mother's drinking was over long before Bristol was born, the stories were legendary. "I'm not surprised. Even if her medical records don't show it, it's often hard to hide heavy drinking from children. There was unde-tected long-term damage to her heart, but her medical charts don't show she was on any medication which makes her condition all the more dangerous."

"What condition?" Bristol whispers fearfully. I grasp her hand so hard, I might be crushing her delicate bones, but she doesn't begin to protest.

We all step into the elevator. When the doors close, Dr. Pilcher turns to us to ask more questions. "Was she ever a smoker?"

"Years ago," I answer. "She gave it up when it started to impact her voice."

He doesn't respond but takes notes on his tablet. My patience at an end, I beg, "Can you please just tell us what's wrong with our mother?"

"Let's get to a private room and I'll explain fully." The doors to the elevator open. We pass by a sign that indicates we're in the

Cardiac Care Unit. Approaching a U-shaped desk, Dr. Pilchner calls out, "Bobbie, is family care room six open?"

"Yes, Doctor. Do you need anything else?"

"Not right now." He begins to lead us down the corridor to a room labeled FC-6. He holds the door for us, and we step inside. "This room will be for your exclusive use," he tells us kindly.

Bristol flops down onto the couch; Simon drops next to her. I take one of the chairs. Dr. Pilchner remains standing. Feeling both appreciative and apprehensive, I gesture to the other chair. "Doctor, please. Have a seat. I imagine whatever you're going to say can't be any easier standing." Bristol's head snaps toward me before turning toward the doctor.

With a sigh, he perches on the end of the remaining chair in the room. "Before we get started, this may be tremendously misplaced, but your mother has provided decades of entertainment to my family." His hard demeanor softens. "I took my daughter to celebrate her graduation from high school to see *Powerhouse*. Ms. Brogan was magnificent."

Feeling both pride and dread, I do what my mother would have wanted me to do. "Thank you. I'll be sure to let her know."

His eyes close behind his wire-rimmed frames. "Ms. Brogan—"

I interrupt. "Evangeline."

He nods. "Evangeline, your mother had what is called a STEMI myocardial infraction."

Out of the corner of my eye, Bristol shakes her head in confusion. "In English, please," I beg.

He takes a deep breath. "She has a complete blockage of several of her coronary arteries. We have her stabilized for now. We need to perform bypass surgery as soon as possible to try to save her life."

The world slows around me. Pilchner is droning on about whether or not my mother has a living will. Bristol is sobbing into Simon's shoulder hysterically. And me? I'm wondering when I'm going to wake up from this nightmare and be able to tell my mother about it before we go on tonight to sing.

Because that's what this is—a living nightmare.

Blindly, I reach down for my purse. Digging through it one-handed, I pull out my cell. We each had all the necessary paperwork drawn up through our lawyer, Eric Shea, years ago to protect our money. While we were there, I vaguely remember him having us sign paperwork just in the event something like this happened. Mom laughed at him and said, "Darling boy, I'm going to live forever."

With a pain in my heart that makes me wonder if I'm not having my own heart attack, I scroll through my contacts. One ring, two. A male voice answers on the other end, brusquely, "Ms. Brogan, what can I do for you?"

Dully, I respond, "My mother's in the hospital with a heart attack. I need her living will paperwork immediately."

There's a long pause before he responds much more gently, "Find out the fax number of the floor you're on, and they'll have it within fifteen minutes. If that's not soon enough, let me talk with the doctor."

Blindly, I hold out the phone to Dr. Pilchner. "Here. It's for you," I say, right before I fall out of the chair. On my knees, I crawl toward my sister and her boyfriend. We're a huddle of whimpering tears while my mother's doctor gives our lawyer the information he needs, puts my phone down, and leaves the room.

All without saying another word to us.

SIX

EVANGELINE

"She kept saying she was fine." My voice is flat. "Every time we'd ask, she blew off our questions."

It's seven thirty the next day. After keeping Mom stable through the night, Dr. Pilchner said her best chance of survival was to attempt a coronary bypass surgery. He warned us it might take close to six hours; the damage to her arteries is so extensive.

It's only been about two hours since the procedure began, but I'm already freaking out.

"We can't make it go any faster," Bristol says practically.

I love her; I do. But practicality is absolutely not what I want right now. I want a million chocolate bars. I want to scrub up and hold my mother's hand. I want to lose myself in dancing...oh, shit. Gulping, I turn to Bristol. "Did you call Veronica?"

Gaping, Bristol accuses, "I thought you would have. You're the one who's her goddaughter, for Christ's sake!"

I groan knowing there's no dance class, no choreography on stilettos, no demeaning comment while I'm at her barre that will make up for the fact I didn't call her last night when all of this went down.

Looking at my watch, I mutter, "I'll call her now. I'm fucked no matter what, but at least she's not in class yet."

Bristol lays a gentle hand on the side of my face before saying seriously, "Make sure you pull your phone away from your ear. You know how she is when she screeches."

Good advice.

Slipping my phone from my jeans, I tap in my godmother's number. "Linnie, I don't have time. I'm late for class. Stefano kept me...let's just say tied up last night."

Ew. I did not want to know that. "Veronica..."

"I hope you're ready for an intense jazz class today, my darling. I plan on working those thighs..."

I try to break in. "Veronica..." But she prattles on.

"Sometimes, I wonder if you've been on the stage too long, my darling. Your form used to be better."

Finally, I've had it.

"*Aunt* Veronica!" I yell. There's dead silence on the other end.

"What's wrong?" she whispers. There's a note of fear now in her voice. I'm not surprised. I haven't called her "Aunt" since she started denying her age, which was right about the time she divorced her second husband, the godfather I no longer speak to.

"Mom..." I have to force the words out. "Mom's in the hospital. She...heart attack. In surgery." My voice is choked with tears.

"Where are you?" Veronica demands.

"NYU. Cardiac Care Unit."

"I'll be there as soon as I can." She disconnects the call.

"I just hope she doesn't bring Stefano," I mutter as I slip the phone into my back pocket.

"Why would she do that?" Simon asks, catching the tail end of my conversation as he comes through the door.

"Because she's banging him," I find a detached sort of amusement as he fumbles handing me my skinny vanilla latte over that announcement. For all his global worldliness, there are just some things Simon can't process. The antics of my godmother happen to be at the top of the list.

Bristol laughs. "Did Mom know?"

I shrug. "No idea. I only found out two days ago when she made me dance with him in class."

Simon looks disgusted. "Your sadist godmother—and yes I can say that as I've taken her classes—made you do a pas de deux with her lover?"

For the first time that day, I smile. "What does that make Pasquale for making me kiss my sister's baby daddy every night?"

Simon and Bristol exchange a smile before my sister pulls out the hand she's been sitting on all morning. "Don't you mean his fiancée?" she whispers.

My mouth falls open. Shoving my cup on a nearby table, I lunge for my sister to catch her close. "Oh, I'm so happy for you." The tears that have been trickling since Mom fell in my arms last night start right up again.

"I decided if I waited for the perfect moment, it might never come. So, I went with the right one," Simon murmurs. His arms wrap around us both.

"Mom's going to be so thrilled." My ordinarily husky voice sounds shredded, but I don't care. For one minute in the last ten hours, I'm happy.

I'll take it.

Who knows when I'll get to feel this way again?

"THE SURGERY WAS DIFFICULT, EVANGELINE," Dr. Pilchner runs his hands over his salt-and-pepper hair. "Your mother has significant tissue damage to her heart as well as the blockage to her arteries. If it weren't for her healthy lifestyle, this would have happened years ago."

Bristol's engagement ring is cutting into my hand. "What can we expect?" I ask bravely when I feel anything but.

"When you're able to go into her room, she will be on a ventilator and strapped down for her own safety should she wake up. Please, one at a time except for Bristol; she and her fiancé are permitted to go in together. If anything happens and the medical team comes in, you move out of the way. Immediately." Pilchner's voice is firm.

Veronica comes forward. "How long do you expect her to be in the ICU?"

"If we're lucky, four days." We all gasp. That's an incredibly long time. "As I said, the damage was extensive." Suddenly there's a loud beeping in the room. Pilchner curses and turns. "Excuse me, I would wait, but this is an emergency."

"Is it Mom?" I ask fearfully.

"No" is all he says before he disappears out of the room. I fall into Veronica's arms while Bristol is swept to the couch by Simon.

We're all quiet for a few minutes before I say, "You two should go in first; tell her your news."

The fluorescent overhead light glints off the diamond on Bristol's hand. "Are you sure, Linnie? I mean, if it wasn't for you..."

I shake my head. "It wasn't me operating on her that has her holding on. Take Simon. Go. See Mom. Tell her. Maybe it will help her wake up sooner." Besides, I want to talk with Veronica about what she knew about my mother's health.

There's an impatient quality to the silence in the room until a fresh-faced young nurse knocks on the door. "I have the doctor's orders to take a family member down to see Ms. Brogan."

I wave toward Bristol and Simon, who are already standing. "Dr. Pilchner said they could go in together," I tell her with an edge to my voice.

Checking her tablet, she looks at my sister and says, "Of course. I'm Cara. I'm one of your mother's nurses on the floor this afternoon. How are you holding up?"

Bristol answers shakily, "I'll be better once I can see my mother for the first time in a day."

Cara makes an appropriate clucking sound, and they disappear. Once I figure they're out of earshot, I turn on Veronica like a wolf on fresh meat. "Did you know?"

Her brows lower in confusion. "Know what?"

"It was her drinking that made this so much worse." Veronica's face pales.

"You're kidding, right? Brielle was one of the healthiest people I know."

Mentally letting out a relieved sigh, I pull her to the couch and tell her everything Pilchner told us. "You heard what he said, Veronica. She should have been gone by now." My voice breaks on the last words.

"Come here, Linnie." I dive into her arms like I used to do after I didn't get a role when I was a little girl. "It will all be okay," she murmurs as she strokes her tiny hands over my long hair. But this close, I can smell memories: the sweet musk of her perfume, the mint of her breath, and the underlying tinge of alcohol. God, it's like a flashback to sitting in Mom's lap when I was a toddler. I push away, unable to bear it.

"It hurts so bad," I curl into myself as my chest heaves up and down.

"I know, sweet girl. And just like your mother, you feel so much. You hide it behind this mask." She brushes her fingers across my cheek. "It makes you so good on the stage and so difficult everywhere else. You don't release it in quite the same way."

I pull out away from her touch. Her fingers fall between us, leaving an awkward silence I don't attempt to break while I order my thoughts. Finally, I let out a tired sigh. "When did you start again?" I feel like I've asked her this question a million times over the years. No matter what, she just can't seem to stay on the wagon.

Veronica turns away. "Now's not the time, Linnie. It's just a little to help calm me down." Yeah, I believe that like I think I'll start drinking cilantro smoothies.

Then again, if it would cause my mother to wake up, I swear I'd swallow those damn things every day and never complain.

"Was she?"

"Who?"

"Mom. Did she start drinking again?"

"Jesus, Linnie, how can you sit here and ask me that?

"Because if there's anyone she'd have taken even a single sip with, it would have been you. You wouldn't have been angry in the same way we would have."

Appeased, Veronica admits, "True. But if she was drinking, it wasn't with me."

Sniffling, I push back. "I'm sorry, but I had to know. Bris will ask..."

"And you didn't want her hurt," she surmises. I nod. Then as a peace offering, I say, "You know if you want Stefano here, you can ask him."

As if I'd gone down on my knees and begged for forgiveness for my assumptions, Veronica's peals of laughter clears the slate between us. "Oh darling, if you think that adorable piece of man meat is going to offer me solace, then you are so wrong. Being near Brielle does that."

Reaching out to squeeze her hand, I whisper, "I know."

My heart feels lighter now that I know my mother hadn't fallen back into her alcoholic habits, something that almost cost her everything when I was a young child. Maybe she will pull through.

Maybe just knowing we're all here pulling for her will give her star enough energy to brighten again.

SEVEN

EVANGELINE

I'm afraid to open the door.

It's not like I can't see into my mother's cubicle since it's made of glass, but sliding open the door is taking a level of courage I'm not entirely sure I have. Closing my eyes, I lay my head on the cool glass while I grip the handle tight in my hand. Even when my father was in a little cubicle like this when he died of cancer, I didn't feel this level of terror. When he passed, all I felt was an overwhelming sadness of a life being cut too short by a disease that wreaked havoc on his body.

After blinking back the burning in my eyes, I pull the handle. I'm hit with the scent of antiseptic and the persistent monotony of pings from the machines keeping my mother alive. "God, Mom," I choke out as I quietly close the door behind me. "This isn't your best look. It won't go with your new Judith Lieber at all."

I want her to sit up and make some smart remark at me. Instead, I take inventory of the incision I can just make out at her collarbone disappearing down beneath her gown that's loosened at her neck. Wires are attached everywhere, not to mention the IVs. There are two poles pumping fluid into her body, including—I wince—bagged blood. When Bristol asked about it earlier, she was told it wasn't uncommon for cardiac patients to need some blood as there might be some bleeding due to the internal incisions.

I'm horrified by the thought my mother could still be bleeding.

But more than anything, it's the ventilator making its hiss and sigh sound that's gutting me. Even though it's keeping her breathing, that damned machine is stopping my mother from drolly replying to me, "Darling, I had no idea about being sick. Stop making such a big deal about it."

At least that's what I want her to say. The ventilator pushing air into her lungs is preventing her from confirming my suspicions. In the meantime, I weave my fingers through the hand with the least amount of wires and squeeze. Hard.

"You got a standing ovation last night, Mom. You were—*are*—brilliant. You're everything. There was no one on that stage who didn't see it was the performance of your career. I'll never play another part I'll be prouder of than this one." Lowering my head to the side of the bed, I whisper, "How am I supposed to get back on that stage without you?"

I don't get an answer.

"You and Bris? You're more than just family; you're my best friends. You're two of the people I trust, and in our business, that's two more than most people have. We're so blessed, Mom. We have Simon and Bris's baby coming. We have family, but we need you. You have to..."

I'm interrupted by a screeching so loud, it mimics the feedback from a microphone gone awry.

Suddenly, Mom's twitching on the bed. "Mom? Mom, it's me, Linnie. Can you hear me?" I squeeze her hand so hard. I have to be digging the IVs in uncomfortably, but I don't care.

Maybe she heard me and is waking up.

The door flies open to her room. Two nurses dressed in dark blue come running in. "Ms. Brogan, please step back."

"She's waking up," I cry out, overjoyed but confused at the grim expressions on the faces of the people coming into the room.

Dr. Pilchner strides into the room. Barely sparing me a glance, he barks, "Get her out of here!" to the third nurse who follows after him.

It's Cara. "But I want to be here when she wakes up," I protest. Cara takes my arm. I rip it away. "No! I need to be here, don't you understand? She's going to wake up, and I need to be here."

Pilchner stops barking orders long enough to come to me. "Evangeline, we have to take your mother back into surgery. Her blood pressure drop indicates there's internal bleeding I need to see to. Now. I don't have time for this." He turns and proceeds to bark more orders.

I'm numb as Cara leads me down the hall toward the room where my family's waiting. Finally, I get my wits about me. "Stop. Please stop."

"Evangeline..." she starts.

"I can't go back in there like this. I..." Spotting the bathroom across the hall, I barely make it into a stall before I begin to vomit. My retching is echoing off the halls, much like Bristol's does since her morning sickness started.

"No! No, damnit!" I punch the side of the stall. I hear the door open and close softly. I appreciate Cara giving me my privacy to get this out because I know I have to be strong when I walk back into that room.

The door opens and closes again. A hand reaches under the stall with a damp towel. "Thanks," I mutter.

"I left some mouthwash on the counter for you," Cara says quietly. "Take your time."

Appreciating her calm practicality in a world so completely out of control, I take a few more minutes to make sure I'm not going to be sick again. Pushing myself to my feet, I flush before exiting the stall. On the vanity is a small hospital Dopp kit that contains a toothbrush, toothpaste, soap, moisturizer, and a comb, among other things. Touched by the simple generosity, I avail myself of the oral products to get the bitterness out of my mouth; nothing will get it out of my soul. Meeting my gaze in the mirror, I find it saturated with fear.

I don't know if I can walk in there and do this. I'm not acting a role; this is my life.

I have to. There's no other choice.

Gathering up the kit and the stained cloth, I move to the door and open it. Cara's waiting outside with a bag. "Here, give me that." She nods at the towel.

I gratefully drop it in. We begin walking down the hallway toward the room where my family is waiting. Laying my hand on her arm, I whisper, "In case I forget to thank you later, I appreciate all you've done. I can't imagine this is the most rewarding part of your job."

Turning, I start to open the door when I hear her say, "No, but moments like this help me get through the others." Her soft-soled shoes squeak as she moves away.

The moment I open the door, Bristol jumps up with an eager look on her face. "How's Mom?"

Tears flood my eyes. "Not good." Bristol's face collapses.

"Shit," Simon bites out.

Veronica's lip trembles.

Taking a deep breath, I tell them what happened. In the end, we're all holding each other up, but we're missing an important piece.

Mom.

HOURS LATER, Dr. Pilchner comes into the room with a defeated look on his face. My heart cracks wide open and is bleeding as surely as Mom's was.

"I'm so sorry," he croaks out. Veronica grips my hand as Bristol falls sobbing into Simon's arms. "We couldn't get her stable again. There was too much damage."

It's Simon who asks, "Can you leave us for now, Doctor? We may have questions later, but right now, we need to be alone."

"Of course. Just have me paged when you would like to speak with me. Again, I'm so terribly sorry."

I can't care about how he's feeling. The tidal wave of pain is crushing as I realize this hurt will never go away.

Mom will never be able to walk my sister down the aisle. Bristol's baby will never get to be loved by its nana. I'll never again hear stories of her and Veronica on the road in their early days as dancers. She'll never get to buy another ridiculous purse or goad Bristol and me into trying some ridiculous restaurant she saw on Food Network.

Broadway will never be the same ever. The lights will come down not only on the theater but in my heart.

Brielle Brogan is dead. Legend, friend, but most importantly, mother.

It's with this thought I break down, my hysterical tears matching those of my sister's.

EIGHT

MONTAGUE

I nova Schar Cancer Institute, in Fairfax, Virginia, is a state-of-the-art cancer center. With a team of nationally renowned doctors and genetic counselors, the treatment plan they've had Ev on for his chronic myeloid leukemia has held him in this static state for more than two years. Two years I've been grateful for every moment not only so I could try to get my shit straight, but it's afforded me time to make critical decisions—the biggest one being move back to the farm. This way Mom doesn't have to watch Ev suffer through this fucking disease alone.

We're waiting while Ev's getting his blood drawn, and she gasps.

"What? What is it?"

Mom's scrolling through a news site on her iPad. "Remember that show we saw on Broadway last week?"

"Of course. You haven't stopped making my ears bleed by trying to sing like the lead since," I gently tease.

She whacks me in the arm. "Cute, Monty. The woman who played the part of the mother died."

That gets my attention. "Seriously?"

"Yes. It says she had sudden cardiac troubles and passed away a few days later. I feel terrible for her family." I sling my arm around Mom's shoulders. She has such a huge heart, I think fondly. Dropping a kiss on her head, I murmur, "That's horrible."

"It is," she agrees. She opens her mouth to add more when a pale Everett steps through the door. I shoot to my feet to grab hold of his arm.

"What did the vamps do this time? Take a gallon of blood instead of a pint?" I try to make a joke as I guide him to the chair I was sitting in.

"Feels like it, son. That it does." Mom looks at him fearfully. "I just got dizzy standing, Char. Nothing to worry about."

"Okay, my love. I won't worry until we talk with the doctor." She lays her head on his chest.

I hope this is a side effect from the meds and the doctor can prescribe something else so Mom can go back to her usual level of fussing and Ev can go back to being...Ev.

Over the years, I've found it's hit-or-miss on whether hopes and dreams are granted. It's worse than luck. It's why I've always tried to make sure I had something stronger at my back.

A way to fight back.

THERE'S no way to fight the news Dr. Spellman's throwing at us.

"Right now, you've moved into an accelerated phase, Everett. We're going to keep up your inhibitors, but we need to start searching the database for a donor."

Ev glances at my mother before saying, "You're concerned though."

Spellman sighs. "I am. You have a rare blood type, and it's one of the main factors we use in HLA—human leukocyte antigen—matching. It's going to be more difficult to match you than some of my other patients."

Crap. Even as I think that, my mother's iPad clatters to the floor. "What can we do?"

"You said you weren't in touch with your family?" Spellman asks Ev.

He nods. "I haven't spoken with them in more than thirty years. Hell, I don't even know if any of them are still alive."

Spellman is brutal. "You have the resources, Ev. Find them. See if one of them is willing to be a donor."

Mom jumps in. "I thought the next level of treatment was a stem cell transplant—where we take Ev's cells and..."

"For CML, we prefer to take the cells from a donor. Otherwise, we could just be putting a Band-Aid on a bullet wound," Spellman says bluntly. Mom's face falls.

I want to punch Ev's doctor in the face half the time, but he gets results. "We can start looking for them tomorrow, Ev. I still have markers I can call in." It seems like forever ago, my life as a federal agent. I look back at that time through a haze of pain now rather than the pride with which I accepted the badge. But in truth, I'd endure my final weeks as an agent over again in a heartbeat for a miracle match.

I can't imagine it would be hard to track down Ev's family. Maybe it's crossing a few ethical lines, but frankly, I'll do whatever I have to. I don't care if I have to wake up every night unraveling even more than I already am if I can help the man who's loved me unconditionally since we met. I'd live with a million more regrets than the one that persistently haunts me. Maybe by helping Ev, it will negate the shot I didn't take—the life I couldn't save.

How am I supposed to atone when I'm never given a chance for redemption?

But Ev's already shaking his head, "I can just hire someone, Monty."

Even as my heart shrivels up a little at hearing this, I lean forward. "Let me do this for you. It won't take long." If there's anything to find, it should take a day—two at most—to find Ev's family.

"We'll talk about it later." He reaches over and squeezes my hand. His attention shifting back to his doctor, he asks, "What do I need to do in the meantime?"

Spellman starts giving a list of directions. Mom leans down to get her iPad so she can take notes. I begin making mental lists of the people I can call to get the ball rolling.

Because we're not losing Ev. No matter what I have to do.

ONCE WE'RE BACK at the farm, I saddle up Hatchet and begin to ride.

There's one good thing about being home full time. I reach down and pat my horse's neck gently. She whinnies in response. I know we could make this climb to the top of the mountain blindfolded; we've taken it so many times.

Slowly, we climb taking our time navigating the well-worn path. I don't want to be at the barn answering a million questions, and I want to give Mom and Ev the time they need at the house. It seems like the only gift I can give anyone right now is distance. And to be honest, I need it myself.

My eyes are drawn to the leaves of the trees around me; the blend of color matches Ev's eyes. I've seen him in so many different moods growing up: amusement, pride, anger, fear. He's gone from being my stepfather to my best friend. The shaft of pain that slices through me is unlike anything else I've ever felt. I could be seventy-five and hearing this news and feel the same way. It's a hole in my soul that's not getting sealed, no matter how I try to fill it.

Hatchet sidesteps. I quickly adjust the reins. "What did you see, girl? A mole or something?" Of course, she doesn't answer me back. If she did, then I'd have a lot more to worry about than the persistent sleepless nights I endure due to my nightmares.

Only, in my case, they're just nocturnal regrets.

A man can only believe he's forgiven for his mistakes when those he's wronged actually forgive him, I think dispassionately. No matter what my job said, they can't absolve me from the guilt consuming me. I thought dealing with that was the worst thing to happen.

That was until I got the news about Ev. It was like a one-two hit to my soul.

I've learned there's only one thing worse than the first punch of hearing someone you love is dying. It's the repeated slaps of hearing the words "I'm sorry" out of every person's mouth when they hear the news.

Pain and shame have no place here, not when I'm expected to be the strength everyone needs to get through. I reach the pinnacle of the mountain and look back at the home Ev built for Mom and me. I know they're waiting for me in the inky darkness of night, but then—then it's on me to handle them. Not anyone else. Pain and shame may show me no mercy.

Just as long as they give it to my family.

NINE

EVANGELINE

The lights are dim in the theater. I'm sitting in the third row, remembering the first time I ever saw my mother onstage performing. Picking up the bottle of club soda tucked into the chair next to me, I take a long pull before putting it back down and wiping my mouth with the back of my hand.

I can still see the way her feet darted across the boards as she made her cue. Her voice soared. It would hover in the air delicately before it ripped the hearts out of each patron in the seats.

Miss Me was shut down for a week before Simon's and my understudies stepped up to bat. Almost two weeks have gone by, and it's still impossible to imagine getting back up on that stage without her. If it were up to me, I'd never step foot up there again. Except, I can hear Mom in my ear telling me I have to. Too many people depend on me for me to just walk away like I want to.

A hand lands on my shoulder. Shifting in my seat, I find Pasquale standing behind me. "What can I do?" he asks.

Reaching up, I squeeze his hand before letting it go. "Nothing. Nobody can."

He sits down in the row behind me. "How's Bristol? Are she and Simon holding up okay?"

If there's one good thing that's come out of this, it's the fact the media's realized the true nature of my sister's relationship with my costar and they've left it alone. For now. I shrug. "We're all messed up, Pas. I feel like the stars are all misaligned, and we don't know which one to follow. There was so much left for her to do with her life..." My voice trails off.

We're both silent thinking of different roles my mother will never experience; Pasquale's probably thinking of the ones who could take place on the stage in front of us whereas I'm thinking of the ones that involve her being called Nana. Still, I speak nothing but the truth when I admit, "I feel closer to her here than I do to her at home. It's easier to imagine that she's going to come out from stage right just in time to hit her cue."

Pasquale drops his head until it rests on my shoulder. I go on. "I can't begin to contemplate finishing out the rest of my life without her, let alone the show. She'd demand I do both in a grand style though—that was her way."

"Yes, it was," he agrees.

"When do I have to be back?" I ask somberly. My understudy has been performing well, but I can only imagine the complaints the office is fielding. Grief or not, the show has to go on. People paid an enormous sum for the tickets, so I don't get the luxury of grief.

"It's only been a week, Linnie. I can hold them off for maybe another..."

I shake my head. "Give me a few more days. Let me talk to Simon. We'll have to prepare Bris, but after that, we'll finish out our contracts."

He lets out a huge sigh. "I figured you'd be telling me you wouldn't be signing a new one."

Tugging the bottle next to me again, I take another drink before offering it to him. He politely declines. I turn to face him before I whisper, "If it was happening to you, would you be able to go more than another few weeks singing the songs that were written to show-case a woman's love for her mother?"

He leans forward and presses his lips to my forehead. "No...but then again, I'm not as strong as you are." Pushing to his feet, Pasquale makes his way down the aisle. I turn and face the stage again.

Wishing this was just a tragedy I was watching onstage and not feeling in my heart.

"YOU DON'T HAVE to go back right away," Bristol argues when I head to her and Simon's condo located three buildings down from mine. "They can't make you, can they?"

Simon and I exchange glances. "Both of our contracts say a 'reasonable bereavement period,'" Simon begins.

"Two weeks isn't reasonable," Bristol snaps. I agree, but I need to point something out to my distraught sister.

"Bris, I might be able to get away with that, but Simon won't be able to. He may love Mom like his own, but our contracts state 'immediate family.'" I knock on wood. "Unless it were Marco, he wouldn't be able to remain out of the show indefinitely."

"What a load of crap." Bristol begins pacing back and forth.

"If Simon goes back, I should as well. We need to show a unified front. Besides—" My voice breaks. "It's what Mom would want."

Bristol stops in place, facing me. Tears fill her eyes. "Yeah, she would."

"I don't think you should go back to the firm until after your doctor's appointment next week though," I argue vehemently. I'm so concerned about the added stress my mother's death has put on my sister's pregnancy.

"I promise, I won't," she assures me.

Turning to Simon, I hesitantly ask, "So, should we say the matinee on Saturday? If it goes well, we'll stay for Saturday night?"

He gives me a tight nod. While we'd both love nothing more than to walk away and not look back, we know we'd essentially be causing the shutdown of *Miss Me*.

Saturday it is.

THE STANDING OVATION at Sunday night's performance leaves me feeling empty. As I lower myself into a curtsy for the third time, the applause thunders through the theater, but it's muffled as if I'm standing in a sound booth. Was the stage supposed to restart the emotions that have been trickling away every moment since Mom died?

Simon gently tugs at my hand. We're both feeling this. Since the first time since he met my sister, he forgot his tradition of dousing his breath with something heinous. Then again, his lips also landed somewhere in the vicinity of one of my dimples. With the way my body was bent, no one could tell but us. It just was another glaring reminder of how off our game we were.

We didn't deserve these ovations; truth be told we didn't deserve to be on the stage. With an aching heart, I make my way back to my dressing room and close the door so I can change and go home. Tomorrow, I'll try to dance away the heartbreak in my soul.

If that's even possible.

TEN

EVANGELINE

JUNE

I 'm about to slip out the door when my cell rings. "What's up, Bris?"

"You need to come over to Mom's." Her voice is subdued.

I take a deep breath and let it out in a shudder. I haven't been to my mother's in weeks, not since the first few days after her death when Bristol and I picked out her outfit for her viewing. Bristol's been back a few times alone to mark the items we decided we wanted to keep before the auctioneers come through. Although the proceeds of Mom's penthouse will be donated to charity, there are still family items which need to be removed.

"I'll be right there." Quickly, I disconnect. Figuring whatever it is won't take too long, I snatch up my dance bag and stride out the door. While I won't make it to the first class, I should be able to get in a decent workout today.

And bury my feelings of grief for a little while longer.

Stepping inside the elevator, I press "2" instead of "L." Mom's building is connected to mine through the fitness facility floor. Pulling out my access pass, I use it to buzz in before striding over to the elevator bank that will lead me directly to her penthouse. I key in the code and use the dongle on my keys to gain access to the elevator that will open directly into her much more modern setup.

I brace myself for the essence of her that hasn't left the space. As I enter, I reach out to touch the cashmere coat handing on a coat tree. She was wearing it the day she had lunch with Bristol and me at Wolf's shortly before her death. Tears gather in my eyes as I remember Lance and his mother backstage. They were so gracious.

Bristol and Simon are waiting on the couch. There's a box sitting on Mom's glass coffee table. "Mom's gonna freak if she sees that on her..." And the realization Mom won't ever see that coffee box is like a shaft of cold steel in my chest. I blink rapidly to keep the tears at bay.

My sister stands, her face pale, and steps around Simon to hold out her hands. "Mom wouldn't care if the box was on her table knowing we found what was in it, Linnie."

Shit. A shiver runs through me. "Why do I just feel like someone danced on my grave?" I bravely try to joke.

"It's not your grave—or should I say ashes—that should be shaking. It's your mother's," Simon says brutally.

Looking at how pale Bristol is, I take a wild guess. "And Dad's?"

She hesitates but then grabs hold of my hands tightly before admitting, "My dad's."

The world spins crazily as the implications of what she's saying starts to sink in.

"Dear God."

"I CAN'T BELIEVE I'm not your sister," I whisper to Bristol as I clutch my mother's letters against my chest.

She shoves me. "We *are* sisters. I never want to hear you say that again." The tears that flood her eyes drown my already broken heart.

Quickly, I rephrase. "I never imagined I wasn't Dad's."

"It never crossed my mind either," she admits. But then her brow furrows. "Do you remember when we were still in school and they separated for a bit?"

Understanding sweeps through me. "It was after that he became so cold toward me. You think he found all of this?"

"We found out about his cancer, and he moved back in." Biting her lip, Bristol turns her head to face the expansive view of Central Park I paid a huge chunk of change for. Simon carried the box out of my mother's place the minute he was confident we were both okay. Right now, he's getting us some cheesecake before we tackle the rest of the box back in the comfort of my home.

"So, we'll never know if they resolved their issues or if he just came home to die," I conclude. Or if he did accept me as his own. Patrick Todd, world-class financier, raised me from the time I was born. Doesn't that count for something? In more ways than the blood running through my veins, wasn't I his?

If not, who do I belong to?

Jumping up from my couch, I head over to the freezer. I pull it open and immediately find what I'm looking for. I snag the pint of ice cream and slam the door. Grabbing two of my coffee spoons that sit in a container next to my coffeepot, I stomp back into the living room and drop on the sofa next to Bristol. Handing her a spoon, I peel back the top and dive in

She doesn't hesitate, though she offers up a logical "Didn't we ask Simon to go get cheesecake?"

I mutter, "I have a feeling we're going to need both."

Leaning her head on my shoulder, she whispers, "You might be right."

And that's how Simon finds us when he gets back, jabbing elongated spoons into a melty tub of Triple Chocolate Brownie. Just being.

And trying to figure out who exactly we are in light of the mess scattered across my coffee table.

BLESS HER ORGANIZED HEART. Bristol has made a list of all the possible things we might need to do, including hiring a psychic to try to converse with our mother on the other side. "I don't think that one's going to work out so well, Bris," I chortle. Laughing is something I never expected to do in this situation. Then again, I never expected to be in this situation to begin with.

"It's better than randomly asking men on the productions she worked on if Mom slept with them." But she's giggling too. She strikes a line through both suggestions before pausing. "Do you really want to know who your father is, Linnie?"

I open my mouth and shut it. In the span of seven hours, I feel like my entire life has changed. I've gone from knowing who I am with a confidence that borderlines arrogance to being so lost I don't even know where to start to be found. I try to explain.

"It isn't just Mom's lie, Bris. How many people knew—people I work with day in and day out? How many of them kept this from me? I don't trust anyone but the people in this room. Is this how I'm supposed to feel the rest of my life?"

"No," she whispers. I reach for her hand and squeeze it hard.

"Maybe he knew and didn't want me. Back then, a single mother still wasn't readily accepted," I admit. I also give my mother credit, knowing she would have raised me come hell or high water. "But once your father knew, she should have figured out a way to tell me. There have been twenty years I could have had with her knowing that after the shock wore off, she was still my mother and I loved her."

Simon, who has remained quiet for most of the night, says, "Knowing Brielle, I bet she was petrified of your reaction, Linnie. You're so much like her." I absorb that quietly before nodding. "But your mother was also like you in another way. She would have confided in her closest friend."

Veronica.

My eyes fly to the clock. It's not quite six. I can still catch her at the studio. Jumping up, I slide into my mules. "I have to go. I need to see Veronica."

Simon pulls Bristol from her seat. "Not without us you don't."

"Fine. We have about an hour before she leaves to go back to her place to bang her newest piece." Both of them wince. "TMI? Sorry, it's going to get more explicit before the night's over."

"That's what I'm afraid of," Simon mutters as I grab my purse. Bristol wisely grabs my mother's diary. The three of us head out on our way to the dance studio to find out what my godmother knew.

And for how long.

ELEVEN

EVANGELINE

The last student files out of the class before I dare to enter in my street shoes, something Veronica in her role as Madame would typically gut me for. But before she can, I hold up Mom's diary that Bristol shoved in my hand while we were waiting and hiss, "Did you know?"

Veronica pales. "How...where did you find that, Linnie?" Swaying on her feet, Stefano steps forward. Her head tips up to him. "Go. I'll be fine."

He shoots me a dirty look before he brushes his lips against her forehead. I'm taken aback when I realize he truly cares about my godmother, something I never cottoned on to until now. But still, I agree. He's not family. Then again, I guess I'm not entirely that either according to this book. But I'll protect my mother's secrets as long as I can.

"I'll shower and call for the car." At her halfhearted smile, he turns his deep-set eyes at me. "Do not upset her."

Bristol jumps in. "Upset her? How about she tells us the goddamn truth and we'll never bother her again?"

Tears begin to slide down Veronica's face. "Darlings," she cries, but my heart is already dead in my chest. Another betrayal. How many would I have to endure so quickly?

"There are exactly two people in this world I trust right now, Veronica. And I only know I can trust them because in the last few hours they've been as devastated by what's in this book as I have."

"Please, come with me so we can talk."

I shake my head adamantly. "Is what she wrote in here true?" My voice is as hard as I want my heart to be.

Her face crumbles right before she whispers, "Yes."

"How could you not tell me?" I demand. I feel Bristol and Simon each lay a hand on my shoulder in support.

"Linnie, you have to understand. She was in love with Patrick, but they were on a break—"

I rudely interrupt. "Because of her drinking." I lash out. Everything that has ultimately gone wrong in my life has had to due to my mother's drinking. Now we can add her death and the fact my father wasn't really my father to the list.

"Yes," she admits. "I knew she had written things down, but I don't know what she wrote exactly. During that time, she met a man named Rhett. They met in a bar while we were touring in Chicago. It was brief, Linnie. She told me she did not know for sure until many years later that you were not Patrick's until he got ill. When they typed his blood, she realized... I may be telling you things you already know."

"You confirmed what she wrote, yes," I agree.

"Well." Veronica swallows. "He was sweet. Funny, she said. They spent most of their free time together during that trip. He left. She left. In the end, she and Patrick worked things out. She loved your father." Her tear-filled eyes drift to Bristol, who's standing stiffly beside me, feeling her own betrayal over our mother's actions.

I believe her. There's too much there that corresponds with what my mother wrote. Except— "I'm certain Bristol's father knew well before his illness, Veronica," I say calmly.

"No, there is no way," she denies emphatically.

"I think he found this book because one day, he went from being my dad to becoming a man with an obligation who allowed me to call him Father. There's a huge difference, you know. Bris and I used to talk about it, wouldn't we?" Blindly reaching out, I grab my sister's hand.

She clasps it. "Yes. I must have been eight; Linnie would have been twelve? But one day he was..." Her voice trails off.

"A stranger. Just like Mom is now," I say sadly.

Veronica approaches us—in my opinion bravely, in our current state of minds. "Your mother loved you both. You were her biggest blessing. She would have spared you any pain," she insists. She lifts her hand to touch my hair.

I jerk back. "Then why did she leave me to find out like this? Why did you?" My voice breaks on the question.

Veronica's hand drops without making contact. "Because it was my hope you would never have found out at all," she whispers.

My stomach churns with nausea I'm barely beating back, but I know the truth. Evangeline Brogan is just another role I've been playing. Only it's the longest one I've had since I've been doing it for thirty-three years.

"Thank you," I say sincerely. Veronica's eyes light with hope. "Thank you for being Mom's confidante when she needed you. Thank you for standing by us during this horrible time, but I think we have it from here."

"Linnie," she whispers.

"Evangeline," I snap. The budding hope dies in her eyes. "Linnie is reserved for the few people I can trust. That's the one name I know is mine. After all..." I let out a bitter laugh. "I'm certainly not Evangeline Katherine Brogan Todd like my birth certificate says I am, right?"

Turning, I stalk out of Veronica's studio with Bristol and Simon at my heels. My heart is breaking at the sounds of my godmother's sobs. Then again, it's been cracked wide open since I read this journal.

★

ONCE WE'RE BACK on the Upper West Side, I don't enter my building right away. "I need to walk. I need to be alone for a while."

Simon pulls me into his arms for a hug. "Do you have your cell on you?"

Nodding into his broad chest, I murmur, "Yes."

"Keys, cards?" Bristol comes up and wraps her hand around my bicep.

"Jesus, Bris. Yes." I sound exasperated, but I release Simon long enough to pull my sister into a long hug. There's no way I could have got through this without these two parts of my heart.

"Okay. Call me if you need me." Simon pulls Bristol to his side as they walk the few buildings to get to their place. I start walking toward Fifth Avenue. Right now, all I want to do is disappear into the crowded streets of tourists.

Blindly, I start walking past stores I'd typically enjoy. I pass by Bergdorf Goodman and Prada. I cross the street to avoid the American Girl Doll store and power past Stuart Weitzman and Cartier. Cutting around people coming up subway entrances and off buses, it isn't until I slam into someone that I realize I've walked almost fifteen blocks. "Excuse me," I murmur. The woman curses at me in three different languages; I only recognize the English.

Shrugging, I step around her and then freeze. Someone slams into me from behind. "It says, 'Walk.' Freaking tourists," a man mutters.

I don't bother to correct him because I'm entranced at what's in front of me. It could be nothing, or it could be everything. Maybe some of the questions plaguing me since last night could be answered by the rainbow shining behind in the Duane Reade drugstore window.

A DNA test.

When they first started becoming popular, Bristol and I used to joke around we should do one to see if we were 100 percent Irish. Bristol—ever the practical mind—would roll her eyes and say, "No one is ever 100 percent anything, Linnie."

That's now truer than ever. We're certainly not 100 percent sisters.

If we'd done it then while we were drunk and stupid, I'd have had the answers while Mom was still alive. I could have confronted her with the million questions running through my brain. Now, my questions are going to be left up to science and luck.

Who knows if Mom really knew who my father was? Maybe she contacted him and he wanted nothing to do with me. Maybe he's married with another family. Or maybe he has no idea there's a woman out there who carries his blood who had no idea until last night that she was even his.

It'd be insane. I'm not on the cover of *People* every day, but I am high profile enough it would be immensely stupid even to contemplate it...

A little voice whispers, *But no one would have to know who you are.* How often am I recognized?

Am I really going to do this?

I'm practically shoved into the middle of Fifth Avenue on the wave of foot traffic. It's pulling me across at the light at Forty-Fifth Street. My breathing accelerates as each step puts me closer to doing the crazy—the inevitable.

I'll figure out all the details with Bristol and Simon later, I decide. The automated door opens for me as I step inside. Making my way into the line, I get behind some guy who's arguing the price of the two cases of water he's buying. Impatiently, I wait my turn until I hear, "Next in line, please."

Pulling out my credit card, I slap it on the counter. "I'll take one of the DNA tests."

"Do you have a Duane Reade card? They're on sale for thirty dollars off..."

"No," I cut the clerk off. "I don't." I'm completely lying. I don't want my name attached to this kit in any way.

"That will be $195.96." I gape at her. "That includes your New York City sales tax. You can buy the kits cheaper online if you like."

"No, this is fine. It's a gift." I stretch the truth. I guess it's a gift when you're trying to find out who your father is. Right?

I stick my debit card into the machine, enter my PIN, and pull it out quickly. The long receipt prints. The clerk bags it all up and says, "Thank you for shopping with us."

"Thanks," I mutter, racing out of the store.

It isn't until I get outside that I realize what I've done.

I've taken the first steps to find my birth father.

Holy shit.

TWELVE

EVANGELINE

JULY

"I'm still pissed you didn't buy me one too," Bristol bitches right before she spits into the tube.

"Shut up and save your saliva." I pause before doing the same.

At first, Bristol and Simon freaked out when I got back and told them what I did. Then Bristol thought about it. She said, "It's not like you have to use your real name, Linnie. I mean, you can be Eva Brogan, Angel Brogan, Lynn Brogan, and no one but us would ever know."

Simon was incredulous. "I can't believe you're encouraging this. The smart way to do this would be to hire a private investigations firm. Marco knows one who would do a fabulous job."

"With what?" I demanded. "We only know a name, and we don't even know if that was his real name or if Mom gave him her real name."

Abashed, he agreed. "True. Okay. So, we do the crazy first, and then if you get any hits, maybe we have him checked out through the firm?"

I acquiesced. "Maybe. If I end up meeting him and if—that's a big if—I feel something wonky."

"You're wonky," he griped. I merely smiled beatifically.

"Aren't you glad your baby only has a quarter of a chance of inheriting these genes?"

He threw the sealed test kit at me.

Now, it's a week later, and Bristol and I are spitting into tubes. "I don't think they'd appreciate if I hocked a loogie, do you?" I laugh. It's either laugh or cry, and I've decided to go with the former.

I spend too much time at night crying.

We all decided the best course of action was to wait until we wrapped the final show in our contract on *Miss Me*. I needed my head free and clear of anything but this. I have the recording of the children's album to do in LA, but I'm not leaving until the week after next for that.

Next week is reserved for all things Bristol. She and Simon are quietly getting married to avoid the media fanfare so close to our mother's death. Since it's just the three of us plus Marco who will be in attendance, it's mainly finding her the perfect outfit, reminding Simon to buy flowers, and deciding on a lavish place for all of us to go to dinner on such short notice. She wants it to be a quiet event, just family. It's going to be beautiful—a perfect memory to take with me when I leave for Los Angeles.

"Shut up and keep going," Bristol tells me. I realize she's almost all the way done with her tube.

"You know, the last time you had spit running down your face like this, you were blowing bubbles at me. I think you were around one and you were teething. You should get used to that."

We grin at each other before resuming our respective *spppt* sounds. Fiercely, I realize I don't care what a DNA test says. Bristol could have no blood relation to me and she'd still be my sister.

"How long does it take to get a match?" Bristol, not one to do things halfway, got me a second brand of DNA kit so we could compare results. "After all, what if your father only is on one site?" So, we've had to set up two profiles and expunge our DNA into a tube two times. We decided for an alias; I should go with Lynn since I'm so used to being called Linnie by my closest family. I agreed because I'm more likely to react to it should I hear it. She even listed her office as the address for both of our kits. "Just in case some schmuck decides to try to find you."

She's seriously crafty.

"I have no idea," I say in response to how fast it takes to get a match. "Hell, I may never know. I may be getting dry mouth for nothing. But if nothing else, I'll at least get information about the medical stuff since now we can't be sure about that."

Bristol is already capping off her sample. "With Dad dying of cancer and Mom of a heart attack, I'm right there with you."

Holding the now filled tube away, I reach for her hand. "You know I love you for doing this for me. I just wish we didn't have to."

"Stop looking at it like that, Linnie. This changes nothing between us. I only wish Mom would have told you while she was alive."

"You and me both, sister. You and me both."

THIRTEEN

EVANGELINE

B eing in LA to record the album was a break I desperately needed. I was in the studio for what seemed like every waking moment trying to record twelve songs in three weeks. It kept me from constantly checking the email account Bristol set up for me. Night after night I'd get notices like, "Your DNA is being processed," or "We're excited for you to get your results! Just a little bit longer now."

I'm in line to board the plane in LA to head back to New York. I want to be with my family and give up on this half-assed idea to find a father who likely doesn't care he has a daughter anyways. It was so stupid. I'm not going to find out a damn thing. All I'm going to be left with are more questions, I think despondently.

"We now welcome our first-class passengers to board the aircraft at this time," the sunny voice of the gate attendant says.

Excellent. I pull up my mobile boarding pass and make my way to the short line. Just as the scanner is about to process the code, my cell goes off with Bristol's distinctive ring. MAGIC! screams out on full blast. Quickly pressing Silent, I start blushing furiously. I send my sister to voicemail. "I am so sorry. So embarrassing."

The gate agent smiles as my boarding pass scans successfully. "It happens more than you think. Don't worry about it. Have a safe flight."

I give her a huge smile. "Thanks. Have a terrific day." Moving past her, I dial Bristol's number. My long legs eat the jetway at a fast clip. By the time the call connects, I'm already nodding at the first-class cabin steward. "What's up?"

"Check your email. My results are back!"

I freeze in place.

"That doesn't mean mine are," I say slowly. I'm afraid to get my hopes up at this point.

"Well, either they are, or we have another half sibling somewhere because it already told me I have a close match."

Holy crap. Excitement begins to pour through my veins.

"Bris, I'm on the plane to come home." I drop my bag in the seat. Shifting my cell to my ear, I lift my larger carry-on to the overhead compartment. My oversized purse easily slides beneath the seat in front of me. Dropping into my chair, I lean my head back. "There's no way I can process this right now." Though, in reality, I want to jump off the plane and spend hours looking over my results.

"Then don't," she replies swiftly. "Go accept my connection and shut off your phone. I won't look at anything else until you come home."

My heart is pounding furiously in my chest. "I can do that."

"Then do it before they close the cabin doors."

"I will if you let me off my phone," I shoot back.

"Oh, yeah." She giggles. "It might work, Linnie."

"Yeah. It's better odds than lotto at least," I laugh.

"Hey, what happened to this being a great idea when we were swapping spit?"

"We didn't swap spit. We spat together but separately," I correct her. The man in the seat next to me begins choking. "Well, that didn't come out right," I mutter.

Bristol is gone laughing. "Are your employees looking at you oddly? Because the man sitting next to me is questioning my sanity," I say with a great deal of amusement. The gentleman in question flushes at so blatantly listening to my conversation. "It's okay," I assure him. "We're talking about a DNA kit."

"My wife and I did one of those. She found out she was part American Indian when she thought her whole life she was Hawaiian. Coolest thing ever." He shakes his head. "One of the craziest things will be if you find out if you like cilantro or not."

"Bris," I whisper. "Did you hear..."

"Yes! It might be genetic?"

We both break up laughing. "Now I can't wait," I admit.

"Me neither. Have a safe flight, honey. Call when you land."

"Will do." We both hang up. I immediately pull up my alternate email account, and sure enough, my results are in there. I log in and accept Bristol's connection. She called it—she's my close match. Not a shock there. As she said, the real shock would have been if there was someone else. Then I immediately shut the site down. I want to dissect the information when I have more time and not more questions.

When the cabin doors are secured, I put my phone into airplane mode and slip my headphones on to watch the in-flight movie.

As the plane taxis down the runway and we take off, so do my hopes. It's way too soon, I know, but something tells me that I'm not only going to get my answers, they might just heal me.

FOURTEEN

MONTAGUE

I jerk awake with my heart pounding. I gasp, trying to inhale hard enough to get enough air. "Christ." I scrub my fingers through my hair. The nightmare I just woke up from has never really gone away—the last case I was involved with before I was encouraged to leave NCIS. It still haunts me, since it wrapped up right before I got the call about Ev's illness.

Knowing it's the only way I'll be able to get back to sleep, I swing out of bed and head over to the wet bar near the bathroom. Grabbing the nearest decanter, I throw a few healthy fingers in a heavy crystal glass and toss it back. The liquid etching its way down toward my stomach helps ease the burn in my heart. Refilling it quickly, I begin to pace back and forth, my mind unable to relax.

How do I make it all go away? There's nothing that comes to mind in the inky darkness. *I can help.* My words from that night echo in my head, making it pound harder. It doesn't matter what miracle mind exercises you're given when you're running from the truth. *That boy died because I wasn't enough.* There's not enough ways to erase the bruises and scars from taking residence in your brain. It fucking kills and I keep reliving it over and over. And compounded with Ev... I take another slug of the bourbon I've managed to not spill in my anxious pacing.

One of the aching pains is the hole I left in my team. By not being able to hack it, I abandoned them to deal with the aftermath of what happened: the negative press, the media, the accusations of mishandling of the case. Everyone's reassured me they don't feel that way, but I can't help but feel like somewhere along the way I've made a mistake that cost so much to so many people.

Finishing my drink, I plunk down the glass on the edge of my nightstand. The sheets get a quick snap to right them before I crawl between them again. Not knowing if trying to get a few extra hours of sleep is even worth the effort, I flip onto my stomach. I punch the pillow, then stare out the wall of windows overlooking the back of the property. Even after all this time, it still takes me forever to fall asleep as I'm still unused to the eery quiet. There's no noise from the streets below. If I listen hard, I might be able to hear a horse in their stall. I brace for another night of loneliness, regrets, and sadness.

It isn't until the sky starts to lighten that I drift back off to sleep.

I'M startled awake by my alarm hours later. Standing in nothing but a pair of boxer briefs, I walk over to the Keurig on the bar in my suite and pop in a cup so I can get the first hit of caffeine down before I start my day. Then I'm finally conscious enough to thank God that it isn't raining. Spring in Northern Virginia is either exquisite or it's trying to bitch-slap you like an errant schoolboy. There is no in-between. Some of the locals joke that we're beginning to turn into our version of Florida going straight from winter into summer. I hope that's not the case; there's something about spring that offers hope around here.

When Ev bought this place, I thought he was insane. What the hell was he going to do with a working horse farm? The man knew software, knew numbers. What I didn't factor in was his enormous heart plus his love for the damn beasts. By opening a small equestrian center that offers riding classes, boarding, and grooming services, he can do what he really wanted to do, which is to fund riding classes for underprivileged children in the area. Growing up in a small Southern town, he taught me what he already knew: working with horses is a soothing balm to a soul that's exhausted by pain.

He could—and still does—wander out from his office to the picket fence surrounding the property and stare at them for hours while figuring things out in his head. It's just now the management of the farm has fallen to my shoulders while he deals with something infinitely harder.

As I slide into jeans, I have to admit my time away from the DC grind has been good for me. Sure, I'm still using a well-trained eye on everything that goes on around me. I might question everyone's moves a little more closely. I'm perhaps just a tad more invasive in the day-to-day operations than Ev was, but I'm pretty confident the men aren't thinking of asking my partner for the names of the criminals I put away to place a hit out on me. I'm damned sure not waking up pulling my gun from under my pillow at the slightest noise. Yeah, I'm still battling a hell of a lot of demons, but one of them isn't the respect of the people I now work with. I'm not just the owner's son anymore. I proved my worth on the farm with hard work months ago.

Tossing back the dregs of my first cup, I quickly wash up and tug on a T-shirt without looking in the mirror. I'm tired of seeing the tattered and droopy look around my eyes first thing in the morning. Snagging a ball cap to pull low over my unruly dark hair, I grab my mug and the glass from last night, then dump the used K-Cup into it before heading down to get something to eat.

"Good morning, my darling." My mother glances up from her copy of *Middleburg Life*, the high-end monthly magazine.

"Morning, Mom. Anything interesting?"

"Well, don't be surprised to see the painted foxes popping up in town again," she laughs as I groan aloud. The painted cow thing was cute when I was a kid. Now, everything is coming up painted. In my travels, I've seen painted bulls, painted cats, painted armadillos, and now in Middleburg, painted foxes for charity.

"Great. Just another thing to block up traffic as people stop and stare," I mutter as I dump my K-Cup in the trash, put the crystal in the sink, and move to the full pot I prayed she'd have brewing for another mug.

"Actually, it says they'll be inside the businesses, restaurants, or as a part of their garden area. So, instead of you being able to avoid them, they'll just spring up on you."

"Kind of like when you used to have girls chase after you when you were a kid. Now they're foxes." Ev laughs at his own joke as he makes his way into the kitchen. "Good morning, my love." He leans over to give my mom a brief kiss.

"Cute, Ev, really cute," I growl. He's not wrong though. After we moved to Middleburg in my teens, there wasn't a time when we would go out to eat when some random family would come up and introduce themselves. Inevitably, they would have a daughter I just had to meet. "Little did they know, I was planning on bailing as quickly as I could."

Ev's hand claps down on my shoulder. "Something I'm still proud of you for, son. When all this becomes yours and your mother's, it will mean that much more to you than if I just handed it over."

A crushing mix of panic and pain washes through me. I don't want to think about that day being sooner than we all anticipated. Instead, I give him a head-to-toe perusal. He's dressed much as I am. "You planning to work for your living today?"

Ev tosses his silver-streaked head back and laughs. His green eyes are sparking with mirth. "I thought I'd come out and see how things are operating, yes."

"Then let me toss some food back and we'll get going. I got a late start this morning."

"Monty, you run operations. You're not expected to be mucking out stalls," Ev says with more than a touch of exasperation.

I grin at him. "You work out your problems your way, Ev; I shovel out mine in an entirely different fashion."

My mother slaps her magazine down. "This is not going to be our breakfast conversation. Do you both understand? Gross. Get out of here so I can go back to being a lady of leisure." Ev and I both chortle. My mother is anything but that. She manages the books for all of Parrish Properties—Ev's multitude of investments—which is a job for at least two people. "Why don't we get you both fed and out of the way before Ashley comes in to clean?"

As she passes by, I drop a kiss on her short, graying hair. "Thanks, Mom."

"No, thank you, son." We exchange a meaningful glance. "Now, do you guys want pancakes or eggs with your bacon?"

"What, no sausage?"

My mother makes a gagging noise. Ever since she saw a television show on how sausage is made, she can't stomach making it.

"You're lucky I didn't turn into a vegetarian after that," she mutters as she makes her way to the refrigerator to get out the bacon. "And since you decided to sass me instead of deciding, I'm making pancakes."

"You're cooking, Mom. Like either was a problem."

"He's got you there, honey." Ev comes up behind her and slides his arms around her waist, nuzzling her neck. It's like watching them when I was a teenager. Hell, they act like teenagers.

It'd be fucking fantastic if deep down we all didn't feel like we have a ticking time bomb over our heads.

Ev's blood type is making matching him for a bone marrow transplant inordinately tricky. Since he has O negative blood, he'd be perfect if he was the one donating the marrow he so desperately needs. The problem is receiving it. Not only can he not have any marrow with any A or B antibodies in it, but it also has to be negative of a specific protein in the red blood cells—the Rh factor. Sure, 9 percent of the global population has the same blood type, but out of the seven and a half billion people on the planet, only thirty million are registered bone marrow donors.

The best chance would be a close match, but Ev can't find one.

We're running out of time. Clenching my hands at my side, I feel an overwhelming need to do something. My jaw tight, I go to open my mouth and ask if we've heard anything when I see Ev lower his head to capture my mother's lips in a soft kiss.

And I realize I am.

I'm already helping them by being here and giving them this time.

Flinging myself into a chair across from where my mother was seated before, I give them a few more moments before I jokingly call out, "I'm not smelling any pork frying, Mom."

I hear the soft, wet sound of their lips breaking apart. "Montague Parrish! You're a thirty-eight-year-old man! If you want bacon and can't wait for me to finish kissing Ev, then get off your ass and do it yourself."

I lift my coffee to my lips to hide my smile.

No, it fucking sucks why I'm here, but I wouldn't trade a single second for anything.

FIFTEEN

MONTAGUE

"Has it really come to this?" Weeks later, Ev's spitting into a tube for us to send out to some genealogy company of crackpots to see if there's someone out there who he might be able to pay for their bone marrow.

"Honey, it's not 'come' to anything. This is just another option Dr. Spellman suggested since Ev's lost contact with his family," my mother soothes me.

I hide my fear behind a laugh of disgust and a quick drain of the crystal tumbler in my hand. "Rightfully so. They were a bunch of abusive shits, Mom. They should have been arrested for neglect. They should have…"

Ev makes a choked sound. "Can you rein in your indignation while I'm trying to procure enough phlegm to fill up this tube, son? I love your passion, but as always, discussing my family leaves a sour taste in my mouth."

"Or in this case, dry mouth?" my mother jests.

He nods. "Now that. I, too, am not overly thrilled I may have to rely upon one of them—worse yet, give them some of the money I worked damn hard to earn to do it. I know I'll be opening a door I can never shut if that happens. But if it means getting to spend even six minutes longer with you both, I'll pay anything."

My heart aching, I move next to my mother. Slinging an arm around her shoulder, I manage to grin at the man who taught me not to be satisfied with the life I could have, only to be happy with the life I wanted. By living that, I've fought for everything.

And I'll help him fight for this.

"What do we do now?" I ask once the kit is safely sealed. Casually, I move away from my mother and pick up the small innocuous box.

"Now, we mail this off and wait," Ev declares as he moves around the counter to pull my mother against him.

"And we pray on every star for a miracle," my mother whispers as she curls into his chest.

His bleak eyes meet mine over her shoulder. Ev's silently telling me he doesn't hold out much hope, but he's willing to do anything to give it to my mother.

"You got it, Mom. Not just one star. I'll pray on all of them."

Ev's face twists in agony before he lays his cheek against the top of my mother's head. The ice in my drink clinks against the heavy crystal as I shake it to find the dredges. Setting my glass on the counter, I'm just about to make my excuses to leave them alone when my mother speaks up.

"I know. Why don't we drop this off at the post office and head down to the Rail Stop for dinner tonight?" Ev quickly masks his despair with one of mild amusement. "Let's just go enjoy each other out for a change."

I'd do anything for my mother in this instant, even slip on a sport coat. That still doesn't mean I won't give her lip about it. "Fine. I guess I can pull on a clean T-shirt..."

"Monty, you will put on a jacket, so help me God..." she threatens.

I walk around and ruffle her hair. "Just kidding, Mom. Listen, for their veal, I'll even clean the manure from the pasture off my boots."

Ev smirks while my mother makes a gagging noise. "Go get ready. And stop talking about shit!"

As I stroll toward the stairs, I call over my shoulder, "It's better than talking shit!"

Both of them laugh, which was my intent. But as I turn to climb the back staircase to reach the second door, I catch my mother burrowing into Ev's chest and sobbing.

Crap.

Even if I were kidding with her before—which I wasn't—I sure as hell would be wishing on all the stars now.

Even the ones I don't know could be out there.

AFTER DINNER, I drop Ev and Mom back at the house before I head to Bar Louie in Gainesville to grab a drink to clear my mind. I'm not immune to the women circling me like hungry prey looking for their chance to get a bite, but I couldn't be throwing off more of a "stay away" vibe if I tried as I nurse the manhattan in front of me.

What are we going to do if we lose Ev?

My piece-of-shit father bailed on my mother almost the minute the sperm hit the egg. Her family wasn't much better. If it weren't for some pretty amazing neighbors where we lived in Rosedale, in a tiny one-room apartment in Queens, there'd have been no way we'd have ever survived.

Until I hit my early teens, Mom and I shared a room. At first, it was easy; I was a baby. But as I grew into a toddler, and throughout elementary school, we slept in a bunk bed. Any expectation of privacy got worse for her as time went on. She was determined I would grow up with "good people" in a "safe community." And if she eventually had to sacrifice her bedroom to her son to do that, she would.

And then she met Ev when he came to stay at the high-end hotel she worked at.

Mom would still describe their first meeting as clumsy and sweet, with him being both. She claims she took one look at his green eyes behind the wire-framed glasses he wore and he knocked over an entire vase of flowers onto the check-in desk. The water splattered all over and dripped onto the floor, but she didn't care.

As Ev tells it, all he cared about was making sure the hazel-eyed, Italian beauty who was too busy mopping up his mess would accept his phone number for something other than his dry-cleaning bill.

It took three days, and his ripping up flowers from the urns flanking the doorway of the Waldorf Astoria hotel, for her to realize he was into her.

It took me convincing her at night that if he asked her out again to say yes.

On their first night out, Ev took her to a hidden gem of a Mexican restaurant he heard about. Amid chilaquiles soaked in cheese and sauce, Mom told him she appreciated his flattery, but this could be their only date. As a single mother, she didn't have much time outside of her son.

Ev got quiet before calling for the check, much to my Mom's disappointment. When they were in a town car—presumably to head back to his hotel—he asked if I had any allergies. Confused, she replied, "No. Not that I'm aware of."

"Great. Driver, can you stop at the light up ahead?" Mom was shocked when he jumped out of the car at Magnolia Bakery, waited in line with the touristy lunatics, and then jumped back into the car fifteen minutes later with a dozen cupcakes. "Now, let's go have dessert with your son."

I don't know who fell for Ev first that night—Mom or me.

It was Ev who said, "You don't need a college education right away, Monty. You have time. Find your passion before you invest your heart." And so I did. I joined the Navy with his full support and Mom's worry. I had an aptitude toward law enforcement. Soon, I was transferred to San Antonio to train to become a master-at-arms. I received specialized training before I was deployed to ships all over the world to help keep law and order at sea. During my tours of duty, I went from being a wet-behind-the-ears rookie just out of A school to helping to detain and interrogate suspects as part of the Navy's force protection duties. It made my transition to NCIS's Special Agent Basic Training Program almost seem like a master's education when I applied for and was offered the position.

Fortunately, I didn't waste my time at sea, otherwise, NCIS would never have been possible. I took online courses to earn my degree. I must be the only graduate alive who has a video of his mother in a rented cap and gown gliding down the grand staircase at his family home to celebrate obtaining his college degree at the ripe old age of twenty-eight while I was in the middle of the Indian Ocean on maneuvers.

Still, while Mom made me laugh while she wore a crimson and gold mortarboard and giving the chop of my new alma mater, Florida State, it was Ev's words of "I knew you'd find your dream and make it come true" that made me wish I was able to walk across that stage for them.

Why can't I make their dreams come true to repay them? I think angrily. Another large swallow of my drink hits the spot, soothing the burning anger bubbling up inside me.

A pretty redhead sidles up next to me. "Can I buy you a new drink?" She bats her eyes at me flirtatiously.

My only response is to narrow my eyes even as I lift my drink again to my lips. I don't want company; I want the burn the alcohol will provide in my stomach. I want the ache I'll feel when it hits my stomach.

Pouting, she mutters, "Right," before she slinks off.

The bartender slides a fresh napkin beneath my drink before I put it down. "Judging by the look on your face, I don't suppose you're interested in the three offers of drinks that I've been asked to slide your way, right, Monty?"

"Not really, Mike. Not tonight."

"You're killing me here, man. You could have anyone you wanted. What are you waiting for?" he asks exasperatedly.

Scanning the room filled with people who don't see beyond their immediate needs, I shrug. Standing, I pull out a few bills and toss them next to my drink. "I think I'm looking for a miracle. And I'm not going to find it here."

"Dude, I could have told you that before you walked in the door," he laughs. Holding out his hand, he reaches over and grabs mine. "Come back when you're in a better mood."

I open my mouth to wish him good night when a petite blonde shoves up against my chest.

"Hey, Monty. How are you doing? It's been a while." Her hand lands on my arm, and she trails her fingers up it in a familiar way. Mentally, I'm shaking my head. This little girl is the daughter of one of Ev's business partners. Doing the calculation, I realize if I got started just early enough, this girl could be my daughter.

"It sure has, Amy. Be sure to tell your dad hi when you get home. Okay?" I pull away and head to the front door. After I make it out into the spring night air, I realize I could have easily had a drink tonight in the pasture with the horses and been more content than I was on the scouting grounds of Bar Louie.

I need a new hangout. Either that or maybe I'll toss a few back with Ev while talking in his study or something. One thing I know is I'm getting too old for this shit. Sliding behind the wheel of my Jag, I sit for a few minutes before I let out my frustration punching the steering wheel as hard as I can.

What am I—what are *we*—going to do if we lose Ev?

SIXTEEN

EVANGELINE

I t's late when the car takes me back to my place after dinner
with Sepi. I didn't expect to enjoy myself as much as I did, but
my agent is just so kind, the night out did me good.

Now every block the town car travels, I feel tension creeping
back in my shoulders. Maybe I should take a vacation and get away
for a while, I think absentmindedly. Not forever—my life is here. My
family is here; my job is here. But maybe for a little while.

The car comes to a stop. Peering out the back window, I see we're
at my building. I quickly give the driver a hefty tip using my phone.
"Thank you," I murmur before I open the door and slide my legs out.

Striding to the entrance of the building, I start to call out a
greeting to Lou, the evening doorman, when he interrupts. "Miss
Linnie, Ms. Bristol is waiting for you upstairs."

"What?" Why didn't she call me? I just paid for the car on my
phone, and there weren't any missed messages. "Did she appear to be
okay?" I'm racing toward my private elevator.

"Yes, but she appeared to be agitated," he calls out just as the
doors open. I use the key card to buzz to my floor before I type in the
code.

"Thanks, Lou." The doors close smoothly between us cutting off his reply. As the elevator ascends, the burden that left me at dinner completely erases. My heart is somewhere in the vicinity of my throat, and all the club soda I drank is churning in my stomach. I burst out of the elevator. My sandals make a little clicking sound on the glossy tile outside my entranceway. Knowing the door won't be locked if Bristol's inside, I fling it open.

"She just got here. I'll call you in a few, honey." Bristol hangs up her phone. She comes directly toward me with her hands outstretched, and I race into her arms.

"What is it? Is it Simon? The baby? Tell me," I demand before she can get a word out.

"I think you need to sit down for this," she tells me quietly, guiding me to the large sectional that dominates my family room.

"Bris, you're scaring the living crap out of me," I tell her shakily.

"I couldn't sleep. I don't know why. I decided to get up for a while, figuring I'd catch up on work."

"Okay," I reply, confused.

"And that's when I got the notification. Swear to God, Linnie, it came in less than thirty minutes ago. If it had been longer, I'd have called you..."

"What was it?" My gut's churning. It could be anything. Maybe Veronica went to the press with my parentage after I confronted her. Shit, why didn't I think of that? Mentally berating myself for not talking with Sepi about it, I miss the first part of what Bristol's saying. Tuning in, I catch her midsentence.

"...it was just like the others except for the words after. That's when I woke up Simon to make sure I wasn't seeing things." Her fingers are like a vice on mine.

"What are you talking about, Bris? What was just like the others?" I'm so confused.

Letting go of one of my hands, she brushes a piece of hair that got loose from the knot on my head away from my face. "You got an email to the dummy account, sister. It said 'DNA confirmed: Close Match.'

When I looked at the profile of the person, their name is Rhett Parrish. Linnie, he's the right age."

I start hyperventilating.

Is this possible?

Did I find my father?

"What the hell do I do?" My heart's thumping erratically.

"Read this and tell me if this works before I hit Send." Bristol lets go of my hands, and I wish she wouldn't. I want her to hold on to me. She's the only thing that's real right now, something honest and true.

I don't know this Rhett Parrish. He's nothing more than a name in an email. No, that's a lie, and I refuse to tell more of them than I have to. Especially than to myself. He's the genetic reason for half the cells in my body. Taking an enormous breath, I read what she wrote.

Mr. Parrish,

My name is Lynn Brogan. If you're the 'Rhett' identified in my mother's, Elle Brogan, diary that I found upon her death earlier this year, then it may be possible I am your biological daughter. This is something I was...

SEVENTEEN

MONTAGUE

I was not aware of until that time. I am not sure if you had any knowledge of this information before now as well. If you didn't, I apologize for the shock this must be causing you as well.

As far as I can piece things together, thirty-four years ago, you met my mother when she was on a break from her long-standing boyfriend. They reconciled shortly after your affair; married soon after that.

You may wonder why my mother and I use her maiden name. At the time you knew her, she had just established a communications firm out of New York City. She was successful at the venture, and I followed into the family business. In doing so, I elected to use her name professionally, although my birth certificate does carry that of the man I thought was my biological father.

I am not trying to intrude on your life, Mr. Parrish. Since my stepfather died early of cancer and my mother recently passed due to undetected heart issues, and the recent discovery about my actual parentage, my half-sister and I decided to have a DNA test performed to identify any medical concerns we could preemptively address.

It led me to you.

I expect nothing from you, but I do hope you may be able to provide me with some medical background for me to be able to ensure my good health and good health to any future children I may have.

With my best regards,

Lynn Brogan

My mother's voice trails off. I toss my head back and finish the drink I poured myself the minute I entered Ev's study after they called me down at the barn to tell me he had a close match. Without a word to the groom I had been talking with, I charged down the path so fast, I thought I was going to be sick.

"Holy crap. You have a daughter." I blurt the first thing that comes to mind.

"That about sums up how I'm feeling." Ev scrubs his hands over his face. He's sitting on the edge of the desk near my mother. He's pale, but I'm not worried it has anything to do with his illness. Pure shock is etched across his features.

"Do you remember her mother?" I ask. Reaching for my mother's hand, he nods.

"I met Elle in a bar in Chicago when I was in my late twenties. I was out there for a conference; she said she was too. It was right after I'd come up with the code and the company was about to go public." Ev's eyes take on a faraway look. Mom goes to stand behind him, not letting go of his hand. "Elle had no idea which button on a computer turned it on." His voice is amused. "She had long dark hair and bright blue eyes. I remember her being very artsy, almost bohemian. Uninhibited. The first time I saw her, she got up on stage and blew the doors off the place singing karaoke. I introduced myself right after."

Mom laughs. "Did your amazing singing voice impress or scare her?" I relax subtly, realizing this isn't going to cause even further strain on them than what they're already facing.

Ev grins. "I didn't get the chance to do either. I scratched my name off the list. You know," he says thoughtfully, "hearing you read that Elle ran a successful communications company astounds me, to be honest. She didn't give the impression of being all that business savvy." Ev's astounded.

"So, there was no concern about corporate espionage?" I wonder aloud.

"Not after the first night, no. When I say she did not know about computers, I mean none. I'd leave her to give a talk on encryption, and her face would be blank. And I'm not talking complex theories here, Monty. The name I used on the profile, Rhett?" He jerks his head toward Mom's laptop. "That's what I was called back home before school. I was already going by Everett by the time I made it through my first week at Tech. She never challenged it. If she ever tried to find me to tell me she was pregnant, she never would have been able to. Rhett Parrish existed...but didn't."

"I understand. You were starting to become high profile, Ev. It's not a crime."

"No, but I wonder if my daughter's going to feel the same way when I tell her that," he says bleakly. Pulling my mother around so she's standing in front of him, he focuses on her. "Char, this was years before I ever met you. I never knew."

"Sweetheart, I know." Leaning forward, she whispers something in his ear that causes his body to sag in relief. "What you did before you met me has nothing to do with how much you love me now."

Except it does, I think grimly. Because we're about to invite this unknown woman into our lives to try to save Ev's.

"I THINK you should let me look her up," I argue. I'm pacing back and forth in front of Ev's desk in his library. Mom's gone off to bed so she can make us her infamous mixed berry galette to celebrate something we didn't have before.

Hope.

I still don't know if what we have is hope. I still feel like we're working on a Hail Mary pass. Acid pitches the alcohol I've been drinking around in my stomach. I rub a hand against it to calm myself down. I'm going to need a half a dozen antacids before bed at this rate.

Ev's sitting behind his computer shaking his head. "No way, Monty. What I learn about my daughter is going to come from her. Do you understand me?" His green eyes narrow in fierce determination. "You don't want to appreciate how disappointed I will be to learn otherwise."

Shit. "Fine," I grit out even though it goes against everything inside me to protect the people I love. Storming over to the decanter of brandy, I pour myself a healthy splash. Turning to Ev, I hold up the decanter. He shakes his head. I keep forgetting the meds he's on don't encourage drinking. Instead, I pour him a glass of soda water. Grabbing both tumblers, I approach his desk. "But the very minute you give me the okay, I'm calling in every favor I have to look this woman up. We can know everything about her in a matter of hours."

"Son." I feel a chill race down my spine at the endearment because I'm not Ev's son. Not really. Not anymore. He has a biological daughter who might be able to do what I can't.

Save him.

"Yeah, Ev?"

"I do need your help with two things."

Taking a swallow, I nod without hesitation. "You don't have to ask."

He takes a small sip of his own. "Even though Char is handling this better than anything I could have predicted, if it gets to the point where we meet Lynn..."

"I'll keep an eye out on Mom," I promise. He lets out a sigh of relief. "What's the other?"

"Would you help me write this letter back to Lynn? I've been thinking about it all night, and I have no idea what to say."

"Ev, I don't think it's insane to ask her for a picture of her mother," I caution. "Maybe you wouldn't recognize a current one, but surely she has an older one that you would. It's not a ridiculous ask." I tick off my list of concerns. "She doesn't have a profile picture. She doesn't list any family surnames. She's not connected to anyone else on the platform."

Brushing his lips across his glass, he contemplates what I'm saying. "So you're concerned it could be a scam. Someone who happens to know me and is exploiting..."

"Let's just say I'd want the picture as a gesture of good faith." I leave it at that.

"Then I'm going to need your help writing back," he says grimly.

Standing, I walk around behind the desk. "Let's write this offline, and you can just copy it in," I suggest.

Pulling up his word processing program, I begin to dictate. *Dear Lynn...*

EIGHTEEN

EVANGELINE

T o say I, too, was shaken by our connection is an understatement. The genetic output, compounded with what you have shared, do lead me to believe I am your biological father. I immediately told my wife and my stepson about you. We appreciate your courtesy while we process the news.

I own a farm in the Northern Virginia area where I'm semi-retired. If you've never been to the area, it's beautiful countryside—rolling green hills in summer and the mountains are covered with the most spectacular foliage in the fall.

You mentioned you are in the communications field in New York City. That sounds like an interesting profession. I was there recently for my wife's and my twenty-fifth wedding anniversary. It's was an exciting city to visit. Very energetic. If your mother is the woman I'm thinking of, I'm both happy and impressed over your success. In part, because the woman I remember as Elle couldn't tell one end of a computer from the other. The only technology I knew she could work adeptly was a microphone. That is if I remember her.

As you have Elle's journal, your memory of what occurred so many years ago is a great deal stronger than mine. I don't know if you *have a picture of your mother from that time; it would help me to recall the past fully. Unfortunately, it was a long time ago, Lynn. Many years have passed. And I'll be terribly embarrassed if I'm sharing memories of the wrong one.*

I hope this finds you well. I look forward to hearing from you.

Rhett Parrish

My hands are shaking as Bristol scrolls through the email that dinged my phone, prompting me to race down to her office. "What do you think? Is it unreasonable to send him a picture of Mom from back then?"

Bristol is thoughtful. "I don't think so. He's cautious, Linnie. You laid out a lot in that initial email. This is a simple request to make certain you're not some sicko. Frankly, he could have asked to have seen Mom's journal, and it wouldn't have been completely unreasonable."

I was thinking the same thing. "Do you have access to the family cloud drive from here?" Years ago, Mom paid a small fortune to have all of her photos and our childhood photos digitally scanned.

She nods. "You know what I wonder..." Her voice trails off.

My lips fall open. "Do you think Mom has a picture of him?"

"I don't know why we didn't think of it." Bristol looks irritated as hell. "We could have gone the normal route and hired an investigator if we'd just thought of that."

"But just think, we know it's likely both our fathers hate cilantro," I joke, trying to lighten the mood.

"There is that. Now, what week was it?"

"Somewhere around November twelfth. She was doing a traveling production of *Anything Goes*, remember?" I give her a wry smile.

"Since you're named after one of the characters, it's kind of hard to forget that. Better than being named after the place you were conceived," she tacks on as her fingers fly across the keyboard.

"I don't know. I've always kind of liked your... Bris, what is it?" Panicked, I surge to my feet and race around her desk.

"Linnie." Shaken eyes raise to meet mine. "I think I might have the perfect picture for you to send to him." Turning her monitor slightly, I see a picture of a dark-haired man with his arm wrapped around Mom. Ignoring the shaft of pain, seeing her so young, vital, and alive does to me, I focus solely on the man. Despite the red eye cameras in that day and age caused more often than not, because Bristol zoomed in I can see the edge of green eyes. Eyes that match my own.

Bristol's arm wraps around me. I whisper, "Do you think we should send him a picture of me as well? Maybe not a professional shot, but one that shows him I'm who I say I am?"

"Maybe once he responds to your next email accepting that he's your father? Let's play it by ear."

Letting out a shuddering breath, I sit down behind Bristol's massive desk and pull up a new message. Attaching the picture, I write a simple email.

Dear Rhett...

NINETEEN

MONTAGUE

I think you'll recognize the man in the picture.

Mom cataloged all of her and my childhood photos not too long ago. We had these on our family cloud drive. I don't know why I didn't think to go through there first. But then, you likely would have been contacted through an investigative agency instead of by me directly.

And yes, you're right. Mom really didn't understand technology all that well. She did have a fantastic rapport with people. It's something that made her a legend in the business.

Best,

Lynn

Even I'm shaken by the image of Ev, one that doesn't look at all different from when I met him. "That was about seven years before I met you both," he murmurs. "I was about to turn thirty. I thought I was on top of the world because of the business." Pulling my mother close, he kisses the top of her head. "Then I walked into a hotel in New York and acted like a bumbling idiot to the most beautiful woman I ever met, and my life changed forever."

Mom shakes him. "Ev, honey, stop thinking this is a bad thing. This could be the miracle we've been hoping for."

He cups her face. "We were never able to have a baby. Why? Was I already sick?"

Mom's face twists in agony. "I don't know. And I don't care. We had Monty and each other. That's all we ever needed."

"Char, if we do this, we're inviting a child I had with another woman into our lives."

"Ev, if we don't, I might not have you in mine," she whispers.

And there it is. My mother wouldn't care if Ev had had an affair at one point and this child was the result. Her love for him is so strong, she'd be willing to sacrifice anything to save him. I turn my back to them to give them a few moments of privacy. Even as I move to the big windows overlooking the barn, I can hear whispers though I can't make out the words. I'm dying to ask someone to investigate the hell out of this woman before Ev risks everything.

But I made a promise. Bracing my arm against the windowsill, I lean against it and let out a long breath. In so many ways, this is wrong. For Ev, for my mother, hell, even for the unknown Lynn. She's about to meet her father after suffering her own tragedy, and then she's going to be propositioned for bone marrow like she's a pharmaceutical rep. I'm dragged back into the conversation when I hear him say, "...meet in person."

"What the hell, Ev?" I turn around and send him a glare. He meets it head-on.

"I think Lynn deserves to meet her father. At least once."

"So, you're going to bring her here? To the farm?" I'm incredulous.

"Give me a little more credit than that. I thought we could meet on neutral grounds. Maybe DC? She could take the shuttle down, we'll meet for lunch, and then she could head back to New York," he adds.

Christ. This is getting complicated. "When do you want to set this up?"

"I don't know." He rubs his hand across his forehead. "I suppose a lot of that depends on her. I don't know her, Monty. Yes, she's my daughter, but what if all she wants is what her first email said? What if all she wants is information to check a box in her orderly life? What if she has no desire actually to meet me?"

"Why do you want to meet her?" I ask him quietly. "You don't need to, you know." I read that plenty of donors don't.

His jaw falls open as if to ask me, *Are you stupid?* "She's my daughter. If for some reason this doesn't work, I don't want regrets. I need to know what she looks like, what her touch feels like, who she is. It's consuming me." His shaking hand reaches for the glass of tea next to him.

I stand and walk back over toward them. "Are you sure this is what you really want?"

Ev lets out a gush of air. "Someday, I hope you understand the beauty and hell of raising a child—the deep-seated pride at their every accomplishment and the depthless agony when they're hurting. It makes all of this"—he lifts his arm holding the glass to encompass the room—"seem worthless by comparison. Now, I just found out I have another one out there who I didn't know existed? Who by chance and sheer desperation on my part I managed to find? Of course I want to meet her. Yes, there is some tiny hope she might be the answers to all our prayers, but I know nothing about that. As her last living parent, I'd do anything to be the answer to hers." He lifts the glass to his lips and drains it, causing the ice to rattle around inside.

Astonished by the vehemence in his words, I deflate. I never thought Ev was seeking out my assistance because he had unfathomable regrets towards a daughter who he just found right at what might be the end of his life. My eyes dart around the room as I try to order my thoughts. On the shelf behind Ev's desk is a picture of Mom, Ev, and me taken the day they got married. Down a few inches to the left is a gag mug I got him for Father's Day years ago that says, "Dad Joke, Loading...please wait" in deference to his love of all things computer. Then there's a picture of just the two of us Mom captured of us riding when I was home on leave where we're both laughing. But as much as I know he loves me, and I love him—God, do I love him—I can't be the biological child he must be craving.

And I can't save his life like she might be able to.

"I don't think," I slowly begin. Ev's eyes cut over to me. "That she's going to necessarily drop everything, jump on a plane, and race down here. She's going to be wary, suspicious. Unless something changes quicker than we expect, you've got some time. You need to establish a relationship with her, Ev. It's going to chafe at you, but the way I see it is that either I pull in my markers, or you hire a firm to investigate her, or..."

"Or I put in the effort to get to know my daughter? I don't push this like I would have a boardroom decision?"

"Pretty much," I tell him bluntly. It's not what he wants to hear, but it's the truth.

"There are so many things I still want to share with you." His voice is rich with emotion.

"Me?" I'm confused. We were talking about his daughter. But at Ev's nod, my head begins to spin. He stands up from behind his desk and walks around to lean against the front of it.

"Yes. I want you to be happy again. Being home has been good for you. I'm starting to see you heal from whatever it is that's hurt you, but I want to see you happy." He leans down and claps my shoulder. "It's a father's prerogative."

"Ev." Just his name and even then, I can barely get the words out. I shake my head as I try to find more, but he goes on.

"I want to watch you fall in love. I want to hold your children from the moment they're born and give them what I couldn't give to you, which is every moment of my time from the first second they open their eyes. If there's any gift that I could give you, it would be more time."

I can't blink fast enough to stop the tears. "Why are you saying all of this now?"

"Because if I can't, if I never get the chance, I want you to know it's been my privilege to be your father all of these years, Montague. Just because I need to settle this part of my life, doesn't mean I regret one minute of my past." Letting go of my shoulder, he moves back behind his desk. He picks up his drink and takes a hefty swallow, staring immobile at the screen in front of him.

I stare out the wall of windows and into the inky darkness. If I were outside, I'd be able to see the stars glittering down like little jewels on the horses as they rest in the paddock. Even though I'm not out there, it's enough to know they are. They always will be.

Kind of like my love for the man in this room. It just is. Nothing will change that.

"Ev, I think you need to tell her how you met her mother. Even if she knows the story from her perspective, she should hear it from yours. There are things you likely remember that her mother didn't write down. Complete the image in her head. Tell her what a day is like for you here. Ask her what a day is like for her in New York." I turn and find him regarding me thoughtfully. "Be you but don't give away your identity just yet, if you know what I mean."

"I do."

"Then you don't need my help sending an email to your daughter. You're a bright guy with a lot of love to share." Crossing the room, I do something I haven't done in too long, and I hate that I haven't. I drop a kiss on the top of his head. "Love you, Ev. Let me know how it goes."

I make my way toward the double doors that guard Ev's study when I hear his cracked voice call out, "Monty?"

I stop in my tracks. "Yeah?"

"I love you too, son."

I let the reminder of that seep through me, igniting parts of my soul that have been slowly losing their light. But I flick up my hand in a quick acknowledgment before I leave Ev to his email, knowing he'll show me what he wrote before he hits Send.

ACT 2 – I'M POSITIVE.

TWENTY

EVANGELINE

AUGUST

"I'm a mess," I confide in Bristol. I'm pacing the Newsroom: Rise Up Suite in the Hamilton Hotel in Washington, DC. After a month of emailing back and forth, Rhett suggested meeting in a neutral location. He generously offered to pay for my ticket to fly down and back, which I politely declined.

Due to the sensitivity of why I'm coming, I decided to charter a jet and fly in and out of Teterboro using their private jet service, which helps reduce the possibility of being followed. And right now, I need every ounce of anonymity I can hold on to. I don't know if the minute I walk through the door at Georgia Browns—a restaurant I've enjoyed in the past when I've performed at the Kennedy Center—whether or not I'll be recognized.

I hope not.

"Linnie, will you calm down? I would hardly call Rhett a stranger. You just haven't met him yet," she points out diplomatically.

"What if I walk in and I forget everything I want to ask, everything I want to say?" Bristol starts laughing. "It's not funny, damnit."

"It sure as hell is. When was the last time that Evangeline Brogan ever flubbed a line?" she teases me.

I open my mouth to retort, but nothing comes out but a grunt, which sets her off further. "At least help take my mind off of it. How's my future niece or nephew cooking in there?"

"Wonderfully. Simon is freaking out. He's looking into animal chipping right now." Bristol's voice is serene.

"Animal chipping?" I repeat to make sure I heard her correctly. There's a clatter on the other end of the phone as someone puts me on speaker.

"You know, like a geolocation chip? The things they put into cats and dogs to find them?" My lips curve as Simon's exasperation comes through loud and clear. "If a pet can have it, why can't my kid?"

"Are you feeding him too much cilantro? That freaking food must do something over time to mess with the brain," I muse.

"Not helping, Linnie," Simon grates out. Bristol doesn't bother to reply; she's laughing too hard. I take pity on my brother-in-law and try to calm him down.

"Simon, I trust so few people around us, it's a wonder the counting doesn't stop on my middle finger." I'm outright grinning when I hear him snort. "That doesn't mean I believe your son is in imminent danger."

"She will be when she's sixteen and looks like her mother," he argues. Aww, now that's sweet. Simon's hoping for a little girl.

"Then you can track he or she down by her phone or whatever technology is available at that time. In fact, wouldn't that be a better use of your time? Maybe by learning how to become a little more internet savvy? Don't be one of those parents who are so easy to fool you become an embarrassment. God, Bris, it wasn't until Rhett brought it up that I remembered how awful Mom was at the computer," I think back nostalgically. Mom was so computer illiterate that she even guilted Bristol and me to do her online shopping for her. We taunted her one Christmas with one of those phones that had only four buttons on it. Imagine our surprise when she started using it.

No wonder Rhett was shocked when I said she owned and operated a "communications firm," I think derisively. But thoughts of

Rhett lead me back to my current problems. "Maybe I should call and tell him I couldn't make it," I whine.

"Maybe you should woman up and realize the search for your father is almost done. After tomorrow, you can choose to have everything or nothing to do with him ever again," Bristol says brutally.

"I hate when you're logical."

"I hate when you're emotional. This is why we work."

"I hate when you both won't shut up and let me look at microchips for my kid," Simon interjects. There's a momentary pause before we both start giggling.

"Now, tell me what you plan on wearing," Bristol asks.

"And with that, take your sister off the speaker. I found a doctor in South America who might be willing to chip..."

"We are not putting a chip in our child." Bristol's voice is firm.

Simon's sigh in the background is his only response.

"Well, I'm down to two outfits." Though I brought eight for an overnight stay.

"Tell me about them," Bristol encourages. I start talking. Soon we're arguing the benefits of what I should wear the first time I meet my father.

We don't get off the phone for another hour, an hour where for now everything's going to be just fine.

It isn't until later when I'm left alone with my thoughts the worry comes rushing back.

SINCE I'VE EATEN at Georgia Browns before, I know the dress at lunchtime is usually business suits since it's so close to the White House. Bristol convinced me last night not to wear the suit from St. John and instead to flaunt my natural style. The trendy skinny jeans I'm wearing have just enough detailed stitching to be dressy. They're paired with a simple violet-red silk tee.

On top of that, I shove my arms into a hip-length leather jacket that's soft enough for me to scrunch up the sleeves. Adding more height to my already long legs, I've paired the look with a pair of leather boots. Finishing the look, I slip on a Tiffany bone cuff and diamond studs.

Grabbing my phone off the charger, I stride over to the full-length mirror and take a picture before texting to Bristol. *Well, I'm as ready as I'm going to be. Now that I'm dressed, I can't throw up.* I press Send.

A few dots come back. *Take your hair down.*

My fingers fly. *Then I'll be playing with it the whole time.*

You look like you made too much of an effort otherwise. Shit, I hate when she's right. Undoing the hair clip, I flip my head upside down and give it a good shake. My long dark brown hair settles down the middle of my back. I take a new picture. *Better?* Before I hit Send, I attach the eye-rolling emoji.

Much comes back almost instantaneously. I capture one side of my lip nervously before I type, *Do I hug him?*

Linnie, do what comes naturally. Only you can make that decision.

Before I can respond, another message pops up. *Just promise me you won't play a part with Rhett. This may be your only shot. Let yourself be and feel whatever you want.*

Right. If I let myself feel what I want, Rhett's going to think he's got a basket case on his hands. Instead, I ask, *Would you tell him the truth? That the background we created was fabricated?*

I'd see how it goes. It's only the first meeting. Now, go. You're going to be late. And remember, everything's going to be just fine.

Fine. Yeah. If we go by the Aerosmith definition of it, sure. It's going to be just fine. I type back. *Yep. Love you. I'll talk to you later.*

Her *XOXO* settles my stomach slightly as I slip my phone into my bag. Leaving the room, I check the door to make sure it's locked. I head over to the elevator, press the button, and wait. The silver mirrored doors open, and inside there's a man nonchalantly leaning against the wall and fiddling with his phone. *Hello, delicious.* Wow, that face is something I'd like to spend more than an elevator ride looking at. "Excuse me," I murmur, slipping on a pair of sunglasses. Then I watch him openly in the mirrored walls of the elevator. Built with long muscles, this man reminds me of a panther; dark and sleek.

"Not a problem at all." His voice washes over me. I feel an unusual chill race up and down my spine. "Hey, Ev. Yeah, I'm in the elevator. I'll be at the restaurant in two minutes. Did Mom buy out half of City Center?" There's a pause before he laughs. "Tell me it's not all waiting at the table and she arranged for it to be delivered. Good. I'm about to get out. See you in about two minutes."

The elevator's slowed, so I know he's not wrong. Unfortunately, that means I have to move and not focus on the eye candy I got to enjoy. As the doors smoothly open, his left hand reaches out to keep them open. "I know this is going to sound insane in a city of almost a million people, but have we met?"

The line is so trite, it has me smiling up at him as I pass. But it helps settle the nerves at meeting my father for the first time. "Sorry, I'm pretty certain we haven't. I don't live in the area."

Stepping out behind me, he asks, "How long are you in town? I'd be happy to show you around." His voice drops further. "Anywhere you want to go."

My breath catches as I stare into eyes that are a swirl of green and brown fringed by dark brown lashes. His dark hair is just beginning to see a few dots of silver, but it does nothing to detract from the sexiness of his strong jaw covered in a light stubble. He's easily got to be six foot three, able to look down on me even while I'm in my power boots. Even if he's a bit leaner than the guys I normally date, he's a delicious package, that's for sure. It's too bad I have much more pressing matters at hand. I can't remember the last time I was so immediately physically attracted to someone.

"It's a damn shame I won't be here long." My fingertips trail over the lapel of his sports coat. "Bad timing." I turn and head out the front door onto K Street.

While a diversion as gorgeous as that certainly would have

distracted me after meeting my father, I don't have the time to arrange a follow-up meeting. I'm supposed to walk into Georgia Browns in less than a minute. As it is, I'm going to be making a grand entrance because I'm already running late.

Way to seek out the spotlight even when you don't want to, Linnie.

TWENTY-ONE

MONTAGUE

I t wasn't just a pickup line. I feel like I've been in the position of watching her walk away from me, but I can't quite remember where or when. There's something about the confidence in her stride, I muse as I follow her a few feet down K Street. The tilt of her head as she pauses to slip her phone out to check something on it before tucking it back into a small shoulder bag. Then my heart stops when I see her duck under the distinctive awning of Georgia Browns. She steps aside as the door's held open for her.

I hold back, lest she thinks I'm deliberately following her. My heart is thumping in my chest as my mind begins to make connections. Long mahogany hair. Dimples in the corners of her mouth when her lips curved a few moments ago. Ev has both of those. What would be the chances the woman I just asked out could be Lynn Brogan?

Inside, the bronze branches crawl their way around the restaurant like the live oaks found in the rich history of Savannah's low country. The carpet is a subtle gray green, giving the feeling of being draped in the Spanish moss that wraps the oaks year-round. The lighting is encased in the restaurant's signature honeybee color, a tribute to the state of Georgia's official insect designated as such in 1975. The restaurant is a work of art; not to mention its delicious food, which is why Ev, Mom, and I make it a point to come here as often as we can.

Since the crowd from the White House hasn't let out for lunch yet, it's easy enough for me to spot them. Ev lifts his hand in acknowledgment. I'm debating whether I should quietly shift around her when she decides for me. Squaring her shoulders, she approaches the maître d'. "Excuse me. My name is Lynn Brogan. I'm supposed to be joining Mr. Parrish for lunch this afternoon."

Before he can open his mouth, I cup her elbow. Startled, she turns. "You!" She tries to yank her arm away, but I tighten my fingers slightly.

"I'll be happy to escort you to your table. I had no idea who you... Ev's been waiting a long time to meet you," I finish lamely.

"Ev? Who are you talking about?" Her eyes dart to the left, and she's ready to bolt. She starts jerking her arm back and forth in my hand. "Lynn, stop," I order.

"How do you know my name?" she whispers, frightened.

"My name is Montague Parrish, though everyone but my mother calls me Monty." The color starts to leech from her face. "Rhett's full name is Everett."

Horror washes over her features. "Do you mean to tell me my half-brother just tried to hit on me?"

"No. I'm merely your stepbrother."

"Oh, well, that's so much better." She runs her free hand through her hair, sending it into complete disarray before the thick strands fall back into place perfectly. "Were you following me?" she demands.

"Not really," I hedge.

This time I let her take the step back. "Care to explain?"

"Did I technically walk behind you from the hotel to here because we're also staying at the Hamilton? Yes. Was I deliberately following you? No." Her indignation deflates at that. A stain blushes her pale cheeks, and she looks away.

"I apologize. I..." Letting go of her elbow, I reach up and give her arm a quick squeeze before letting it go. "Listen, would it help you to know he's as nervous as you are?" I don't feel like I'm betraying Ev by sharing that. One look at the table and she'll know that for herself.

"Honestly? Yes, it does. Thank you." She closes her eyes for one heartbeat, two, before opening them. "Lynn Brogan." She extends her hand.

"Monty Parrish." I glance over her shoulder at the maître d' and give him a jerk of my head, dismissing him. He discreetly moves away. "May I escort you to meet your father and my mother?"

The panicked look that had receded from her face comes rushing back. "Your mother's here too? Why would Rhett do this to me?"

"I think he had some idea that meeting all of us at once might be easier on you."

"Yeah, well, a little warning next time," she mutters adorably.

I cock my head to the side. "Is there going to be a next time? Are you a genetic phenom who has three sets of parents?"

Lynn hauls off and smacks me in the arm before realizing what she did. "Oh. My. God. I am so sorry. Did I hurt you?"

I grin. "You need a drink if you think a little thing like you can hurt me." I hold out my arm for hers.

Tucking her fingers beneath my elbow, she mutters, "I don't drink alcohol. But a rocking Shirley Temple sounds great right about now."

I halt our progression around the bar. "Seriously? You don't drink?"

"No. I don't even really like food cooked with alcohol."

Interesting. "Okay. I'd ask about any sauces you're unfamiliar with, but most of the food here is just amazing low-country Southern cooking."

Lynn shakes her head. "I've eaten here before and I still don't know what that means."

Pulling back, I scan her from head to toe. "It means you should know you're going to wish you didn't eat for three days once you get started."

As I start moving us forward again, I think I hear her say, "I didn't eat because I was so nervous."

Ah, well, crap.

As we approach the table, I give my mother and Ev a reassuring smile. "Look who I ran into at the hostess station." I drop Lynn's arm and place a hand at the small of her back.

Ev gets to his feet slowly. "Lynn?" he whispers in shock. "You look just like Elle did but..."

She holds out her hand. "With your eyes. I always wondered where they came from. Mom said it was from a distant relative."

He scrambles around the table and clutches both of Lynn's hands in his. They stare at each other as I move around to Mom. It's beautiful, awful, and painful to watch. I curl Mom into my chest when I hear Lynn ask, "So, which do you prefer? Everett, Ev, or Rhett? Monty gave away your full name earlier when he was trying to prevent me from screaming holy hell after he accosted me in the foyer."

Mom bursts out laughing. I have to defend myself. "I did not 'accost' you. I was merely trying to detain you as you looked like you were ready to bolt."

She snickers. "What are you? A cop or something?"

Mom and Ev answer, "Something," in unison. I tack on, "I was, but I recently changed jobs." Her lips part in surprise.

"Let's sit. Get some drinks. I'm Charlotte—Char—Monty's mother." Mom holds out her hand for Lynn to shake. Lynn reaches past me and squeezes.

"It's a pleasure. And please, everyone, make it Linnie. That's what my close friends and my family call me."

Linnie. It suits the sharp, funky woman sitting next to me much better than Lynn does. "So, who's sitting where?" I ask.

Ev's still in a state of shock. He's barely moved since his daughter approached the table. "Why don't you sit next to Linnie, sweetheart. This way, I can snap Ev out of his stupor," Mom suggests.

"Probably a good idea," I joke.

"So, it is Ev," Linnie confirms, as I hold her chair for her.

Since he seems incapable of speech, I answer for him. "Yes."

She turns to her father and asks, "Then why use Rhett on your profile?"

Ev opens and closes his mouth like a fish. It's Mom who answers. "When Ev was younger, a lot of people knew him by that name. If they wanted to make a connection, he figured that would be the name they recognized."

Linnie's about to respond when the waiter approaches our table for drinks. She orders a Shirley Temple with crushed mint in the bottom. Mom looks at her appraisingly. "That sounds...delicious. Can I have one as well?"

Linnie blushes. "I don't drink, but please don't think you don't have to on my account."

"I host luncheons all the time, and people are always trying to top one another for the menu. You'll excuse the fact if this taste as good as it sounds, I'm totally going to steal the idea." Both women laugh.

"Be my guest. I had it once with lemonade at a restaurant, but I decided to nix the lemonade."

"You do you, Linnie." I toast her with the water glass sitting at my right.

"So, how was your flight down?" Ev's voice is low and quiet, but at least he's broken his self-imposed silence.

Linnie picks up her glass of water and takes a small sip. "A bit bumpy. I had some rough weather."

Ev frowns. "It's been a beautiful day."

She shrugs. "It was horrible yesterday. I flew through torrential rain over Delaware. I swear, I thought the state wanted to keep me it seemed to take so long to go over it."

"Why didn't you say you were coming in last night? You were all alone?"

"Sometimes, I need a little downtime. Time to just...be. I'm not a huge fan of flying to begin with, and I knew I'd be anxious meeting you. I decided to come in a day early so I could curl up with a bowl of ice cream, reread your emails, and be talked off the ledge of insanity by my sister. Who, by the way, says hello. Since she's read every email you sent, she feels she knows you already." Ev's face is a mixture of humorous tragedy.

Mom tries to steer the conversation to neutral ground. "Where did you stay last night? There are so many lovely places in the area."

Linnie lets out a low laugh that hits me right in the gut. As she tosses her hair over her shoulder, I can't help but stare at her. God, she's beautiful. "Funny enough, I stayed next door." At the startled expression on my mother's face, she laughs. "I know. That's why I accused Monty of accosting me in the foyer. He and I rode in the elevator together from the Hamilton."

"That's before I tried to ask her out," I toss out casually.

Both Ev and Mom's eyes turn on me like I'm fifteen again and was just caught with my hands down Natalie Wells's pants on our first date. "You didn't," Ev breathes.

I point a finger at him. "Don't go there. I believe I'm the one who recommended asking Linnie for a current picture."

"True," Ev gives in. "But even I recognized she looks just like Elle."

"Who was more than just a single photograph on your brain, Ev," I counter. The waiter approaches with our drinks. After putting them down, I lift my Kentucky lemonade. "A toast, to families. Those who are with us now." I nod to Linnie. "Those who are in our hearts always." I smile at my mother.

"Beautifully said." Linnie's lips curves, showing off both of her dimples. I ignore the punch to my gut and tip my glass forward. The four of our glasses clink together in the center of the table before we all take a sip. Suddenly my mother bursts out with, "Linnie, this is delicious. I am absolutely serving this at my next event."

The woman sitting next to me sends my mother a dazzling smile that could light up a room. "Have at it, Char. Ugh. I still need to figure out what to eat. This place is divine."

"Tell me what you were thinking," my mother encourages. And

soon, the two most important women in Everett Parrish's life are chatting away inconsequentially about lunch choices. I know Ev wants to break in and ask more in-depth questions, but for now, he sits back and sips his drink, reveling in the moment.

Taking my cue from a man who's taught me so much, I decide to do the same.

TWENTY-TWO

EVANGELINE

"Tell me what working in communications is like, Linnie." I freeze at the question my father asks me.

"I do a lot of talking." And singing, but I keep that to myself. I hope that answer satisfies my father, who has come out of his shell during our meal. After all, I have no idea what someone who works in communications actually does.

When I panicked one night after my father asked what I did for a living, Bristol suggested I tell him I'm in communications. "After all, you do 'vocalize' a lot to people." She grinned.

"True," I'd readily agreed at the time.

By explaining that Brogan LLC was a communications firm instead of the way I pay my publicist, lawyers, agent, accountant, and her, it seemed like the perfect solution. Mom and I used to run everything through the same overhead corporation, with our own individual sub corporations to handle our separate finances. Bristol and my accountant handle everything with ease. I drag myself in tirelessly for quarterly updates where I'm assured the government is getting their healthy chunk of my earnings and the rest is being invested soundly.

"Do you have to travel a lot?" Monty asks me. Gratefully, I can answer that one honestly.

"No. There are occasional trips where I have to handle something outside of New York, but I've been very fortunate. I pretty much get to pick and choose my...clients." I almost flubbed up and said roles.

"Is it going to be a lot more stress on you now that your mother is gone?" Char asks gently. I bite my lip to keep the tears from overflowing. My voice is scratchy when I answer her.

"Emotionally, it's already been an overload of stress. I feel like there's this huge weight on my shoulders I can't let go of. But if you mean work? No. She picked and chose what she did at this point. There won't be any additional workload felt by anyone." Even though some are still grieving her loss, they're already salivating over the opportunities Brielle Brogan's death means.

Monty jumps into the conversation. "So, is it nine-to-five? Do you have an office?"

Thank God Bristol prepped me to answer this. "We tend to go on-site to work." I stretch the truth so thin, you could read my next Playbill through it. "And no, my hours are not a straight forty; more often than not, I work six days a week."

Char laughs. "You inherited that from both your parents, then." She points at Ev. His cheeks pink. "He was a complete workaholic. Even now, if I don't open the door to his office around mealtime, I'd never see him."

I laugh at the imagery. "So, the adage is true but slightly modified? It's not the way to a man's heart, but the way to see if he exists?"

"Exactly," she agrees.

"I'm so glad my daughter and my wife are ganging up against me. Monty, you're still on my team, right, son?" Something catches a little inside at hearing my father call another man his son, but I dismiss it. After all, Patrick was a decent father, I guess, until he found out I wasn't his. And I can't blame him after my reaction. I just feel sad we were never able to reconnect since he died.

"I'm remaining neutral, Ev. Since I came back to work for you, I've rather enjoyed not having to cook for myself." He smiles. His eyes crinkle at the corners, causing little flutters in my stomach the way they did when he stopped me at the hotel a few hours earlier.

"What is it you do? Did?" I correct myself. By steering the conversation away from myself, I hope to learn more about my father. Certainly, it's not to find out more about my new stepbrother.

"We own a farm in Northern Virginia," Monty answers. "Since Ev is getting old, I left my previous job to help him with the day-to-day operations of it."

"Thanks for the 'old' crack," Ev grumbles. But he's grinning, nonetheless. I see the same dimples that grace my face on his. Even though Monty said earlier we shared the same smile, now I can see it. That sends a shaft of shock through me since I always believed I had Mom's. Pulling myself out of my stupor, I ask more about the farm.

"So, cows, goats, things like that?"

He's shaking his head. "Horses. Northern Virginia is prime horse country. There are some beautiful places to ride."

I nod, though I'd never heard that. The only horses I've been behind pull a carriage around Central Park. "You must have enjoyed growing up on a farm."

"I didn't buy the farm until later in life," Ev explains. He reaches over and squeezes Char's hand. "I didn't meet Char until Monty was twelve."

Startled, I find Char smiling at me. "It's true. I was working in a hotel, and Ev dumped the vase of flowers all over me."

"I was so blinded by how beautiful you were I was clumsy." He lifts her hand to his lips.

"Where were you when you met? Here in DC?" I ask as I take a small sip of coffee.

"I was working in a hotel in Manhattan at the time."

I choke a bit. "Seriously? You're from the city? Where's your accent?" I demand.

Char laughs. "I'm originally from the Midwest. Since I never talked like a typical New Yorker, I never passed that on to Monty."

"How does one earn the name Montague anyway?"

Monty groans and buries his head in his hands. "Try a mother who was a theater major in college and obsessed with all things Shakespeare. That's how," he grumbles.

A theater major from New York? I can feel the walls closing in on me. To push them back a little while longer, I decide to turn the tables a bit. "So, Montague." He lifts his head and glares at me. "Before you went to help out with the family farm, what did you do?"

"Ev never told you?" He frowns at his stepfather.

"No. I had just started to talk about my family when we decided to meet in person. And I apologize for springing them on you as a surprise, Linnie. I just figured it might be best to get all the uncomfortableness out of the way."

I wave off his concern. "I appreciate your line of thinking. Now. When I was at the maître d' station earlier, not so much."

"I'm glad you can understand his logic," Monty mutters. "Even as a trained investigator, I have trouble with it sometimes."

My head whips around. "A trained investigator? What do you mean? Was I investigated?" Have these lovely people known I've been lying to them the entire time?

Monty scowls at Ev. "No, because Ev asked me to not call in the markers I'm still owed. Why? Hiding any skeletons in your closet?"

Oh, only my name, who my mother really was, and what I do for a living. Nothing major. "No more than the average person." As much as I'm withholding information, I can feel Monty doing the same thing. "Is it a place I'd recognize?"

"You might. When I got out of the Navy, I went to work for the Naval Criminal Investigative Services."

Faintly, I say, "NCIS? Like the shows on TV?"

He shakes his head. "No. Nothing like the shows. It's tougher and a lot harder, but we're just as determined to find out all the answers."

Suddenly, swallowing seems like an improbability. Here I am stretching the truth—okay, lying—to a former government agent. Can they arrest me for that? I'm just about to open my mouth to admit to who I am when the waiter comes up with our desserts.

"Ma'am, I believe you selected the sweet potato cheesecake?" The young waiter slips a dish in front of me.

"I did. Thank you." If I'm about to be sent to the pokey because I've been lying to my father, stepmother, and her son—the fed—I plan on eating every damn bite of this dessert that's drowning in caramel sauce and whipped cream.

Who knows? I might find a dance partner in prison who can work it off of me.

BEING on the stage my whole career has been a great adventure I wouldn't trade for the world. I've sung and danced for people who want to escape their world for a little while. It's been exhilarating every moment I've played a role. Except for right now when I'd give anything to be just the woman I've sworn for the last few hours I am to my birth father.

"So, when do you fly back, Linnie?" We're all standing outside Georgia Browns. It's a weird feeling; after all, we're all heading back to the same hotel.

"Anytime," I blurt out without thinking. Three sets of eyes give me different looks of confusion. "I, um, have an open-ended ticket." Probably because the pilot knows I'll give him twelve hours' notice when I'm ready to leave.

"Really? I was hoping we might have a chance for another chance to talk. Just us." Ev's nervousness starts to make an appearance. I do what comes naturally, what I'd do if I were backstage with a nervous fan. I reach over and squeeze his arm. He lets out a deep breath.

"That'd be lovely. What are you doing tomorrow? I flew into

Dulles, so I thought I might hit Tyson's Corner on my way out of town."

His eyes grow wide and flick toward Char before they meet mine. "I have a doctor's appointment in the morning, but if you don't mind a late lunch..."

"I don't mind at all." Lunch was enjoyable, but I feel so much more of a connection to Char, and even Monty, than I do Ev right now. I attribute it to the fact that they're naturally more outgoing than he is.

We need this time together—my father and me.

"There's a restaurant in Tyson's called Coastal Oaks," Char suggests. "It's part of a local chain. You can't go wrong with anything on the menu."

I smile at her warmly. "Sounds like we have a winner. You mentioned a doctor's appointment? If you let me know what time that is, I'll plan to meet you a few hours later."

Monty barks out a laugh. "What?" I ask innocently. "Just because I think doctors should send out a text message like restaurants do when your table is ready..."

Now everyone is laughing. "I'll be sure to mention that to mine tomorrow." My father grins. "Now, I understand why you're so successful at your job, Linnie. You have a very natural way of putting people at ease."

Except myself, I think guiltily. I hate lying to these kind people, but I had to be sure my father was as genuine as he appeared in email. "Thank you," I say sincerely. "But I think that's just something I learned."

"Then your mother did a spectacular job raising you," Char declares. Laying a hand on my shoulder, she brushes her cheek next to mine. "Thank you for being so lovely in person, Linnie. I hope we'll meet again."

"Me too, Char. And thank you for being here. It was a nice surprise." I mean it. My father's wife complements him beautifully.

She pulls back, and then Monty's in front of me. "There's still something about you," he murmurs. He brushes his hand casually over my shoulder. I feel the jolt down to my toes.

"Is that a good thing or a bad thing," I joke.

His head tilts. He purses his lips while he considers his words. "It's something. I'll let you know when I figure it out. In the meantime, safe travels." He leans down and brushes his lips against my cheek. Thank God he can't feel the way my heart skips a beat in my chest as I inhale the scent of the rain mixed with the woods that's clinging to his skin. As I so rarely get to smell fresh scents in the city, it's intoxicating to my senses. "Thank you for making it a pleasure."

I pull back just enough, and our eyes connect like magnets; a compelling mystery arcs between us. Even beyond the half-truths, it's like he can see me. The real me—the Linnie that only a handful of people get to know. In my fright, I step back. I can't find words, so I nod. He lingers a moment before stepping back to let Ev move in.

"Should we exchange numbers?" he asks with some hesitation.

Well, laughing is one way to regain whatever breath I seemed to have given to Montague Parrish. "I guess that would help." I grin. Quickly, Ev and I exchange contact information.

"I'll text you when they call me back," he promises.

"Don't be surprised if I'm already there," I warn him. "It's rare I get time to just putter in stores."

He lifts a hand cautiously and cups my cheek. I still. "I won't be. Do you need a ride? We can drop you off along the way," he offers.

I shake my head. "I have transportation, but thank you."

His hand drops. "Of course. I'll see you at lunch, then." He turns and reaches for Char's hand. The three of them start to walk into the Hamilton.

I can't leave it like this. "Ev?" I call out.

He stops and turns. "Yes?"

I take the few steps that span us and give him a gentle hug. "Thank you for asking me to come down. I know this wasn't easy for you."

He drops Char's hand to wrap his arms around me. We stand

there for a moment in silence. "Linnie, if you knew what this moment means to me, you'd understand that I'm so overwhelmed I don't know what to do."

"Then why don't we take it one day at a time. See where this goes," I suggest.

"That sounds good. How about letting your father escort you back to your hotel? It's a long walk and all." He has this adorable, quirky sense of humor that just dives in and grabs my heart in the sweetest way.

"I'd be honored." He holds out his arm, and I let my father escort me into the lobby of the Hamilton before we finally part for the night.

TWENTY-THREE

MONTAGUE

"Well, I have good news for you, Ev. It appears you've slipped back into a chronic state." Dr. Spellman's voice arrogant voice holds a tinge of relief. "It gives us more time to find you a donor."

I'm about to speak up to let him know about Linnie when Ev shakes his head sharply at me. Frowning, I sit back in my chair and listen to Spellman. "I'd like you to keep taking the Imatinib, but let's change the dosage back down to 400mg now that your bloodwork is showing an improvement." Making some notes in Ev's online computer record, he turns to ask, "How are you for pills?"

Ev replies, "I have enough to last about another three weeks on the adjusted dose."

"I'll order you some more."

I'm seething as I wait for Ev to wrap up his appointment. It's a good thing my mother's in the middle of a financial meeting. Otherwise, my fingers would be flying asking her what the fuck Ev's doing?

Soon, Spellman leaves, and I turn on my stepfather like he's a hunk of juicy meat to a hungry lion. "Not here, Monty. Let's go grab some food, and I'll explain."

"You up to driving after, old man? Because I want a drink," I snap.

Sighing, he bends enough to tell me, "Yeah. You might need one."

Crap. Doing a quick mental inventory of the restaurants between here and Middleburg, I settle on Ford's Fish Shack. I have a feeling a good dark and stormy plus a lobster roll might suit what Ev's about to tell me. When I mention one of our favorite haunts, his face lights up. "Your mother hates the spice on their calamari," he muses.

"I know. Let's go get some food, and you can tell me why you stopped me from telling Spellman about Linnie." The look that crosses his face does nothing to encourage my appetite.

For food.

"Yeah. Let's get settled. I'll text Char the good news for when she's done with her call and let her know we'll be home in a while," he agrees.

I don't let him see the way his capitulation affects me. We make our way down the halls after we stop to check out. Soon, we're flying down US-50. I'm keeping an eye out for cops as there's little traffic at this time of day and I can open up the car a little bit, a rarity around here.

Besides, I want to get to Ford's so I can find out what the hell is going through Ev's head.

"WHAT THE HELL do you mean you don't plan on telling Linnie you're sick?" I demand. A copper mug is set down next to me. Snatching it up with a muttered "Thanks," I take a giant slug of the rum-and-ginger brew combination. Before the waitress can leave after putting Ev's iced tea down, I stop her. "You might want to put in an order for another one of these."

Ev raises an eyebrow but even if he's concerned, he doesn't say anything. He knows the bomb he just dropped on me has rattled me to the core. We spent months trying to find someone who might be a match for him. Finally, we found someone—his daughter for Christ's sake—and now he's balking at the last fence. "Why? Can you tell me that at least?"

Ev runs his finger in the water ring left by the glass on the wood table. "I don't know if you'll understand."

I lift my drink to my lips again, but before I take another large swallow, I bite out, "Try me."

He sighs. "Monty, you've known me for almost thirty years. You know the kind of person I am. Linnie's met me twice? And the lunch we had alone wasn't exactly easy on either of us."

Silently, I give him that. After his doctor's appointment in August, Ev had lunch with Linnie in Tyson's Corner. It was, per his description, awkward. "Linnie's lost since the death of her mother. Her whole world's been shaken," Ev begins.

And mine hasn't? The thought flashes through my mind, bitterly. Finding out someone you love and respect may have less time than you anticipate is an insidious feeling that grabs you by the throat when you least expect it. I'm just about to speak when our calamari and my second drink arrive at the table. I tip my head back to drink as much of the first as I can before the ice starts to angle itself toward my face dangerously. "Here you go." I hand the waitress my glass. Ignoring the flash of surprise on her face, I reach for one of the small plates. "So, you're going to lie to your daughter instead?'

Ev flinches at my words. "I wouldn't call it that..."

I interrupt him. "Of course you wouldn't."

He gives me a narrow-eyed glare. "But until I get to know Linnie a little bit better, I feel like she needs to get to know me and not the me who's ill." He pops a piece of calamari into his mouth, chewing silently, something I've always appreciated since the sound of people eating drives me up a wall. I do the same.

"I'm just going on record as I think you're not giving her enough credit," I state firmly before I pop my bite into my mouth.

Ev swallows before dabbing his lips with his napkin. "So noted." Reaching across the table, he places a firm hand on mine. "Monty, I get you're pissed, but understand it's my decision. I have time, and I've been given a huge gift. Maybe one day you'll realize the importance of this, but I don't want that woman to look back and think any part of her time with me was a mistake."

I open my mouth and immediately close it because I can see where he'd feel that way. This isn't a stranger the system matched him with that he can coolly negotiate a deal with; this is a life that he helped to create. And despite not knowing it before fate and circumstance forced the issue, he's already beginning to feel something deep inside for her.

"It's your decision, Ev," I concede. "But soon, you're going to have to answer her questions that you're avoiding. All the questions about the medical health on your side of the family. It is why she reached out after all."

"I know." His eyes remain steady on mine. "I just want some time."

I shore up on the inside, adding the weight of this additional burden to the others I carry. I don't think it's the right decision, but as Ev's already declared, it's not mine to make. "Then let's toast to the fact you're back in a chronic state." Lifting my glass, I paste a smile on my face and clink my glass against his.

A broad smile spreads across Ev's face, causing a dimple to appear. Absently, I note it's a dimple he shares with his daughter. I don't point it out because this is the kind of discovery he should realize for himself.

Over time.

Time that he now has to get to know her.

TWENTY-FOUR

EVANGELINE

"Y ou're heading down to DC again?" Bristol flops back on my bed as I pack my weekender again.

My shoulders droop slightly. "Yes. I have the next few days off, so I'm going to meet Ev in Alexandria. I figure this way we can do a few touristy things." I don't add on *And we have something to talk about*, but I don't need to. Bristol knows my lunch with my biological father was pretty much an unmitigated disaster.

With his family around to help ease the conversation burden, Everett Parrish is warm, if a little bit quiet. Without them, he's nervous, anxious, and it was left up to me to find topics of conversation to cover our lunch together at Coastal Oaks. It was a good thing they had these fantastic little rolls that tasted more like donuts that I could stuff in my mouth otherwise I'm pretty confident I'd have run out of topics by the time our meal was over.

But by the time I got back to New York, there was another warm email from him. I realized quickly, Ev's just an introvert. With a little snort, it makes me wonder if he'd had a few to drink when he approached my mother all those years ago because I can't imagine the man he is now would have caught the eye of Brielle Brogan. It isn't that my father isn't attractive, even now in his early sixties. He's sporting the Richard Gere style about him. But if he couldn't deal with my mother's known outrageousness, I'm surprised they ever made it into bed to, well, create me.

"What's that laugh for?" Bristol rubs her hands over a slightly protruding stomach. Distracted, I sit, laying my hand on top of hers.

"Next week we get to see another picture," I murmur. Our fingers tangle on top of her little son or daughter resting inside.

"I know. I hope he or she cooperates when it's time so I can make plans."

I roll my eyes at that. "You know there's a chance they could get the sex wrong," I remind her.

"If the baby is as...blessed... as Simon is, there's no chance of that."

Immediately, I start making vomiting noises over the side of the bed. Bristol starts laughing before she says anxiously, "You promise no matter what you'll be back for that, right?"

"I swear to you, Bris, I'll be here for every moment of your pregnancy you want me to be," I vow.

Calmer, she relaxes back against my pillows. "So, what's in Alexandria? I've been to DC, but I've never been there."

"Honestly, when Ev suggested it, I had to look it up myself," I admit. We both start giggling. "It's on the waterfront, has a ton of shopping and restaurants, but looks like something out of the Revolutionary and Civil Wars."

Thoughtful, Bristol says, "I wonder if Simon would like it for a quick babymoon."

"What the hell is a babymoon?" I demand.

"Oh, it's a last-minute trip you take before the bundle of joy arrives."

"Sounds like an opportunity for the father to get some before his wife starts ignoring him," I laugh.

"It's that too," she agrees.

We're a mess of laughter and tears when the door to my penthouse opens and Simon calls out, "Do you know what a pain in the ass it is to walk through Fifth Avenue traffic holding three milkshakes as well as a sack of burgers?"

Bristol, never one to put up with any crap, yells back, "Then you shouldn't have got yourself one!"

There's silence from the other room. Simon has no comeback for that. He should have known better than to open his mouth against his smart-ass pregnant wife.

I hold out my fist for Bristol to bump it. She does, before asking, "How many days are you staying?"

"I agreed to three, but I have the option to fly back early since I'm chartering a jet," I explain.

She nods. "Then I'd leave about half of what you intend to pack home. Knowing you, you're likely to find a store you love and buy it out."

Thoughtfully, I look at the outfits I'd planned on bringing. "Makes sense." I begin to put hangers back into my massive walk-in closet. "But I'm taking all the shoes."

"Of course. You don't want to be walking around in new shoes and get a blister," she calls out, voice horrified.

When I step back into my bedroom, the tension is gone from her face. "I'm just worried about you, Linnie. It's wonderful you found your father, but I still feel like we know next to nothing about him. Maybe it's the baby hormones, but I'm just concerned. You're you. That makes you a target."

Sitting down next to her, I lean my dark head next to her blonde one. "I know. This weekend I will find out more to help ease your mind."

And my own. As much as I hate to admit it to Bristol, I relish the days off where I don't have to act. Right now, when I spend time with my father, I'm not getting that break to be me, Linnie Brogan. I'm playing a role, so I hope I don't trip up and tell him who I really am.

OLD TOWN ALEXANDRIA is quite possibly one of the loveliest places I've ever been to. With its cobblestone streets and historic waterfront, it's almost mind-boggling to think this little gem is only ten miles from the insanity of the nation's capital. I mean, there's even an adorable red trolley car that zips up and down King Street.

Bristol was spot-on when she told me to leave half of my clothes at home. What we failed to take into account was I'd find a multitude of stores I'd buy out—much to Ev's amusement—and I'd have to buy luggage to get all of my finds home with me. "Obviously, the communications business pays well," he says when I come strolling out of Sara Campbell's boutique with a garment bag over my shoulder.

Blushing, I try to stammer out a reply, but all Ev does is lift the bag from me and say, "How about a bite to eat? You shop like Char does."

"How's that?" I ask, truly curious.

"Like all the stores are going to go out of business," he says dryly.

I laugh, heartily.

We end up at Sonoma Cellar, a wine and tasting bistro. I order sparkling water, and Ev orders an iced tea. We decide to split the West Coast Cheese Plate to start. I begin fiddling with my utensils before I blurt out, "You don't drink either?"

Ev levels a solemn look on me. "No, I take some medication that alcohol interferes with, Linnie. I haven't had a drink in several years."

My filter must have been left in New York because my inner thoughts just come flying out. "I saw you and Char and it makes complete sense. You two are like two halves of a whole." His face softens. "But trying to picture you with Mom is an impossibility to me."

There's a long pause between us. Suddenly, Ev begins to make a choking sound. "Ev?" Shit, did I just kill my biological father? "Damn, do you have any allergies? Do I need to call for help?" I'm practically hysterical.

His choking erupts into a deep laugh that has him waving his hand in front of his face. "So, you thought your mother and I must have been drunk to have conceived you? That we were so different?"

"The thought did cross my mind," I admit. "Unfortunately, with Mom, it wouldn't have been all that far-fetched back then." That sobers him up as nothing else would.

"What do you mean?" I don't respond right away as the waitress arrives with our cheese board. My eyes widen at the size of it.

"Um, Ev? Do our rooms have refrigerators?"

Picking up a slice of toasted bread, he slathers a creamy brie on it. "Dive in. And tell me what you meant about your mother."

Telling myself I'll run an extra few miles on the treadmill tomorrow to make up for this, I do.

By the end of it, Ev's face is pale. To say he's shaken when he realizes the woman he thought was a flamboyant bohemian was quite simply a very functioning alcoholic is an understatement.

He's rocked to his core to realize that for years a fond memory has been nothing more than an image, an act.

And I'm the result of it.

TWENTY-FIVE

EVANGELINE

A few days later, I'm due to fly back home and more at ease with my father than I was before the trip started. Ev's admitted a few of his own truths along the way. He's not just some nobody; he's a retired software mogul. He was thrown I didn't recognize his name when Char first used it.

"To be honest, Linnie, I kept thinking I'd get an email from you accusing me of lying to you," he admitted last night at dinner. This was right before he invited me to come to stay at his farm in nearby Middleburg for as long as I want to get to know him and Char better.

I told him then, I'd need to think about it, but all it took was a FaceTime to Bristol. She practically fell off her bed when I told her the truth. "He's that Everett Parrish? Holy hell, Linnie, we handle some of his accounts." Her voice was faint. "The man is worth millions—like maybe closer to billions."

"So, I take it that your concerns..."

"Are completely eradicated. The man is responsible for some of the breakthroughs of the early days of the internet. He was doing the same thing we were with your identity." Even over the Wi-Fi connection, I can see how stunned Bristol is.

"He wants me to come to visit," I blurt out. Her eyes widen.

"For how long?"

"For as long as I'm comfortable with."

"Whoa. What are you going to do?"

I begin pacing the hotel suite; now I know how Ev could afford two of them. "There's the side of me that wants to get to know him and his family. But then there's the side of me that wants to be with you and with Simon."

She's quiet—so quiet I think I've lost her. I begin pressing buttons on the phone until she snaps, "Will you stop flipping the camera around? I'm beginning to get dizzy."

"You were so quiet I thought I'd lost you."

"You're worse than some of the people I work with," she complains. I smile because Bristol has some great stories about the computer-illiterate people who work at her brokerage firm. "Listen, you already told me you'd be here for all of the major moments with the baby, so what's holding you back?"

An image of Monty flashes through my brain. Thoughts of Ev's dark-haired stepson send warning signs screaming in my head and my heart. But he doesn't factor in. Not when it comes to this. "Nothing. I'm not scheduled for anything."

"And you can always come home."

"True," I concede. Ending my call with Bristol shortly after that, I know what I'm going to do. It just feels crazy to put it into words.

"I'm thrilled you're going to be able to come down for an extended stay," my father says softly. We're out to lunch before the car service takes me back to the Dulles VIP terminal. If it weren't for the cobblestone streets of Old Town, I'd swear I was back in New York City with the amount of swearing that comes from people's mouths when you make an accidental wrong turn. Sheesh.

"It wasn't that difficult to get the time off." That's not an exaggeration of the truth. It isn't like I have a nine-to-five job. Everything Bristol said made sense. I want—no, need—to get to know my father better.

"Still, it means a lot. If your job is going to cause any problems for you financially, well." He looks embarrassed for a moment before he mutters, "You know you just have to ask."

A flash of anger whips through me that he thinks I'd be sitting here right now for money when I can almost hear my mother whispering in my head, *Take a deep breath, darling.* "Ev, I have no need for your money. I don't want your money. That's not why I'm here," I remind him firmly.

Green eyes—the same shade as my own—look at me with amusement. "And that, I know without a doubt, you got from your mother. In the very short time we were together, she wouldn't let me pay for a thing."

Placing the menu aside, I lean forward. "Really?"

His smile holds fondness. "Oh yeah. Elle was all about sharing the bill. She continuously paid her way. I called her a stubborn Irishwoman more than once in the few weeks we spent together."

Laughing, I pick up my water. "She was that," I murmur.

"You said she was in the same business you are? I know you said last night she was a recovering alcoholic, but did stress contribute to her illness? Should you get checked out?" His evident concern about my well-being causes warmth to steal through me. I'm saved from having to answer when our waiter comes up. We both place our orders, and I realize I can't do it anymore.

I can't hide who I am.

After the waiter departs, I angle my body toward his. "Part of the reason I went through the DNA testing portion of the genealogy kit was to see if there were any underlying medical issues. I'm covered through an excellent plan I pay out of pocket for." I'm not shocked by his gasp of outrage. He believes I work for a communications firm. "Please, let me finish?" He nods. "But my medical history was under the presumption that Bristol's father's family lineage was my background. I can more than afford to have the right medical care, but I needed information first. And if something came up, until I could find that data—" I grimace. "—well, I could deal with my doctor. Ev, what Mom and I did, what I do, for a living is extremely physical."

His eyes narrow in contemplation. "Dealing with clients, running events..." His voice trails off as I shake my head back and forth.

"No." I take a deep breath and let it out. Just as I'm about to tell him, the waiter arrives with our appetizer. Tipping my head back, I smile brilliantly. "Thank you."

The waiter stumbles backward. "Umm, you're welcome?"

The food sits between us untouched. "Linnie, what do you actually do for a living?" Ev asks me quietly.

Reaching into my bag, I pull out my cell. Pulling up my Wikipedia page, I take a deep breath. I turn my phone around to slide it across the table. He tags it and starts to read. A choked gurgle escapes.

"I haven't been entirely truthful about what I do either. I think," I whisper, as his eyes shoot up to meet mine, "you might understand why."

His fingers slowly scroll the article. A lance of pain crosses his face when he murmurs, "Brielle, not Elle."

"Everett, not Rhett," I reply back. His head snaps up; chastisement and pain chase across his face. "You couldn't have found her, nor she you. Not back in those days."

"It would have been almost impossible," he acknowledges. I relax slightly. "But if I'd known about you, I damn sure would have tried."

The prick of tears in the back of my eyes burn.

He twists his arm under mine. Clasping my forearm, he grips tightly. "Linnie." We sit in silence for a few moments until the waiter comes back to ask if there's a problem with our food.

Grinning at each other, we pull apart and begin to dive in.

WE'RE in the middle of our main course when Ev asks, "What do you need for an extended stay?"

I chew the bite of my sandwich before answering him thoughtfully. "I have to look into renting some studio space of some sort. I can't let myself get out of shape."

Ev snickers. "Because I can see you're out of shape now. What did you say you ran? Five miles yesterday on top of all the walking we did?"

"I've not been eating like normal," I protest.

"So, what you're saying is we can't make this kind of meal a regular occurrence."

I look at the plate of goodness in front of me. "Sadly, but no. This isn't what I normally consume when I'm working, though I do give myself some leeway when I'm not on the stage. I normally weight five pounds less?" I estimate.

He frowns. "That's too tiny."

"Now I know how Mom and Char fell for you." His eyebrows raise. "Charm."

His laughter booms out.

"I'm considered both tall and large for a dancer," I tell him. Now that I can talk openly, it's such a relief. "When I did a stint in the New York City Ballet..."

Ev holds up the hand not filled with his sandwich. "I didn't get that far reading. You were in the ballet?"

I grin. "Yep. I towered over the other dancers in the corps when I was *en pointe*."

"So, what kind of dance can you do?"

"Probably the better question is what can't I do." Leaning back against the red leather booth, I begin to rattle off a list. After a few minutes, I add, "I have to keep my skills sharp. There's always someone younger, prettier, more talented who wants the same roles I do."

"I doubt that."

"It's true."

We each take a bite of our food before Ev says oddly, "You were a gift."

"Excuse me?" I don't know how I'm supposed to take this. No one's ever said anything like this to me before.

"From Monty to me and Charlotte. We saw you and...wow. I just realized Elle was on stage too." He looks dumbfounded. "It was our anniversary. Char wanted to see *Miss Me*. Monty spent a fortune on them."

"They're less expensive now," I offer, slightly embarrassed.

My father rolls his eyes. "Of course they are. You're not starring in it. But what I'm trying to say is, yes, Char hogged the binoculars, but I did get to look through them. How did I not recognize...?"

My heart breaks for him. My father is analytical and is trying to figure out how even if he didn't recognize me, how he didn't know my mother. I pick up the phone I never put away and unlock it. Pulling up the photo app, I scroll quickly to a picture of my mother and I hugging each other from opening night. Simon has his arms wrapped around both of us. We're all beaming because Bristol took the picture. My smile is bittersweet, and my eyes fill with tears as I trace my mother's face. "Would you have recognized us?" Mom and I are in heavy stage makeup, and both of us have wigs on. I hand my phone back to my father.

Putting what's left of his sandwich down, he takes my phone after wiping his hands. For a few minutes, he stares at the photo, two weeks' worth of memories living and dying in his eyes. If I learn nothing else in the next few months, I know this: my father did have feelings for my mother during their affair. It was wrong from my mother's standpoint. It ended up hurting people. But for the person who was created from it, it's small comfort.

His voice interrupts my thoughts. "Since you showed me the article earlier, that's exactly what I remember from when Char would let me have the binoculars. Do you have a picture of the two of you without all of...this?"

My throat tight, I reach over and pluck the phone from his hand. Within seconds, there's a selfie of Mom and me at my condo laughing. You can see her beautiful hair, lightly made-up face, and unforgettable smile. Without a word, I hand it back to him. With just a table separating us, I can see his eyes flare. "I...I take it you would have recognized her?"

The answer's already evident by the moisture in Ev's eyes. He gives her picture another long look before he hands my phone back to me. "Will you excuse me for just a moment?"

"Certainly."

My father stands and walks around the perimeter of the restaurant. I put away my phone, my lunch forgotten. Opening myself up to Ev has opened all of my wounds from the last few months.

My head is in my hands, so I don't realize he's back until I hear him ask, "You mentioned a studio space. What size do you need?"

Grabbing hold of the reprieve with both hands, I explain the reason for the large amount of space I dance in. "I have to be able to do multiple spins and jumps without injury. I plan on having someone send me workouts while I'm away."

Ev shakes his head, trying to absorb everything I've just told him. "How many hours a week does that entail?"

"When I'm in a performance? I do only one day of full classes. When I'm not—like now? I'd normally go in three or four days a week to keep at peak level. On off days I run about five miles for endurance." At my father's shocked look, I try to explain, "I have to be ready for the next role. It could come up at any time."

"Do you have another role in mind?"

I shake my head. "No. There's not even a project that interests me at the moment." And I frown a bit at that. The offers Sepi keeps bringing up are singularly uninteresting. I wonder briefly if she's trying to ease my way back onstage.

His face reflects his shock. "My agent's sent me several things, but nothing's piqued my interest. This...it's more important for me to get to know you, to figure out who I am and who I come from." And since I have no idea who I am without the spotlight, it is going to be an interesting journey.

Tentatively, his hand reaches across the table and squeezes mine. "If I haven't said it enough, thank you for agreeing to come down."

"I hope it will be worth it."

His hand clenches harder. "I already know it is."

TWENTY-SIX

MONTAGUE

I'm leaning against the paddock fence when I hear Ev's SUV drive up.

She's here.

Unfortunately for Lynn Brogan, I'm not in the best of moods after having had the kind of nightmare that sends me straight to the bourbon bottle in my suite of rooms. In the light of day, I can reason with myself it was a crazy mash-up of my last case as an NCIS agent combined with my worry for Ev that placed Ev in the center of the room pulling the trigger of the gun on himself instead of that last victim I was trying to help save. But instead of being one of our team in the immediate circle who was splattered with the victim's brain matter like it was the actual night it occurred, I was one of the ones who thundered up the stairs seconds too late, looking accusatorially at those in that tight circle. The circle compromised instead of Mom, my former partner Shaun, and another agent.

And the agent closest—like I was that day—when she turned to face me was Linnie. But her lips were painted a deep glossy red, her head tilted as if she was trying to ask me something.

I woke up sweating, cursing, and turned on. If I thought I wanted to punch a hole in the wall of my room before, it was nothing like what I wanted to do last night.

Yanking my Nationals cap off my head, I flip it around backward and twist it so it settles correctly on my head. My heart rate finally settled back down to something resembling normal, and I was able to pass out sometime before my alarm went off. Rolling to the side of the bed, I mentally prepared myself to face the day. Then I remembered what day it was. Even coffee, bacon, and my mother's blueberry rolls couldn't brighten my morning. I decided I'd be better off mucking out some stalls to improve my mood while my mother and Ev went to retrieve Linnie from the airport on their own.

My focus still on the horses, I don't see them move when the delicate crunch of gravel alerts me to someone coming up behind me. So it's not a surprise when my mother announces, "Did you work out whatever was causing you to be a snot this morning?"

"I tried," I admit.

"I'm glad," she says. "Because otherwise, I was going to cheerfully set you on fire with the way you stink. Jesus, Monty." She pulls away to my uproarious laughter. "Did you roll around in the horse dung this morning."

Grinning, I stalk after her to give her a sweat-soaked hug. "It's called shit, Mom."

"No, that's what you smell like," she retorts. "Stay away!" She takes off screeching with laughter.

I stop chasing her as she makes it up to the deck. "Dinner in a few hours. Can you make yourself presentable by then?"

"I can try," I call back. Flapping her hand at me in the way only a mother can, she ducks inside the kitchen. But now that she's mentioned dinner, my stomach growls when it realizes it missed lunch.

Knowing there will be something to eat somewhere in the tack room, I head in that direction. Passing by any number of kids ranging from six to eighteen, I nod as I make my way toward the back of the barn. I open the fridge and spy a bag of apples that are marked, "For

Humans." Knowing this is my mother's handiwork, I snag two and a bottle of water before shutting the door.

Something's changed about Ev in the last few weeks. There's something he's hiding. Panic rips through me as I wonder if he's sick again, but then I think back to the times I've caught him with a small smile playing about his mouth at the oddest times. I quickly dismiss the idea of an affair because more often than not, he's wearing that look when he's talking to Mom.

So that leaves one thing: Linnie. There's something about Linnie I don't know.

Well, the time for not asking questions is over. She's staying with us now—that means the gloves can come off. I promised Ev I wouldn't investigate her. I didn't promise I wouldn't try to find out everything possible about her.

And now my ability to do so just got a hell of a lot easier.

Sinking my teeth into the crisp apple, I wander back out into the September sunshine, wondering what Mom's going to make for dinner.

"THIS IS WAY TOO MUCH FOOD," Linnie protests. I can't help but grin. I didn't forget how tiny she is, and the amount of food Mom's piled on her plate must look like someone swapped her plate with mine at an all-you-can-eat buffet. Terrified eyes meet mine across the table. I try to school my features, but I can't. I'm snickering as she shoots me a death glare. "Char, I appreciate your warm welcome, but there is no way I can eat all of this. I'll finish maybe a third."

Calmly, Mom plucks Linnie's plate back up and slides half of it onto mine. "Hey!" I protest. I already had a small mountain of home-made enchiladas, beans, and rice on my plate.

"Did you eat lunch?" Mom asks.

"I ate." It's not a lie, though two apples for the amount of physical labor I did hardly counts.

"Shut it, Monty."

Shaking my head, I slide my chair back and walk over to the fully stocked bar. I begin to mix a pitcher of margaritas expertly. "Ev, I know you're good with tea. Mom, margarita?"

"Yes, sweetheart."

"Linnie?" I remember her saying she doesn't drink, but right now, she looks like she could use one. Her eyes are enormous in her face, and she looks like a skittish colt, ready to bolt at any second.

"No, thank you."

Clearing my throat from the bar, I ask, "Then what would you like to drink?"

"Oh, water's fine with me." Everyone around the table laughs.

"Linnie, you're going to need something to wash the spice down," I assure her. "If alcohol's not your thing, we've got soda, tea, or I can make you a virgin margarita."

Her lips curve in a smile. "A virgin margarita sounds delicious. Thank you."

Grabbing a second pitcher, I quickly mix up some of the fresh lime juice we keep on hand with orange juice and simple syrup. Sticking a slice of fresh orange on top so I can be sure which pitcher is which, I bring both back to the table. "Here you go." I place the pitcher next to her. Pouring for Mom, I reach over to pour for Linnie just as she's about to grab ahold of the pitcher's handle. Our fingers brush and that electricity that sparked between us in the lobby of the Hamilton shimmers again. Her lips part slightly just like they did in my dream. Only they're not bright red but instead stained in pale pink.

Tugging, I pull the pitcher away and quickly pour her drink. After putting it down, I lift the one well doused with alcohol for myself. I'm about to take a sip when Ev stands. Pausing with the glass so close to my lips, I put it back on the table.

What's he about to say? Panic assails me. A glance at the other table occupants shows no outwardly indication that there's anything wrong, so I try to calm my racing heart.

"I'd like to propose a toast. Linnie, we're honored you're able to take the time away from your job to join us at our table. Having found you has been a surprise, yes, but a wonderful one. I hope you know we'll all do what we can to make you feel welcome in this family."

"Thank you, Ev. I'm honored to be here." Father and daughter share identical smiles.

Mom tears up. "Excuse me," she sniffs. She jumps up from the table to go dab at her eyes. Linnie's eyes follow my mom with some concern whereas Ev looks on indulgently.

Way to go, Ev, I think bitingly. We can't even get through a family meal together without some drama.

"Ev, should I..." Linnie starts, but Ev cuts her off.

"No, darling. She's okay. She's just as happy to have you here as I am," Ev reassures her. Linnie relaxes slightly in her chair. He remains standing until my mother comes back just a few moments later, her eyes slightly damp but a huge smile on her face.

"Now, look at the trouble I've caused. I hope dinner isn't too cool."

"Mom, if you cooked it, even if it's as cold as an iceberg, it's still going to require a pitcher of drinks to get through."

Linnie reaches for her drink while eyeing her plate askance.

I laugh out loud, absorbing her small movements. "If you don't like it hot, don't eat in Char Parrish's kitchen," I warn her wickedly.

"Let's finish the toast before you terrify the poor girl, Monty," Ev chastises me. "Welcome, Linnie. It may not seem like it now, but we hope you will come to think of this place as a second home. Cheers." He leans forward with his glass.

"Cheers." Mom lifts her glass.

"Cheers," Linnie repeats, a hint of doubt in her voice.

I touch my glass to all of theirs, not saying a word. Instead, I take a long pull of my drink when we separate before I ask, "So, Linnie, have you ever been riding?"

A self-deprecating smile crosses her face. "Does riding in a carriage behind a horse around Central Park count?"

"Umm, not exactly," I laugh. I appreciate her honesty. Watching skilled people on a horse make riding look easy when it's anything but.

"Then no, I've never been on a horse in my life."

"Well, I'm sure you'll have a chance while you're here," Ev says consolingly.

"I feel like I'm Alice in Wonderland," Linnie bemoans. Everyone laughs.

I give her a brief once-over. "You're about the right size. How do you look with blonde hair?" I tease.

Imagine my shock when Ev shoves away from the table with his hand clapped over his mouth. "What did I say?" I ask my mother. She shakes her head, her face wreathed in mirth.

Linnie's the only one able to speak. "Ask me that again some other time. So, what kind of horse do you recommend for someone who's frankly scared of losing a foot?"

I explain how gentle all of our horses on the property are as we teach classes for children of all ages and skill level. Linnie asks a few questions, and soon the conversation around the table turns to the farm, how certain horses are faring, and Mom promising Linnie a full tour soon.

Where the questions don't go is to the mysterious brunette whose eyes sparkle as she takes small bites of the delicious food Mom prepared even as I shovel it in.

I didn't realize before I sat down how hungry I was, both for information and food.

TWENTY-SEVEN

MONTAGUE

"Linnie, I hope this tastes good. They didn't have the brand you mentioned you liked, so I asked the store clerk, and they said this is just as good." My mother looks on anxiously while sliding a small bowl of greek yogurt and berries in front of Ev's daughter. It's impossible to think of Linnie as my stepsister, especially since very lucid images of her have been easing their way past the nightmares that plague me each night. It's not stopping me from waking up bathed in sweat, or being unable to go back to sleep without a little help from my friend Maker's Mark, but thinking of Linnie Brogan is that calm that eases me back into slumber with less anxiety despite the liquor tearing a hole in my stomach.

Linnie shoots her a dazzling smile, which relieves none of the tension I'm feeling but which draws an equal one from my mother. "Thanks, Char. This is perfect." She plucks a ripe strawberry out of the dish and dips it into the yogurt. "Delicious! And these berries are so fresh! Where did you get them?"

My mother beams. "I'll take you shopping with me next time we go. This store is insane. You have to go in with a list, and then you have to expect to spend 20 percent more than what you think you're going to..."

"Is that what happens to the grocery budget," Ev gripes as he shoves a bite of food into his mouth.

"Everett!" Mom snaps at him. I grin.

This should be weird, but it feels right. Linnie fit into our early-morning routine on the farm quickly. When we explained we rise early, she merely shrugged and said, "I'm normally done with my run by then. It gets too hot in the city otherwise."

That sends something niggling in the back of my brain that I just can't let go of. Then again, maybe it's the sight of her luscious body in tight leggings that reminds me I'd have to be dead not to notice. Her ample breasts have to be suffocating in whatever sports bra she's wearing under the sweaty, ragged tank that says "Will Dance for Food."

"How many miles did you get in this morning?" Ev asks as he passes her the carafe of coffee.

I almost choke when she says in a disgusted voice, "Only four. I normally can get in more, but I forgot something." Jesus, four miles? That's insane for a new runner around this area. Middleburg is nestled in the valley of the Blue Ridge Mountains, and driving in a car is like taking a roller-coaster ride at Disney.

"What's that?" he asks.

"You're all insane trying to run up and down mountains." The table breaks out into gales of laughter.

Ev's still chuckling when he says, "Not used to our little bumps in the road?"

"Not in the slightest. I thought I was going to have to crawl back up the driveway." I cough to try to disguise my laughter but fail miserably based on the narrow-eyed glare I'm receiving.

"Let me guess, this is nothing for you?"

I offer her a smile, which, to my surprise, she returns. Maybe her stay with my family won't be as frustrating as I initially anticipated. "When I was in the Navy, they had us run five miles before breakfast, eat, do maneuvers, and mentally, I'd be praying to God I didn't puke. Then later, we'd run another five with full gear on."

Linnie's chewing, but her gaze is thoughtful. "How long did you serve?"

"About twelve years."

I'm floored when she says, "Thank you for your service. With everything that happened during the first time we met, I don't think I said that, and I try to. Since I've lived in New York my whole life, my city's landscape—and I don't just mean our skyline—was changed after September 11. I hold great admiration for the bravery of our first responders and our armed forces."

The sincerity behind her words touches me deeply. It doesn't change anything though, I tell myself firmly. Neither her words nor the way she looks is deterring me from wanting to know all her secrets, but I figure they'll all come out in due time. Everyone's does.

"Appreciate that." As my mother brings over a basket of warmed rolls to the table, I don't miss her subtle slap to the back of the shoulder.

"Linnie, so if today was a running day, does that mean you're not going to be working out?" Ev asks, casually. In the weeks since she's been gone, Ev had contractors turning an unused barn into a blank space that almost resembles a dance studio for reasons he wouldn't share. "Listen, Monty, women like these kinds of things. They can do yoga and shit. Linnie will love it. In bad weather, your mother can use the space for indoor functions." He was right. Mom was delighted, but I'm not convinced if this wasn't something the little bombshell across the table asked her rich daddy for.

She shakes her head. "I'd like to get my bags unpacked, and then I have a few calls to make. I know we talked about renting some space for me to work. A place was recommended in"—her brow furrows —"Ashburn? Does that sound right? They seem to be the right fit for what I need, and the cost is reasonable."

Huh. Linnie has no idea what Ev did for her. I flick my eyes over to him.

Mom lays her hand on Linnie's arm. "Why don't you finish up, get comfortable, and then we'll give you the tour of the grounds before you get started. How about that?"

Her smile raises the warmth in the room by at least five degrees. "I'd love that, Char. Thank you so much for your hospitality. It truly does mean a great deal."

Mom squeezes her arm before letting it go. "Good. And then you can tell me if you'll eat what I have planned for tonight's dinner or if there's something else you want me to add on the menu."

"You're sweet, but I'm used to making do."

"Are you like a vegan or something?" Getting narrow-eyed stares from the two people who raised me, I backtrack quickly, "Not that there's anything wrong with that."

Linnie tips her lips up. "No, but with what I do, I can't afford to put on more than a few pounds. I have to be very careful about my diet. I can't overindulge too often, and like I've said, I never drink alcohol."

"Communications jobs are strict about that kind of thing?" I'm confused. I understand the no-alcohol deal is her rule, but the rest seems like a recipe for an HR disaster.

"Let's just say Linnie's in the spotlight a lot," Ev says smoothly. Linnie ducks her head but not before I catch the mischievous smile she shares with her biological father.

There's so more to this woman. I know it.

I just can't put my finger on it.

"OKAY, Ev. Spill it. What is the deal?" I manage to corner him as my mother and Linnie are walking around the pool area toward the back steps.

"I don't understand your question, Monty."

"What changed between you and Linnie during your last visit together?" *What miraculously sprouted out of her mouth to make you suddenly trust her like you've known her for decades* is what I want to ask, but I hold my tongue.

"I learned more about her. It cleared up several things."

"Like?" I demand.

He shakes his head. "If she chooses to share them with you, that's her prerogative." We're following my mother and Linnie through the manicured backyard toward the first horse barn.

"You got to give me something here, Ev."

I'm surprised when he spins around and gets into my personal space. "No, Monty, I really don't. That's my daughter you're speaking of, not some stranger. I know this adjustment is unsettling, but I won't have you persistently questioning every word out of her mouth."

I take a step back in shock. Ev holds up his hands placatingly. "While I appreciate everything you've done for me, especially since I've become sick, I won't have you treating her like that. You don't have to accept her, but you do have to be polite. She is my family. If she isn't yours, so be it. But she's a guest in our home, and you will treat her with the respect that is due." Ev leaves me standing there shell-shocked to join my mother and Linnie. And ever since the first time I was caught stealing from his liquor cabinet, I feel ashamed.

Taking a deep breath, I relax every muscle in my body. All around me, little sounds fill the air: a buzz of a fly, a horse's tail swooshing through the air. Just as a horse lets out a snuff of welcome, I hear Linnie's peal of laughter. My heart starts racing.

How can she be accepted so readily when I feel like it took half my life to find my way to belong? I tip my head back as bitterness and shame wash over me. Ev's right. I'm not expected to embrace her, but she is essential to him. So, unless I can figure out what is bothering me about her, I will respect her.

After giving them a few more minutes alone, I head in their direction, rejoining them just in time to catch Linnie reach out to touch a delicate bloom growing on the far side of the barn. Her fascination isn't faked. I imagine with the hard stone and steel of New York, the lush landscape of Virginia has to be an anomaly to her. "This is like visiting a park or a zoo. I can't imagine the effort that goes into maintaining it."

My mother laughs. "If it wasn't for my love of flowers, and Ev and Monty's love of me, I guarantee it wouldn't look this pretty. They'd likely have bushes all over the place and call it a day. But if it weren't for Monty taking over recently, none of the farm would run the way it does, would it, Ev?"

"Not at all. He's an amazing manager and a terrific son."

From where I'm standing, I have a clear view of Linnie's fingers leaving the flower and touching Ev's. A hesitant but solid bond is being built there that damn if I'm not a little jealous of. How is it she manages to obliterate all of my preconceptions when she says, "I'm so glad you had that—that you all have that. Family ties are...everything."

Her husky voice is filled with pain.

"Come here, sweetheart." Mom steps forward. Linnie resists for half a second before accepting her embrace. "Even as you get to know your father, you're going to grieve your mother. That's perfectly normal. We understand that."

And Linnie bursts into sobs.

I back away again, giving them this moment because although it's vastly different, I too know what it's like to not have a parent.

And like Linnie, I know what it's like to gain Everett Parrish as one.

TWENTY-EIGHT

EVANGELINE

"I'm so sorry." I wipe my eyes on the handkerchief Ev hands me.

"Why? Is grief supposed to have a time limit?" he questions simply. I shake my head no. Of course not. "Then don't apologize for loving someone so much you feel so much pain when they're gone."

The sound of my breath is wobbly, but my words are clear when I say, "Virginia may be good for me in many ways."

"I hope so. Now, there's one more building we wanted to show you. There's a barn on the right up ahead."

"Do you also churn your own milk or something?" I joke. "Maybe make your own cheese?"

Ev snorts. "After seeing the amount you ate of that cheese board, that wouldn't be a bad thing."

I push him lightly. "Hey, wasn't it you who asked the waiter where all the cheese was from, and if you could buy pounds of it to go?"

Char laughs. "You two are like peas in a pod."

Immediately, I feel awful. Here I am, her husband's unknown daughter, and I feel like we're leaving her out when she's done so much for me. I begin stammering, "I'm so sorry... I didn't mean... I never meant..."

Char slides under Ev's outstretched arm. "Linnie, sweetheart, Ev and I have no secrets. None. We both know we had pasts. Was it a shock to find out you existed? Certainly. I think what was harder was the facade you put up because you were afraid of being used."

My eyes dart to Ev before they accurately read Charlotte's serene face. "You know."

"Yes, Ev wouldn't keep something that huge from me. But we will keep it from everyone else until you're ready."

"Or unless I'm recognized," I joke.

She tips her head. "Does it happen often?"

"No." I think back to the lunch at Wolf's Deli with my family. "More often in New York than anywhere else."

"I'm honored to know such a strong and fierce woman," she admits.

Ev kisses her head. "Char, honey, I think those are the same thing."

She adamantly shakes her head. "They are not. Linnie's strength comes from inside. She didn't crumble when everything fell on her heart. Her fierceness is because she's determined to do what's right for herself, her career, and her life. They are different."

I blink away tears. I have a feeling when I eventually go back to New York, it's going to be just as hard to leave Char as it will be to leave Ev. I change the subject. "So, you were saying something about a second barn?"

Ev's smile grows wide; Char's goes wonky. "Oh, Lord. Do you butcher cows there or something?"

They both break out into gales of laughter. Extending the arm not wrapped around his wife in front of him, he says, "Let's go see."

I walk behind them along the flagstone path to the well-maintained barn.

It's dark when we step in. There's air of some type running. "Well, there's no smell of sacrificed animals. That's good."

Char laughs.

"Give me a moment to find the light switch... Ah, here it is." Ev turns on the overhead lights.

I gasp and feel the smooth bar hit me in the lower hips. It still doesn't jolt me from my shock.

I never expected this. Never.

The studio gleams, beckoning me.

Almost in a trance, I can't control the need to do a *chasse en tournant* on the beautiful maple floors. Without realizing it, I flick off my shoes and begin dancing to the music that naturally flows out of my mouth. To the background of my voice singing "Use Somebody," I lose myself. Even though I'm not *en pointe*, I'm gliding around the room executing grande pliés, *detournes*, pirouettes, and fouettés. My voice fades as I sink to the floor.

Suddenly, I remember where I am, and my head snaps up mortified.

My father has tears brimming over while Char is swiping hers away from her cheeks. "I'm sorry." I flush horribly.

"For what? For giving us the honor of seeing what you do close up?" Char whispers.

"I assumed..."

"Correctly. When you told me how much effort you put in to doing what you do, how hard you work, how often you'd be away to maintain your fitness levels, I decided to do this. I want to get to know you here, not wonder if you're safe while you're driving on unfamiliar roads commuting to another city to train." I open my mouth to protest, to offer to pay for it, but Ev steps forward. "Linnie, I'm a rich man. A wealthy man. I can't take any of this with me when I go, only the knowledge I made my family happy. We're adjusting to that, but you're a part of that now. Please accept this gift as a selfish man who wants to be able to pop in on his daughter—if she permits that?"

I swallow hard so I can get one simple word out. "Yes."

The next thing you know, I'm enveloped in Ev's arms. It's the first time since Mom died I feel those places deep inside of me partially fill back up. When Char's arms wrap around us both, they top off a little more.

Hours later, I'm helping Char in the kitchen when I finally ask, "Who's coming over tonight?"

"Oh, it's just Monty's former partner. He's like another member of the family," she says breezily.

"His partner? I didn't know he was involved with anyone." I'm not surprised he's involved with someone. I didn't realize he was already spoken for when he asked me out. I get lost for a second remembering the look in those dark lashes over those intoxicating eyes as he asked if he could give me a tour of the city.

Charlotte breaks me out of my reverie. "Not that kind of partner, sweetheart." At my pronounced confusion, she clarifies, "Remember, when Monty left the military, he went to work for the NCIS? Shaun was his partner there."

"That's right. So, what I know about NCIS is summed up through the very special agent I get to see through reruns of the TV show. But I have to ask if Monty did half of what they do on the show, how did you not know who I was?"

A slow smile breaks out across Char's face. "Ev made Monty swear he wouldn't use his old contacts to look into you. Quite simply, it's driving him insane."

I still. "But it won't stop them after they meet me tonight," I whisper.

Char lays her hand across mine. "Is there a reason it's so important to keep this under wraps, Linnie? I know if it were up to Ev, he'd be shouting it from the rooftop."

"Part of it has to do with Mom. The press has been particularly tenacious trying to figure out what in her past might have caused her to die so young..." I feel the warm pressure from her hand, which helps me to go on. "Also, I wanted the time to get to establish a more solid relationship with all of you before I brought you into the spotlight. Little did I know who my father really was." My tone is dry.

"I know. I imagine someone's going to put it together soon."

"Or like they did with my brother-in-law, they'll make something up. Say someone will write that I'm having some scandalous affair with the very wealthy Everett Parrish. See page 12 for the scoop," I drawl scathingly

"Is Simon Houde really that dreamy?" Char's eyes take on a faraway cast. I burst out laughing.

"Let me just say that *People Magazine* doesn't do him justice."

"On behalf of women everywhere, can I say I hate you for getting to kiss him every night?"

"It isn't that great." I quickly tell her about our ongoing battle with cilantro and onion. Soon, Char is doubled over.

"Your sister must be amazing. Not only to put up with all the noise from the tabloids but to deal with cilantro breath?" Charlotte pulls out some vegetables to chop.

"Do you have an extra cutting board and a knife?" She smiles and pushes her board and knife over. "How do you want these cut?"

"For dipping. We'll munch on those."

I begin to chop a head of broccoli up into bite-size florets. "Bris is terrific," I say, bringing us back to our earlier topic. "She's due in late January." I smile at the joyful gasp. "She's been a bedrock for me. Where I'm emotional, she's logical. We balance each other out. I don't want to add any undue burden to her when all of this comes to light."

Char frowns as she cuts a carrot into sticks. "I see what you mean."

I try to explain. "It's a relief to have you and Ev know. I feel like this weight has been lifted from me. But I have to be careful about how far that circle expands. Protecting Bris, Simon, and this baby means everything to me."

Laying down her knife, Charlotte gathers up her carrots and arranges them artfully around the large platter. "Then we'll try to keep it in the family. But Shaun will respect Ev by not poking and prodding. I promise you that."

Putting my trust in people has never been easy, but without being able to fall back on my mom, I have to rely on something I haven't used in far too long—my instincts.

"I appreciate that. Everything you've done to welcome me into your home has been so appreciated." My voice breaks. "When I came to find out more about my birth father, I didn't expect to get his family too."

She quickly rounds the counter and pulls me into her arms. "I'm glad that worked out for all of us."

There's a door slamming in the front hallway followed by the sound of boisterous men. "Oh, I guess he's here early." Char pulls away, dabbing at her eyes. Discreetly, I do the same. "We should finish up with this platter. Shaun will be in here shortly scrounging for some food, I'm sure."

I give Char's outfit the once-over; she's dressed in what I'll term casual country chic: white linen shorts, leather flats, and a pale pink button-down shirt neatly tucked in with a trim belt around her waist. "Do I need to run up and change?" In complete contrast, I've got on camouflage short shorts, a tight black T-shirt, a goodly amount of silver jewelry, with my hair loose down my back. My flip-flops are somewhere under the stool I'm perched on.

"Sweetheart, if I could pull that outfit off, I'd work it." She grins at me before sliding a few peppers onto my empty cutting board. Happily, I julienne them before popping one into my mouth.

"Thanks, I got it at..." Before I can tell Char I scored my outfit online at Old Navy, the kitchen fills with people. I keep chopping—albeit with a grin on my face—as an African American male swoops up Char like she weighs as much as a gallon of milk. He grabs her cheeks and plants a smacking kiss on her lips. I stifle a giggle when she blushes to the roots of her frosted hair. I finish up the peppers on my board and am just about to reach for the zucchini that has been abandoned on Charlotte's when I hear my name called. Only it's not the one I'm expecting.

"Well, holy crap. Evangeline Brogan is in the house. What a surprise!" The man I presume is Monty's partner has an arm slung around Char and is eyeing me up and down with appreciation. "I'm a huge fan. I've caught you the few times you've toured at the Kennedy Center."

I send a quick look of regret over to Monty, who has just entered the door with a frown at his partner, before finding my flip-flops. With my stage smile in place, I hold out my hand. "Shaun, I presume."

"Indeed. Has my reputation preceded me?" He winks.

"No, just Char's mouth," I assure him. We both laugh.

As we shake, I hear Monty ask Ev, "Will someone explain to me how in the hell you know Ev's daughter?"

TWENTY-NINE

MONTAGUE

"This is funny, Monty."

"It really isn't." I'm beyond annoyed right now.

"It is." Shaun's tickled I had no idea Ev's daughter is *the* Evangeline Brogan. I've been taking shit from him all night like, "Next time, try Google," or "Do I contact Glynco to see if you really graduated?"

Asshole.

I'm irritated at Linnie, Ev, and by the looks of it, my mother, since she clearly knew as well. I don't get what the big deal is. If anything, it might have alleviated my fears that Ev's daughter was just out for his money...

Ah shit. Suddenly I realize why she didn't blurt out who she was right away. Until the weekend they were in Old Town together, Linnie had no idea that her father and Everett Parrish, the software genius, were one and the same. She's a celebrity who recently lost a celebrity parent, reported on most major news outlets. The media swirl around her only just quieted down. She was protecting herself the same way I recommended he defend himself. With that, a large part of my frustration dissipates.

After being introduced to Shaun, Linnie's been hanging out in the background, helping out, giving my mother a much needed reprieve. I don't know if that's to keep herself out of the line of fire, but as I hear my mother's peal of laughter—something I hear far too rarely as of late—it's appreciated.

Promising to return with dessert, Mom and Linnie both scurried off a few moments ago. I'm keeping a close eye on the door, so I walk away from Shaun's incessant prattling when I notice Mom's heading down toward us holding a carafe of coffee while Linnie's carefully balancing a heavy tray of desserts, cups, and accouterments. Mom flaps her hand at me, so I deliberately get in Linnie's way. "Let me get that for you." Quickly shifting the heavy tray from her arms to mine, I'll admit I'm impressed by her strength. "Where do you want this?"

"Oh, thank you. I guess...wherever your mother wants it?" She searches for where my Mom went, but I figure Mom will set up dessert on the closest table to the firepit where everyone is currently relaxing. I stride off in that direction.

Linnie's long legs quickly fall in step.

After I've set the tray down on the table, I turn toward her. She's ducked her head. "I just wanted Ev to get to know me before I told him who I was." Curtains of long dark hair hide her face as her hands brace on the tabletop. Reaching down, I pull her hair away. Frustration marks her face. "I just wanted a little time to be me, but then Ev asked me to visit. He got worried I wouldn't have enough money. I had to tell him who I was. I'm sorry you found out the way you did." Her eyes—Ev's eyes in such a beautiful feminine face—lock onto mine. "I truly am."

There is no artifice about this woman. I blurt out the first thing that comes to my head. "How on earth are you an actress? You have absolutely no capacity for hiding anything."

Her lips tip up, and I feel it like a punch to my gut. The Indian summer air is heavy but somehow light now that there are no more secrets.

Well, except one, and I've been ordered I can't share it.

"I don't hide who I am with family." She shrugs. "The only secrets I keep are for their own good, not to harm them."

With that, I let out a jagged sigh. Maybe Linnie will understand then. Perhaps she won't hate her father for not telling her right away why he completed that damn genealogy kit.

Her eyes narrow, but before she can open her mouth, Mom calls over to her. "Linnie, come sit down!"

If I weren't standing right in front of her, I'd have missed the flash of humor across her face before she calls back, "Be right there."

She slips around me to make her way back over to the group. Before I join them, I turn and rest my hips near the desserts. Ev slips away and joins me.

"How mad are you?" he asks bluntly.

"I was until I realized she did it to protect herself. Now, I'm more worried about how she's going to react when she realizes your still hiding something from her."

Ev frowns. We both jerk when we hear Linnie's musical laughter at something Shaun said—damn, that should have been a clue too. Everything she does has sway and movement. She's always in motion. Even now by the firelight, her foot is tapping to an internal beat in her head.

And she's never looked more beautiful.

"Give me time. Then I'll tell her." Ev sighs. "She just lost one parent. Things are under control. I hate even to give her the idea that one day she might lose another." He pushes away from the table.

"Ev," I say, stopping him. "Miracles can happen."

He grips my shoulder tightly. "They already have. Don't you see? I have your mother, you, and now Linnie."

I bow my head as he walks away, unable to come to grips with the emotions coursing through my system.

★

WE'VE DECIMATED DESSERT. Even Linnie couldn't resist the novelty of roasting a marshmallow. We all laughed at her when she screamed, "Fire! Fire!" when her first one lit up like a torch though. Doing my duties as the wiser, more experienced marshmallow roaster, I blew it out. And then I ate it directly from the stick.

She made a disgusted face that caused everyone to howl with laughter. Me? My teeth were stuck together with the sticky goodness.

Shaun merely shook his head. "You can't dive headfirst into the heat. You have to let it warm up around the edges. Then when it's ready to catch on fire, that's when it's ready to devour."

I muttered to Ev, "Is he talking about roasting marshmallows or..."

"I don't want to know, son. I don't want to know."

"Linnie, so is the adjustment out here on the farm tough since you grew up in the city?" Shaun asks her.

"How do you..." I begin.

Shaun shoves me in the shoulder. "Dude. Look. Her. Up. Now that you know who she is, will you—for all that's holy—find out exactly who your new stepsister is?" His voice must carry loud enough because when I turn across the fire pit, Linnie's eyes are resting on me.

I shake my head back and forth without losing her gaze. "Nah. I think I'll let her tell me. I think that's important to her." Linnie sends me a smile so bright, it makes the flames jumping in between us look dim.

And besides, I can't think of Linnie as my stepsister.

Now Shaun's randomly plucking at the guitar he always brings along, and he asks Linnie, "Do you always listen to Broadway music?"

She counters by asking, "Do you always read crime reports?" knowing he used to be my partner.

"Not a chance in hell. That's morbid!"

She leans back in the chair she's curled up in with a snicker.

"There's your answer. I listen to all kinds of music because I love all kinds of music."

"Classical." Shaun's lip curls in a sneer.

"Of course. I was in the ballet." My eyebrows shoot to my hairline.

"Pop," he counters.

"Shawn Mendes and OneRepublic."

"Rock," I throw out.

She sneers, "Rush. Best band ever. I might have sold my soul to play the lead if Neal Peart ever wrote a musical." Everyone breaks out into laughter.

"Hip-hop," Ev asks curiously.

"I'm a throwback. I dance all the time to '90s hip-hop. I love me some Blackstreet," she sighs nostalgically before we all chuckle.

"How about this? Can't claim to have a family from this area and not know this group," Shaun teases. He strums a few notes.

Her smile quirks. "Bris and I saw them in concert...oh, like ten or so times since I was in college? My crush on Marc Roberge is ongoing." Everyone doubles over laughing.

"You and every other woman who hears him sing," Ev calls out from where his arms are wrapped around my mom, who's nodding emphatically.

Shaun thrums the chords to one of O.A.R.'s most popular songs. He nods over to Linnie, who begins to tap out the beat on her bare thighs. Her voice joins in about their famous song about giving up comfort and ease to create something more. It's a song that teaches people how to move forward through all kinds of adversity to find a new triumph. Her hips shift back and forth in her chair, her long hair swaying around her as she embraces the fast-paced lyrics.

There's a quiet that descends upon the group. Mom breaks it by saying, "Why aren't you recording an album of your own?"

Linnie squirms in her seat. "Well, I kinda just did."

My jaw drops. Everyone gapes at her in astonishment. "It really isn't a big deal. I've done cast recordings before," she hurriedly explains.

"My daughter just recorded her first record?" Ev confirms slowly.

"It's lullabies, Ev. They wanted me to sing some holiday music, and I turned that down. I wanted to do something that meant something special to me. So, I recorded a bunch of lullabies and children's music. I wouldn't expect it to hit the top of the charts or anything," she jokes, embarrassed.

"What made you decide to do that?" Mom asks.

"Remember I told you about Bristol?" Mom makes an "Ah" in assent. To the rest of us, Linnie explains, "My sister is having her first baby."

I've never given much thought to celebrities before. I mean, I've seen their images on all the tabloids during the checkout aisles, of course. But I imagine very few of them are like Linnie, who rises out of her chair to begin clearing the mess so my mother can sit within the confines of her father's arms. "Thanks, sweetheart."

Linnie waves her off with a smile.

"Beautiful and nice? Dude, you might be in some serious trouble with her around. More so than you already were," Shaun mutters to my left as he randomly picks out some notes on his guitar.

Maybe it's her core of humility that trips my heart into an erratic beat when out of the corner of my eye, I watch Linnie head back from inside to plop down into her chair. It can't be those ridiculous long legs showcased in shorts or her long glossy hair hanging down her back.

Or a heart I'm beginning to realize is going to be shattered when the news about Ev's illness hits her.

THIRTY

EVANGELINE

I'm in New York for the week at a charity event I promised Sepi I'd attend even before Mom died as an alumni of NYU to help raise money for their theatrical scholarship program. As I walk the red carpet outside of the Waldorf Astoria Hotel, I'm overwhelmed by the number of flashes. The trick is to look beyond the cameras so you're not looking at any one photographer.

Because the dress specified cocktail attire, I slipped into a crepe cap sheath dress with a gold zipper that runs down the back. My shoes are embellished slingbacks I expect I'll be ready to chuck at someone's head by the end of the night. Bristol said it perfectly when I was complaining while getting ready, "You're getting too used to the peacefulness of the farm."

Sliding on a chunky Tiffany gold ball-and-chain bracelet on my wrist, I agreed with her. "I am. You should come down to visit. I know Ev and Char would love to meet you."

Bristol laughed. "Maybe. I need my routine, just as you need the time to get to know your family, Linnie."

Seriously, I clasped both of her hands in mine. "You are my family, Bristol. Even though I found Ev, it's...different."

"Of course it is, silly. Ev's your father. He's never going to be the one who knows you let Campbell Frost get to third base in the laundry room of his apartment building when you were only thirteen." Her face is angelic. Glaring, I yank my hands away from hers.

"It was second base, and I was fifteen, thank you very much," I grouse at her.

Bristol laughed before stepping back into my space and wrapping her arms around me. "No matter what, there's enough room in your heart for all of us, Linnie. I'm sure of it."

I finished getting ready and waited with an impatient tap of my foot for the car to pick me so I could make my grand entrance on the red carpet. I used the time wisely though. I took a few selfies and shot them to my father with the bewildered question of "Did you ever have to do ridiculous stuff like this before you retired?"

The laughing emoji I got in return didn't help. However, his text of "You look beautiful. Enjoy yourself and your time with your sister. We'll see you next week" went a long way to soothing my frayed emotions.

I pose at the front of the Waldorf for one more round of photos, before the doors are held open for me and I slip inside. Letting out a deep breath, I turn and run smack into Pasquale. "Pas! I didn't know you'd be here," I exclaim. I take a step forward to move into his arms, but he takes a firm grip on mine to hold me back.

What on earth?

"Evangeline, always a pleasure to see you." His voice is cold. It completely lacks the warmth and care he gave me the last time we were together in the theater after Mom died.

I'm about to question what's wrong when Veronica slides up to him and wraps her lanky arm around his waist. "Hello, Evangeline. How have you been?" God, I'll never be glad my mother is gone. If she were still alive, would she be as horrified as I am at the degeneration of her best friend?

It's been only a few months since I've seen her, and even I can see the physical changes that have come over my godmother. Her makeup on her face is heavier than normal, likely covering the effects of a bender. Her normally thin body is almost waiflike, her bones beginning to push up under her skin. Her hands are trembling even as she clings onto Pasquale to remain standing. She looks worse than when she came off a monthlong bender and almost lost her job at BDC before Mom intervened. A silent bell of alarm goes off inside my head making me wonder if our confrontation pushed her over the edge into drinking again.

God, I'm furious with her. We just lost Mom to the effects of the bottle and she thinks the answers can be found at the bottom of it? But how can I be the only one seeing this? Is it because everyone else sees her day after day?

My heart hurts when I nod my head and answer. "Actually, Veronica, I'm doing quite well since my father and I reunited."

Her eyes bug out. "Excuse me? Did you say your father? What did you do, hire someone from the Village to hold a seance to talk to Patrick again?" Pasquale doesn't bother to hide his snicker.

I want to laugh and cry simultaneously. What does she think this little confrontation will do but further my bitterness against her? "Yes, I found my biological father. Of course, you remember me discussing him with you? Bristol and Simon were there? This was, of course, before I dared you to ever speak to me again for withholding that information from me."

Pasquale's laughter abruptly dries up. He takes a step back, whispering, "What?" I don't bother to give him my attention. Being a part of their inner circle for almost as long as I've been alive, he should have realized that nothing short of treason would have ever caused me to stop speaking to my godmother.

Veronica neither confirms nor denies my accusations, but the high color along her cheekbones tells its own story. I step closer. "Get help. You need it more than Mom ever did. Some people still could love you. I just don't know why you won't let me be one of them," I reprimand softly.

Instead of answering me, or making excuses for her behavior, my godmother turns on her heel and disappears into the crowd.

Pasquale's eyes follow her for a moment before they meet mine. Now they're filled with the wretched sorrow I expected. I have no idea what she told him. I'm too emotionally exhausted to care. "I'm sorry, Linnie. I never..."

I nod, accepting the apology for what it's worth, which is next to nothing. Mom always warned me about being in this business—that you keep your close circle of friends close and everyone else just close enough. While Pasquale's known me since I was three, none of that mattered when the gossip was flying. To me, he should have known better than to listen to a woman who was filling his head with nonsense while undoubtedly getting him off.

I don't bother to say anything else. Instead, I feel nothing but pity for the woman I grew up with, knowing there's no way she'll ever find happiness at the bottom of a bottle. As for me, knowing the way it could impact my life, I'd be a complete moron to touch a drop of alcohol in this lifetime.

BRISTOL TOSSES another news rag into a growing pile that's spilled onto the floor. Practically every word I exchanged with Veronica made the tabloids last night. Unfortunately, they put a spin on it that we were fighting for Pasquale.

Ew. I'm so disgusted I want to vomit.

"I know! Let's see what your friend at The Fallen Curtain has to say," she says brightly. I groan. Bristol pulls her iPad into her lap and pulls up yet another gossip website. "Well, well, well." Her voice is smug.

"What?" Not another recount of how I'm trying to buy my next part by sleeping with my former director.

"Sepi should be hiring her as your publicist. Listen to this:

Last night's fund-raiser for NYU's Tisch School of the Arts was horribly disrupted by Broadway Dance Center's veteran dancer Veronica Solomone.

Solomone's exclusive dance classes have become much less sought-after since Broadway star Evangeline Brogan recently changed studios. Solomone was selected by Brielle Brogan to act as her oldest daughter's godmother.

Solomone approached Brogan at the charity event yesterday evening right after Brogan stepped off the red carpet. As always, the Broadway star stood her ground with class, letting the older woman embarrass herself with her date, Pasquale Beecher. Sources close to the trio note that Brogan showed the class she was known for while she held her godmother—who obviously had an agenda—at bay while one individual willing to speak off the record said, "It's obvious Veronica needs help for her grief."

Ms. Brogan hasn't had nearly enough time to mourn the loss of her mother, who collapsed in her arms on stage during a performance of Miss Me, *with Evangeline in the starring role as "Kate Hynes." This all-star cast also included Simon Houde as her love interest, "Michael Kirby." Although Brogan was nominated for this year's Tony Award for her performance as Hynes, neither she nor Houde walked the red carpet out of respect for their deceased family member. She was instead in Los Angeles recording an album of lullabies to be released just in time for the birth of her younger sister's first baby with costar Houde.*

While we wish the entire Brogan family nothing but peace as they come to terms with their new family dynamic, Broadway isn't the same without the combined force of their voices.

"Is it wrong to be both grateful and a little scared that Courtney Jackson was in the crowd that close to me and I have no idea who she is?" I wonder aloud.

"Maybe it's Pasquale," Bristol suggests.

My eyes widen. "You don't think..."

"Of course I don't! Jesus, we can pull up her picture on the website," Bristol exclaims and does just that. Seeing the petite blonde from The Fallen Curtain's image, I vaguely remember her in the crowd around us. Out loud, I say, "Remind me to send her a bouquet of flowers."

Bristol types in a reminder on the iPad. "Done. Do you think things are going to get better?" she frets. I talked to her right after I called a furious Sepi last night.

"I don't know," I tell her. "Right now, I'm not sure I care. I care more about getting answers to know who the hell I am."

"And that's not happening here," Bristol concludes sadly.

I wish it could, but I have to agree. "No, it isn't."

We've spent the better part of the last few days with my telling her all about Ev and Char. I've even ventured into talking about Monty, though it's odd every time I do. Bristol will start to ask a question, and I'll deflect it. Just saying his name conjures up images of his gorgeous face that linger for hours.

I haven't slept well since Bristol and I have been up all hours talking.

"With the way your luck is going, you're going to end up madly in love with your new stepbrother and living in there..." She trails off, picking up something in the tensing of my shoulder, she correctly guesses, "You like him."

"I find him attractive," I admit. "He's warmed up some since he realized I'm not after Ev's money."

"He's your stepbrother!" Bristol shouts.

"So? Simon wanted me to date Marco. What's the difference if it were to happen? Not that I think it will."

Bristol opens and closes her mouth a few times. "Nothing. I've got nothing. Be honest now: what's he like?"

I think back to the night of the dinner where he easily could have looked up everything about me. And one word pops out of my mouth.

"Understanding."

Bristol shoves the rest of the papers to the floor. She drops her iPad on top of them and lies down on the couch. "Okay, start from the beginning."

And so, I tell her about how we first met in the lobby of the Hamilton, the wary vibes Montague Parrish gives off, and yet how protective he is of his family, including me.

"I never thought I'd say I'm ready to be gone for a while, especially to the country. But after your sonogram this week, I'm looking forward to heading back," I admit.

"To see Monty?"

I flop onto my back so my head's next to hers. "No, for the peace of the farm. I'm just beginning to relax there. I think it will be good for me."

Bristol turns her head toward the ceiling. "I wonder why he left his job."

"Me too, but it's not like I'm his confidante. Besides, I still have plenty of secrets." I run my fingers through my hair and squeeze. Hard. I feel her hands reach back and grab mine.

"So, you're just kind of seeing where all of this takes you? With Everett? With his family?"

"I am. I mean, what's the worst that happens? I walk away and come back to New York?" I shrug.

"No, the worst is you come back with a broken heart," she argues.

"You're assuming I'm going to get in that deep."

"I think you're already starting to."

THIRTY-ONE

EVANGELINE

The rest of the week in New York was almost carefree in comparison to the night at the Waldorf. After we found out Bristol is carrying a little boy, Marco joined us for dinner at the Club A Steakhouse where we joyfully passed around the sonogram photos. Bristol and I managed to outfit the nursery using Mom's purple Judith Lieber purse as a kickoff for a fun, funky zoo theme. She and Simon plan on staying at my place while the amazing mural painter I found comes in next week to create a charming and bright-colored room for their future son.

And on display in a glass box will be his nana's purse.

I'm texting Bristol to let her know I landed when I hear, "Hey, lady, looking for a ride?" My head snaps to the side, and I see Monty leaning negligently against a wall. Even though mirrored shades cover the top half of his face, a smile creases the lower half. Not for the first time since I saw him in the lobby do I think, *Damn*.

I tug my sunglasses off my face and tuck them on top of my head. Inside, I try to tamper down the anxiousness bubbling up over our first time alone together. "I guess that depends on what kind of wheels you got out there," I deadpan.

Unable to maintain his look of stoicism, Monty pulls off his shades. Dark hazel eyes twinkle. "If you had half a clue what to do with this much power, I'd let you drive."

"The last time I drove, I think it was before college," I shyly admit as we make our way over to the baggage retrieval area. I know I've shocked him; I mean, what grown adult doesn't regularly drive? Except I grew up in a city where mass transit is everywhere, and with private drivers, I didn't need to.

Monty is stunned speechless. That is until he sees the amount of luggage I packed for this trip. "Four separate suitcases? Are you planning on moving in permanently?"

Embarrassed, I duck my head. Even though I did pack a lot, I also brought gifts from New York. Still, with everything that happened in the city, I thought I'd feel the warm welcome I did the first time I came here. During a quick text, Ev said to bring as much stuff down as I wanted, that I could leave it here.

Deciding to ignore Monty, I reach for the heaviest of the suitcases and hoist it with two hands. "What the hell do you think you're doing?" He rips it away from me, and our combined strength has the bag flying away a few feet. "Geez, He-Man, I was teasing. Ev said you'd have a lot of stuff."

"Oh." I yank my glasses back down, knowing they're big enough shield my face so my hurt can't be seen. I'm unsuccessful as Monty gently removes them.

"Hey, I didn't mean to upset you." He briefly touches my cheek before removing his hand, leaving a tingle in its wake. We both turn our heads toward the bag that went flying. I wince as I realize what bag it is. "Was there something breakable in there? Perfume or anything?"

"No, but you might regret it anyway."

"Why?"

"Because that's the one with all the food in it from the city."

"Do you want to..."

I shake my head. "Only because if I open that bag and something's broke, you're going to be pissed you don't get to eat it."

"Well, crap." We exchange pained expressions. "Why don't you inspect the damage while I get your other bags?"

"There are two more big cases like this and a dress bag. All the same color."

"The lime green makes them easy to spot. That's both good and bad considering."

I've lowered the first case to the ground and quickly unzip it. Smells of delicious New York bagels assail me. I quickly check the bubble-wrapped packages to make sure the deli mustard and other breakables didn't shatter. Letting out a relieved sigh, I close it back up. "Considering what?"

"Considering who you are. In a lot of ways, you wouldn't want to be noticed. I mean, it's fine right now, but you don't want to be recognizable so someone could tamper with your stuff," he tells me.

"I don't know whether to be petrified or touched you care," I tell him bluntly.

"Figure it out while we're in the car. I about died when you opened that bag and I got a good whiff of the bagels. I might break land-speed records getting us back to the farm."

I laugh, which was Monty's intent. Together we wheel my bags out. Stopping in front of a sexy red vehicle, I can almost feel Monty's pain when I say, "I like the red color of your truck."

"Okay, this isn't a truck; it's a Jaguar SUV."

"Is that supposed to mean something to me?" Yep, there's no denying the sick look that's now taken residence on his face.

"You're a star, Evangeline! Do you mean to tell me you don't know anything about cars?" he demands.

"Sure. If I don't want to ride in a nasty one, I order an Uber Black."

After using a button to close the trunk once my bags are loaded, he rests his head on the back window. "Think of this as Uber Platinum. No, Uber Titanium."

My lips part in a silent O.

"A Jaguar is an experience, Linnie. And that 'red color' is Firenze."

"Umm, Florence. I love that city." I head toward the passenger-side door.

Monty opens his door and slides in. I quickly follow suit before he decides to take my bag of goodies and drive off without me. "So, you know Italy, but you don't know cars?"

I shrug. "I spent my time walking through Italy to experience it. What about you?"

He gives me a wolfish grin. "I spent my time eating and drinking my way through it. That is if I wasn't driving like a bat out of hell." Pushing a button to start the car, I'm fascinated when I can barely detect the engine, let alone any sounds outside the window. "Are you hungry?"

I shake my head.

"Want to stop for coffee on the way back to the farm?" he throws out casually. "Unless something in the bag is going to spoil, we've got plenty of time. Ev and Mom are running a few errands."

"That sounds..." Disappointing Ev and Char won't be there when we arrive but on the other hand... "Good."

With a broad smile, Monty takes off. By the time we hit the highway, I have a newfound appreciation for Jaguars. As much as I'm clutching the door handle, I wonder if even the police could keep up with us as we speed westward.

"OKAY, I TAKE IT BACK."

"What's that?" Monty asks. We're waiting in line to get our coffee, and the smells infiltrating my nose are changing my mind from earlier.

"That sandwich in the display case looks delicious." My stomach gives a deep growl as if to back me up.

Monty bursts out laughing. "Not hungry at all?" he teases me as we step up to order. "Hey, Amy. How about we try a Mosby, a Federal, I'll have a large dark roast and..." He turns to me.

"A medium caramel mocha latte," I add on. "What did you order anyway?" I ask curiously.

Monty grabs one of the menus in front of us and holds it out to me. "Which one of us is eating which?" Because both sound delicious.

"I'll make sure the sandwiches are cut in half," our cashier, Amy, assures me. "This way, you don't have to choose. Soup or salad?"

"Salad for me," I interject.

"The soup," Monty says.

"Okay, that will be..." I don't wait. I'm shoving my card into her hands.

"To say thank you for picking me up at the airport," I explain when Monty squawks in protest.

"You won't be so quick the next time, Linnie," he growls.

I shrug. It's this time that mattered.

"Since we're slow right now, I'll bring your food out to you in just a few minutes," Amy assures us.

Turning, I spy a table near the old stone fireplace. "Do you mind if we sit over there?"

"Not at all."

Moments later, I'm being warmed by the fire crackling when a sweet dog comes up and butts his head against my leg. "Hey there, gorgeous."

"That's Cody," Amy says as she drops off our drinks. "He's completely friendly." I immediately reach down and scratch behind his ear. "And he just became your new best friend," she laughs. "When you're ready to eat, just tell him to lie down. He won't beg too much."

"Thanks, Amy," Monty calls out as he takes a pull of his coffee.

"My pleasure." She scurries away. I'm picking up my glass to take a drink when I notice the pumpkin drawn in chocolate over the foam.

"No way! Did you see this?" I exclaim. I stop scratching Cody, who whines pathetically. Monty laughs and resumes my job petting him while I pull out my cell, take a shot, and send it to Bristol. Picking it up, I murmur, "If it's half as good as it looks..." Then I take a sip.

"This mug holds liquid heaven. After the crap I dealt with while I was away, I'm being given a reward."

Monty frowns. "You didn't enjoy the time with your sister?"

"Oh, no. Not that. Never. Bris is wonderful. The baby is healthy and growing. There was other crap I had to deal with that was unpleasant."

"Do you want to talk about it?" he offers. I open my mouth to say no automatically, but something makes me want to say yes.

"Can I take a rain check on that?"

"Of course."

"It's not that I don't appreciate the offer. It's just all twisted up with emotions about my Mom I'm not ready to face yet."

His sharp eyes narrow over the rim of his cup. "The offer doesn't have a time limit, Linnie. And as you might have noticed, I'm not going anywhere." His voice holds a wry note of self-deprecation. I tip my head to the side. I'm just about to ask him why not when Amy arrives with our sandwiches.

And suddenly, I'm not just hungry; I'm ravenous.

Picking up one half of the delicious-looking cheesy jalapeño bread, I take a bite. My teeth sink into the nutty gruyère and the tangy mustard before I reach the salty ham. "Twisissogwood," I mumble even as I'm trying to take the next bite.

Monty barks out a laugh. "Are you going to give me my half of that?"

Do I want to give up the other half of this deliciousness to the unknown? Monty takes the decision out of my hands by holding his sandwich across the table. "Come on," he coaxes. "You know you want to give it a try."

I manage to swallow down the bite despite the intensity that just settled over us.

"Give in. Who knows when you'll have the chance again?" he murmurs. And somehow, we're talking about lunch, and we're not.

And we both know it.

But I'm not ready.

"I'm content for now." Even as the words come out of my mouth, they settle my mind but disturb my soul.

"You don't seem like the kind of woman where being content is enough."

"What makes you think you know me?" I'm mildly offended. We might be living in the same house, but our interactions have been relatively limited. While I spent my last visit getting to know Ev and Char, Monty was working hard. And when I had some downtime, he was sleeping. Our schedules have never seemed to mesh.

Until now.

Putting down his sandwich, Monty leans forward. "Because I studied your emails. I looked for some clue about who you are. Despite my promise to Ev, if something had set off alarms about you, there's no way you'd have got near him. What I read was a woman who is both intelligent and sharp. She's also looking for adventure, whether she's willing to admit it to herself or not."

"What if I told you Bris wrote those emails?"

"Then I'd tell you that you were lying. I may not be an active investigator, but I used to specialize in interrogation. You can't lie worth a damn."

Shit. Throwing him a mock glare, I sigh. "Maybe. Maybe not. Maybe that's who I needed to be. Maybe I'm always acting, and for the first time, I'm trying to figure out who I am without a role to play."

Monty's taken aback. "You think that we're not all acting to get through life? Wasn't it Shakespeare who said 'All the world's a stage'?"

"Yes, but..." I'm not allowed to finish. But his words cause me to freeze just as I'm about to sit back.

"We're all acting. Every one of us. We all have our grief and pain that latch on and refuse to let go." He sits back and picks up his sandwich. Tearing off a bite, he focuses on chewing while I've lost all interest in food.

Monty's words hit me hard. Whether by purpose or by accident, I'm being forced to confront who I am. "I think it's the idea of not knowing who I was, that the expectations were changing," I say slowly.

"Why did your expectations change?" He asks.

"Because I did." My voice is firm. "A whole half of myself I thought I knew as intimately as...a lover...was just gone. Dead as much as my mother was. How am I supposed to embrace this part of me that's been living there all the while?"

"Seems to me you're making it harder on yourself than you have to." Monty takes another bite of his sandwich.

"Why?" I challenge him. Picking up my coffee, I take a sip. The silkiness of the caramel and mocha slide down my throat. The combination works, just like I thought my life did.

"Because regardless, life continues. You just have to figure out what you're going to do to cope."

Monty's words echo in my head long after we leave the coffee shop and head back to the farm. They ricochet through my head after he lugs the heaviest suitcases into the kitchen. As I unpack it to put the goodies from New York away, he graciously takes my other cases up to the suite of rooms Ev and Char declared as mine.

But when I get upstairs, I don't unpack. I throw open the bag which I know has my dance clothes. I find a pair of leggings and a ratty tee and throw them on. Slipping a pair of worn sneakers on my feet, I quickly braid my hair before racing from the bedroom and down the stairs.

I know of one way to cope. And it involves losing myself to the rhythm and music as quickly as I can.

THIRTY-TWO

MONTAGUE

I'm standing at my bedroom window on the opposite floor of the house as Linnie's. Mine overlooks the backyard, so I get a full view of her sprinting single-mindedly out the back door like the fires of hell are licking at her feet, her braid flying. I feel a stirring inside of me. And it's like my body and my mind finally have a conversation far too long denied. Long legs were whipping past me on a crowded city street. A body that lightly bumping into mine. My body's instinctive reaction as I turn to catch her from behind.

I was trained to notice details.

How did I not put it together before now?

Linnie was that long-ago woman on the streets of New York, pushing her body in a grueling workout just hours after she had sung her heart out on stage. Closing my eyes, I pull out the details of the runner from my memory bank. It fits. I was hanging around Central Park waiting for Ev and Mom, which happens to be near Linnie's home in the city. She mentioned in passing her home is around the city's infamous park. Groaning aloud, I wonder how many other times our lives brushed up against each other before they entwined.

I guess we'll never know.

The cell in my pocket rings. Absentmindedly, I answer it. "Yeah?"

"Hello to you too, son." My mother's voice comes out as dry as the fall leaves beginning to dry on the trees outside. "Did I interrupt something?"

I bark out a laugh. How do I answer this? *Yeah, I was busy realizing the reason I have a mild obsession for Ev's daughter. Nothing to concern yourself with. Just a little fantasy I've had since New York. I'll get a grip on it later.* Instead, I reply, "Everything's good here. What about on your end?"

"Right as rain," Mom chirps. "We were thinking of celebrating another good month by going out to eat. Which do you think Linnie would like better, Eddie Merlot's or Rail Stop?"

"Rail Stop," I reply immediately.

"You think so?" Mom says, doubtfully.

"More low-key. Besides, she just took off for the studio." I turn back toward the window. "I'd hate to interrupt her right now."

"Then Rail Stop it is. We should be home in an hour," Ev announces.

"More like an hour and twenty with this traffic."

"Right. So, let's plan on leaving for dinner in a few hours? Can you let Linnie know?"

I want to dive through the phone and give my mother a huge kiss on the cheek for giving me the excuse to seek her out. "Of course." Making my way over to the bar, I debate pouring a small measure of bourbon and throwing it back but decide against it. "Happy to."

"Great. We'll talk to you later, honey." Mom disconnects. I put the crystal tumbler down on the bar before I wander back over to the window again.

I wonder what else Linnie does in her studio beside dance. I guess I'm about to find out.

⭐

A SOUNDTRACK IS BLARING through the high-priced stereo system as I slip in unnoticed. She's spinning barefoot, her long dark hair unbraided, flying around her. Her back to me, she plants her feet as her hips sway. "Life should be more!" Her voice reverberates in the room.

I realize she's singing one of the large cast numbers from *Miss Me*, and my heart thumps wildly in my chest. Quietly, I shuffle to the side. "Don't let your chance slip away. Reach out and grab it." She flings her arm out as she spins around before she goes up on the ball of her foot. If I remember correctly, this is a dance where she partnered with the male lead. Waiting for a beat, she begins to scissor her legs back and forth while racing across the floor.

It's like walking into a dream. The pulsing throb of the music sets my blood humming to the same beat. Quietly, I close the door behind me. Leaning back, I admire the seductive way her hips roll. I wonder if they move that smoothly when she's not dancing. Chastising myself, I tune back in to hear her sing. "Grab a hold... It's your chance..." She performs a series of spins before leaping into the air. God, I remember when she did that on stage. She was—is—like lightning.

Just as the music begins to wane, she strikes a pose. I call out, not wanting to scare her, "Wasn't that dance for two?"

"Jesus Christ!" Linnie stumbles. I straighten away from the wall, automatically reaching out to catch her. "I had no idea you were there!"

"I wouldn't have thought you would mind an audience?" After all, this is a woman who's performed in front of thousands of strangers throughout her career.

A look of pain crosses her face. "I haven't sung a single song from *Miss Me* since Mom died." She walks over to the remote sitting on top of the bar. She presses the Pause button and the music cuts off. "I wasn't sure if I'd ever be able to."

I take in the vulnerability in her stance, the graceful arms that were swinging in the air moments ago now wrapped around herself protectively. "Shit. I'm sorry."

"You had no idea. I figured if there were a place where I could try, it would be here. There's nothing here to remind me of her." Linnie shrugs as if it's no big deal, but I know the truth. It's a monumental step in her path towards healing. Linnie rocks her foot back and forth as if her body can't not be moving when it's ready to dance.

"What was she like? The mom, not the actress." Brielle Brogan was a legend. It's hard to imagine the mother inside.

Linnie's face lights with a glow. "She was crazy practical about some things and insanely ludicrous about others. She helped with homework and then said, 'So what?' to Dad—Patrick—when it was all wrong. She'd argue that she tried and that it was just as important to teach us that as it was to show us the right answer." I nod because it seems a good lesson for kids to learn. Linnie continues. "When we got older, she'd get the wildest ideas. There was one time when she... the balloons." Linnie's voice trails off as she starts laughing. "God, with everything going on, I'd forgotten all about that. I can't remind Bris about it. I may have to do it for her as a baby gift."

"What did she do?" The look in her bright green eyes is addicting. Her face lit with joy that radiates around the room.

Linnie proceeds to tell me how Brielle sent a gift to Bristol at college where she flooded the young girl's on-campus apartment with balloons in the school's colors. "It took Bris forever to navigate her way to her bedroom to be able to call Mom. The ribbons from them took up every inch of floor space." Then, much to my surprise, she begins to sing.

My heart was filled with pain,
I'll be with you wherever you go,
I'll be with you whenever,
Forgive me,
Our love is forever.
Miss me no more.

The tears streaming down her face aren't of laughter, they're from pain. It's the kind pain that embeds itself into your soul and clutches onto your heart with talons made out of love. When Linnie looks at me, she's weighed down by it. "We were singing that song when she collapsed into my arms. Unless you'd seen the show before, you'd never have known there was anything wrong. But I knew. I knew my mom down to my soul, Monty. And I had to wait with her in my arms knowing there was something wrong." Her hands raise to cover her face.

There's no way I can passively stand there watching her grief. Taking a few giant steps forward, I pull her into my arms. Holding her against my chest, I feel the shaking of her body against mine. "I'm sorry." The words seem so inadequate in comparison to the grief she's feeling.

She nods, her face still cocooned in her hands, but I feel the motion. I hold her tightly, not offering any words, just physical comfort.

Right now, it seems to be enough.

Slowly, she shifts. I loosen my arms to let her go. "I don't know what brought you here, but I appreciate the shoulder to lean on."

"Well, technically, it was my chest." The corners of her lips tip up as was my intention. "But it was nothing. Anytime."

She puts space between us by moving over to the bar and picking up a bottle of water to drink. "Why did you come in here anyway?"

Crap. With everything else, I forgot about dinner. "Mom called. She doesn't feel like cooking," I lie glibly, feeling like absolute shit for doing so. This woman doesn't need more lies; she deserves the truth. "So, we're going to take you to one of our favorite places to eat."

"Does it mean dressing up?"

With the freedom to give her a head-to-toe once-over, I shrug. "You might want to dig out something other than Lycra."

"How much time do I have?" Linnie slams the cap back on her water. Her head snaps back and forth in search of something—ah, her shoes. I suppress a smile as she dashes from one to the other, then hops as she slips them on her feet.

"I'd say about—" I check my watch. "—forty-five minutes?"

"There's no way I'll be ready in time!" She races to the door and dashes out. I'm beginning to realize Linnie Brogan doesn't slow down for much.

Strolling out the door behind her, I call out, "Don't worry, I'll shut everything off!"

"Thanks!" she calls back as she runs down the path toward the house.

I lean against the jamb as she runs, admiring her for the second time that day.

Only this time, I'm just as close as I was that morning in New York. There's no doubt in my mind now. It was Linnie I saw running outside of the park. Whistling, I head back inside, turn off the sound equipment, flick off the lights, and turn the bottom lock before heading back to change.

Because as much as I'm looking forward to the food, it's the company I know I'll be spending time with that has me walking a little more rapidly.

THIRTY-THREE

EVANGELINE

There's no doubt something's changed between Monty and me. Ever since last week when I broke down in the studio, things are just more intimate, like there's a secret between the two of us no one else knows about. I dash down the stairs, trying to avoid holding up breakfast for the others. I spent most of the night twisting and turning in bed thinking about Montague Parrish and realizing that for a man who's consuming my thoughts, I know so very little about him.

And I wonder why beyond the natural extension of getting to know my father, there's a desire to know more.

Ev and I have spent hours each day talking. I have a new appreciation for his brilliance. When he tried to explain how he went from being a too often backhanded, malnourished, genius kid to one of the wealthiest men in the nation, I was enthralled and captivated.

"It started because I had to get out, Linnie." We were walking toward the paddocks. Horses were grazing around hay strategically placed around the lush green grass. I could see Monty talking with a group of men, wiping the sweat from his brow beneath a red ball cap with a white *W* emblazoned on it. "There was one wealthy family who lived in a nearby town. It was a damn fiefdom. If these people wanted to spit on you, you would let them. They controlled whether you worked, you ate, you had a home, clothes—anything."

When we'd stopped some distance away, he rested his arms against the top of the split rail. "I didn't want to rely on anyone. My pa? He worked in their factory and then expected my ma to do his every bidding for him like he was a king. He was a huge man who swung a belt with unerring accuracy. I was so grateful to have won a scholarship to Virginia Tech. It was my ticket to freedom."

I laid my hand on top of his briefly before pulling it away. "I'm so sorry."

He barked out a bitter laugh. "I used to be until I met Char. Then I realized I'd live through every moment all over again to knock over those damn flowers. I felt this spark the minute I laid eyes on her, but until that moment, she never saw me."

"Have you ever told her that?"

He turned his head away from the horses he'd been studying to smile at me. "Many, many times. I could lose it all tomorrow." He waves an arm to encompass the land and the house behind us. "But if I kept the love my family has for me at this moment, I'd be richer than I would be if *Fortune* told me I made the top 500 wealthiest people in the world."

I froze and asked him, "Umm, you're not on that list, right? I mean, I guess that'd be cool for you, but frankly, money can be a pain in the ass. At least I find it to be. That's why I let Bris deal with mine."

Chuckling, he slung a friendly arm over my shoulder. "I think that's the first time I ever heard anything to that effect."

"Don't get me wrong. I like my creature comforts, but Bris donates a bunch." I shook my head. "What the hell am I going to do with all of it? She keeps making more," I tack on in disgust.

Ev tossed his head back and laughed. "You are priceless, Linnie."

I gave him a quick wink.

Even Char and I have spent time getting to know one another.

She made a trip to Gainesville this week for some extra groceries and asked me if I wanted to come along. We took her Lexus SUV—a vastly different driving experience than riding with Monty—and by the time we left Wegmans, I was indignant there wasn't one closer to me in New York. "What complete crap," I declared, much to Char's amusement. "I'd love to be able to get the groceries we just got in one store. I have to get Whole Foods to deliver, go to Zabar's, and hit a few specialty stores to get half of what's in the trunk. You can walk in one freaking store and get everything." I'm in awe.

"This is why I suggested we eat first. Can you imagine if we went in there hungry?"

"We'd have bought out the entire hot bar," I said faintly. "As it was, we needed two shopping carts, Char. Two."

Char reached over and patted my knee. "I only shop like this once every few weeks. It's not as bad as it looks."

Like the baby on *The Exorcist*, my head revolved around to her. "Every. Few. Weeks? Are you feeding the horses people food?" I demanded.

Char's laughter exploded over the music in her car. Shaking my head, I grinned out the window as Char drove us back to the house explaining the town we were driving through, littered with town-homes and shopping centers, used to be huge farms which were sold off for housing developments closer to the nation's capital.

But despite shared meals, the one member of this family I still don't have a pulse on is Monty. Wandering over to the fence where my father so often stands, I lean against a post, lost in thought.

What do I know about him? He loves his family. Char explained Monty left his job because of a personal decision. He's patriotic, loyal, and I know very intuitive about human nature. He understood the idea of him looking into me would be disturbing. But there's something else, something I can't put my finger on that's floating just out of reach.

Scraping the toe of my sneaker back and forth against the blades of grass, I don't notice anything different about my surroundings until

I realize the sun's ducked behind a cloud. Glancing up, I jump back-ward when I'm startled by the fact it's not a cloud that's blocked the sun but a man on a horse.

Monty and the beast he's sitting astride sure know how to make an entrance. A tiny smirk touches my lips wondering if there's a chance in hell of ever getting both man and beast up on a stage—whoever cast them would make a mint. It would undoubtedly cause a stir in audiences everywhere, that's for sure.

"Whatever you're thinking can't be good," Monty declares as he throws his leg over the saddle, slides his body down the side, and loops the reins over the horse's neck with ease. Holding them loosely in one hand, he makes his way around the front of the dark-maned beauty.

"Why do you say that?"

"Because you and Ev have the same smile." Again, I'm startled, since I always thought I had my mother's smile. I take a step back to regain my balance. As if he hasn't just rocked my world, he continues. "When you laugh, you both get dimples right here." Monty points on his cheeks where I do have two dimples. "When you concentrate, you both make this face." He puckers his lips until he looks like a goldfish.

An involuntary laugh breaks free. "Oh God. I don't look like that. Do I?"

With his eyes twinkling and his lips still pursed, Monty replies, "Yes, you do." Quirking his lips, his sexy smile causes my stomach to flutter. "So, fess up. What were you thinking about?"

"You and your horse," I blurt out.

His brows raise a bit. "Come again?"

I begin babbling. "I was thinking you both would make one hell of an impression coming out on a Broadway stage. If you rode on out, the awe on the audience's faces would be insane."

I'm pretty sure Monty thinks I'm insane if the disbelief on his face is anything to go by. To cover my embarrassment, I keep talking. "I mean, you looked impressive up there. All...tough. Masculine. Not that I know anything about it. Riding, I mean. Well, I don't know about being a man either. I've never been asked to play one. Though, that might be interesting..." I frown in thought. Then I shake my head. "Never mind. If I did that, it could never be a musical." I focus back on Monty to find him more than just a little amused.

"Did you just have an entire conversation with yourself about whether or not you'd be able to play the part of a man and then rule it out because you wouldn't be able to sing?"

"So? People talk to themselves all the time," I defend myself.

His lips twitch, but it sets off a chain reaction. I start giggling. "It was pretty insane, wasn't it?"

Casually, he reaches out and tucks a strand of hair off my cheek. "Just a bit. Got anything to tie back your hair?"

"Sure."

"With you now?"

Confused, I reach for the hair tie on my wrist to show it to him. "Do you need it for your horse or something?"

That must cross some inner threshold he can't contain. Monty grips the top rail of the fence as he howls.

Bristling, I start to turn away. Quick as a snake, he grabs my elbow over the top of the rail. "Don't. It's been too long since I laughed like that. And God knows, I needed it." Rubbing the inside of my elbow, he says, "Come for a ride with me."

I shake my head. "I can't. Remember? I've never been on a horse."

Turning back to face me, his often far-too-serious eyes are smiling. "You can trust me not to let you fall."

Oh, but if only I could trust myself. Wordlessly, I nod. Stepping back, I look up and down the long rails for a break in the fence to walk to enter the pasture. Monty shakes his head.

"There's no gate on this side." He drops the reins. Holding out a hand, he motions me closer. "Put your hands on my shoulders and step on the lower rail. I'll lift you over."

"Okay." Using my lower body strength to push up, soon I'm being swung over by Monty's strong arms. As I slide down the front of his body, my breath whooshes out of me softly, barely a puff against his chest. I don't think he notices as he picks up the reins and then quickly guides me to the beautiful horse. Fortunately, he can't feel what being pressed up against his body did to my heart. Otherwise, there'd be no way I could survive this ride.

Soon, Monty has helped me mount and is swinging up behind me. Clucking softly, the horse beneath me begins to walk. I let out a slight yelp, much to my horror and Monty's amusement. "Who is our ride today, and can I pet her or him?"

"Her registered name is Crimson Seminole. I call her Hatchet." I go from thinking what a beautiful name to rocking back against Monty with laughter. His arm tightens around my middle.

"Ha-ha-Hatchet?" And I'll be damned if the horse's ears don't twitch.

Monty's chin comes to rest on my shoulder as the three of us walk along. "She was a gift from Ev when I graduated from college."

"I'm confused. She doesn't look twenty."

Monty's chuckles. "She's only nine. I graduated college while I was still in the Navy," he explains.

"Oh. That makes more sense, but why do you call her Hatchet?" I twist my head slightly, only to find his face right there.

Oh.

His chiseled lips curve. "I received my degree through the online program from Florida State. Colors are crimson and gold; mascot is the Seminole."

"That explains her name but..."

"Hatchet comes from the arm motion all FSU fans do at their games." Monty lets go of me with one arm. As his arm goes up and down like an ax, I begin to cackle. I don't know how I'm staying upright. When he's done, his arm settles back around me, making me feel cocooned in safety.

Deciding there's nothing to lose, I decide to ask what's been on my mind. "What made you come to work for Ev?"

The quiet clop of Hatchet's hoofs against the turf is the only sound as Monty struggles to answer me. "You don't have to answer. I was just wondering," I rush out.

"It's not that. I was trying to figure out how to answer." He doesn't offer more, and I don't push.

We go on for a few more minutes before he speaks. "There were a few things Ev needed assistance with. The timing coincided with an incident at work." I feel the tremor in his body behind me. Instinctively, I do what comes naturally.

I hold on tighter.

"It started as a much-needed break," he admits. "I officially resigned, though I did give thought about returning to my team. But soon the days turned into weeks into months. And I couldn't bear to wear my shield again. I realized I came home," he concludes. "As much as I miss it some days, I can't go back."

"Did something happen? Something that made you not want to be an agent anymore?" I ask cautiously.

"You could say that." His voice is tight. I decide to steer the getting-to-know-you questions in a different direction.

"So, how hard was it to make the transition from the city to the farm? I have to admit, I'm having some difficulty without the lack of noise outside my window." I can feel the vibrations from Monty's laugh against my back.

"At first, it was like a massive power outage. Like a grid went out or something," he agrees.

"Yes! That describes it perfectly. Like some buildings were smart enough to have power but not ours!" I twist a little only to find him smiling down at me beneath the brim of his hat with warm hazel eyes. I clear my throat and break our eye contact. "Anyway, you were saying?"

"It wasn't completely atrocious since I used to live here and then visited often enough. What was difficult was the men looking to Ev for confirmation when I was directing their work. Here I was supposed to be relieving his stress, and they were bringing him more of it."

"Relieving his stress? Is everything okay?" The panic in my voice is real.

"Nothing for you to be concerned with, Linnie." There's a stretch of silence as Monty guides us between some trees at the ridge. I didn't realize we'd traveled so far until he turns Hatchet around and we look back at the property. Ev's home looks like a dollhouse from the distance we're at. We've stopped at the top of a crest covered in lush wildflowers. Monty keeps a firm rein on Hatchet to keep her from nibbling on more than a few of the beautiful blooms.

"How far away are we?"

"About a mile. Nothing too far."

"It's beautiful. I've never seen anything like it." And it's true. New York is filled with a sharp edge, but this is quietly filling a different part of me I didn't know I had to be topped off.

"It's home," Monty affirms. "Maybe that's why it was easy for me to come back to."

And maybe that's why I'm having such a hard time adjusting. Because as welcoming as Ev and his family have been, as generous as they are, it still doesn't feel like home to me.

It may never be.

THIRTY-FOUR

MONTAGUE

"No. Hire a tour bus if you need to, but none of you are driving into the district." I sound like a parent lecturing three teenagers instead of my parents and Linnie. And by the look on all of their faces, they're all thinking the same thing. Sticking my fork out at my mother, I tell her, "You and Ev get lost trying to drive down in DC, and Linnie shouldn't drive for all our sakes."

"That's it, sell me out," Linnie jokes as Mom and Ev turn to gape at her. "I haven't driven since I was a kid," she explains. "If I needed to get somewhere, I walked."

"Or called Uber."

Linnie tosses her hair over her shoulder. "There is nothing wrong with Uber Black."

"No rideshare with your fellow New Yorkers?" I tease her.

"Listen, I take plenty of subways. When I'm in a car, I like my privacy," she retorts.

I shake my head in mock sadness. "Now see? If you knew how to drive, you could see all the sights without a chauffeur."

Linnie throws her roll at me. I catch it before forking a bit of chicken and shoving it in. "Delicious, Mom."

She shakes her head and uses her fork to point at Linnie. "Thanking the wrong cook, son."

My brows arch. "Wait just a second. You know how to cook? You don't have a staff of twelve who waits on you?"

Rolling her eyes, Linnie cuts off a bite of her own grilled chicken breast atop spicy ginger noodles. "Do you? I mean Ev's home is much larger than mine." She shoves the small bite in her mouth and chews. Swallowing, she continues. "And aside from the people who work at the farm, I haven't seen anyone around here to help your mom with the house, which is why I offered to cook dinner." She blushes before turning her attention back to her meal.

"We do have people who come in, Linnie," Ev says gently. "They're just not live-in. We prefer our privacy that way."

"Char let me know when I was cooking. It was a relief, that's for sure. I had visions of her pushing a vacuum, and all I could hear was my own mother saying, 'Darling, at my age, there are certain things a woman just doesn't do.'" Linnie mimics her mother's voice beautifully before her face falters. Her fork clatters to the side of her dish.

Mom reaches over and squeezes her hand. "Well, I for one am glad not to be taken for granted."

Linnie nods rapidly.

Is this what I'm going to feel like if something happens to Ev? So broken that the mention of the good memories brings nothing but pain? Tossing back the rest of my drink, I stand to get something a little stronger. On my way back around the table, I see Linnie's eyes are latched on the glass. Her lips are compressed together slightly. In part to divert her attention, and truly because the idea of any of them driving in the District truly scares the hell out of me, I find myself saying, "There's no way we can do DC in one day because I refuse to get up that early."

"Also, it's unlikely you won't take her by to see Shaun at the office," Mom says brightly.

I roll my eyes as Linnie's eyes snap up, excited instead of tragic.

"You know the NCIS office looks nothing like the show," I warn.

"Neither is backstage at a Broadway show and people still want to visit it," she says wryly.

"But backstage for you has Simon Houde," Mom says dreamily.

Ev shakes his head while I remind her, "He's young enough to be your other son!"

She waves me off. "Semantics."

I groan. My mother has a massive crush on Linnie's brother-in-law. "So, we have a deal?" I ask. If I'm going to DC tomorrow, I need to shore up tonight mentally.

"Wait? Are you serious? I couldn't take you away from your work, Monty!"

I wave it off as no big deal when the reality is that it's going to drive me to drink. Being back in the city aggravates my nightmares. But the pleasure that washes over her face makes it worth it.

"Just tell me when you want to go and I'll be ready," Her face is flushed with excitement.

"We'll leave tomorrow at ten. Dress nice, but wear comfortable shoes. We'll be doing a lot of walking."

LINNIE'S still somber as we walk out into the sunlight from the Holocaust Museum. "I'd always wanted to see it, I just never had the time."

"It's not something you can put into words. It's something you have to experience," I say honestly.

She lifts a shaky hand to her stomach. "Those videos, Monty. Who would ever..." Her voice trails off.

"One thing I learned in my years in law enforcement was that understanding the criminal mind is fascinating." Linnie's head whips toward me. "Not because of what it does, but because what makes it twist and do something so off-kilter. Take you, for example." Linnie stops while we are walking.

Indignantly, she glares at me. "Are you trying to say..."

I steamroll over her. "You could have someone with a perfect life on the outside, but what would make you fall apart on the inside? What could drive you to do something crazy? The insane? The foolish? People have tried scientific study during a criminal's life, and even after their death, and I don't know if they'll ever get it right."

"Any theories?" We resume walking to where the car is parked. We have to drive over the Anacostia River and get on base to get to my old office. Shaun agreed to get us both in. "Listen, she's part of your family. Happy to give her a quick tour." I didn't mention how much that statement weirds me out when I can't get her out of my thoughts.

Or my dreams.

A glance at my watch tells me traffic won't start to pick up for at least another two hours. "Come on. We can discuss this in the car."

We reach the lot where I parked the Jag. After we slide in, I pick up where we left off. "Greed, insanity, or revenge. So far, those are the three main reasons I've seen criminals commit the acts they do."

Linnie's thoughtful as we zip down South Capitol Street. "So what you're saying is that anyone has the capacity for certain crimes with the right incentive."

We pull up to the Joint Base Anacostia-Bolling Main Gate when we're stopped by a MA who I know damn well would have no problem shooting us if we posed a threat. I should—I helped train him when I was still at sea. "I need your ID."

Reaching into my back pocket, I present both of our IDs to the guards while I patiently wait for the dogs with the other to do a walk around of the car.

Linnie's eyes get huge. "Holy shit," she whispers. "This is what you had to go through every day?"

I nod. "Coming on base is serious." I'm about to run through a typical day's protocols when I'm given the go-ahead to drive through.

"You're all clear. It's good to see you, sir." I nod at the young lieutenant, who's run my ID and Linnie's. I know by the time I pull up to the NCIS headquarters, Shaun and whomever he chose to escort Linnie will be waiting outside. Taking our IDs back, I toss mine on the dash while Linnie slips hers away.

"Every day," I confirm.

Her eyes get big, but before she can gather her thoughts for comment, we're pulling up in the parking lot near the nondescript brick building that holds so many of my memories and even more of my nightmares. A bead of sweat trickles down my back. I rub my hand across my neck. I nod. "So, this is it. NCIS Headquarters."

Linnie doesn't say anything. I twist in my seat to face her only to find her not looking at the building but me. "Is everything all right?" Her voice reflects the concern etched on her face.

I turn off the Jaguar, leaving us cocooned in silence. "Everything's fine." Until I pulled up to my old office, I thought I was improving. Now, I realize I'm no closer to stepping in through those doors than I was six months ago, the first time I received a call to determine my mental readiness to return to the job. Back then, I had Ev's medical health to shield me. Now, there's nothing but my fears.

Even as I'm reaching for the handle, I give Linnie a quick rundown of what she can expect. "You'll be escorted everywhere inside the building, even the restroom. You have to wear a badge at all times. There's going to be areas you'll pass that you may have questions about, but we won't be able to answer, no matter how much you try to dig. If you can't handle that, tell me now, and I'll call Shaun over to say hi." Part of me wants her to say no so desperately. I can almost taste the bile rising in my stomach at the idea of walking into my old life.

Linnie nods. "I understand."

No, you don't! I want to shout at her. *You have no idea what the men and women inside that building go through daily.* Flashes of the acceptance on Shaun's face when he realized if I took the shot the through-and-through would be likely to hit him almost make me want to upend the lunch Linnie and I enjoyed near the museum. The horror of Tim McMann's face as he ate the bullet. The devastation and ultimate blame turned on me by Commander Cindy McMann when she learned the full extent of what happened to her son.

And the weight of it all in my mind.

"Then let's go," I say brusquely, shoving my door open. Linnie follows at a slower pace. She silently keeps pace with my long strides, which I do not attempt to slow down. We reach Shaun and a female agent I recognize as Sandra Raines. After a quick introduction, the issuance of badges, and another briefing, the four of us enter the building. Linnie surrenders her purse for inspection. We both walk through metal detectors and into the shielded elevator to the third floor where my old team sits.

As the door closes, I feel myself start to hyperventilate. Then whether by accident or design, a smooth hand jostles against mine.

Linnie.

She doesn't say a word, but she doesn't move away either. It was her presence that made stepping off the elevator possible.

And the next few hours bearable.

SOMEHOW, Shaun's unearthed an official NCIS hat and T-shirt for Linnie. She's charmed by the gesture until he casually says, "You should make sure there's no blood on them. I stole them from Sandra's locker."

Linnie turns a pale shade of green. "Umm..."

I snicker, knowing Shaun would be more likely to have requested them for Linnie than ever do something like that.

Sandra, who just wrapped up taking a call on a possible lead, throws him the finger. "He did not, Linnie. Don't let him mess with your head. He got those just for you," she says, confirming my suspicions.

Linnie pokes Shaun in the chest. "You're trouble, Shaun."

Sandra gets belligerent. "How is it Monty's new woman has your number already?"

Linnie and I choke on her assumption simultaneously. Linnie recovers her aplomb quicker though. Giving me a wink, she drops her voice and adds a touch of venom. "New woman? Darling, I thought I was the only woman."

I pretend to placate her. "Now, sweetheart, you know there were others before you."

"According to Sandra, it appears I'm one of a crowd. I'm not sure how I feel about that," she sniffs. I want to howl with laughter. Based on the look on Shaun's face, he wants to as well.

"Do I need a song to go along with this little dramatic fit?" I drawl. This is way too fun. Leaning against the secure file cabinet next to Shaun's desk, I cross my arms and my legs at the ankle.

Linnie looks tempted. Her eyes narrow. "Don't think I won't. You know by now I have no problem with randomly bursting into song. It's embarrassed you enough times. Particularly when we got into that fight at the coffee shop."

Shaun's doing everything not to laugh, but Sandra looks enthralled. "Tell me, what song fits this little squabble?" I dare her.

And damn if she doesn't start to sing about someone having six wives and arsenic. I'm bracing myself on my knees to hold myself upright. Shaun's pounding my back, wheezing with his laughter. And Sandra declares, "You just became my new best friend."

Linnie pops out of the pissed-off girlfriend role. "What's even funnier is that we're not together." She shrugs. Giving me a warm smile, she tells the other agent, "We're just good friends."

A familiar male voice comes up behind us. "That's a pity. And here I was hoping former Special Agent Parrish had got his head on straight long enough to get back to work."

Ah, fuck. Just who I didn't want to run into: the director. Then I see Shaun and Sandra stand and Linnie's eyes widen. Shit. That can only mean someone else walked up as well. Someone important.

Taking a deep breath, I turn around to both of the men I wanted to avoid at all costs. "Mr. Secretary. Director Troy. A pleasure to see you both."

"We're glad you think so, Parrish. How about a quick chat before you head out? I'm sure Johnson and Raines can watch your guest."

Knowing there is absolutely no way out of my current predicament, I nod. Turning to Linnie, I hide all of my churning emotions. "Stick with Shaun and Sandra, no matter what."

She reaches up and brushes her hand gently on my chest. A simple gesture but one I appreciate. The brand of her fingertips transfers much-needed strength. It's enough for me to turn and follow my former bosses to the director's office one floor up.

This exact confrontation was what I was hoping to avoid.

THIRTY-FIVE

EVANGELINE

We're driving back from the tour, and Monty's quiet. I'm not sure if that's due to the storm outside or the one I saw brewing in him as we made our way to his SUV. Things were fine until he went into a closed-door meeting. When he came out, his face was a blank mask. Instead, I scrambled to comply when he said, "There's a storm coming. We need to go."

Shaun and Sandra escorted us downstairs. I thanked them profusely, but it wasn't until we were off base and well on our way that I realized I left my gift on Shaun's desk. In the grand scheme of things, it means nothing in comparison to getting Monty away from that place as soon as possible.

I want to ask him what's wrong, but the pounding rain slamming against the glass needs his attention. He has on a local radio station. After a few more minutes of crawling along, he jerks the car to the right, abruptly pulling off at a turnoff overlooking the Potomac River that he pointed out on the way into the city. "It's only supposed to last a little while longer," he assures me, though his voice is flat.

"Whatever you think is best," I concede quietly.

Suddenly, out of nowhere, his hand slams against the steering wheel in frustration. I jump in my seat. "It was supposed to be a quick in-and-out tour—not that."

"Not what?" I seize the opportunity to help. As an actress, I usually see when someone's playing a role—Monty's good at it, no doubt. But the masks can only be held up for so long before they disintegrate. Unfortunately, Monty's just did.

Finally, I'm about to see the man underneath the rock that everyone leans on.

"Not an ambush to come back. I've barely got to the point where it doesn't require drugging myself to be able to sleep and even now the nightmares..." His voice trails off. A crackle of lightning rips out overhead.

"Have you talked to your Mom or Ev about it?"

"With everything that's going on at home? Hell no, I haven't."

"Why not?"

A bitter laugh boils up. "It's just one more piece of crap piled on top of all the others they're dealing with. I almost couldn't handle it. I was such a mess after I quit, and when I got the news about that, I decided to stay drunk for an extra day."

Something about what he says niggles at the back of my mind, but I push past it. Monty's my concern at the moment. "What happened, Monty?" I lay my hand on his arm. He stiffens beneath me. "There's no one here but you and me. And I'm not here to judge you."

"Everyone else has; from the secretary down to Shaun. What makes you so different?"

"Because I know what it's like for the whole world to look at your life and say what they would do differently or better. Until they've stood in your shoes, they have no idea what decisions they'd make."

His jaw goes slack as the impact of my words hits him. Scrubbing his hand down his face, he mutters, "I never thought of it like that."

"Not many people do," I say quietly.

The rain pounds on the windows outside. The force of the wind rocks the car a little bit, but I've never felt safer. We're not two strangers right now; we're two survivors of our brand of pain. Our pain bonds us at this moment more surely than if he leaned over and laid his lips on mine. I don't pressure him; knowing from experience, he'll speak when he's ready. It doesn't take him long.

"None of my—our—cases were easy. From the moment I joined the agency, I was challenged. God, I'm not supposed to talk about them."

"Then how are you supposed to get back to where they want you to be to do the job they want you to consider doing again?" I ask pragmatically.

"The hell if I know. They seem to think a few sessions with a shrink and..." His voice trails off before his whole body shudders. "I can't go into the details. I'm under a sworn vow; it's part of the reason I haven't told anyone at home. But that's helping—working with the family, seeing happy, healthy kids. Helping those Ev sponsors who aren't well off enough. Seeing their smiles, their frustration, their hope, that's helping."

"He sponsors kids to ride?" I've seen kids of all ages around the farm, but I assumed they were there for the classes I'd heard people talking about. It never occurred to me there might be more than just that. In my quest to get to know my father, we've never really talked about the business. It doesn't surprise me though. Knowing what he's told me about his background and the kind of people I know Ev and Char are, I can totally see them sponsoring underprivileged kids. Another part of my heart warms toward my father and his wife. I feel Monty relax a little beneath my hand.

"Yeah." Even though I can't see his face, I can hear the smile in his voice. "These kids come in with no confidence, and the idea is to get them to build up trust. Build up their faith in the world around them."

"Has it done the same for you?"

My question lies in between us in the small confines of the car. Monty's harsh breathing is all I can hear despite the raging storm outside. "I'm not prying, but I'm assuming this involved a child. You don't have to tell me," I add on quickly.

"It's always worse when there are children involved." There's a sting in the back of my eyes I ignore. If he wants to talk, I'll listen to every detail without showing a single ounce of emotion. "And when decisions have to be made in a split second, time is only a luxury in the aftermath." He lowers his head to his clenched hands. I doubt he notices my hand smoothing up and down his broad back. "Should I have made a different call? Would things have turned out differently?"

"In the aftermath of my mother's death, I asked myself that and a lot of different questions." His head whips around to mine. "I noticed some oddities that she waved off; she overheated at the oddest times, out of breath. Did I dismiss them because she wanted me to or because I didn't want to see? Would she still be alive if I trusted my intuition more?" The tears I swore I wouldn't shed spill over. I swipe at them angrily. "I'm sorry, this isn't about me."

"I had a choice of trying to talk a boy down from taking his own life or taking a shot to disarm him that almost certainly would have taken Shaun's." I can't hold the gasp in no matter how hard I try. "Turns out he was too far gone to leave it up to my decision. How do I live with that? How do I trust my judgment when I spent the next month being berated for making the wrong call? By my chain of command? By his mother?"

"How do they know he wouldn't have tried at another time?" I wonder aloud.

"Excuse me?" Monty whispers. I struggle as I try to clarify the question.

"Not knowing anything more than what you just said, it seems like this poor soul was determined, Monty. It's a horrible tragedy. It happened, and you feel you made the wrong decision, but if he was willing to do something so tragic in front of strangers..." I shake my head. "He would have found a way to do it alone for sure. He was searching for a way out, not for a way to be helped."

"How can you be so sure?" The uncertainty in his voice is my undoing.

"Because he may not have thought there was a reason to get help when he saw no way out. He couldn't see past his own pain to see who else would be impacted by the decision he made. He was just a kid, Monty. His reasoning was impaired by what happened. There was no way for him to know it might have been the hardest fight of his life, but he could have survived."

At his doubtful look, I give him my truth. "It took a long time, but my mother realized her drinking while pregnant with me caused me lifelong complications. It's not my fault she drank; I wasn't even born yet. She was determined to get help though. Even though she spiraled on and off in her journey, she kept trying. Eventually, she had a reason inside why she was trying to get sober." Sitting back, I wrap my arms around myself to ward off the chill that runs through me.

Monty hasn't moved a muscle. I push forward. "Don't you get it? You're a victim of what happened just as he is. That's why you don't want to go back. Whatever happened is eating away at your soul because you're carrying the burden for everyone."

"How..." he chokes out. There's a single tear running down his face. No one's ever explained it from this point of view to him because he felt he had to be a hero and hold it all in.

"Because you have the same look on your face that I remember seeing on mine when Patrick told me that rehab failed for my mother. Again. You look lost and terrified."

Shifting in his seat, he faces me. "How old were you?"

"Which time?"

"Any, all of them."

"My earliest memories of my mother drinking and cheating on Dad—Patrick? God, I was no older than two."

"What did your father—" He shakes his head. "—Patrick do?"

"Kept trying to get my mother help. He loved her—God. If I'm sure of anything, it's that. When she was sober and saw what her actions were doing to me, well, that might have been her compass to save herself. But she had to be her own north. Nothing else would have saved her. With addicts, I don't know if anything else does." I glance over at Monty, something about the shadows under his eyes sparking a disquieting memory, but I push it aside. If he's been carrying these kind of burdens, it's no wonder he's not getting enough sleep.

Monty's quiet as the storm starts to let up. I hope this doesn't put a wedge between us. "I didn't tell you all of that to redirect the subject. What I was trying to drive home was I don't think there was anything you could have done. Unless the person is willing to change, nothing will compel someone to let go of something toxic for something beautiful otherwise."

Shifting back, he looks at the homes directly across from us. "His mother told me I betrayed the badge I wore."

"That's someone else lashing out in their grief," I declare resolutely.

"Maybe. But it made me question my judgment enough that I leapt at the opportunity to get away. I couldn't be responsible for the lives of other people while I used the job to try to find my confidence," he admits.

"That sounds reasonable."

"Tell that to SecNav and the director. Both of them are putting the pressure on for me to come back." Monty pushes the button to start his Jag.

"And do you want to jump back into the saddle?" I probe as he puts the car into gear.

"Only the kind that has Hatchet beneath. I still don't trust myself to make the right choices." He swings the car out onto the tree-lined two-lane road and punches the gas. Soon, we're flying down the highway in a dizzying blur of twists and turns with no other words between us.

My heart hurts for the man sitting next to me. He feels so much more than he lets on. He's got scars on his heart, on his soul, yet he still manages to find the smile on his face for family day after day.

It isn't until we're back on Route 50 that I feel a hand reach out and clasp my own. Monty lifts my hand to his lips and brushes a kiss on the back of it. "I've been trying to think of the right words to say thank you for your help. For opening up the way you did. I haven't found them yet."

Faintly, my heart bumping up against my ribs, I answer, "I think you just did."

He squeezes my hand before letting it go. "No, but it's a start."

I DIDN'T NOTICE any discernible change with Monty that night or the next. All I could hope was that he was thinking about the things I said and taking them to heart.

It wasn't until three days after we got back from DC when I walked into my room and I found a bouquet of the wildflowers that I remember grew at the top of the hill where he first took me riding that I knew he was thinking about more than just what I said.

He was thinking about me.

THIRTY-SIX

MONTAGUE

In the middle of the night, I'm sipping a large tumbler of bourbon while I stare out the windows over the vast darkness. I can't see the moon or any stars tonight. Fortunately, there's the small ember of one that's been lighting the house for weeks.

The dream woke me up again tonight, but instead of my hesitation waking me up screaming, I woke up with tears on my face. Rubbing my hand across my chest, I remember the words Commander McMann hurled at me: "You're a disgusting representative of your badge and this Navy. You should have taken the shot! Maybe my son would still be alive!" My breathing speeds up as I try to reconcile that with Linnie's soft but resolute "That's someone else lashing out in their grief."

Could it be that Linnie was right? Was Commander McMann lashing out in her grief? Which should I believe? What am I? Someone who was caught up in circumstances or a disgrace of a man?

Even as I lift the tumbler against my lips, I feel the liquid warmed from my hands slosh over the side. Taking a few short breaths, I steady myself before I throw back the rest of the drink. Sucking in a tight breath, the burning down the back of my throat causes a sound-less whistle.

The hand holding the tumbler falls to my side as I lean my head against the glass. If I squint just hard enough, I can make out Linnie's studio. God, if there was ever someone I'd taken at face value, it was Evangeline Brogan.

I likely can't see the stars because she's dulled them out, I think whimsically. I've never met anyone so incredibly beautiful as the woman who's safely bedded down just a few doors away. I wonder if she lies awake as I do. What does she think about in the middle of the night? Turning, I begin making my way to the door to find out when I realize I'm more than a little unsteady on my feet. I slam into the side of the wet bar with such force, I send the bottles rattling.

Well, since I'm here... Lifting my glass onto the counter, I pour a quick refill. Resting against the back, I sip the drink and think about long dark hair and bright green eyes.

How on earth did she not hate her mother? I wonder. How did she know she wanted to follow in her mother's footsteps? Do her lips taste as good as they look? Will she hate all of us when she finds out about Ev? That and a million other questions about her run through my suddenly sleep-addled brain.

Bed. I think I can sleep now. With a clink, what's left of the glass goes down on the counter before I shuffle off to my king-sized bed. I'm practically asleep before my face plants in the center of my pillows.

IN THE MORNING, as I get ready, I put on my usual cup of coffee as I get ready to hit the shower. Noticing there's a little left of my middle-of-the-night bourbon sleep aid, I quickly down it before I go to brush my teeth.

Good bourbon is never something to waste. And besides, it's just this once. It's not like it's going to be a regular thing.

THIRTY-SEVEN

EVANGELINE

"**H**ave you heard the latest, Linnie?" Sepi and I are finally getting a chance to connect while I'm out for my morning run a few days after Monty left the flowers for me.

"About what?"

"About Veronica. Madame Solomone." Something inside me hurts at hearing her name, but I know Sepi wouldn't bring her into our conversation unless it were necessary.

"The only people I've spoken with are Bris, Simon, and you. If I haven't heard anything from the three of you, then I haven't heard anything at all." My heart is pounding though. It isn't like Sepi to gossip.

"BDC let her go. She came to class, was apparently intoxicated, and there was a verbal altercation with a student," Sepi tells me somberly.

"What?" My shock and outrage are conveyed in that single word.

"I know. At first, I couldn't believe it. But Stefano had to restrain her while another dancer went to go get Liz." Sepi names one of the other instructors at BDC. "By then, the screaming could be heard in the other studios. Linnie, she's a mess..."

"I can't believe it." I say that and yet, I can. Veronica has been deteriorating rapidly since my mother's death. It's like Mom was the conscience on her shoulder keeping her from drowning. Since she's been gone, nothing and no one has been there to hold her back.

Certainly not me.

"Yes." Sepi takes a deep breath. "Liz wants to know if you'd reconsider your patronage to the studio now that Veronica is gone. She understands you are on an undetermined leave of absence. She said she'd personally choreograph training routines for you and send them to you."

"I don't know what to say." It's a mutually beneficial offer—a very tempting one. Liz, next to Veronica, is a beast of an instructor. She'll know where to push me to keep me in top shape while I'm gone. But... "I want her under an NDA, Sepi. I won't be subject to the same vitriol if it all goes wrong and I decide to leave," I warn.

"Done. I'll get with your attorney and get one over to her today. I think you'll both be pleased with this working relationship, Evangeline."

I do too. But I don't say it out loud. Instead, I stretch in preparation for a long run. Now that the days are getting colder and I'm more comfortable running the diabolical hills, I can start a little later. "What else have you got for me?"

"The parts that are coming in are much more interesting, but they're roles Brielle would have played." I frown. "It's like people are expecting you to slide into your mother's shoes."

"No." I shake my head in repugnance even though Sepi can't see. "I don't think so," I declare.

"We may have to consider taking one of them unless you want to reconsider London or doing a film." I'm quiet as I ponder what she's saying.

My mother would tell me to look at the parts and think of the audience, but I worked damn hard for my reputation. I still have a few more years of lead roles before my age forces me to slow down.

It's going to be harder as certain obstacles I've had to deal with become even harder due to age. I refuse to back down now.

"Keep that on the back burner, but let me know if there's anything that would make me leave Virginia right away. Oh, what are they saying about Simon's hiatus?" Simon declared in a press release he doesn't plan on working until after his and Bristol's child is safely born. I released a statement through Sepi my wholehearted support for my brother-in-law and costar.

"They're salivating to see whose stage he graces when he comes back." Her voice is wry. Of course. Simon's a male. It drives most actresses insane that men's time on the stage isn't limited by age. There are so few meaty roles for women in that in-between age.

"Of course."

"He also said that he'd be disappointed to work with anyone but you again. So, I wonder if that's not part of the reason people are tossing supporting parts at you. Directors may be saving the larger roles for when the Wonder Twins can get back on stage together," Sepi thinks aloud.

"I'm not worried," I lie. "In the meantime, keep me informed."

"Will do. Talk soon." Sepi disconnects the call. I slip my phone into the pocket of my warm-up jacket, plug in my earbuds, and take off at a brisk stride.

Alcohol has stolen so much from me: my mother, my godmother, and my sanity. As I run, I flash back to the tests I endured for my difficulty learning, seeing school psychologists because I wasn't able to pass standardized tests, Mom and Dad—Patrick—fighting for me because I couldn't keep up with the other kids in my grade, but there was no clear reason why. And although it was never confirmed it was due to Mom's drinking, I'd see the guilt in her eyes when I'd be struggling.

My feet slapping against the pavement, I remember the times in college I'd struggle with requirements because of the intense amount of reading until Bris recommended having someone read my homework to me like a book on tape. Later, I did the same with my scripts, putting them into my long-term memory.

My whole life has been affected by alcohol from the minute I was born, and I've never had a drink of it. To do so would practically be suicide. I've been subject to everyone else's reaction to alcohol my entire life.

What I want to know is can't someone be saved from it? Just once? Why am I a target for the hurt and pain of alcohol abuse? Am I not worth fighting for—giving up the bottle for? Then I remember what my mother said to me: "Liquor complicates an already complicated person, Linnie. But they have to be willing to put it down and walk away. Giving it up has nothing to do with how much they love or don't love someone else; it has everything to do with how much they love or hate themselves."

Tears blur my eyes as I think about how much pain Veronica must be feeling. If my mother was her heart, BDC was her soul. Maybe this will be the catalyst for her to get her life in order.

Hitting the halfway mark, I turn and run hard back toward the house where I've been welcomed with open arms. My thoughts and heart heavy. Even though I usually don't dance on the same days I run, I think I'll spend a little time in the studio today just thinking of my godmother and hoping the thoughts land on her heart through the many miles between us.

THIRTY-EIGHT

EVANGELINE

I t's almost Halloween. I didn't realize it gets as cold as it does in Northern Virginia. My breath is cold as I dash after breakfast from the house to the studio to dance.

After properly warming up, I feel like something sassy. My feet are flying across the dance floor, and my fingers are snapping. My voice echoes beautifully in the room as I taunt an imaginary audience. Okay. If I'm honest with myself, I imagine Monty as I tease him with this particular dance which is seductive and playful.

Since we came back from DC that day, he's been more open about laughing with me. He hasn't held back from casually touching me, which sets my body aflame. The problem is I can't tell if it's just me feeling this way. How do I know if he's naturally this personable and I helped release some of the pressure built up in him so he can once again be himself?

Twirling around, I kick one leg up and then the other. I admire the long length the stiletto point gives to my kick. Slowly, I sway my hips back and forth as I walk around an empty chair. This particular show would generally have me wearing much more of a flimsy outfit than the running shorts and tank I'm presently dancing in, but it's fun as I sink into a grande plié and then shift my hand to the ground to slide into a split in front of my "customer." I fling my head down to my knee, still singing. Rolling my shoulders back, I finish with my back arched, one hand up, the other bracing my core.

Then I hear a slow clap. My head snaps toward the door.

"That's one hell of a show, Linnie." Monty's eyes are burning down at me. "Though I imagine if I were sitting in the chair, it would have been even more entertaining."

Swinging my back leg around, I push myself to my feet. "It's from *Sweet Charity*. I haven't done stiletto work in a while, so I figured I needed to bone up on it. Can't let the skills get rusty from lack of use."

Monty lets out a choked sound. I realize what I said, and I want to slap myself in the head. Instead, I make my way over to the bar and grab the towel and bottle of water I keep there. Just as the next number starts, I hit Pause. "What's up?"

"Ev and Mom had a few things to do this afternoon. They'll grab dinner out. Thought I'd see if you wanted to go for a ride," he tosses out casually.

"On a horse?" I've been up on a horse a time or two around the ring with the beginner students. They find it cute that someone who's as old as their instructor is taking the beginner class.

"No. But dress comfortably. We'll be out a while ourselves." Monty turns to leave. "I'll grab some food for us to eat on the way. An hour enough time for you?"

"Sounds good." Ever since we went downtown, Monty's been different. He's held himself back less and less from me even though there's still a weary edge to him. His hair looks like it's about two weeks past due for a cut. Normally, it frames the lines around his face. Today, with the smile on his face, it makes me wonder what slipping my fingers through the dark strands would feel like.

"Take your time. We're not in any big hurry." He opens the door and is about to pass through it when he drops a bomb on me. "But the next time you do that number, I might have to hunt you down after. You may not be used to that kind of response to one of your shows." He steps through the door and closes it behind him.

I grab the counter to stabilize myself on the heels I'm wearing. It wouldn't do well to roll an ankle at this juncture because if I'm not mistaken Monty just fanned the flames of the interest sparking between us.

And I just agreed to spend the afternoon with him?

Oh boy.

DRESSED IN A VEST, long-sleeve T-shirt, and jeans, I meet Monty in the kitchen about an hour later. "I hope this works?" I twirl to indicate my outfit.

"You might be hot while we're in the car, but otherwise it's perfect."

"Are you going to give me a hint to where we're going?" I ask as we make our way out through the drop zone toward the garage.

He keeps walking. Holding the door for me, he purses his lips. "Nah. I am enjoying the fact you know nothing about the area, so everything is so new to you."

I stick my tongue out at him as I pass by. Quick as a snake, he snatches me around the waist. "I recommend for your sanity, you keep that inside your mouth unless you plan to put it to use."

I smack him on the chest. "Flirt," I accuse.

"Maybe," he agrees. "Then again, there's only one way for you to find out."

"Do your parents know how you behave when they're not at home," I tease over my shoulder.

Monty's laugh in conjunction with the doors being unlocked is my only answer. But when I slide into the seat, a familiar-looking to-go cup is waiting for me. "Wait? Is this from..."

"You seemed to like their caramel mocha well enough when we stopped on the way in from the airport. I picked us up some food and drinks." He shrugs like it's no big deal.

"What are we doing?" I whisper, turning toward him before I put on my seat belt.

"Giving up on being 'just friends.'" His hand cups my cheek. "I'm spending way too much time with you on my mind. What do you think?"

Slowly, I nod, my cheek brushing the inside of his hand. Am I seriously agreeing to this? My heart picks up in anticipation and nerves.

"Then why don't we get our first date started." Monty drags his fingers through my hair as he lets me go, and I let out the breath I've been holding. I slide back against the luxurious leather seat and reach for my seatbelt.

Then a thought occurs to me. "Are Ev and Char truly out running errands?"

A smile slashes across his face. "They might have been encouraged to once they knew we already had plans."

I laugh as he backs the SUV out of the garage. "Find something for us to listen to. It's going to take about forty-five minutes for us to get there." Monty unlocks his phone so that I can scroll through his music choices.

Soon we're zooming down I-66 talking and laughing about my riding lessons. "And to think I was going to suggest you get driving lessons soon," Monty teases me.

I punch him in the arm right before I take a sip of the coffee he bought me. Like the first time, it's delicious. It's an unexpected sweet treat.

Much like the man next to me.

"THIS PLACE IS BEAUTIFUL."

"I agree. Skyline Drive is a special place."

"What is it exactly?"

"It's a road that runs along the Blue Ridge Mountains inside Shenandoah National Park. It's spectacular at this time of the year. The views are incomparable, which is why"—a note of humor enters his voice, and I swivel my head toward him—"we've already stopped four times."

"That's not my fault!"

Monty mocks me. "Not at all. I'm sure your sister wants every picture of every leaf sent to her. I figured we'd drive down to Thornton Gap. With all the times you're going to want to stop and get out, that's going to take us hours."

I'm practically bouncing in my seat. "Why will it take so long?"

"Trust me when I say there's going to be places we'll want to get out."

"I assume one of these places has a bathroom."

"What if I told you that you'd have to pee in the woods?" He takes his attention away from the curvy mountain road briefly to see my reaction.

I'm about to blast him, but I see the glint of humor in his eyes. I grab a balled-up napkin and throw it at him. "Cute."

"If you think I am, why don't you take a picture? You know, add it to the ones you're sending to your sister?" Monty's teasing, but *hmm*, Bristol's been asking what he looks like. Lifting my phone, I take a few quick shots while he's driving.

"Could you look over for just a second?" Monty whips his head over, and I take a snap of his stunned face. I save a copy and send it to Bristol with a "Caption this."

The blue dots move while Monty sputters next to me. "Did you seriously..."

"Send that to Bris? Of course I did. Don't dare me to do anything you don't want me to..." I begin howling with laughter when I get Bristol's reply. *Simon's more my type. Monty seems more...rugged? Enjoy your date with my blessing.*

I quickly write back. *It's not a date!* But before I can shut off my phone's screen, Monty snags it out of my hands. "Hey! That's a private message. And you're not supposed to be texting and driving."

"I'm not texting. I'm reading." Monty grins. "By the way, tell your sister she's right. It is a date." He tosses my phone back into my lap.

"Oh, holy hell," I mutter, my cheeks bright red with embarrassment. I lean my head against the window to try to cool down my flushed face.

"Do you know what I did the first time I ever saw you?"

"You asked me out. Then we had lunch with my father." There's a thread of humor in my voice. I mean, come on? How many people can say that?

"Actually, no," Monty says casually. "The first time I ever saw you, I had just put Ev and Mom in a horse-drawn carriage at Central Park for a ride during their anniversary weekend. We'd seen your show the night before. I bet if I told you the date, you'd be able to tell me that you were out for a run the next morning; you keep to such a strict routine. While I was waiting for them, a knockout brunette accidentally bumped into me when she was running. I turned around and watched her run half the block before she crossed into her building by the Plaza." I gape at him. "I wished I was staying in New York for a few more days because I couldn't get her off my mind. Then I happened to meet someone in the lobby of the Hamilton who stirred the same feelings inside of me."

"That's impossible." The words escape past my lips

Monty pulls the car off into the Visitor Center parking lot. Killing the engine, he turns to me. "Nothing's impossible. Impossible is only something you believe in because you won't see what's beyond it."

My mouth opens and closes. I need space and air. "I..." Quickly my hand goes to disengage my seat belt, but Monty lays his on top of it.

"Come with me and give it a shot." His hand tightens on mine briefly.

I pull my hand from his. Undoing my seat belt, I slide from the car. Monty meets me at the back of the vehicle.

Clasping hands, we walk past the picnic area until we're overlooking the vista. The orange, gold, and red leaves make up a patchwork quilt in the foothills and valleys. You can barely make out tiny homes spotting the grassy plains in the valleys. What must life be like in those homes? I wonder. Unknowingly, I squeeze Monty's hand.

"A penny for your thoughts," he asks, squeezing back.

I shake my head. Then I smile. "I'll take a leaf for them though."

Searching my face, he quickly agrees. "That's a deal." Bending down, he scoops up a handful of leaves. Dividing them between us, he says, "Ask me any question you want, but you have to pay for it with a leaf. I'll do the same for you."

"And when I run out?" I look down at the three leaves in my hand.

"We'll find more at the next stop," he says confidently.

"But what if I like the leaf and want to keep it?" I'm looking down at a red maple leaf that's enormous with a bit of regret. I don't want to let it go. It's brazen and beautiful yet fragile. It's a symbol of the moment he's creating between us.

It requires special care if I want it to last.

"You can keep them all if you answer one question for me?"

I close my eyes. Here it is, I think cynically. He wants to know something about me I haven't told anyone.

"Why do you want to keep it?"

Without thinking, I answer in confusion. "Doesn't every girl want to keep a memento from a first date?"

"Good answer." Grabbing the wrist holding my leaves, he pushes the bunch of leaves down and out of the way before he wraps his arm around my waist and yanks me toward him. Lowering his head, the red leaves from the maple tree above us form a canopy to block out the blue sky so that I can see his eyes. "Tell me now if you don't want my lips on yours."

My answer is to drop the leaves and to lift my hands to his dark hair. I sink my fingers full of the rich sable strands to pull his face down to mine.

Monty slants his head, and my head falls back. He cradles me against one arm as his tongue traces the seam of my lips, seeking entrance. I part mine, and he slips in. He tastes of coffee and mint and more. He steals my breath more than the Virginia hills I've run up and down.

He's right. The thought barely registers through my brain as Monty warms my lips with his own in the fresh mountain air. The spark between us has been dormant, but I'd be lying if I don't admit I haven't wondered what this would feel like.

Our bodies shift into better alignment, so I'm able to wrap my arms around his shoulders, fitting myself as tightly against his body as the puffiness of my vest will allow. His hands don't remain dormant. One slides into my hair, holding my head prisoner to his ministrations while the other grips my hip to rock me into the cradle of his hips.

We both are so lost in each other we forget we're standing in the middle of a public space until the shrill shrieking of childish giggles penetrates my brain. Tearing my mouth away, I gape up at him.

Never in my life has there been anyone who's made me feel like that with a single kiss.

"So, for my question, I'd like to know if you're ready to discuss the fact we've pretty much blown the idea we're not attracted to each other out of the water?" Monty says with a perfectly straight face.

"All right. I admit there might be a slight attraction," I allow, my lips twitching.

"Sweetheart, if those kids didn't show up, we might've be arrested for starting a forest fire in a national park." He winks at me before bending over to pick up my leaves. "Come on. You can ask your questions in the car on the way to the next stop."

I want to protest, but he holds out his hand so sweetly, it's all I can do to not fall in his arms again. "If you think I won't be asking them, you don't know me as well as you think you do," I tell him haughtily as I pass by.

Wrapping an arm around me, he breathes, "Certainly not as well as I hope to either."

Damn. I came to stay in Virginia to get closer to my father.

Not his stepson.

THIRTY-NINE

MONTAGUE

"Put your hands up!" I yell. I'm sweating bullets. *Don't make me take this shot. Please, God. Just let him drop the gun.*

The shooter—a fourteen-year-old kid who had been sexually assaulted by the father in the home he was staying in while his mother was deployed—holds the gun with the stillness I've seen only in battle fatigued soldiers. "I can't. I won't."

"Just put the gun down. I know what happened. I can help," I plead with the kid as my partner, Shaun, moves to the back side of him. Saunders and Rogers are slowly climbing the back stairs so they don't startle him into shooting. He's surrounded. There's nowhere to go.

"No one can help. No one! Don't you get it! I won't admit I did anything wrong. No matter who I talked to, they said I was making it up!" he screams.

I'm not so sure he's wrong for putting holes with the .45 he's holding in the chest of his molester either, but that's not up to me. It's up to a criminal justice system that's overrun with too many cases like his. "I can try," I whisper.

"I can do better." He lifts the gun to his head and squeezes.

"*No!*"

I shoot up in bed on a scream the same way I have for the last eight months since the night we solved the case but failed to save the victim.

Tim McMann died because he didn't believe. And I no longer know how to.

Shaking, I get out of bed and stand in front of the window, searching for something to calm my aching heart. Wildly, desperately, I race over to the bar and reach for a glass. I pour myself a drink and pound it back.

As soon as the burning liquor hits my churning stomach, I race to the bathroom, dropping to my knees. I begin to wretch. Loud, violent heaves. Over and over until I'm sweating with snot and tears coursing down my face.

When will it end?

Wearily, I put my head down onto the vomit-ridden toilet seat for just a moment and close my eyes. I know I'll have to shower before I crawl back into bed, but I don't have the energy to right now.

And all I want is peace. Somewhere to escape all the pain.

FORTY

MONTAGUE

I don't know why I seek Linnie out the next morning. She wasn't at breakfast, which was unusual. She hasn't missed eating with us once since she's arrived.

I try her dance studio first, and I'm shocked when the door's locked. Pulling out my phone, I give Ev a quick call. "Do you know where Linnie is?"

"She mentioned going for a walk, but I didn't ask where."

"Okay. Thanks." Disconnecting, I think. Where would she go? Deciding to saddle up Hatchet, I wander off to the horse barn where I stop in my tracks. The woman I've been looking for is sitting on the floor of the dirty barn in designer jeans having an in-depth conversation with a little girl who's been sponsored through Ev's scholarship program. Lorrie lives with her elderly grandmother on the outskirts of Leesburg. She's been a tough nut to crack with the horses. She's more than willing to groom them but refuses to get up on them. I can't figure out why.

But apparently, she's a marshmallow for Linnie, who's making her giggle.

Lingering in the shadows, I blatantly listen to their conversation with interest. I'm astounded by what I hear.

"Grandma doesn't know how to do fancy braids like that." Lorrie reaches up to touch the french braid that runs down Linnie's back. "All she can do is pigtails." She lets out a beleaguered sigh. "And every day she threatens to cut my hair anyway."

"Why's that?" Linnie asks, not putting pity or sympathy in her voice though God knows she has to feel both.

"Well, we can't afford conditioner. So it hurts when she pulls a comb through," Lorrie replies. "Grandma says it'd be easier if my hair were shorter, but then she realizes it'd have to be cut more. Instead, she slaps my hand with the comb if I get too loud."

"Does it hurt?" Linnie digs in her bag in front of her, pulling out a bristle brush. As she gets up on her knees, she spots me. She gives me a negative shake of her head, which I acknowledge with a slight tip of my head.

"Nah. It's kinda like this." And from the shadows, I watch as Lorrie pops Linnie lightly on the fingers. The tension in Linnie relaxes.

"Are you going to do that to me if I try to brush out your hair to braid it?" Linnie teases. The little girl's face lights up.

"I might," she teases back, twisting her head back and grinning at Linnie, showing off where she's missing a few teeth. Spotting me, she goes, "Uh-oh, Miss Linnie. Now might not be a good time though. There's Mr. Monty."

Linnie makes a scoffing sound. "I'll bet you mucking out Hatchet's stall he'll let me braid your hair."

Lorrie wrinkles her nose. "I'm not so sure about that."

It's then I step forward. "I think she was betting me, Lorrie. And what do I get if I win?"

Linnie sits back on her heels for a moment in thought, "Hmm. I have no idea what you want."

I do. The thought floats through my mind and drifts into hers because Linnie's lips part. "How about you sing for me? And Lorrie," I tack on, catching the little girl's glare.

"Deal." Linnie turns and barely lifts the brush to the ends of Lorrie's hair when we're both startled by a howling screech from the child.

"Good heavens, Lorrie." Linnie's startled. "Is your head that sensitive, sweetheart?"

Mischievously, the little girl throws me a wink. I'm taken aback. "Nah. I didn't feel a thing. I just want to hear you sing."

Linnie bursts out into laughter. "Next time, how about asking versus taking a year off my life?" Lifting the brush back to the ends of the girl's hair before she unravels the band, Linnie begins to hum before singing a beautiful song about loving yourself as you are.

Uncaring of what has to be done around the farm, I drop in front of the two girls dappled in the sunlight as Linnie's fingers quickly separate, tug, and twist. As the first braid finishes, her voice climbs higher, but she calmly scoots behind an unmoving Lorrie. She repeats the process over again with Lorrie held captive by the power of her voice. Even as she ties off the last band, she spends the time brushing out the ends until she finishes the song. "Now, how's that?"

I'm entirely unprepared for Lorrie to toss herself into Linnie's arms. "Maybe now the riding hat will fit better so I can ride. Thank you, Miss Linnie. Thank you!"

"My pleasure, sweetie. Next week, I'll start teaching you how to braid your hair so you can do it on your own. Now, why don't you let Mr. Monty take you to the tack room for a helmet?"

Linnie's words jerk me out of my stupor. That's why this little girl didn't want to get on a horse? Because her head didn't fit into a helmet?

"We need to talk," I murmur as I pass by Linnie, who's already putting her brush away.

"You have precious cargo to take care of. I'll be in my studio."

"Come on, sprout. Let's go try on a helmet. Then let's get you up and walking today." I hold out an arm to gesture to the tack room.

Lorrie's shining black eyes are beaming up at me. Then she dashes to the tack room.

I'm not far behind her.

HOURS LATER, I walk into Linnie's studio where she's clad in a pair of tight shorts that barely skim the curve of her ass. As I close the door behind me, she goes up in ballerina pointe shoes and performs a series of spins that frankly leave me as off-kilter as the scene in the barn earlier. Her arms are almost as fast as her legs. Open. Spin. Close. Spin. I'm dizzy.

And her hair's flying behind her in a perfect braid.

I wait until she's finished in a pose where her arm's thrust above her head before I ask, "How did you know?"

"There's something to be said for saying hello," She doesn't turn around. I walk around until I'm in her direct line of vision.

"How, Linnie? Ev, Mom, we've all tried to break through to that little girl for months." My voice is accusatory, but damn if I'm not a little frustrated.

She reaches behind her and pulls her mane of dark brown hair forward. "Maybe because I was in the same boat?"

Understanding flashes through me. "I didn't..."

Pushing up on the toes of her shoes, she saunters over to me. I don't know how she manages to balance on just her toes. "Of course not. I wouldn't have assumed you would have. Maybe Lorrie would have trusted you eventually, but she saw me struggle with my helmet the first day. I put it down in the dirt to braid my hair lower. She took a chance to form a bond—something I thought *we* were doing. I don't get it. I'd thought you'd be happy; why are you upset?"

I don't have a good answer, so I do what I think is the wise thing and keep silent.

"You don't get to come in here and take out your frustration on me." Still, on her toes, she goes to spin away, but I catch her around her waist. "This isn't a pas de deux, Montague," she grits out.

"No, it's an apology." She's rigid beneath my hands for several heartbeats before she lowers herself down to her heels and steps back. My hands drop.

"Fine. Now, if you'll excuse me, I have a few hours of work left before I can call it a day." She lifts her leg in a perfect P while rising on the other foot unaided.

"Hours?" It seems incomprehensible the delicately boned woman in front of me punishes her body like this day after day.

She shrugs before beginning the same exercises on the other foot. "I'm going easy on myself."

Suddenly her cell phone rings with an incoming FaceTime. "Excuse me." Her feet angled outward, she dashes over and picks up the phone. Her face illuminates when she answers. "Marco!"

"*Mon petit oiseau chanteur*," comes a lightly accented voice from the other end of the line. "You are well?"

"Well enough." And then she gives him *my* dimples. An unreasonable irritation starts to form. I lean against the wall, blatantly listening. "How's New York?"

"Dimly lit without you, Linnie. Your former *la chorégraphie* was in my club last night. She was asking if I'd seen you since the incident at the Waldorf. She was quite...flustered...when I told her I don't discuss my family."

Linnie snorts. "Veronica was trying to get gossip about me from you? What a joke."

"I know, *chérie*." They both laugh. I want to move, to give her the privacy she deserves, but I can't force my legs to work. The tone of this man implies a long intimacy with the woman I'm developing feelings for. And as much as I want to despise him for that alone, I applaud his protectiveness of her.

Linnie clucks in mock sympathy. "Did she screech when you escorted her out?" As if such behavior would automatically earn such retribution from the man on the other line.

"It was loud, yes. I still have ringing in my ears where I should only hear your lovely voice. When are you coming home?"

"Christmas, maybe," she says. I blink in surprise. The last I heard she was going to ask her sister how she felt about spending the holiday here depending on what her doctor said about her due date.

"I thought—"

Linnie shakes her head with a glance in my direction. "Not now, Marco."

"Very well. I'm sure we'll talk later. Just let me know if I need to cancel my plans."

"I will. *À bientôt, mon ami*," Linnie concludes.

"*À bientôt*," Marco blips off. Linnie holds her phone for another moment before I step back in front of her to regain her attention.

"Why don't we go out to dinner and talk?" I say quietly. Her nostrils flare. Just as her mouth opens, I add, "We can run to Target and pick up a few things that you might want to get for Lorrie. You were right, and I'm sorry."

Her shoulders slump, and I press my advantage. "There's a great hole-in-the-wall Mexican joint that will feed you enough food for five days near Target," I encourage her gently.

"Go away, Monty." She turns her back to me to put her phone on the counter. I remain planted where I am, waiting for her decision. "If I'm going to eat my body weight in Mexican later, I need to work out for at least another two hours. No distractions." She turns and gives me a mock glare, but the spark is again back in her eyes.

I'm not forgiven for storming in here like a braying jackass, but I'll work on redeeming myself over dinner.

"I'll see you in a few hours, then." I head toward the door when she calls my name. "Yeah?"

"Marco's my brother-in-law—Simon's brother. We're affectionate, and he's very protective, but that's all there's ever been." I turn and head back in her direction.

"You didn't need to tell me that."

"Yes, I did."

"Why?"

"Because." She bites her lower lip. "You didn't ask. And I'd wonder if the shoe was on the other foot. Especially after our kiss."

Lifting a hand to cup her cheek, I murmur, "I don't know how you make a living as an actress."

She shrugs. "I don't play games with people I care about."

Thank God for that. Leaning down, I nuzzle her nose. If I kiss her now, she'll never get her workout in. "Two hours, okay?"

Her dimples pop out as does her smile.

And this time they're all mine.

FORTY-ONE

EVANGELINE

"Long intimate walks down the aisles of Target. My perfect date." I smile winningly at Monty, who looks like he's ready to weave the hair accessories together to form a noose.

"So, El Tio was a bust, but hair accessories does it for you?"

"I wouldn't say that." I laugh at the disgruntled look on his face. "This is just more fun."

"Says you."

"Says any woman who doesn't have easy access to one of the greatest stores ever created."

He stops dead in his tracks, rattling together some of the items in our cart. We came in for hair products for Lorrie, and somehow, we've almost managed to fill a cart. "I don't understand. You live near Saks, yet Target is the greatest store in the world?"

"Listen, at one time it was possible to get McQueen and Jean Paul Gaultier at Target. It is, however, not, possible to get Kind bars, Starbucks, and Goody hair ties at Saks," I declare triumphantly.

Monty opens and closes his mouth repeatedly before throwing up his hands. I'm about to launch into a more man-friendly explanation when I see the mecca of all Target shoppers.

The end cap. The sale items of all sale items. It calls to me like diamonds call to some women.

"If you'll excuse me," I say faintly.

"Linnie? Are you okay?"

"I...I don't know yet. Give me a moment...holy shit! They have Essie nail polish on sale! Bring the cart, Monty! Quick!"

He approaches me slowly. "I'm scared. I'm telling you this because I want you to know if I go running out to the car in fear and leave you stranded, I need to make sure you have Ev's number so you can get back to the house."

Rolling my eyes, I stomp over and snatch the cart out of his hands. "Stop being such a man and get your ass over here. They only have six left."

"Only six. Right."

After I precariously pile the nail polish in the cart, I let out a sigh of happiness. "This is the best date ever."

"Well, if that's the case..." He pulls me to him and wraps his arms around me before lowering his lips down onto mine.

I've never kissed a man while laughing. We're grinning into each other's mouths so huge we can't even do it right. But just like this date, it's fantastic. I shove to the back of my mind the margarita Monty drank with dinner. He's a big enough guy that by the time we're done shopping he should be good to drive. The taste of Mexican on him is delicious though.

Echoing some of my thoughts, he whispers, "I've never laughed during a kiss."

"Me neither."

Putting another gentle one across my lips, he breathes against my lips. "There's another sale rack two aisles over. Go for it, baby."

My heartbeat picks up in anticipation. I'm just not sure if that's because of what Monty said or what he did.

After all, accepting me for being me is a pretty huge deal.

FORTY-TWO

MONTAGUE

L ong after we get home, I step out onto the balcony off my deck. Only wanting a breath of fresh air, I didn't expect to hear the deep breathing of someone trying to rein in their emotions.

Leaning over the edge, I call out, "Linnie, are you okay?"

There's a muffled gasp in the dark. "I'm here if you want to talk," I offer. "Sometimes, it helps to get things out." And maybe one day I should listen to my own advice. I shove the thought aside.

"Is that personal experience talking?"

I admit, "Yeah."

"Will you tell me?" The thought of putting the horrifying images of my last case into her head appalls me, so I hedge.

"What I can."

There's silence from the other balcony. I can hear the soft nicker of the horses in the distance before she starts talking. "I don't know. I was just feeling lonely because I couldn't talk to my mom about tonight. I mean, I called Bristol, but she's in baby mode. Mom? She'd have loved hearing about every detail. There are so few people I'm able to trust deep down. It's weird that I find it's here I get to be just

Linnie, when I never have before. To protect myself, I built my life keeping people at a distance."

"That must have been incredibly lonely," I think aloud.

"Am I allowed to say yes to that when it was by my choice?"

"I don't know. But I wonder if Ev ever feels like that."

"I never thought of talking to..."

"Your father?"

"Yeah." The nights are getting cold. I shiver despite the sweater I'm wearing. Her next words surprise me. "I was so afraid to come here."

"Why?" I lean over the edge.

"I don't know. Maybe I was afraid I wouldn't be accepted."

"If you think you were worried, you should have seen Ev." Her soft chuckle warms me. "What did you mean when you said this was the first time you got to be just Linnie?"

I hear a chair scrape back. Then I hear the soles of Linnie's shoes as she approaches the railing closest to where I'm standing.

"I've been to parties where I've worn jewelry worth more than people's homes. I've danced in dresses that cost more than their cars. And the person people want to talk to is Evangeline, not Linnie. Their interest in me extends to how I can help boost their career. The funeral for my mother was a spectacle—I mean a true media circus. Only a small handful of us care that she's gone." I can hear her exhale across the feet of darkness shrouding us.

"For well over a year, it was speculated I was having an affair with my male lead." Before I can ask, she adds dryly, "Even if Simon and I weren't the closest of friends, my sister would have killed me since he's her husband, father of her child, and the love of her life. They wouldn't care about redone barns, or a little girl's hair. Is any of this making sense?"

"Not really."

"I was always too busy chasing the next spotlight. I thought if I earned enough awards, I could substitute them in place for my father's lack of love for me when there's no substitute for that. So, I'm angry right now, Monty. Maybe I could have had all of this for fucking years. And I'm upset because I'm angry with my dead mother who I loved more than anyone in the world." Bewildered, she asks, "How am I supposed to handle that?"

"Not easily," I admit.

"The week before she died, my mother reminded me of something I'll always have in my memory. 'Look beyond the lights of the stage.' She used to say it to me all the time. It was her way of reminding me there was life beyond the theater." The air goes still for a moment before her voice penetrates it again. "I guess we all have versions of ourselves we show to the world."

"I would agree," I tell her gently. But in my mind, I'm thinking of the nightmares, the unraveling, the excuses I give myself for my nocturnal behavior.

"Yeah."

The night cloaks us, so it gives me the courage to ask something I've been curious about. "Do you think she was meant to be with Ev or your father?"

"Neither. She was meant to sing to the heavens, dance for the angels, be worshiped in the arms of strangers. She was supposed to be everyone's best friend, no one's worst enemy, and could do it all as easily as I breathe. She would have been horrible for Ev whereas Char is his perfect match," Linnie tells me firmly.

"You sound certain about that."

"I am. For me, it's a job I'm damn good at, but since I've been here, I realized I want more from life than a game of empty spotlights and faces I can't see beyond the edge of them. I want to know the people whose lives I touch." I don't know if it's the darkness that enshrouds us, but she admits, "I fear I was becoming a diva in the truest sense of the word. I'm not like that."

"You're not?" My voice is mocking as I think back to our early meeting at Georgia Browns where she meticulously ordered her drink.

She makes a scoffing noise.

"All I'm saying is they made a movie about a woman who ordered just like that. It's called *When Harry Met Sally.*"

Linnie's giggle twinkles into the night.

"This wasn't what I was expecting when I came out here," she murmurs once she's gotten herself under control.

"No?"

"I figured I'd cry, be angry for a while under the stars. Then I figured I'd go to bed and do more of the same."

"Schedules suck."

"Says the man who's changed mine so I'm running before breakfast."

"Those hills are easier to conquer earlier in the morning."

"Ah, so that's the trick."

"No, the trick is to run them more often." Her infectious laughter lights up the night between us before the silence lapses again.

"Monty?"

"Yeah?"

"Did I say thank you?"

"For what?"

"For not looking me up the minute you knew who I was. That...it meant something to me." Her voice is hesitant.

"I caught on to that. The media doesn't like you?"

"In general, no. But I'm more than that. I...I want you to know that from me."

I'm fighting a war with myself because I already know she's more than just the acclaimed Broadway actress. That's not the problem. The real issue is that she's also digging her way deep into my heart.

"I promise. I'll wait to learn what I need to from you."

Her heartfelt words almost feel like a touch on my skin.

"Thank you."

AFTER SAYING good night to Linnie, I go back inside. Stripping out of my clothes, I turn on the shower while I stare at my reflection over the mirror. I turn away when I see what I always do: an unworthy man who looks beat to shit. Now, I can see a new layer of guilt on top of all the others that were seeping into my skin, making me look years older than I actually am. An already complicated situation just became more so with Linnie Brogan's arrival.

I'm lying to a woman I'm beginning to deeply care for.

I've got to figure out a way to get Ev to tell her and soon. These might be the last few months of his life. I can't screw anything up by not honoring the promise I made to him. The problem is the closer I get to Linnie, the more I'm betraying her.

Stepping into the shower, I duck my head under the spray, wishing the water sluicing over me would drown me in wisdom. Instead, all it does is makes me ache for the weight of my mind to be lifted. I could follow my gut, which is pointing me to protect the woman right next door, not the man one floor up and across the other side of the house.

FORTY-THREE

EVANGELINE

Chaos reigns at breakfast the next morning. There are two entirely different conversations going on at very high volumes. My father and Monty are arguing about baseball. Across the room, Char is on the phone discussing an upcoming 5K for the American Cancer Society being held in downtown DC that is sure to muck up traffic.

I'm grinning when Ev catches my eye and winks. "Typical," he mouths at me.

"Fun," I mouth back right before the knife I'm using to slice up some fresh strawberries slips and catches me across two fingers. "Shit!" I cry out in pain. Throwing the knife so I don't ruin breakfast, I pull my bloody hand away. Char, hearing me cry out, spins around. Her face takes on a whitish hue seeing the blood. I feel horrible for ruining everyone's morning this way.

Ev's heading toward the pantry. "I'll get the first aid kit," he calls out.

Monty is at my side in seconds, even as I'm grabbing a towel to wrap it up. "Let me see," he demands.

"It's fine. I feel like an idiot though." I try to pull my hand away but hiss in pain when his fingers tighten slightly. "Damn you, that hurts!"

"I'm trying to apply pressure to stop the bleeding," he tells me calmly.

"Do you have to be perfect?" I gripe.

Leaning down, he whispers close to my ear, "Yes. It's part of my charm."

"Yeah, well, right now your charm sucks."

Monty squeezes tighter, which makes me whimper. "Linnie, we've got to try to get the bleeding to stop. Even from where I was sitting, I saw the ooze of blood."

"Great, with my blood type, I'll probably need a freaking transfusion," I overdramatize, lifting my other hand to my forehead. Monty chuckles.

"Calm down there, sweetheart. This isn't Broadway. About five minutes of pressure should do the trick. If not, then we might need to get you to urgent care for some stitches."

I start to pull away. "No. No stitches."

"Afraid of needles?"

"Yeah, it's called all the vamps who have tried to harvest my blood since I was eighteen. They sucked at it. I left all these blood drives with so many bruises, and I began to get a ridiculous phobia. So, either you manage to fix this or I'll ruin one of your mother's kitchen towels." Both of our eyes drop to the one wrapped around my hand.

"You haven't even bled through this one..."

I interrupt him. "Much."

"Much," he agrees. "I think we're safe to say... Hey. What did you mean about people harvesting your blood?"

Forgetting there's anyone else in the room, I glibly say, "I have a somewhat rare blood type. I'm what doctor's call a universal donor? So, every few weeks, the Red Cross is asking for my blood. I give as often as I can, but as I said..."

"You're afraid of needles." His eyes are swirling with something profound.

"What is it?" Even through my pain, I can tell something much more serious is happening. Monty squeezes my fingers harder. Char drops the phone, startled. Ev makes his way over to her. He lifts the phone, murmurs a few indistinct words, and presses the Off button.

"Ev?" Monty calls out to my father without losing my eyes. "You have exactly ten minutes to tell her or I'm breaking my promise. I swear to fucking God, I'm not holding a thing back at this point."

"Get her fixed up and bring her into the library." I turn my head and watch as Ev wearily pushes his hand through his hair. "Charlotte and I will meet you both in there."

"Ev?" I call out. My father's eyes cut to mine. In them is sadness, despair, and so much love, I'm knocked back into Monty with the force of it.

"In the library." He slips an arm around his wife, and they make their way out of the kitchen.

I'm almost nauseous by the time Monty stops the bleeding enough to bandage my hand before I race out of the kitchen. He catches up with me and grabs me by the shoulders. "Linnie..."

"Tell me," I demand.

"I can't. Just promise me you'll meet me later to talk about everything you're about to hear." His hazel eyes bore into mine.

"You want me to promise you something when you won't give me anything in return?" I demand.

He nods. "You're right." Trailing a finger from my temple down to my chin, he whispers, "When you first came here, I was afraid and not just for Ev. Now, I'm hopeful for exactly the same reasons." His simple touch sends shivers coursing through my body. As he steps back, he whispers, "Come on. It's time for you to know everything."

Side by side, we make our way into the library.

THIRTY MINUTES LATER, I burst out of the library with tears streaking down my face.

I only just found my father, and now I could lose him too.

How in the hell is life fair?

Racing through the house, I find the nearest exit and run hell-bent for leather toward the studio my father gave me as a welcome-home gift.

Except this may not be home for long since he may be dying.

FORTY-FOUR

MONTAGUE

"Could that have gone any worse?" Ev asks, running a shaky hand through his hair. Mom lays her hand on his knee, offering what comfort she can.

I have nothing to say right now because all I want is to run out the door behind Linnie. I need to find her and hold her, to let her know we'll get through this together. Somehow in my heart, I knew she'd feel like this—wounded and in pain.

I've reached the point where I'm tired of keeping so many secrets. It's destroying the relationship I have with my soul, and this one might have just destroyed the one that was blooming with Linnie.

"There's one good thing," Mom says softly.

"There is?" I ask incredulously.

"She didn't leave."

"That you know of," I spew bitterly. Standing, I look down at the two people who raised me. "You forget the only reason she's been here has been to get to know us. What did we show her? That we're all a bunch of lying..."

"Montague!" Ev snaps. My mother's hurt is stained on her cheeks.

"I'm sorry, Ev, but I warned you this was going to happen." I turn and stalk to the door.

"Where are you going?" he calls out.

"To try to find Linnie. To see if she'll forgive one member of this family for their duplicity." Hopefully, the one that's developing feelings for her. As my fingers twist on the knob, I hear a soft laugh behind me. "I really can't find anything about this funny," I growl.

"One day, I'll tell you what I think is both sad and funny about this moment, Monty. Now, go find your girl," Ev says with a break in his voice.

Looking over my shoulder, I see my mother's fingers being brushed back and forth across Ev's lips as they have been so many time over the years. But his eyes are fixed on me. He nods, a crooked smile of sadness across his face. "Go, son. Find your woman to make sure she's all right."

If it wasn't for the handle holding me up, I might have fallen to the floor. "And don't try to tell me otherwise, Monty. For us Parrishes, sometimes all it takes is one look." Mom's head drops to Ev's shoulder.

I gather my bearings before I say something I know I don't say often enough. "I love you both. No matter what." Before they can respond, I head out of the library in search of Linnie.

I CHECK THE STUDIO FIRST. She's not there dancing out her anger and pain. Then I walk the perimeter of the farm along the fence line. I go through the stables; still no sign of her.

I'm about to give up and call her when I happen to glance up at the house and see movement on my balcony when I know damn well I didn't leave the doors open earlier. Taking a chance, I jog through the kitchen and up the back stairs. There's a light sheen of sweat on my skin despite the cold November air.

Sprinting down the hall to our side of the house, I fling open the door to my suite of rooms. The door crashes against the far wall, startling the woman curled up in the chair. She rises, and half a dozen tissues fall from her lap to the floor. The breeze picks them up. She bends quickly to grab them, her hair falling in front of her face. I can't tell if she's still crying or not.

My heart rate starts to even out, and I turn and close the door, flipping the lock. About thirty feet lies between us, but it might as well be miles. "I wanted to tell you," I choke out. "From the first moment you were in this house."

Her head tips back. "Ev didn't?" I start to make my way closer, but she holds up her hand. "No, don't come any closer."

"Linnie." I can feel, literally *feel* my heart start to crack inside my chest. "I didn't keep any secrets of my own from you."

"No, you just helped keep the fact my father might be dying from me," she lashes out. "There's no way a man can—"

"Can what?" Ignoring what she said, I move closer. She twists the crumpled tissues in her hand.

She flings out her arm and the tissues she had in her hand come flying at me. I bet she wishes they were rocks, I think grimly. Instead, they land on the floor between us like the barrier Ev's words created. "There's no way a man can start feeling things for you while lying to you with every breath he takes," she hurls at me. "And to think after yesterday, I'd begun to think..."

"Think what?" I demand. Because last night, for the first time in as long as I can remember, I slept through without a damn nightmare. Who knew if or when that would happen again.

She wasn't the only one who'd begun to think—to need.

"I'd begun to think you cared about me. That's impossible though, isn't it."

"That's true." I edge closer to the tissues. Caring is such a politically correct, pansy-ass word for what I feel for her. I need her more than my next breath. And if Ev fucked this up by making me hold back from her, I don't know what the hell I'm going to do.

Her face pales before she squares her shoulders. "Then tell me what it is you want," she demands. She's practically dancing in place. She's on the balls of her feet, rocking back and forth in her anger, her pain.

Her passion.

"There's exactly one thing I want. It's the only thing I've ever wanted since the minute I saw you." Deliberately, I let my foot crush the fragile tissue barrier between us.

She holds her ground. My nostrils flare.

"And what's that?" she hisses. God, she looks like a warrior ready to do battle, refusing to surrender. Only there will be no white flag.

"This." And I tug her hand to pull her close. Wrapping my arms around her, I lower my head.

Dimly in the back of my mind, I'm a little in shock to realize the stars let their most precious one go so she could light up in my arms as her arms slide around my neck to return my kiss. Passion flares between us, switching despair and anger to hard-core yearning and need in the time it takes for my tongue to slip between the seam of her lips. I tilt her head back to make sure this is what she wants. Her lips curve in a sensual smile as my tongue dips out to capture our combined taste. To memorize it. To hold it deep in my soul.

But I have the answer I need.

My hands roughly slide into her thick hair as she slides her arms under my sweater and begins shoving it up as our lips collide. My eyes drop to half-mast when she rakes her nails over the lower edge of my spine over my pants.

Dropping my head forward, I scatter kisses to her forehead, her cheeks, trailing them down her neck until she lets out a breathless moan in my ear. "Monty, don't let go." Then as she arches her throat, she murmurs something incomprehensible to everything but my heart. It's a plea to hold on.

In my own, I promise to kiss her every morning, every night, and every moment in between. While my hands skim under the tight-fitting running shirt, over her smooth skin, I swear to be a better man

—a man worthy of skin kissed by the moon, hair drenched by the dark sky, and eyes shot through by magic.

Out of the corner of my eye, I catch the sun gleaming off the leaded crystal, and I swear to myself before I drop to my knees to pull off her running shoes that I'm through with dulling my pain. *I'll find a way*, I swear to the three souls in the room: Linnie, myself, and the specter of the alcohol that's been tying me to the past. No more.

After quickly removing one of her sneakers, then the other, I reach for the elastic waistband of her running pants. They fall prey to my shaking hands as I hear the seams rip in my haste. Leaning forward, I can inhale her pure, clean scent from this angle. I run my nose along the seam of her panties. She gasps, her hands, which had been braced on my shoulders, sinking deep against my scalp. "I didn't like these pants much anyway," she says, her voice husky.

I can't help but smile. Shoving to my feet, I grab the hem of her shirt, leaving her clad in nothing but a sports bra and panties. My hands carefully trace the alabaster beauty of her skin. I know I could sip a thousand kisses from it and become drunk from every one.

"This is just the beginning," I murmur. "All I need is you."

Contorting her arms through the straitjacket-like contraption women have to suffer through to exercise, she whips it off. "Then show me," she dares.

I'm not entirely sure if I'm talking about Linnie and me, her and Ev, or the conclusion of my drinking, but whatever combination, I mean what I say. In response, I pick her up and stalk over to my bed before tossing her lightly upon it. She bounces a few times before edging up on her elbows as I begin to strip off my clothes.

I've never seen anything quite so beautiful.

I'll never taste anything quite so smooth.

And I know as sure as I'm about to touch her, no moment will be as life-altering as this one.

Not a single one.

FORTY-FIVE

EVANGELINE

He's the most rugged-looking man I've ever seen, muscular yet graceful. His body is ropes of muscles woven together to form a twisted pattern that makes my hands itch to run my fingers up and down it. Long legs, slim hips leading to an almost overly trim stomach. He's lean almost to the point of thin, but knowing how hard he works, I'm not surprised. Unclothed, there's nothing holding back the power that everyone, including me, relies heavily upon. It's much more apparent without the barrier of clothes to hide it.

His jeans are riding low down on his hips so I can just see the band of his underwear. My lips part as he bends down to unlace one boot and then the other; I get a fantastic view of his traps and deltoids rippling. I don't know if it's his years of service, the shape he had to remain in for his job, or the work he's done on the farm, but I could combust looking at his back. A dreamy sigh escapes my lips.

When he stands, I know he's heard it by the hungry look on his face. An answering growl leaves his throat. Quickly, he unsnaps and lowers the zipper on his jeans before moving toward the bed with the grace of a cat—quiet, stealthy, predatory.

My heart speeds up in anticipation. Soon, that body will be next to mine, over it. I shiver, lying trapped by the fierceness in Monty's face and yet protected by it. My legs begin to scissor back and forth, but even that small motion highlights the need aching between them. Nothing seems to take away my need for Montague Parrish. Short of him thrusting his hard cock inside of me, I know the ache will continue to grow until it consumes me.

In the dimly lit room, his dark hair gleams as if the moon itself decided to rise early and cast its glow on this, us. My fingers clench on the duvet covers as I anticipate running them through the soft strands while I arch into his powerful thrusts. But he stops by the side of the bed, laying a hand over my quivering stomach to still me.

"I never wished for anything until before you." His hand trembles on my skin. "How do I do someone as perfect as you justice?" His hand begins to make little circles. My stomach hollows out in reaction.

"Just want me." Releasing the bedspread, I capture his hand and drag it up my body, over my ribs, between my breasts, until his hand is cupping my face.

"I already do." Lifting one leg, then the other, he wraps them around his hips as he comes down on top of me, his hips aligning with mine.

"Yes," I hiss, as I rock my hips up to meet his. His hand slides down the back of my panties and pull my hips tighter against his.

"Think of how good this will feel when it's just us," he rasps against my ear. "Nothing but our skin connecting. Nothing but my hands, my lips, on your body. What do you think about that?" He sinks his teeth against the cord between my shoulder and my neck.

I moan, knowing if I'd been standing, I'd have fallen. The feelings Monty causes to erupt inside of me are just that strong, just that powerful. Nothing, not even the stage, has ever made my body sing like this.

He lowers himself on top of me, and every inch of him aligns perfectly to me. Bracing his weight on his elbows, he moves his hips slowly. I want him closer—every inch of his skin on every inch of mine.

But he has other ideas.

Removing his hands from me, he rolls us until I'm straddling him. *Some moves*, I think wildly, as Monty's hands cup my sensitive breasts. My nipples elongate as he rolls each one gently but diabolically with his callused thumb and forefingers. "Ohh," I moan out my pleasure. My hips move of their own accord in his lap.

"The first time I watched you dance in the studio, I wondered if your body would move like that in bed." My mouth opens on a gasp as he curls up to capture my lips in a searing kiss. "I'm so fucking excited to know I'm going to find out."

Looping my arms over his neck, I press my lips against the skin of his neck. It's a feast to my senses: the satiny texture over the rippled muscle, the scent of his woodsy cologne mixed with sweat drying on his skin, the warmth of his body. I rake my teeth over his shoulder joint just before Monty tips me back to capture the tip of one of my nipples in his mouth and sucks it tightly against the roof of his mouth.

"Oh my God." The fingers of one hand score down his back while the other tunnels into his hair. "Don't stop," I plead.

He immediately lets the nipple loose. I protest with a small mew only to be granted a boon from some merciful god as he quickly latches onto the other. His other hand resumes the tweaking it was doing earlier, bringing me right to the edge. "More. Harder," I beg.

Monty complies. Pushing my breasts together, he alternates between one and the other, leaving the nipples exposed to the cold November air floating in from the balcony doors I never closed. "Monty, I'm going to..." I mewl, just as small shivers contract my pussy. I slump in his arms slightly. He releases my breasts to wrap them tight around me. As our lips align when he raises his head, I practically devour him. I want to consume him, absorb him into my skin.

He's an addiction I don't mind having—definitely the first and quite possibly the last.

"I want to be inside you the next time it happens," he murmurs against my lips. I squirm against him, anxious to feel the power of his body against mine. "But first, I want to make you forget your name."

My heart stutters before regaining its normal rhythm. "It's Evangeline," I blurt out.

A roguish look crosses his face as he lays me back on the bed. "I'll be sure to ask you that again in a few minutes." Gripping the sides of my panties, he drags them down my legs. I lift my legs to assist him.

Once he's tossed them aside, I go to wrap my legs behind his back, but he presses them gently to the side of the bed. Kissing me, he leaves me partially dazed as he begins a descent, trailing kisses over the peaks and valleys of each rib, my hips before coming to the smooth juncture between my legs.

I arch my back, practically begging for his lips and tongue to taste me.

And he does.

"Perfect," he mutters as he circles my clit with his tongue. I let out a harsh groan and call out his name.

"Monty!"

"Can you take more?" he wonders as he slips one, no, two fingers inside of me. I practically levitate off the bed.

"No!" I cry out. I'm going to come again with what he's doing, and I want to with him.

I need to go again with him.

With a wicked laugh, he moves his mouth to the side, leaving a gentle kiss on my inner thigh. After a moment, he slides his fingers out and promptly slides them inside his lips. Pushing to his knees, he shoves down the rest of his clothes and kicks them off the side of the bed. His hand drops down to his cock, touching the thing I want most in this world. And quite simply, I break.

I scramble out and frantically push him onto his back. "Condom?" I demand.

He nods to his end table. I yank it open and almost send the drawer flying. Finding an unopened box both excites and infuriates me at this moment—I'm thrilled because the box was bought with me in mind, but I'm so resentful of the extra seconds to rip it open and tear off the square packet.

"Give it to me," he growls, then tears it open with his teeth before quickly sheathing himself. I'm bitter by the fact he once again got to touch his cock and I was denied the pleasure, so I don't wait for him.

Shoving him back, I straddle him and rub my wetness all over him so I can take him deep.

But Monty has other ideas.

Rolling me onto my back, he lifts one leg under my knee until it's arched almost to my shoulder. Sliding the head in, he lets me adjust to his size before pushing in.

"Yes," I groan next to his ear before I take a nip at it. Like it was the signal he was waiting for, he pulls out slightly and thrusts back in. And again, and again. Soon, I'm coming around his cock, and he picks up speed. Moaning out his release, he's a couple of quick thrusts behind me.

We're both panting like we just did back-to-back shows with no break when he lifts his head and grins. "Do you still remember your name?"

I'm not sure how I have use of my arms, but I do. Running my hand up and around his neck, I whisper, "Yours," and watch the teasing look melt from his face.

"You know that goes both ways, right? I'm not letting you go through this alone."

"I wouldn't be here if I thought you were," I tell him honestly.

Muttering something incoherent, he lowers his head to my chest and listens to my heart for a while. I hope he's not offended that's it's saying I'm scared as hell, but I'm going to give this a try.

FORTY-SIX

EVANGELINE

"**A**s a master-at-arms, I rarely had time when I wasn't on duty. But there was one night in San Diego..." Monty trails off. His fingers sift through my hair rhythmically. I arch against him, purring like a cat.

We've been lying in bed for hours making love and talking after a quick raid of the kitchen. I was mortally embarrassed when Monty's phone rang about thirty minutes ago. He answered it with a gruff "Hey Mom." I tried to push out of his arms, but the bands tightened. "No, she's with me." There was a long pause. "I think we'll be all right if you and Ev want to go out to eat." His voice is sardonic when he tacks on after another pause, "No, I think we're okay just where we're at." Even as my face flamed hotter than the sex we'd already shared, his softened. "We're good, Mom. Tell Ev things will be just fine. We'll see you both in the morning." Closing his phone, he rolled into me before announcing, "We've got about thirty minutes, and then we can pillage the kitchen. I don't know about you, but I'm starved."

After I beat him over the head with a nearby pillow, I had to give up my righteous indignation when my stomach agreed quite vociferously it needed food.

Now that we're both done consuming our smorgasbord of fruit, cheese, and bread, we're lying with our heads cradled by one arm, our fingers interlocked with the other. Monty's been recounting some of the stories about the military experience. I'm avidly listening as each one reveals another part of his character: the autocratic leader, the loyal friend, the mentor. But this one's holding me captive for a different reason.

"We were going to be in town for a few days. And even though I knew Mom and Ev were planning on meeting me early the next morning, we decided to hit the bars in Gas Lamp."

I snicker. "Sounds like a wise life choice."

His broad chest shakes in front of me. "Right? So, here we are, a bunch of drunk idiots wandering the unsuspecting streets of San Diego..."

"Uh-oh," I singsong.

He smooths his hand down my side, tickling me slightly. "We weren't that bad. Cocky as all hell, sure. But we knew we'd have to answer to the XO if we did something stupid. But as we were trying to find our next watering hole, we make a wrong turn and end up on the street littered with art galleries."

Pushing up, I lay a hand over the center of his chest. A V's formed between his brows. "What happened?"

"I fell in love." My heart lodges in my throat. "Through the window, I saw her. Magnificent. Powerful. Wretched. And I wanted her badly."

Somehow, I manage to scrape out, "So what happened when you went to talk with her?"

His lips curve. "I found out she was $32,000."

I jerk back. "She was a prostitute?"

"She was a painting. A renowned local artist named Marie T. Williams had painted her. The painting was of Virginia during one of the most violent of storms to hit in recent memory. But to me, it was every emotion I had brewing deep inside me." I feel the rise and fall of his chest. "I stood there for hours staring at it—no, absorbing it until the guys came back for me." With a sad smile, he says, "They were such a hot mess, the owner threw us all out."

"What happened?"

"I went back to the gallery the next day with Mom and Ev. The owner was appalled when I walked in with them, not realizing, of course, I had been a serious buyer."

"And?"

"He'd sold it to a couple from the West Coast who were looking for something for the foyer of their vineyard after I left. I was devastated. To this day, I still want to find out what vineyard so that I can go and see it."

Curiously, I ask, "Have you found it online?"

He shakes his head. "Either they don't have it publicly displayed, or it's been resold."

"Did it have a name?" My heart aches. As an artist, this is precisely the kind of emotion we want to elicit—an ongoing love affair.

"Yeah. It was called *Forgiveness*. I always wondered if the artist named it that because of the storm or for some other reason."

"I know some people..." I begin, but Monty lays a finger across my lips.

"I appreciate that, sweetheart. But I wasn't going to let Ev buy it for me. I knew then, and I know now, to own something like that is something I'd have to earn. If it ends up in my hands, it's because it was meant to."

I accept what he's saying, but I wish I could hand it to him. It takes someone with such emotional fortitude to want something so badly and to not accept it out of hand. It takes a sense of honor that I've never brushed up against before. It makes me want to stay where I am.

Here. With Monty. Figuring all the rest out.

Because maybe with his strength to lean on, I won't collapse as I try.

FORTY-SEVEN
MONTAGUE

Her skin feels like a bolt of satin beneath my worn hands. I'm afraid my fingers are going to catch and snag against my fingertips as I brush them up and down her arms, her hips, her stomach. It's terrifying and intoxicating to hold a woman so delicate, so perfect.

I bury my face in her hair the color of dark mink, inhaling the scent of lemon. Shyly, she explained she only washes her hair every few days, so she hoped I wouldn't be grossed out by it. I'm selfish for wanting to wake her so I can see if her eyes will be as bright as the grass or as dark as the fir trees when the long lashes flutter open. Is it daylight that changes them? Her mood?

Everything about her is perfect. Everything that is, except her feet, which are hard and calloused as they rub against my legs in her sleep. It's a relief, to be honest, to know there are parts of her that aren't, that she won't expect me to be that way.

That there are imperfections within her just as there are in me.

I want to take her breath away. I want to shatter her soul. I want to become her purpose.

But then I catch sight of myself in the mirror across the room and realize I still haven't earned the right for all of that.

The ache and pain begin to settle in for their nightly visit. My eyes drift to the one thing I know can chase it all away. I start to shift away until a slender thigh pins me to the bed.

Trapping me.

Holding me back.

Imprisoning me simultaneously in heaven and hell, unable to move, unable to breathe.

Unable to escape.

It doesn't matter to me how she makes me feel; it's how I can't be without the burn.

Unburdened.

FORTY-EIGHT

EVANGELINE

"I grew up in a world where vows of fidelity wilted due to pressure to perform. There was a race to stay ahead because of age and ego required for both. The constant temptations of drugs and booze to enhance the highs and bounce from the lows."

"How did you handle it?"

I shrug, dislodging the blanket Monty pulled over me to keep me warm after our last round. "It wasn't hard in my case. The cost was too high to pay."

He frowns up at me. "What do you mean?"

I disengage our bodies and stand. Tugging the blanket, I use it as a cloak as I wander over to the window to find the night sky. I've become accustomed to seeing the stars while finding my peace of mind—dangerous considering my life is back in New York.

But I don't regret what happened yesterday—not one moment.

I needed Monty— hell, I still do. And I need him to know more about me than the glamour and the body he spent hours exploring dedicated to my pleasure. I need him to understand why I'm the way I am—a dedicated professional, pathologically organized, and perpetually damaged.

"You learn the only person you can truly control is yourself. Need is a different motivator than influence and love. I need things in my life because I have to function in a certain way. It doesn't always make sense to others, but they respect me enough to let me figure out what's best." I turn away. "Until it's not."

I hear the rustle of the soft sheets. The swoosh of a sheet approaching behind me is my warning he's left the bed. Therefore I'm not wholly unsurprised when his hands land on my shoulders as I stare out into the ink giving way to blush in the sky. "Tell me," he commands lightly.

In the flimsy shadows of Monty's room, the words come from the depth of me, bursting forth as if they've been waiting for this moment, this man. "I don't take lovers lightly." His fingers tighten. "It always seemed to expose a part of myself I had to protect, but I can't seem to do that with you."

"Don't distract me, Linnie." His tone is light, but when I turn to face him, his expression isn't. It's filled with the kind of turbulent chaos I recognized right before he pulled me beneath him to love me senseless. My lips part of their own accord; my body's already accustomed to the need he generates in it. He lets out a rough laugh. "Talk to me."

Pulling the blanket tighter, I think about how to explain the fact I'm essentially a fraud. I decide to start from the beginning.

"When I was maybe seven, there was a school play. It was *The Wizard of Oz*. I didn't get cast as Dorothy." Even though my heart races when I imagine his reaction as to why, there's still a sneer in my voice twenty-six years later. His light laughter makes me feel better though.

"What did you do? Chop off the lead's braids or something?"

Thoughtfully, I mutter, "I wish I knew you back then."

"Competitive little thing, aren't you?"

"You have no idea." Regulating my breathing, I continue. "I was cast as Auntie Em. There were fewer appearances on stage and fewer lines to memorize. But the songs she sang are some of the most haunting in that show."

Monty drops one arm to wrap around my waist. "It sounds like you got a better role."

I neither agree nor disagree with his conclusion. I go on. "I owned that stage during my solos. Suddenly, the focus shifted to the director for his poor casting." Lowering my head, I was ashamed when I admitted, "But he was right. Back then, I should never have been lead."

Monty turns me in his arms. "Why not?"

"Because I can't remember things worth a damn."

Monty laughs. *Here it is*, I think painfully. "How is that possible, Linnie? You remember scripts much more difficult than that today. You sing more songs..."

"I have a problem learning," I blurt out. Pulling away from his arms, I lean back against the cold glass.

"How?" The sheet he pulled from the bed is knotted at his waist, allowing him to cross his arms comfortably across his chest.

With the ends of the blanket still in my hands, I must look like a bat trying to sleep as I pull the ends toward my face to scrub at my eyes. "I have to put things into my long-term memory to memorize them. I went to doctor after doctor when I was a kid, but no one was willing to diagnose it as anything specific. Mom always suspected..." I trail off.

"So you don't drink?" It's a statement and a question. I lower the blanket to meet his confusion head-on.

"No. Mom did heavily while she was pregnant with me. The problem is, she was also given drugs to help with her labor and delivery. Either, both, could have caused problems with my learning issues." And there it is: the dawning horror I've seen on the faces of doctors, teachers, and the occasional person we've let close enough into our family fold to be told the truth.

Ignoring the beginning of anger that's just forming inside, I plow on.

"The only reason I can memorize scripts is that I have someone read the lines into an audio recording—you know, like an audiobook. It was a fluke I ever learned that trick. I was studying for a class where the professor happened to mention he was friends with the audio narrator, and this was another professional path we could go down. The idea of being a narrator intrigued me; I could use my talent without having to memorize anything. So, I downloaded the book we were reading. Imagine my surprise when I could answer questions in class later that week." Even I can hear the bitterness in my voice. "I made an appointment with the professor, had him sign an NDA, and explained everything I'm telling you."

"What did he say?" It's the first thing Monty's said.

"He got me in touch with his friend, who happens to own the small company. We had a long discussion about what I was looking for. I didn't even know if it would work. But I agreed to pay him thousands of dollars from my savings—I like to call it my mother's old guilt fund—to see if having one of his lesser-known narrators read me my textbooks would help put the materials into my long-term memory. I could listen to it while I was working out, while I was on the subway, anywhere."

Monty brushes a lock of hair off my shoulder. "How quickly did you see results?"

"Oh, about six weeks. So much of literature is already on audiobook format. It was just a matter of getting the right recordings. All I was paying for was my regular textbooks like science." Rubbing my fingers against my temples, I try to soothe the headache beginning to form. "As we started to get into my theater classes, it became more complicated."

"Why's that?"

"Because even though it was for personal use, we were still making an unofficial audiobook of a rented production. We were essentially licensing our copy of the production. I had to bring Mom's attorneys in at that point." Bemused, I tack on, "She never once protested."

"I should hope not." He's angry. "How..."

"She was my mother," I answer. "Do I continue to punish her? No. Do I love her less because she was ill? No. Instead of being an adult, when I had to deal with thinking about a parent being ill, I just had to do it before I hit school." His sharp inhalation of breath soothes me. "It's just what my life was, Monty. So many have so much worse."

"They're not you." The simplicity of his words do more than any more flattery ever will. They undo me. Stepping closer, I'm both gratified and terrified when he sweeps me into his arms and carries me back to his bed. Quickly pulling the blanket away, I shiver under his concerned perusal. But he unties the sheet at his waist, draping first that, then the blanket over me before sliding in next to me.

"Hold me while we sleep," I murmur, so drained after telling him my truths I don't realize he's nowhere near the lethargy I am.

"As long as you'll let me," he promises. Trusting that, trusting him, I roll to my side within the cradle of his arms as the pink makes a more valiant effort to push away the black of the night.

I never realize Monty doesn't sleep a wink.

FORTY-NINE

MONTAGUE

"**D**r. Spellman, I would like for you to meet Evangeline Brogan." Mom and I sit back as Ev introduces Linnie to the doctor who's kept him healthy the last few years. It's been just a few weeks since Dad and Linnie talked about his illness. Thanksgiving Day has come and past. We had a hysterical time watching Mom drool over Linnie's brother-in-law on FaceTime while Linnie, Bristol, Ev, and I laughed in the background. Ev invited Bristol and Simon down for Christmas. And barring any complications with the baby, they accepted.

Linnie demanded to come with us to Ev's monthly checkup with Dr. Spellman. "Listen to me right now, Everett Parrish," she demanded with her hands on her hips. "Like it or not, I am at least as half as stubborn as you are."

His lips thinned.

"Your doctor wanted you to find a donor for a reason."

"Yes, but..."

"Likely to increase your chances at living, gee, I don't know, beyond the next few years?" she yelled at him.

Ev had the good grace to blush. "So, we go in. I get tested. What's the worst he says—no? We're no worse off than where we are now. But Ev." Linnie dropped to her knees in front of him. "What if your doctor says yes? What if we're close enough of a match for me to help you?"

Ev lifted a trembling hand to her hair. "You'd do that for me?"

"Without question." And that settled it.

"An honor, Ms. Brogan. Truly. I saw you perform on Broadway years ago."

"Thank you," Linnie says demurely, but I see the way she's pursing her lips. I can almost hear her thoughts; we've become so in tune with each other. Flattery? At a time like this?

"This is an honor, indeed. Are you visiting the Parrishes?" Spellman sits down on the edge of his desk and gestures for all of us to as well.

Linnie defers to Ev, who reaches over and takes her hand to give it a brief squeeze. "Actually, Linnie has a much greater significance than that in our lives."

Spellman says, "Oh?" before crossing his arms over his chest.

Clearing his throat, Ev admits, "This isn't easy to say..."

Spellman jerks back. "Ms. Brogan, if you tell me you're pregnant with Mr. Parrish's child, I've already discussed with him the chances of cord blood producing the cells he needs are going to be less effective than..."

"Ew!" Linnie exclaims. "Seriously?" She twists in her seat with a disgruntled sneer. When we were in bed last night, I told her that Spellman was a hell of a doctor but had the social skills of a petrified turd. I burst out laughing, remembering her saying, "Oh, he can't be that bad." Mom shakes her head at our antics.

"Doctor," Ev placates while shooting me a look filled with retribution, "we have reason to believe Evangeline—Linnie—will be a close match."

He looks down his superior nose at Ev. "Oh? What makes you think so?"

And hot damn, I'd give up the Caps winning the Stanley Cup

again to capture the look on the good doctor's face when Linnie says, "Maybe the DNA test proving I'm his biological daughter? We kinda thought it might be important for me to be tested."

I can't restrain my grin as Spellman begins sputtering, "You... he..." But he becomes very still when they both smile—an identical smile.

Spellman starts wheezing. And I can't control the laughter. My mother elbows me and asks, "Can you behave?"

"No, I'm sorry. I've been waiting for this day for way too long." It just happens to be a bonus that it's being handed to me by the woman I'm falling for who has eyes and a smile that's identical to the father figure I've respected, admired, and yes, loved for years. The first time I saw it, a man handed me cupcakes for no other reason than he didn't want me to be left out. And the last time it was directed at me with such openness, Linnie was fluttering her lashes before I rolled her onto her back this morning and kissed her good morning.

Singularly, each of those smiles could light up the room, give power to the sun, and rejuvenate a soul. Together, I think they can perform a miracle. And by determination washing over Spellman's face, so does he.

Picking up the phone sitting by the side of his hip, he lifts the receiver to his ear. "I need to arrange for an immediate HLA-match testing done for Everett Parrish." His face contorts in frustration. "No, I'm not sending them down to the lab. Have a technician come to my office. This is a VIP situation. Both he and the potential donor are sitting right in front of me." There's a pause. "Fifteen minutes? Fine."

The receiver slides off his cheek. He places it back in the cradle. "Ms. Brogan, we have VIP status at the hospital to protect patients like Mr. Parrish and yourself." He winces a little. "I'm not going to lie and say there haven't been breeches in the protocol where information hasn't leaked in the past."

Linnie flaps her hand at him. "My relationship with my father isn't going to remain a secret forever, Doctor."

"Adding additional stress during a procedure such as this could..."

"I don't plan on having a news conference," she says exasperatedly. "If it comes out that I'm here, all you need to say is that I know him through a mutual acquaintance. Since our blood types were the same, I was tested to see if I was a compatible donor."

Spellman looks at her with something like admiration. "You know, if you ever give up acting, you'd have a great career in communications or public relations."

He has no idea why we all start laughing and can't stop until there's a knock on his door signaling the arrival of the technician,

"NOW, please be aware, it could take weeks for us to get the results."

"Weeks?" I'm shocked.

"There are many things that are done to the blood, Mr. Parrish," Dr. Spellman explains calmly.

"Is there anything I should do differently in the meantime?" Ev says as he rolls down the cuff to his shirtsleeve.

"Yes, relax. Enjoy the holidays. Nothing's going to change between now and then," Spellman says bluntly.

Right. Relax. I wonder how the hell that's supposed to be possible when I look over at Linnie. Her eyes are shining with unshed tears. "No matter what, we tried, right, Ev?"

"Right, darlin'." He pulls her in for a close hug. "Thank you for even coming this far with me."

"Of course," she replies shakily. Burying her head in his chest, I hear her say, "That's what family's supposed to do, right?"

And it guts me when Ev's eyes pass through me as he says, "They never have before, Linnie. That's what makes this so special."

Turning my back, I try to modulate my breathing while absorbing the ache, the pain that never quite seems to disappear over knowing I wasn't enough to save another person.

No matter if it's trying to talk them down off a ledge or give them the blood from my own body.

FIFTY

EVANGELINE

The weeks seem to fly by even as they've crawled. My emotions are all over the place, turning on a dime. I know why. I miss Mom with every inhale and worry about Ev with every exhale. It's only in my heart I can acknowledge my growing feelings for Monty, that he's what pushes air into my lungs at all.

And it's Christmas.

Char has gone whole hog around the farm, demanding every building be lit up like something out of a Martha Stewart fairy tale. I'm both terrified and astounded that the men who work here bend so easily to her will. And then there's Lorrie, who brought me a present of one of her school pictures framed after the holiday riding demonstration, which her grandmother attended. Lorrie and I spent hours together over the weeks talking. She told me not too long ago, her grandmother apologized to her. "It isn't that Grandma didn't want to do my hair, Miss Linnie. It was that she couldn't. She isn't capable. It's hard to be angry at someone who just can't do something," the bright young girl explained.

Monty's gone to the airport to pick up my sister and Simon while Ev and Charlotte finish a few things around the house. At loose ends, I decide to get in my workout while I can since I know it's going to be a crapshoot while they're in town visiting. It's going to be wonderful to have them here, but there's still going to be a piece of my heart missing. Twirling in a cutoff gray sweatshirt, I wonder what my mother would think about this. Was I judging her too harshly when I never had an opportunity to ask her about any of this? Especially when it's led me to such happiness?

I lunge. My voice comes out strong when I start singing another song from *Miss Me*.

Can't you see?
His love for me is real.
Don't be mad at me, just feel,
That he's the only one for me.

That's when I hear a voice behind me that sends my heart soaring in a different kind of way.

I will never love again,
She's my heart until the end.
Stop trying to pretend.
You don't want her will to bend.

I turn around and find Simon singing. Lounging against the doorway is a very pregnant Bristol with Monty hovering behind her. "Go on," she encourages us both. Simon meets me in the center of the room and clasps my hand before spinning me out and back. We fall into the easy pas de deux as we sing the refrain.

I miss you now
I miss you more
Take me back to what was before
I miss you now
I miss your heart
Don't let time keep us apart
Don't let love tear us apart

I end up bent back over Simon's leg in a swoony move. Normally we'd kiss at this point, thereby ending the scene but beginning the cilantro war. Instead, he whoops and lifts me, swinging me around in circles. "Good God, I missed you."

"Oh, what perfect timing you have." I hug him back hard.

"As always, darling."

I laugh before I start beating him on the shoulder so I can run over to Bristol. Her stomach reaches us before I can fully get my arms around her. "Damnit, Bris. I thought I said to come only if it was safe." I feel such overwhelming guilt. I wanted my whole family here for the holidays, sure, but not at risk to my sister or future nephew's health.

"Please. I wouldn't have got on the very comfortable jet where Simon proceeded to throw back the Scotch and sodas..."

"It was only a few," Simon protests. Bristol's eyes roll so far I'm afraid she's going to pass out.

"Is this why is your sister is pissed at her husband?" Monty comes to stand at my side. "She bitched at him the whole ride here." He drops a kiss on my head before nuzzling his cheek against the top of it.

"Hi," I murmur up at him. "Oh, they're both—"

"Petrified to fly. So by tossing down a few, my darling husband decided to worry more about entertaining the in-flight crew than holding my hand. I might forgive him by the time Alex is born."

My head snaps up. "Alex? You named him and didn't tell me?"

Simon plants his hands on his hips and glares at my sister. "I thought we weren't telling anyone."

"You forfeited that right when you told the entire crew the baby's name, you ass. Or don't you remember that? If it doesn't end up in *People Magazine* by next week, I'll eat healthy for a whole week," she fires right back. This is a serious threat because Bristol has been sending Simon to Juniors for cheesecake almost nightly. Simon has the good grace to look ashamed.

"Oops."

I'm shaking with laughter from the confines of Monty's strong arms. "Better tell Marco you're naming the baby after your dad, then, Simon. If he reads about it in *People*, he's going to be pissed."

"Actually, it's Alexandre Patrick." Bristol bites her lip anxiously. "After both our fathers."

"That's perfect." And it is. Before I was able to separate everything Dad—Patrick—did for me, I think it would have been harder to accept Bristol honoring him this way. Now, I understand more because he was a good man, a good father. He just wasn't mine and unable to work through those emotions to circle back to who we were before he died. I am grateful to him for everything he did for the time he was in my life though.

And then in a perfectly timed entry, my father and Char walk in the studio door. "So this is where all the fun is," Ev jokes. We all break into laughter.

"Bris, I'd like you to meet my father, Everett Parrish, and Monty's mother, Charlotte." Bristol holds out her hand, and it's swatted away by Char.

"We're huggers in this family, darling. Welcome. And make it Char."

Bristol laughs. "Thank you for having us." She turns to Ev and before she can offer her hand, he wraps her in a quick embrace. "I don't think I've been hugged by a client before," she teases him.

Ev tilts his head to the side. "Wait, you're Bristol Todd?" She nods. "Linnie mentioned your name, but I never put it together until you just said that. Well, I'll be damned. You do damn fine work."

"I didn't think you'd know who I was, sir," she says respectfully, resting her palms on her protruding stomach.

"Your bosses have wonderful things to say about you. I'm wondering how much my portfolio is going to go down while you're out on maternity leave," he jokes.

"Fortunately, I don't have that problem," Simon smirks. Bristol punches him in the arm, still clearly pissed from his earlier showmanship, and Char wheezes. "Oh, Lord."

"Here we go," Monty mutters.

"And Ev, Char, my brother-in-law, Simon Houde. Otherwise known as the worst kisser in America," I tack on devilishly. Monty squeezes me so hard, I feel like my ribs are about to crack. "Hey," I protest.

"I don't think your new—geez, Linnie? How do we refer to Monty? Your stepbrother? Your boyfriend?" Bristol really should have gone into acting as her voice drops, "Your lover, appreciates the idea you've kissed my husband in the past. Or that you're likely to do so again."

If she weren't nine thousand months pregnant with my nephew, I'd shove a cilantro smoothie down her damn throat for prodding the not-so-sleeping tiger at my back. Twisting around in Monty's stronghold, I lay my hands on his chest. "Now, sweetheart, let me explain a few things about acting," I begin.

"No, why don't I," Simon butts in. Smoothly moving over to Char, he captures her hand and yanks her to him. Her face is shocked stupid when Simon bends her back over his arm and lays his lips on hers. Monty's jaw drops while I shake my head at the bemused expression on my father's face. As he swings her back up, he grins unrepentantly. "And that's how you do a stage kiss. Thank you for your help, Char. I'm—"

"A freaking dumbass!" I yell loudly. "Jesus, will you at least tell me you didn't eat something repulsive before you kissed her?"

Simon throws up his hands. "There's nothing repulsive about cilantro."

Bristol and I say simultaneously, "Yes, there is."

Simon haughtily proclaims, "This—this is the reason I eat it night after night. To annoy the crap out of her." He stabs his finger in my direction.

"Where's the closest brick of nasty-ass gorgonzola?" I threaten. Simon shudders and immediately goes to hide behind his wife.

She shoves him aside. "You're on your own, buddy."

"You're my wife!"

"You told an entire group of strangers our baby's name!"

Monty's shaking with laughter behind me. The three of us turn on him and all yell, "What?"

"Mom" is all he manages to choke out. He points a shaking finger in her direction.

Char has a dreamy look on her face as she stands next to Ev. She's being held by her husband of twenty-five years, who I know she thinks the sun and moon rise on, when she says dreamily, "I like cilantro."

We all burst out laughing, including Ev. "Why doesn't everyone come back up to the house? Char has some snacks ready, and we can all get to know one another."

"Sounds perfect, Everett," Bristol agrees.

"Make it Ev, sweetheart. After all—" He sends a warm look in my direction. "—you're family." Guiding a still-stunned Char out the door, he leaves the four of us standing there.

"Linnie, I never thought I'd say this, but who knew that day when you spit in that tube you'd hit the jackpot." Raking her eyes over Monty, she adds on, "Possibly in more ways than one."

"I'm just as amazed as you are. Now, let's go get something to eat."

IF SNACKS with my family were hysterical, dinner is riotous. We're all lounging around the kitchen trading jokes back and forth. It's a testament to how much I've bonded with my additional family and how wonderful they are in general. They would have made terrific parents to a houseful of kids, I think sadly.

"What put that look on your face?" Monty asks me as I'm pulling coffee mugs down while Char is being told a story from Simon about his time in London.

"I was thinking about how wonderful your Mom and Ev are as parents. Wondering why they never had more kids." Placing the last mug on the counter, I lean against it while the coffee brews.

Monty shrugs, but I see the wounds in his eyes. "I'm sorry if it's too difficult..." I stammer.

"No, it's not that." He sighs and pulls me to him. "They tried for several years. Did the whole gamut of doctors, what's wrong, and in the end they were told it could be a combination of things. Ultimately, they decided the stress it was putting them under wasn't worth trying anymore. So, they changed their energy to helping others." He shakes me a bit. "That's why I was worried at first when we heard about you."

"About me? Why?" And then suddenly it hits me. Because I was a child Ev had created with another woman. What would that do to Char inside? My heart crumbles when I think about how warm and gracious she's been since the moment we first met. "Oh. Monty." My heart hurts at the additional burden she carried.

"Hey, none of that. She's okay." He swipes his thumb across my cheek.

I reach up and squeeze his wrist. "Now I know where you get it."

His brow lowers. "Get what?"

"You have this unconquerable strength that allows me to just trust you in a way I've never done before." Reaching up, I pull his head down for a quick kiss. "It's obviously inherited from your mom. For me, I spent a lot of time trying to build up that circle of trust. You were lucky to be born with it." I brush his lips with mine one more time, then rejoin my family at the table.

But I do stop by Char and give her an extra-warm squeeze. "What's that for?" Her lips curve.

"Just for being a great mom," I tell her honestly and loud enough so Monty can hear me where he's still standing near the coffeepot. He shakes his head before he grabs a handful of mugs.

But it's true. If I ever get a chance to be a parent one day, I'd like to think I'd learn from the fearlessness of my mother and the soft heart of Monty's. *I could do it with the right man,* I think, my heart jumping as Monty plunks down the mugs before turning to grab the coffee. There's no reason I couldn't soar to the skies and cuddle on the couch. No reason at all.

What about life says they can't go together?

FIFTY-ONE

MONTAGUE

I t was simpler if I didn't know how she felt about the whole thing, when I assumed she'd hate me if I crossed the room in the middle of the night. Then the choice wasn't mine, but hers in a way. Then I knew I'd lose her if I took a drink. Then her brother-in-law came in drinking and she didn't care. Beads of sweat pop out across my skin as Linnie's body curled next to me boosts our combined temperature. Slowly, I lower the blanket down to relieve some of the heat.

Not because I'm going to move.

Little puffs of air that both soothe me and keep me awake at the same time. Even though I know it's her breath as she inhales and exhales from her mouth, it feels like someone is sitting on my shoulder whispering lies where there should only be promises.

I shake my head to clear it, and it disturbs Linnie enough that she rolls away from me. *Roll back*, I mentally beg her. She doesn't know it, but she's the sentry keeping all the mistakes I can't find the words for in the light of day at bay. *Come closer and protect me from the pain.* But she's been fighting so much. I can't ask her to fight one more battle, to take on one more burden.

Especially when she needs me.

I feel like I'm being tested, pulled in a tug-o'-war I can't win without being split in two. *Be strong enough. Be tough enough to be with her.* My soul is screaming while the other side taunts, *You weren't enough before. People died.*

Abruptly, I sit up in bed. I can't handle it. I need relief. I'm about to swing my legs over when I feel a reprieve.

Then I feel the cool brush of her fingertips across my spine.

"Is everything okay, baby?" she murmurs sleepily.

"Yeah." My breath comes out harshly. "Go back to sleep." But she doesn't. She crawls up behind me and drapes herself over my back.

"Bad dream?"

"You could say that." More like a living nightmare.

"Come back to bed. I'll hold you until you sleep," Linnie whispers, pressing a kiss between my shoulder blades. I ease my back against the pillows. She curls up and begins stroking my chest.

Once again, the strength of the woman I've fallen for has saved me from the uncontrollable thing that wants to see me crumble.

FIFTY-TWO

EVANGELINE

JANUARY

I've got the post-holiday blues. I'm running in the gym in Ev's basement because I refuse to injure myself on Virginia's icy roads. Apparently, this state gets snow, something Monty thoroughly enjoyed my shock over. "I thought you people below the Mason-Dixon Line avoided fluffy white crap," I accused.

Monty kissed me hard before replying, "You New Yorkers avoid it too. It's black sludgy crap up there."

Char and Ev laughed at us both while serving up a delicious meal of homemade lasagna.

We're all on pins and needles waiting for the test results to come back. Ev shrugs, but he's exuding anxiety. I've walked in his study in the afternoons to find him staring out the window. Char has been trying out new recipes like mad to distract herself, and Monty? He's decided it's his mission to try to teach me how to ride outside of the beginner's class I've been enjoying with Lorrie and the kids. He's a lot more patient with a class of six-year-olds than he is with just me.

I feel like Dr. Spellman's silence is causing us to reach a breaking point. If we were going to have good news, we'd have heard something by now. Increasing the speed and incline on the treadmill, my legs pump harder and harder, trying to run away from the inevitable conclusion staring me in the face.

Shawn Mendes is blasting in my ear, so I let out a yelp when I feel my earbud being yanked out. I almost face-plant when Monty steps in front of me. "Slow it down, baby."

Planting my hands on the handrails, I lift my knees and jump to the sides of the rapidly moving tread. Quickly, I slap the Stop button. "What's wrong?" I pant, yanking out the other bud.

He rests his arms on the treadmill as it lowers back into place. "We just got the call from Spellman. He wants us in his office in two hours."

My legs wobble as I jump down and they hit the solid floor of the gym. I'm about to sprint up the two flights of stairs to Monty's room—the room I've basically moved into—when he stops me. "Hold on a second." Cupping my overheated, sweaty face between his fingers, he lowers his mouth to mine.

The kiss is gentle. It's not meant to arouse but to soothe. My eyes drift shut just before it ends. "I want you to understand before we move an inch that even if this only started by giving him hope, you gave Ev—all of us—so much more." My eyes fly open to reveal Monty saying a million words with his eyes we don't have time for.

We're about to find out if I'm a close enough match to help save my father's life. Yet— "I just got this feeling in the pit of my stomach our whole life is going to change." I drag my fingers down his cheek.

Turning, I fly up the stairs.

A LITTLE LESS THAN two hours later, we're escorted into Dr. Spellman's office. "Hell, if I'd known the bastard was going to be on time for once, maybe I'd have driven faster," Monty mutters.

"If you'd have driven any faster, I'd have needed air sickness bags," I retort. "Those curves right by the house are hell on my stomach."

Ev looks a little green himself as he collapses into a chair. "All I have to say is thank God we have an E-ZPass. Jesus, did you see the traffic in the other lane?"

Char flaps her hand. "Those poor people who deal with that commute every day. I can't even begin to imagine."

"If we're lucky, maybe some of them can 'remote work' like Linnie does. Isn't that what you said when we first met?" Monty lifts my hand to his lips. I'm tempted to squeeze his lips together to get back at him for taunting me, but I realize he's only trying to put the room at ease.

"Not all of us are lucky enough to have your job, buddy." I can give as good as I get. "Roll out of bed, have food ready, stroll out to work at whatever time suits us. It's going to be hell on your system when I'm not there to convince you to stay in bed."

Monty flushes as Char bursts out laughing. Ev chokes, coughing just as Dr. Spellman comes in the room. He frowns at my father. "Everett, I hope you're not getting ill. After all the trouble you went through to find a donor, it would be poor timing to have to ask the poor girl to wait for you to get better."

The collective air is sucked out of the room. My head is spinning dizzily. "Wait, you mean..."

The stick-up-his-ass doctor smiles. "Yes, Evangeline. I wanted to be completely certain, so I asked for the tests to be run twice."

Ev interrupts. "That's the reason for the delay?" Relief is evident in his voice. Char is curled under his arm, quietly sobbing. My father's eyes are bright as well.

"Correct. Normally a perfect match is considered eight to ten or more HLA markers. Evangeline is what we call a close match: six. Because Evangeline is Everett's biological daughter, I'm confident enough he won't reject your cells—or that we could counteract any reaction. Therefore, I feel confident we should proceed with allogeneic transplant." Spellman lifts his hands. "Ultimately, it's up to both of you."

My hands are shaking. I couldn't save Mom, but I can save my father. In my mind, there's no doubt, no question at all. But... "Ev? This is your life. It's your decision."

"You're asking me if I want the chance to extend my life by an infinite amount of time or be living on borrowed time?" he asks me incredulously.

"I'd like to remind you all of the processes by which both Evangeline and most especially Everett will go through for this procedure to be a success." He quickly describes the harvesting process I'll endure, which sounds more discomforting than anything else. Then I get chills as he explains the "conditioning" Ev will endure: high doses of chemotherapy to kill off his cancerous cells. "We may need to do radiation as well; we won't know until we see the effects of the initial treatment."

"Reading between the lines, you're going to have to kill me before you cure me," Ev says pragmatically.

Char's hands are covering her mouth, and a sob escapes. Monty, who's been silent this whole time, hands her a box of tissues. His jaw is locked so tight, I don't think a bolt cutter could get through it. Even I let out a little squeak of sound I can't entirely control.

Ev winces when he realizes the effect his blunt words have on the rest of the occupants of the room. "I'm sorry, everyone, I didn't mean..."

"It's the truth though, Doctor, isn't it?" Monty's voice is harsh.

"Yes, Monty. I'm afraid it is. If the worst happened and there was a total transplant failure, we would be looking at a situation where Everett's life expectancy would be rapidly reduced."

"Are we talking about years? Months?" Char whispers.

Spellman's voice softens. The doctor knows the news he's delivering isn't easy. "I'm sorry, Char. We could be talking about days. That's why this decision is the most important one he'll ever make."

Char turns to Ev like a she-cat. "I know I encouraged you to do this, but don't," she begs. Tears fall hot and heavy over my cheeks. "We have Linnie in our lives, and that's a miracle enough. We'll have a few more years together. How can we ask for more?" She collapses in his arms, sobbing.

"I have to do this, Char. How can I not when I can have a few more years plus another day with you?" I swipe my arm under my eyes. "We've all been granted the miracle of each other. I've never heard of anyone declining a miracle, have you?"

She shakes her head in his shoulder, still not lifting her head. I curl my legs up in my chair and bury my face into them. *That's the kind of love everyone should hope for.* I don't realize I've said it out loud until I feel myself being lifted by strong arms. Monty sits down with me in his lap. "I've always said they were a perfect match," he murmurs in my ear. "Let's just hope between the two of you, he gets through this."

And you get through it too, I think, but I don't say it, because Monty begins asking about timelines even as his arms tighten around me. And I again thank God for his strength.

Because I fear we're all going to need it.

FIFTY-THREE

MONTAGUE

The information floating through my head is making me dizzy. The numbers are making my head blurry.

Fourteen days of outpatient therapy where Ev will be home as we slowly help him to kill off his immune system; the medicine will swim through each cell, killing them off, destroying what's left.

Three days of intense chemotherapy. The dangerous kind—one that will have Ev tethered to a catheter to flush out his bladder so it doesn't fall victim to the toxicity of the drugs. Cytoxan. They say it's standard, but there could be significant side effects at his age, so he'll be continuously monitored—another fucking number. I shiver in the cold.

One day of rest before the transplant, but what kind of rest will he have? After his system's been systematically abused and destroyed for the seventeen days prior, he gets one day for one shot at this one life.

And above all the other numbers, one is the number repeating over and over and over again.

I just want one fucking drink.

I want the salt cracking my lips to be a result of a tequila shot, not as a result of my tears. I'd love to taste the smoke of bourbon to fog out the doctor's words, the buttery taste of Jameson to smooth away the burn. I want something to make me forget all these numbers, make me forget anything except...

I jump when a cold hand lands on my bare forearm. "Monty, you're going to freeze." Linnie's teeth are chattering. "Come inside. Your mother's made cider, and Ev wants to talk."

Quickly, I wipe my fingers under my eyes before I turn to face her.

Even though silence and the bottom of a bottle sound like a better way to process my thoughts, the concern in her eyes causes me to choke that statement back. Not when it's her strength that's going to flow into Ev's body to heal us all. No, even as I brush a long lock of her hair back and her face turns to kiss my hand, even as much as I know it's a perfect night to pour a glug of Irish into the cider she mentioned earlier, I'll get drunk on this woman instead. Because in her eyes, I pray, lies the path to all of our futures.

"I hope you don't mind if I dream about dousing mine with a good shot of Irish," I joke as I slide my arm around her shoulders, careful to keep my expression casual. Her nose wrinkles, but she doesn't say anything more. My breath is calm on the outside, but inside, my heart is quaking in anticipation.

In excitement.

In yearning.

Not only for the woman next to me but for the fact she really doesn't mind if I have a drink and love her anyway.

Because I don't know how I can live anymore without one or the other.

FIFTY-FOUR
EVANGELINE

"What does this mean? In English, please?" I'm sitting with a patient advocate in Inova Fairfax discussing the process about donating my bone marrow. I thought it would be relatively straightforward—especially since Ev refuses to let me pay for a dime. Instead, I've been in hour after hour of meeting with doctors, physician assistants, and now the patient advocate. Yes, I understand I will be undergoing a surgical procedure. Yes, I know there are risks involved. I realize I will experience soreness, bruising, pain afterward. I have a ridiculous lack of care about the amount of time it will take for me to return to my "normal" life when what I care about is giving my father more time to live in this one.

I want to give Ev this hope of a longer life with the wife he adores and the man he has called his son who I have fallen in love with. I want to get to know my father even more than I already have, build memories that I'll be able to pass along to my children one day the same way I'll be able to tell them about the ones I have about my mother. I want to have my father sitting front and center at one of my performances.

With Monty right beside him.

Life, it turns out, is more complicated than wants. After all, if it were based on wants, my mother would still be alive, and I'd have learned about my father in a much more conventional way than spitting in a tube mailed in a rainbow-tinted box.

My hand shakes as I reach for the glass of water on the table in front of me. "Go ahead."

"As I was saying, Ms. Brogan, this document is a commitment between you and the patient..."

"My father," I interrupt, angrily. The time for hiding is long gone. After this is over, Ev and I need to make some decisions on how to announce this. It was my mother's secret, not mine.

"Yes, Mr. Parrish. This document is a letter of understanding that once the protocol begins, you understand if you back out...well, there is no going back for your father." A high-pitched sound of pain comes from somewhere. It takes a few moments to realize it's from me.

The advocate fiddles with the pen on the table anxiously. "Ms. Brogan, you do understand what that means, correct?"

It means I'm literally signing Ev's life away. If something happens between the time they start his transplant and when I give him my bone marrow, my father will die. I want to run away, but I have nowhere to go. Not physically. Mentally, I retreat to the only safe place I've found in the last few months. And that's where my heart is.

Monty, I know, is with Ev somewhere in the hospital going through a similar briefing. I received a text from him earlier that said, *They just had Ev sign something... Well, let's just say, this day had better end up with you, me, and a glass of something. Fuck, Linnie.*

Now I understand. "Did my father sign something like this?" I ask quietly, still not picking up the pen.

"I'm not at liberty to discuss—"

And I lose my mind. "Yes or no! Was my father asked to sign a paper like this?" I shout.

"No." I sag in relief. Much too soon, she continues. "All transplant patients—speaking generally, of course—are advised they may not make it through the conditioning period. That"—my arms grip the sides of my chair—"if something happens to their donor, they understand their condition is considered to be terminal if they don't have a backup donor."

Picking up the phone instead of the pen, I send a quick message to Monty. *I don't drink, but it seems like a good night for it.*

As I'm signing my legal name on the most critical form I've ever signed—more important than any binding contract—I get back a single word.

Amen.

I'M SITTING on Monty's balcony wrapped in the comforter from his bed. Tears are frozen against my cheeks as I crush my phone between my hands. It all starts next week, but the soul crushing continues as soon as I press Send on the call I need to make.

Will she understand?

I'm not choosing one family over another. I have to break a promise to save my father's life. I guess there's only one way to find out.

I press the green button and hold the phone up to my ear. One ring. Two. "Bristol Todd...Houde."

I smirk. "After all these months, still not used to saying it?"

"Simon didn't care if I changed my name for work, and honest to God, Linnie? I'm beginning to wonder if I should have started the process to change it. It's a royal pain in the ass. Half of my log-ins are in one name, half in the other. I figure they might have my access figured out just in time for me to go out on maternity leave in a few weeks," she grumbles.

"It can't be that bad." While I'd typically pounce on her count-down like a lioness on fresh meat, I avoid it for now.

"It is. I think the baby shower my assistant threw for me today was a 'get the hell out of here so I can get some damn work done' party." Jesus, I forgot today was her shower at work. My head falls forward in gratitude over the fact my sister didn't want a private shower, so I just bombarded her with gifts at Christmas when she was here—something Simon gave me a raft of shit over. "How the hell are we supposed to get all this crap home, Linnie? We flew?"

I remember telling him, "On a private jet, you schmuck."

He'd sheepishly wrapped his arms around a chuckling Bristol. "Oh, yeah. Oops. Thanks!"

Everyone laughed as I threw part of a diaper cake I had made in his face.

She chatters on in my ear. "I think once Alex is here, it will become more real—that we're all Houdes." Her voice is buoyant, happy, excited.

I'm about to ruin all of that.

"Bristol."

I've only said her name when she interrupts me. "What's wrong?"

Can one right balance out the incredible wrong I'm about to deliver? I rub my hand over my forehead as I try to find the right words.

I must take too long, or she knows me too well.

"You're not coming home in time for Alex to be born," she says flatly. I wince at the complete void of emotion in her voice.

"Let me explain," I plead, but before I can get another word out, I'm again cut off.

This time at the knees.

"I've been there for you since the moment I found that damn diary! I'm the one who held your hand while you grieved, but you can't hold mine while I celebrate?" Bristol takes in a shaky breath. "You made me a promise!"

"Please, Bristol." I'm begging her. "Let me explain. Ev's sick."

That gets her attention.

"What do you mean, sick?" she demands.

"It's cancer," I manage to get out.

And just like that, her anger deflates. "Jesus, Linnie," Across hundreds of miles, the horror of what's happening is understood. "Is there anything we can do?" I know from the limited amount of time they spent together, Bristol and Simon respect and admire Ev and Char.

And it's so like my sister to put aside her feelings of disappointment to ask.

"There's only one thing that can be done." I take a deep breath. "And I have to help him do it."

"What do you mean?"

And slowly, I reveal the real reason it was so easy to find my close match—because my father needed a bone marrow donor. I explain about the procedure Ev's about to undergo and how I'm going to help.

"I'm feeling so much right now: regret because I can't be there with you, agony over what Ev's about to endure, and drained."

"Because you feel like you're holding the world up on your shoulders?" Bristol interjects.

I frown. "No, I think Monty's the one who's doing that."

"Is he really? Or is he leaning on you like a crutch, Linnie?"

"What makes you say that? I thought you liked him." I'm confused

"I don't know. Since I've been back, I've been thinking about him. There's something about him that reminds me of someone. I just can't put my finger on it."

My hackles rise in defense of the man I love. "Don't judge him based on one week when he's a lot more than that, Bris. Don't define him by that. You're not with him the way I am. You don't understand the pressure he's been under, the pain he's endured, and how he's come out the other side."

There's a long pause. "You're right. I'm only basing my judgment on what I saw in such a limited time. You're the one living with him day in and day out."

"I worry he's punishing himself: for Ev, for things that happened with his former job," I confess. "But I know he's strong enough to get through. He is so much *more*. It might just take time."

"And right now, your focus has to be on Ev."

"I wish I could be there. I want to hold your hand when Alex comes into this world, but Dr. Spellman has basically forbidden it."

"I hate Dr. Spellman," Bristol grumbles, but I know what she's doing. She's trying to get me to laugh when all I want to do is cry.

I'm about to agree when she says something that takes my breath away. "For too many years, you've had to be strong. Yes, there are days when everyone needs to be strong. But I need you to know I love you no matter what. This is your home. You can always rely on me to love you, Linnie. No matter what."

I try to speak, but I can't. For a long time, there's just the sound of our breathing on the phone. I finally manage to get out, "I love you, Bris."

"Love you too, Linnie." She doesn't speak again. Eventually, I pull the phone away to see Call Ended. I drop the phone in my lap.

And in the fading light of the sun, I just sit and be. I'm scared of what's to come. I'm out of sorts.

I feel like I did when Mom died: alone, and petrified of letting everyone down.

"JESUS CHRIST, Linnie. It's like twenty degrees out." Monty's voice interrupts my mental inventory of everything I've done wrong. His concern begins to warm the place inside of me that's slowly frozen over in the hours I've been huddled inside the blanket thinking of Bristol.

From the first time I held my sister to Christmas, a million memories pass through my mind. Not all of them are good, but they're all wrapped in reciprocated love. That is until today's phone call. My face contorts in pain.

He reaches down and touches my cheek. "You're like ice. Get

inside before you get sick. You have more than just your own health to think about now."

Of course. It's not about me; it's about saving Ev. I don't know how pain can penetrate the numbness I blissfully felt until Monty walked out onto the balcony, but it can. I unwrap myself from the blanket to reveal the heavy North Face coat I'm wearing. Without a word, I grab the blanket and drag it past him as I head back inside.

"What's wrong?" he demands as I carefully spread it back across his bed.

"Nothing. I just need a few moments to..." But I'm not given them as Monty's up in my face.

"You've been crying," he accuses me as he grips my arms to hold me in place.

I shrug. I'm not going to deny it.

"Look, if this is too much, tell us now. The minute Ev swallows that first pill, there's no going back," he warns me. As if I need another reminder.

Then my eye catches the dying sun glinting off the bottle of amber liquid on the wet bar in the room. "What does that taste like?" I ask.

Monty looks over his shoulder. His frame locks. "Why?"

Hurt, I wrench away and stalk over to the bar. Trailing my fingers along the crystal decanter, I whisper, "It's been a really shitty day. I just...I just wanted to know what it tasted like to make all these people want to use it to obliterate their pain."

A flash of something crosses his face. He stalks over and takes the decanter from me. Lifting it to his lips, he takes a swallow. "Taste it from me, then," he says before crushing his lips down on mine.

I wanted to understand, and in some weird way through his kiss, I do—pain, suffering, and a feeling that falls just short of love. I didn't want anything to do with alcohol before this moment, and I know for damn sure I don't now.

Pushing him away, I wipe my arm across my mouth to rid myself of the taste on my lips. "I wasn't out there trying to get sick. I was already sick—sick at heart because I had to tell my sister I'm going to miss the birth of my nephew because I agreed to donate bone marrow to my father. I don't like breaking promises to people I've made them to. Particularly those I love."

Pain lashes across his features. "Sweetheart," He reaches for me, but I step out of reach.

"Tell your mother I'm sorry, I'm not feeling very hungry." Turning, I make my way into the connecting bath and lock the door.

The emptiness I feel at this moment is so consuming it brings me to my knees without a sound. I don't know how long it is I stay there, my arms wrapped around myself just trying to hold on to something because God knows I don't feel like I have anyone else I can hold on to.

FIFTY-FIVE

MONTAGUE

All she asked me was what alcohol tasted like, and I flipped like she was playing judge and jury. When her soft voice whispered, "It's been a really shitty day. I was just...I just wanted to know what it tasted like to make all these people use it to obliterate their pain," I realized she was looking for comfort.

Of course, that's not what she took that kiss as.

I realized that the minute she walked out of the room and I heard the lock of the bathroom snick behind her. I downed two glasses of bourbon before having enough courage to go downstairs and explain her absence.

At dinner, Ev looked haggard over the events of the day. "It's too much for her. We don't have to do this."

"Ev, I don't think you can stop her now." The force of my words caused him to blanch. "Let me worry about Linnie."

Maybe he sees how much I'm in love with his daughter, but I don't care. After tonight, she'll have no doubt how I feel. But when I walked back into my suite after dinner, it was to find her huddled on the side of the bed, her long hair undone, fast asleep.

It wasn't until I pushed her hair off her face that I saw the dried tear tracks on her face and took them like a kick in the chest. *God, help me say the right words to her to heal whatever part of this pain I caused.* Shifting from my knees to my full height, all I feel is the need to drop back down to them to wake her to beg her for forgiveness.

My woman cried herself to sleep tonight. Unlike me, she doesn't hold in her pain. Instead, her face is painted by her heartbreak. Every overwhelming emotion she's been put through has scored her cheeks with wetness.

Her father.

Her sister.

Me.

I can smell the very thing that caused me to flip at her earlier. Like a siren, the bourbon's seductive scent calls to me, whispering at me to come to have another taste since I've already had her once today. Like a body driven by primitive instincts, I move away from the woman I know I need to care for in favor of the thing I yearn for.

A burn that wrenches my gut so painfully it obliterates the ones in my heart.

Not bothering with a glass, I tip the bottle to my lips and swallow again and again, until I gasp for breath. The heat hits and suffocates the ache. My eyes dart over to the bed.

Linnie's rolled over to her back. Her hand's reached over to my side, seeking me in her dreams. Thank God I didn't fuck this up, I think woozily. Stripping out of my clothes, I leave a trail of them as I stumble across the room. Lifting the covers, I slide her hand out of the way. I crawl in beside her and gather her close. Her brows scrunch close together, but she doesn't wake.

The bubble I'm wrapped in doesn't allow for a filter. "I love you." My words seem to echo off the walls of the room, but I'm sure I must have whispered them. After all, they're only echoing in my head over and over. I didn't just yell them for the first time at a sleeping woman who's carrying so much on her delicate shoulders.

As I pass out, it never crosses my mind I might have bellowed them in my drunken state to the woman I do love, who startles awake at my declaration.

FIFTY-SIX

EVANGELINE

Did that just happen?

Monty's naked in bed beside me having just shouted his love before passing out. He smells like a distillery. The smell reminds me of the nights Mom would come in to tuck me in when I was a child. But Monty's been through so much; he's under such a strain with trying to be the strength we all need him to be. I don't want him to come to bed with alcohol on his breath for the rest of our lives, but tonight? I almost understand.

Before I can travel too far down a path sure to bring back bitter memories, the words that bounced off the walls, yanking me from my sleep, bring me fully awake.

Did he just yell to anyone in hearing distance that he loves me?

Snuggling against his chest, I disregard his fuzzy alcohol breath as he snores deeply. Brushing a kiss across his cheek that desperately needs a shave, I wrinkle my nose at the smell of alcohol, which is so different when combined with sweat and odor. Laying my head against his heart, I murmur, "I love you too."

I came to some conclusions earlier that made my heart hurt. Life is all about the choices we make. And in this case, it's about my decision to give someone life. It hurts—God, does it hurt—but I can't stop agonizing over the what-ifs.

"Oh, Mom. If you only you had just told me," I whisper sadly in the dark. "How much of this would be different?" As if he can hear me, Monty's arms tighten on me to pull me closer to his already warm body. Shifting to get more comfortable, I lay my head down on the pillow and close my eyes thinking of promises, declarations, and hopes.

Sometimes people have to come in and out of your life to become better versions of themselves. Sometimes it isn't to hurt you, though it does. No matter what you do, you can't make them better on your own.

I just don't want the latest person to be my father.

Finally, as I drift off to sleep, I vaugely wonder if Monty's going to have a drink every night before bed. If so, I'm going to need him to brush his teeth and shower before he crawls between the sheets. After the initial burst of flavor from his lips, the smell's noxious as hell.

FIFTY-SEVEN

EVANGELINE

No one talks about how real cancer is until they live it. We're on day seven of the conditioning, and my father's fading away and dying right before my very eyes.

I don't know what's worse: what happened to Mom or what's happening to him.

Throwing myself into a series of turns, I make myself deliberately as dizzy as the medicine is making my father. Catching myself against the far wall, I'm out of breath, and the room is spinning wildly. Now if only my hair would start to fall out in chunks, I think bitterly.

Everett Parrish started taking the protocol to begin killing off his immune system and in a matter of days went from being a capable man in his sixties to a man who visually would have no problem passing for early eighties. His appetite has been nonexistent when he's not violently ill. And Char—bless her. She's been at his side every moment with mouthwash, weak ginger ale, and ice chips.

And all I can do is wait.

Dr. Spellman notified us they'd bring me in for the aspiration on the day they admit Ev into the hospital. That will give them enough time for the extract, to use the Cytoxan, and for Ev to have his day of rest before they introduce the new marrow into his system. Until then, there's pretty much nothing I can't do. "Except get sick," he said sternly.

Which is why I can't hop up to New York to be there for Alex's birth.

But no matter how much I want to scream, all it would do is echo back at me. My pain is nothing in comparison to the people I love.

Even Monty.

He thinks he's so strong, but even he's breaking. He doesn't think I notice. He hasn't touched me other than in a superficial fashion since the night he admitted to loving me. It's like he revealed some deep secret and now is pulling back. He holds me every night, but it feels like it's more out of obligation. It would be like tearing out the final piece of a heart that's been finely shredded, but I'm beginning to wonder if I should move back to my original room.

Leaning down against the bar, I put my head in my hands and pant in exhaustion.

"When this is over..." I don't finish the thought because I'm interrupted.

"I think we should go away," Monty says from the door. "Anywhere we can find that makes us want to forget the last few weeks."

I shrug, turning my back to him. "I don't think a place like that exists."

He comes up behind me and brushes a few strands of hair that have escaped my braid off my shoulder. "Then we'll hole up somewhere and create it."

"Why?" I ask blankly.

"Why what?"

"Why me?" At his sharply inhaled breath, I turn around. His hands fall from my shoulders. "I mean, I get that you need to be away for a while, but don't feel obligated to take me." A bitter laugh escapes. I wrap my arms around myself to accept a hug from the only person capable of giving me one right now.

Me.

Monty studies me for a few moments in uncomfortable silence. I plow through. "If you don't mind, I need to work out since I won't be able to for a few weeks."

"Talk to me." He deliberately steps in my way.

"Why?" It isn't meant to come out cruel; it's just an honest question. But by the way he recoils, it's as if I struck him.

"Why? Maybe because I'm a nice guy and I care about the woman sleeping in my bed every night." It looks like I've poked at Monty's anger too.

I don't have the energy to care.

"I was thinking about that. You, me—don't feel obligated to me just because of everything going on with Ev." I turn my back to him because just saying the words slash another wound into me.

"Obligated?" he says carefully. I can practically feel the waves of his temper wash over me. But the words have been spoken, and I can't take them back.

"I understand your focus is with your family, as it should be." I open my mouth to continue, but Monty steps in front of me, eyes blazing.

"And you're a part of that family."

I shake my head. "Am I?" Before he can answer, I rush on. "Ever since the day at the hospital, you don't hold me. You tolerate me. I don't belong anywhere. Not anymore."

"I think the stress of this is getting to you," he tells me bluntly. My eyes widen.

"Me? I'm not the one who has to drink to force himself to crawl into bed with a woman every night. Just forget it. I'm moving back into my old room tonight," I declare, ripping myself out of his arms to turn away. If I hadn't turned at just the wrong moment, I might have seen the shock on his face.

"Linnie, sweetheart, no. That's not it." I feel his fingers graze my bare arms.

My heart wrenches. I'm forcing myself to wake up from all of the illusions of my life and face reality. Nothing lasts forever—not the spotlight, not family, and certainly not love. In my case, it lasted the duration of time for a man to shout it out right before he passed out next to me.

"Yes, I'm having a drink, but you're not the reason why."

"It doesn't matter." I ache in all the wrong places having this conversation. I want to be left to the one thing that's not let me down so far.

Pain.

"It does." He grabs me and spins me around.

"I understand, Monty. I only wish you'd talked with me about it." *Before you'd broken my heart.* But I don't add on the last part. "Let me finish working out and I'll..."

He spins me into his arms. "How am I supposed to pick up the pieces of you when I'm falling apart at your feet? How can I hold you when I'm doing something I know you disapprove of? You walked away the last time and cried because of it. How can I tell you I've fallen so deeply in love with you when I'm not strong enough to promise to be what you need?"

My heart thumps hard beats inside my chest. "I didn't walk away. I've been here the whole time," I say quietly.

His fingers tighten even as his face contorts in pain. "I hope you mean that, because I'm not capable of letting go. Not anymore." Monty lowers his head down to mine, so close our eyes are centimeters away from each other.

We don't kiss. We don't move. What we've just shared is too overwhelming to shatter the moment by moving a fraction of an inch to capture each other's lips. Instead, it's the delicate flutter of our lashes as they tangle that exchange the power of our declaration.

We're in this together.

We'll figure out the miscommunication later, but right now, he's not letting me go. He's holding on.

Even as the air passes my lips and reaches his, I feel my soul sigh in the same way.

An oasis found in the storm that we both know is coming.

THAT NIGHT as we get ready for bed, I'm washing my face when Monty comes in behind me in the bathroom. I smile when he reaches for his toothbrush. "I just had a drink, baby. I don't want that on my breath when I kiss you in a few."

I shock the hell out of him when I say, "I didn't mind it that day, Monty. Why wouldn't you kiss me?"

His toothbrush falls out of his hands and into the basin. "Then why did you walk away?" His confusion and self-loathing are evident. I feel terrible I've played a part in this without him knowing.

"Because I didn't want to add to your burden." Placing my hand on his chest, my fingernails rake through it before settling over his heart. "You already shoulder the burden for so much, too much. I needed to have a good cry. It was too much that day. Dad, telling Bristol I couldn't be there for her..." I swallow hard.

"Prove it," he challenges.

"How?"

"Kiss me," he demands. And I understand what he's saying. He's had a drink. He was willing to scrape off the taste so I didn't need to absorb it. But if it wasn't him who hurt me, then I should have no problem laying my lips on his.

Stepping even closer, I slide my hands into his thick hair and tug his head down a little. He obliges by ducking down a little. I seal our lips together with a tenderness I think we both need. His arms wrap around me. I nibble at his full lower lip before taking a nip. He parts his lips in surprise—my tongue darts inside for a long stroke, a taste. I shudder in joy and longing.

Monty groans before taking over the kiss, backing me up against the vanity. His head slants, and he tangles his fingers in my hair to hold my head steady as he plunders my mouth.

Long moments pass where there's only the sounds of our harsh breath and sighs. When he pulls back, he whispers, "Sometimes I forget until I look at you, there are miracles in this world. Don't ever let me forget that." Pulling away, he leaves me standing there stunned as he quickly brushes his teeth.

Monty swipes a hand over his wet mouth. "Come on, my love. We need a good night's sleep. Neither of us has had one of those lately."

While a small part of me is a bit disappointed he's not planning on ravishing me, I know he's right. I'm wobbling on my feet as we make our way to bed. Crawling in next to him, I roll to my side, my position of the last week. I'm well on my way to la-la land when Monty hauls me onto my other side so I'm curled into him.

"Much better," he mutters.

And I have to admit, he's right. Hearing his heart so close to my ear is so much better. Within seconds, I'm asleep.

I have no idea how long it takes him to drift off.

FIFTY-EIGHT

MONTAGUE

I slip from her side in the middle of the night and head straight to the bar. I didn't have a nightmare because I haven't slept. What do you call your life repeatedly flashing before your eyes in the middle of the night while your heart beats erratically?

A wake-up call. Maybe a never-sleep-again call. Either way, I need a drink.

The marks are fresh on my soul from what happened today even though it worked out okay. Linnie's mine and I'll do anything, say anything, and protect her from anyone.

As the golden liquid slides down my throat, I berate myself. What was I thinking? I should have known better than to think there wouldn't be scars on someone whose mother was an alcoholic, that she wouldn't misinterpret my drinking to be about her.

I am surprised she said she didn't mind. Then again, in the world she grew up in, alcohol is likely as commonplace as water consumption. What she doesn't want it to be is because of her, which I gave her the impression of. Swallowing the last of the lowball I poured, I admire the way the moon makes the ivory of her skin glow. The way her dark hair floats around her like a cloud.

I feel a stirring deep in my loins the way I haven't since the day Ev began the at-home protocol.

I cross the room and move back into bed. Sliding a hand over the silk covering Linnie's hip, she stirs in her sleep. "Monty?"

"Hmm?"

"What time is it?" she mumbles.

"It's time for me to show you how much you mean to me." I press a warm kiss to the center of her stomach before I work my way down.

It's a long while before I work my way back up her body, and only after she's breathlessly called out my name. It's even longer before I join our bodies.

But not before I tell her the most important thing. "I love you, Linnie." And then, only then, do I slide home inside of her. Her body trembles beneath me when she whispers, "I love you too." Then, I begin slowly moving in and out of her.

Instead of being tired and alone fighting these battles raging inside of me, I'm able to hold her next to me as I sip at another drink before I finally fall asleep.

THE FOLLOWING day while Linnie's in the shower, I make myself a cup of coffee. Looking at the mostly empty decanter, I say, "To hell with it," and pour the rest of it into my coffee. I'm not planning on driving anywhere today.

And besides, this way it can be cleaned. I honestly can't remember the last time that thing was scrubbed out.

After a day where Linnie helps the beginner students muck out some stalls, she has to change to be fit to eat lunch. "I'm a disgusting mess, Monty!"

"You realize I'd make you wear it if your father wouldn't likely get ill if he smelled the manure," I tease her about the horse shit that ended up in her braid.

Giving me the finger, she walks into the bathroom and strips. Quickly starting the shower, she purrs, "Planning on joining me?"

I tell myself it was that invitation and not my spying the newly full decanter sitting on the bar that caused my heart to leap in anticipation. With a smirk, I start unbuttoning my shirt. "What do you think?"

FIFTY-NINE

EVANGELINE

"**K**ick your foot out of the stirrup!"

"Oh my God, Monty!" I'm freaking out and screaming with laughter at the same time. And God help me, it feels good to laugh. Lord, I can't remember the last time I did. Was it a month ago? More? I know it's been at least fourteen days—that's when Ev popped the first pill to kill off his immune system. It's been about a week since Monty's tender declaration of love—not the one where he shouted it randomly to the whole household. And in the time between, we've clung to each other as Ev's deteriorated even more each day.

Yesterday morning, Char drove him to the hospital. She told Monty she'd be back later to see us before we all go tomorrow for my procedure.

In the meantime, Monty's determined if I'm not going to be able to walk, it should be for a reason like being up on a horse. I told him there were more fun ways. Even though his eyes sparkled with interest, he still told me to "Braid your hair, sweetheart. Let's see if you can manage a lap around the ring on your own." I agreed because it's beautiful out. The sky's an incredible cerulean blue without a streak of white marring it. Knowing I'm going to be housebound for the next few days after the procedure, some fresh air sounded like a good idea.

That was until Hatchet realized I was "in charge."

Horses must have this innate sense of knowing who's doing the riding, I muse, giggling, while Monty curses a streak as blue as the sky. She walked docilely around the ring to show off before deciding she had an itch and just had to scratch it. Unfortunately, she didn't care I was still in the saddle.

"Hatchet, you crazy horse. Get up," Monty orders. But even he can't keep the humor from his voice. Hatchet, realizing neither of us is angry, rolls partially off my trapped leg enough so I can free it from the stirrup. I shuffle back while she proceeds to scratch her side in the dirt animatedly.

"This is a fine example of my skills of a horsewoman," I declare, pulling my knees up to brace my arms against them. Hatchet continues to ignore me as she smooths her face and side back and forth in the dirt before attempting a full roll, saddle and all.

Monty's look of disgust as he tries to right his horse sets me off in hysterics again. "What in the world is wrong with you?" he demands of the 1800-pound animal. Finally getting her to her feet, he finds me exactly where I've been the whole time—on my ass. "Up and at 'em, Brogan. Time to teach you both who's boss in the saddle."

"If you think I'm getting back up on her, you're crazy."

Monty leans down and wraps an arm around my waist while holding Hatchet's reins away. "Crazy about you, that's for damn sure."

"Then you won't make me get up on that horse again."

"Sweetheart, life's already thrown you much harder than this. How did you face it? By giving up?" he challenges me.

"No," I answer, truthfully.

"Just like riding, you dug in your heels and didn't let go. Now, I'm going to boost you up so you can do the exact same thing."

My breath hitches. Monty's face is so close I can see each spike of his eyelashes. I realize if I'd had him supporting me along the way, the knocks I took after Mom died wouldn't have been so devastating.

I can do this, not just because he's autocratically ordering me to, but because I'm not the same person I was before. There isn't anything in my heart and soul that he hasn't seen and accepted. It has nothing to do with who I am on a stage, but who I am off of it. I could choose never to play another role, never sing or dance again, and the man who's muscular arm is pulling me to my feet would support that.

Support me.

And just that quickly, I realize home isn't New York, nor is it the farm.

Home is Monty.

Because when you find the one place you know no matter what you'll always be able to lay your head down and find peace, it doesn't matter if that's a penthouse, a barn floor, or a street corner. That place is home.

And the right one can give you the strength to conquer all of your fears.

"Okay." I wrap my arms around his neck.

He pulls me the rest of the way to my feet before ordering, "Now, get control of your horse."

"Don't you mean your horse?"

He rolls his eyes at me. "Whatever. Get Hatchet on her feet and get back in the saddle."

"HOW ARE YOU DOING?" I'm on the phone with my father. I couldn't talk to him yesterday because he was too ill every time Monty or I tried to get him on the phone. We were in the middle of preparing lunch when Char said she was going upstairs for a nap. After she woke up, she said, "Let's give Ev a try. I know he wants to talk with both of you."

Monty spoke with him first. I let the two of them have their time alone. God, when Monty came out of the room shaking, I could feel the blood drain from my face. He shook his head and muttered, "I need some time and a drink. He's on the phone waiting for you."

Torn between the man I love and my father, I hurried into the study uncertain of how much energy my father would have. And I knew there were things I wanted to say.

"Tired, sweetheart. And if I ever mention wanting ginger ale after this, shoot me." I'm curled up in the chair in his office. But at his weak attempt at a joke, I laugh softly.

"I'll remember that if you do," I tease him. I spy a photo of the two of us that Char took on Christmas Day on his desk. I'd found a T-shirt shop online to make up a shirt that read "World's Best Biological Dad." He slid it on with pride. Char took the shot. I reach for it as I cradle the phone in between my cheek and shoulder. Was the love between us so evident even then? I wonder. I trace my fingers over his face, lingering on the eyes and dimples that exactly match mine. I haven't seen them in the last few weeks.

I wonder if I ever will again.

It's that thought that drives me to blurt out, "I don't regret a single minute of getting to know you, Dad."

There's a pregnant pause on the other end of the line before he rasps out, "What did you say?"

"You heard me. I wish we had more time—that I could hug you one more time. I would give anything to know this is going to work, so that I could call you Dad to your face for the first time instead of over the phone."

"Just hearing it at all...Linnie, it's more than I ever hoped for." There's sniffling on the other end of the line.

"You have to promise me no matter what you'll fight," I say fiercely. "Think of it like some software you have to conquer or something. Figure out a way to make my cells work for you, damnit. You're some sort of super genius or something; you can do it."

He starts laughing in my ear. "I'll do my best, sweetheart. Linnie, I love you. You know that, right? No matter what happens."

Now, I'm the one with tears falling faster than I can wipe them up. "I don't want to talk about what might happen. Only what will. Now, I have to go rest up. I have a pretty big day myself tomorrow."

"Listen to the doctors," he says sternly.

"I will if you will."

"That's the only thing I can do, sweetheart."

"Then try to rest. I know they're going to start another round soon, right?"

"In a few hours." His voice is resigned but determined. As long as he doesn't lose that determination, I think he'll be okay. At least I hope so. Otherwise, it will be just a few... *No, don't think about it.*

"Then I'll talk with you on the flip side. Hey, Dad?"

"Yes?"

"I love you too." Quickly, I hang up the phone. Suddenly my stomach lurches at the idea this might be it. Tomorrow, I'm having surgery for the first time. Even though I've been tested for this, I've never had a major medical procedure performed. As fear washes over me, I grab my phone and send a text to Bristol. *I love you. I always will. I hope you, Simon, and Alex will always be blessed and happy.* Pressing Send, I lean back in my father's chair.

And think about after all is said and done, the day my father met me was the day he began to die.

It's one hell of a legacy for a daughter to have.

With a weariness I didn't realize was permeating my bones, I push myself out of the chair and head upstairs. Figuring I'll run into Monty there at some point, I realize I ache all over. I want to submerge myself in the massive tub in his room and think of nothing for a little while.

SIXTY

EVANGELINE

The heat is scalding, but it's the only thing penetrating the aches permeating my body and soul. There's a searing tension that's taken residence inside me. The nerves that were gripping me earlier starts to come back, making me face reality head-on.

Tomorrow is the day. Tomorrow morning we'll drive to the hospital, and I'll undergo the procedure to give my bone marrow to my father, to the man I called Dad for the first time on the phone when I spoke with him only hours ago. To the father I might lose if this doesn't work out.

No, I tell myself firmly. Positive thoughts. Nothing terrible will happen to him. Besides, Dr. Spellman is adamant. This is Ev—Dad's —best chance at long-term remission. But it's hard not to wonder what can go wrong.

"I should go find Char to make sure she's okay," I murmur out loud.

"She's fine." I jump. Water threatens to spill over the side of the tub at my sudden movement.

"Monty." My voice comes out somewhere between a plea and a

prayer; which is merely a reflection of what my heart feels when I first see him. As I take in his dark hair and chiseled jaw, I'm swamped with love. I never knew I could feel even a fraction of the way I do for this man.

He takes a drink from the glass he's holding before setting it on top of the vanity. Reaching behind his neck, he grips the back of his sweater and tugs it over his head. His head pops out, and his gaze returns to mine in the dimly lit room.

Toeing off his shoes, he doesn't speak a word as he makes swift work of his pants, socks, and boxers. Picking up the glass, he moves toward me, his cock jutting upward, but it's the look in his eyes that traps me in place. I lick my lips involuntarily at the devastating sight. I'm helpless at the crippling combination of strength, faith, and devotion that emanates from him. The love he has for me leeches all of the doubt from my mind about whatever lies on the road ahead for us. After all, people aren't perfect, so why should love be? I shove all my doubts aside, instead focusing on the fact that he's here and he's mine.

Rising to my knees in the slippery tub, water sluices away from my body, but bubbles cling to my skin. I hold out my arms to this man who isn't perfect but has become embedded in my skin, my bones, my DNA. If this bone marrow transplant works for my father, it's as much Monty going into him as me, I think whimsically as his hard body pops the tiny bubbles between us.

His hand smooths over my skin slowly. "Are you trying to shed your skin like a snake with the water that hot, baby? I mean, a few more degrees and I could probably skim off the bubbles and sell the bathwater as l'essence de Linnie." His tone is wry, but his face is wreathed in concern.

"I was cold and hurting," I explain softly.

Nodding solemnly, he lets me go briefly. Moving near the head of the tub, he swings his long legs over the side so he can slide in behind me. "C'mere." Holding his arms open, his chest is exposed, calling for me to lay my head on it.

I fall back against him and nuzzle close. Sighing, the whooshing of the water around us sets the rhythm for the beats of our hearts, slow and steady. "How's Char?" I ask.

"Surprisingly calm. Either she should be on the stage with you, or she's at peace with what's going to happen tomorrow." His hand tangles in the hair I twisted up earlier, causing the loose knot to fall. Tipping my head back, I look back at the man who has become everything to me in such a short amount of time.

"And you?"

Sliding his hands to my waist, he pulls me astride him. My breath catches as my breasts nestle against the scratchy hair of his chest when he sits up against me. Water splashes over the sides. Neither of us gives it any attention. "I sleep, and I hold a miracle in my arms, one sent straight from the stars. I know it's going to be fine."

I drop my forehead until it touches his. "No pressure," I manage to get out.

"Baby, look at me," I lift my lashes, and they brush against him as I do just that. "Ev made this choice. His doctors recommended this option, but it was his choice. You are the closest match he will likely ever find. Spellman said that to all of us." He takes a deep breath I can feel against my chest and lets it out. "That makes it the greatest chance he will ever have. You know your father—he's as analytical as they come. Do you think he'd be satisfied with for now when he can have forever?" I can see how difficult it is for Monty to get the words out.

"But what if it doesn't work?" I voice my greatest fear. Because if it doesn't, it's not just my pain I'll have to absorb. It's Char and Monty's. And they've loved Ev for so long. I don't know how I'll survive their disappointment.

How I'll survive Monty turning away and breaking my heart when he realizes I'm not a hero, I'm just me.

"I don't know," he admits honestly. A knife of pain slices through my heart. "I do know I'm grateful you've forgiven me for not telling you the truth."

I shake my head. "It wasn't yours to share. I understood."

A soapy hand pushes my hair away from my face. "Still. It wasn't my choice."

No, I don't imagine it was. Cupping his face, I brush a kiss across his lips. A low hum of pleasure emits from his throat. My soul sighs. Since the first time we made love, Monty hasn't hidden a single reaction from me. "This isn't another thing to carry guilt about, Montague." The pleasure turns to a growl at the use of his full name. I smile against his lips before retaking them, this time tracing the seam with my tongue. He parts them to let me inside.

Our tongues duel back and forth in a slow dance. Steam billows up around us as we continued to convey everything in our kiss: fear, apologies, acceptance, and love.

Monty's hand slides from the curve of my hip up my slick skin to play with my breast. Cupping its heavy weight, he thumbs the nipple back and forth slowly as I grip his shoulders. Ripping my lips away from his, I suck in some of the humid air. "Monty," I whisper.

"Are you too sore from earlier?" he murmurs. Wordlessly, I shake my head no. "I need you, Linnie. I need you to stop the dreams tonight."

"Yes." Sliding my hands down, I find his flat nipples and tweak them. Monty lets out a harsh groan.

"Or maybe like this?" I ask as I duck my head and take one of the dark nubs into my mouth and suck. He bellows out a strangled "Aah!"

In the dark bathroom, as our bodies grasp for one another, we touch and share our strength. We kiss and share our hearts. I'm taken with a single thrust but give everything. There are no roles. I'm just me, but to him, I am everything.

I'm close to the edge. I know I'm going to soar high. The water we've splashed out of the tub has likely flooded the floor of the bathroom, but I can't care. Monty's fingers are working their magic on my clit, his mouth furious against my neck. So, I'm shocked when he pulls me down and holds me hard against his hips. His lips take my ear into his teeth and graze it before he speaks.

"You and I will be lost and found a thousand times before this is all over, Linnie. What's ahead isn't going to be easy," the deep timbre of his voice says softly. My head lifts. I'm trapped not only by the strength of his arms but by the conviction of his words. "I promise you: we're strong enough to last through the worst of this. This love we've found will survive anything." He thrusts up hard against me, the heat of him jettisoning into me, his promise warming me from the inside out.

At that moment, I dive after Monty over the edge. My whispered "Yes" is a vow to him.

After, as I rest on his chest, he reaches for the drink he placed on the floor earlier, and my anxiety starts to seep back in about tomorrow, about all my tomorrows. But then I remember his vow—my vow —and I settle against him in the lukewarm water and dream, not knowing the pledge would be something I'd need to cling to in the most desperate darkness that would soon follow in the upcoming weeks and months ahead.

SIXTY-ONE

MONTAGUE

I'm shaking in the dark as I hold her. If I didn't need to drive in the morning, more than the amount I drank earlier would be warming my stomach. Part of me wants to vomit it all up. I replay my conversation with Ev over and over in my head while Linnie sleeps restlessly at my side.

"Monty, I want you to know I'm so proud of the man you are." Ev's weak voice had me leaning against the desk in his office for support. I got my legs under me enough to get to his liquor as he kept talking. "So strong throughout all this; so strong for your Mom, for me, for Linnie. I don't know what I did in this life to deserve you, but I thank the Lord every day for it."

"Don't." I wince, knowing I don't deserve his praise but his condemnation. I'm so weak inside where it counts, I'm surprised I haven't buckled under the weight of my burdens. My mind has no idea how to handle what's happening, but I can't admit it because to do so is to show weakness I can't admit to.

They need my strength, the illusion of it, even if it doesn't really exist. So, I keep silent all the while screaming in pain.

My mind's as broken as my heart right now as I recall Ev talking about how he knows if the worst happens, he can rely on me to take care of Char and Linnie. Absolutely, I assured him—without a doubt.

Take care of Linnie.

Ev's words seem to be stuck on repeat in my head. From the beginning, I've been drawn to her, protective toward her. She's worth everything, even the things I can't figure out how to give to her. Ev thinks I need to give her strength, but the reality is she gives it to me. I'd be drowning in a puddle if not for her tampering down my need. But this woman? She makes me want to try.

Rolling over slightly, I lift a trembling hand to her glorious mane of hair. We leave in just a few hours so they can prepare her for surgery. If fortune shines on us, we'll be back here tomorrow night while Ev will rest in preparation to receive the miracle this woman is about to deliver.

SIXTY-TWO

MONTAGUE

I'm terrified right now. The doctors performing the aspiration just left, letting us know that Linnie's in recovery, but she's not breathing well. Her oxygen levels aren't stabilizing the way they want them to. Mom's clutching at me, leaning on me, when a phone in my left pocket starts to vibrate. I frown and pull away. It's Linnie's cell. She didn't want to include it in her personal belongings, so she handed it to me.

Pulling it out, I check who could be calling, and my breathing accelerates. I press the small green button as I step away from my mother. "Yes?" I growl into the phone.

"Monty? It's Simon. Is Linnie there? Bristol wants to talk with her. We had the baby and..."

"Linnie's a little busy right now."

"Look, I know what's going on. Bristol told me." I move farther away from my mother so she can't hear me rip a new asshole into someone she welcomed into her home.

"Did she tell you about the surgery being today?"

There's a sharp inhale on the other end of the line. "What

surgery? I know she was going to donate some blood or something to help him out."

A bitter laugh escapes. "It's a lot more complicated than that. Linnie went under anesthesia today to donate her bone marrow for Ev." The words get stuck in my throat. "We just got word she's having difficulty breathing now. So, when I say she's a little busy, it's because her oxygen rate is so low, they have a nasal cannula shoved up to keep her breathing regulated."

"Jesus Christ," Simon snaps, fear in his voice evident. Through the phone, I hear the slap, slap of his feet against the floor as he runs. Presumably, he stepped out of Bristol's hospital room to make the call.

"I don't think you get the full implications of what we've been dealing with." I don't realize I'm yelling until my mother plucks the phone from my hands.

"Hello, Simon. It's Char." Mom pauses. "No, honey. We're still waiting for news." Her voice cracks. "We hate to bring such worry to you under such a monumental occasion." She pauses again. "I'm certain she'd appreciate hearing from her sister when she's recovered, yes. No, I'm not sure how long that will be. It was supposed to be an easy procedure. She should have been able to come home today, but now..." Mom shakes off her anxiety, which I know is rising. She plows on, briefing Linnie's family much more calmly than I would have. My stress is through the roof over the idea that Linnie is back there incapacitated and I can't do a damn thing to help her. "We were told during the advocate briefings Linnie's recovery from the aspiration can take several weeks. Of course, you're welcome to come to see her when you are able to travel. No, Ev won't be home for some time." There's a long pause. So long, I begin to wonder what's going on until I hear, "Bristol, please stop crying. I don't think I can handle any more tears other than my own right now." Simon must have made it back into his wife's room and put us on speaker.

A haze of fury envelops me. "Give me the phone, Mom," I demand. This is not what she needs right now. None of us do. I need to be focused on saving the core of our family before we're incapable of keeping it safe any longer from the cancer trying to kill it.

Literally.

She delicately wipes her lashes. "We're so happy for all of you, Bristol. Our congratulations to you. I'll be sure to tell Linnie about her nephew when—" Mom's voice breaks. "—she's awake in recovery. Bye for now, honey."

Even as Mom's handing me back Linnie's phone, I'm demanding, "I was fine. Why didn't you let me...?"

"Because, Monty, you're so angry because things aren't going well with Linnie. You're looking for someone to take your frustration out on, but Bristol and Simon aren't it. Linnie's family is important to her," Mom scolds me gently.

"My way would have made me feel better," I mutter.

"For now, because you're worried about Linnie and Ev. Later, you would have regretted it." She pats my arm.

Sighing, I ask, "Think anyone would mind if I take the flask in my jacket and whip it out?"

Mom laughs, thinking I'm joking. I'm not. If I don't suck back something to calm my nerves soon, I'm going to storm through the doors of the recovery room and take out my fury on the unsuspecting hospital staff. "If you have things under control here, I'm off to find some coffee. Do you want some?"

"Sure. Thanks, Mom." I kiss her brow. After she disappears, I reach into the inner pocket of my coat and yank out the leather-encased flask. Unscrewing the top, I tip it up to my lips. The vodka goes down smooth. Not knowing what lies ahead, I don't drink the whole thing. Recapping it, I slip it into my pocket only to meet sets of shocked eyes. Slowly, people who had been sitting next to Mom and I begin standing and moving to chairs in the far corners of the waiting room. They begin whispering among themselves while looking at me.

Crossing my arms over my chest, I glare at them.

Only one has more audacity than the others. He plops in the seat next to me, and I mean mug him. He holds up his hands. "Dude, I was just wondering if you think I could get one of those at the gift shop."

"I brought this one from home." And I should have brought more than one, I think hazily as the vodka begins to trail warmly through my system.

"Yeah, you look like the kind of guy who might have had a backup plan." My eyes narrow. What the hell does he mean by that? But before I can ask, he gripes, "Should have thought to have brought one of my own with the crazy-ass lunatics from my wife's family who just had to come with me."

I grin at the older gentleman before telling him regretfully, "Sorry, I don't think they sell them downstairs."

"They damn well should," he mutters, giving a loud group of people a few feet away a mild sneer.

As I think about Linnie fighting for her breath which comes so smoothly when she sings, or even how I cause her to lose it when I kiss her, I don't disagree with him in the slightest.

Beads of sweat start to pop out as I wonder how long it will be before they let me back to see her.

"MONTY..."

"Are you sure you're up to call your family back?" She's safe and in my arms. I'm stroking her long braid, and I don't want to let her go. Six hours later, Linnie's in a private room for the night as a "precaution." Dr. Spellman's even come to see her, disquieted by the fact that apparently she reacted to the anesthetic, which never came up on pre-op testing.

Linnie assured him she didn't fault him. "How would I have known? I'm just pleased your team was so efficient in handling it." He patted her shoulder over and over, making sure she was all right as he explained what would happen next. Linnie's bone marrow was being processed so it could go into her father starting tomorrow. "But

I'm confident we're looking at a positive outlook. We'll know within a few days."

Now, Linnie's looking at the room service menu like it's going to disappear and arguing with me about calling her sister. The relief permeating through me is enormous. When I finally got back to see her paper-white face in recovery, I was petrified.

As if her nose is itching from 900 miles away, the phone jumps in Linnie's hands, cutting our argument short. Linnie looks down. There's a picture of a smiling Bristol and Simon holding baby Alex that Bristol texted. "Yeah, I'm totally up to calling her." Quickly punching in her sister's number, she waits for her to answer the call. "Congratulations, Bris. To all of you." Her voice is tender.

There's a lengthy pause. "Stop. I'm fine. I had no idea either. I thought it would be an easy in-and-out procedure. I know we talked about it, but no one could have predicted this would happen." Another pause. "Besides, that's not what we're focusing on today. Tell me about your beautiful new son." She reaches for my hand.

Quickly, I walk around the bed to take it. "Bristol, honey. I am so thrilled for you. You deserve this happiness. It's a miracle you made. And stop worrying about me. Besides, you have to be just as exhausted." A shorter pause before Linnie starts snickering. "Um, yeah. Of course you told Simon to get you cheesecake. Did he really think that your cravings were over just because Alex was born? Does he realize that now you're a mother that he has a lifetime of being in your debt?" Linnie's laughter is the most beautiful sound in the world. "I'm so sorry this caused even the smallest blemish on your perfect day, love."

"She needs to eat," I call out. Linnie glares at me. Then her face softens.

"No, he's not wrong. I'm tired, hungry, and all I want to do is sleep. I imagine you're feeling the same way." Another pause. But when she talks again, her voice is much softer. "I love you." Pause. "Always. And that little one had better be getting extra kisses from me. I'll be there as soon as I can to give him a million more." God, that sends shards of panic through me at the idea of Linnie leaving, but I tamp them down. "Now, get some rest. It might be the last night you get to sleep for eighteen years." She laughs. "You bet your ass I enjoyed reminding you of that. To the moon, Bristol. Always."

Linnie pulls her phone away from her ear and presses the End button. "I love her so much. I don't know how I would have got through everything without her."

I growl. Linnie lets loose a light laugh. "Part of me loves that you're so protective of me, but you don't need to protect me from the people I love."

Something twists inside me when she says that. "I feel like I need to protect you from everyone." *Including me.*

"I don't give up on the people I love. You fix the problems that are buried deep inside them." My heart races when her hand that has a capped-off IV reaches up and cups my cheek. "Same goes for you, buster. Not that I expect you to step out of line anytime soon."

"I'll try not to." I chuck her chin lightly.

"Good." She plops back against the pillows. "Now, how about a cheeseburger?"

"I believe the nurse said a light dinner. See? They even have them marked with an *L*?" I point out to her.

She pouts in response.

"The creamy chicken..." I start to read, but she interrupts.

"Sounds like it will taste like ass. I want real food." And that's when I grin. She's going to be just fine.

Now we just have Ev to worry about.

SIXTY-THREE

EVANGELINE

"You're positive?" Char asks Dr. Spellman excitedly.

"Absolutely. His bloodwork is showing a positive improvement, and there's no sign of graft versus host transplant."

"Oh my God. We'll have to do something to celebrate. How much longer until he can come home?" I lean forward. Char is squeezing the life out of my hand.

"I'd say another few weeks. His immune system, while growing, is still weak. We don't mind healthy visitors who wash and suit up. But too many people? Too much exposure? At his age, I'm still cautious about it."

"A few weeks," Char breathes. Her face is alight with happiness. Then again, whose wouldn't be after being told their husband is going to have years to live and not just days? "Oh, Linnie, I don't know how to thank you." And the next thing you know, I'm being toppled backward in my chair by armfuls of my stepmother.

Monty chuckles from his perch on the far side of the room. His face has an ease to it I haven't seen in weeks, months. "Why don't we let Dr. Spellman get back to doing his rounds, Mom can visit Ev, then I'll take you both out to lunch," Monty suggests.

"I think that sounds perfect." I detach a weeping Char from my arms. "Come on, Char. You can't go into Dad's room crying."

"No, you're right. He'll wonder if somethings wrong—like maybe I've spent all of his money on shoes or donated it to some charity that sponsors growing wheat in the rain forest."

Spellman, who had just made it to the door, barks out a laugh. "It's always a pleasure when I get to enjoy the results of my work." Shaking his head, he steps past Monty after they exchange a handshake.

Standing, I grin. "Let's go celebrate."

Monty holds out his hand, first to me, then to his mother. And the three of us leave, promising to meet in the courtyard in an hour. As Monty and I make our way into the late-February sunshine, I spin into a series of pirouettes. "It worked!" I'm so happy, I could fly.

"That it did. How does it feel to be a hero?" There's an undercurrent to his voice I can't quite pick up on.

Ignoring it, I shake my head. "This was a team effort. If anyone's the hero, it's Ev. It's one hell of a decision he made."

Monty goes to open his mouth but closes it. "That it was. So, what do you want to do for the next hour?"

"This." And I throw myself into his arms. Pulling his head down to mine, I kiss him senseless.

I feel him smile against my lips. "Good choice." He slants his head as he captures my lips under his.

I thought so too, I think smugly before abandoning my heart and soul into the kiss and the man delivering it.

SIXTY-FOUR

MONTAGUE

"I promise I won't be too long," I tell a laughing Linnie. "I just want to go up to see Ev before he conks out for the night."

"Want me to come with you?" She steps into my arms and tips her head back.

"I'll be okay." The reality is, now that Ev's on the mend, I want to talk with him about some of the stuff clogging my head. Now that I don't have this overwhelming fear he's leaving us, I need to unburden myself of everything that's been going on.

The worry. The pain. The drinking.

And I can't have the woman I love there while I humiliate myself.

"Then be careful driving." She rises on her toes. "I'm just glad I got a hold of your mom before she got too far down the road."

"Me too. Text me when you get home." It's a request, but I know it comes out more like an order when she rolls her eyes.

"Yes, sir." She throws off a mock salute which, in the history of salutes, should never be seen by a military officer for the crime against nature it truly is.

"I'll see you later." After Linnie and Mom are safely on their way, I head back inside the hospital. Taking the elevator up to Ev's floor, I make my way down the hall toward his room. I'm scrubbing up when a nurse steps out. "Oh, hello, Mr. Parrish. Were you hoping to see your father?" A frown appears on her face.

"Well, yes. Why? Is that a problem?" There hasn't been set visiting hours before, so I'm a little confused.

"Your father was experiencing a little fatigue this evening and asked for us not to have him disturbed. I'm sorry, when a patient requests that, it includes family unless otherwise specified." She lays a hand gently on my arm. "How about coming back first thing in the morning when he's a little bit fresher."

An erratic beat begins to thrum in my heart. "Sure, that's fine." Stripping off the paper gown, I toss it into the trash receptacle. "I'll see you in the morning."

Distracted while she makes notes on the chart, the nurse smiles briefly before returning to her work.

I'm walking past the nurses' monitoring station when I pick up bits of conversation. I slow my stride to hear more. "...doing so well. It came on so suddenly." "It's so sad; he's such a nice man." "Well, you know the donor was only a close match. There's always a chance the transplant is being rejected."

Turning abruptly, I give them my broadest smile. "Hello, ladies. Could you let me know what time I'll be able to come back to see Everett Parrish in the morning?"

All of their faces close up. "He has a do-not-disturb order for his room. It's probably best if you call," one says gently.

"Yes, that's for the best," the other agrees.

"Thanks," I choke out. Turning, I practically run for the elevator.

Oh, God. They were talking about Ev.

It's Ev rejecting the transplant.

Linnie was unable to save him. She wasn't a miracle, after all.

PANIC AND FURY drove me out of Inova. I didn't bother to slow down to gather my thoughts. I only know I need a drink fast.

I drive past several popular haunts, not wanting to make conversation. I want to forget what I just heard. I need to obliterate the nurses' words from my mind. There's a chance the transplant is being rejected. The next forty-eight hours are critical.

Finally, I see a broken neon light up ahead announcing what I so desperately need.

B-A-R

I swing the Jag into the gravel parking lot. I hear ping after ping of rock hit the body before one flies up and nicks the windshield. I don't care.

All I need right now is behind the front doors of a place that looks like it's going to ask no questions and demand no answers.

Perfect.

Pulling open the door, I stalk up to the mostly empty bar. Reaching for my wallet, I pull out all the bills before shoving it back inside my back pocket. I feel my cell buzz in my pocket, but I ignore it. Slapping the money on the counter in front of the startled bartender, I snarl, "Take 20 percent off the top for yourself, and then just keep the vodka coming."

"Will do, hoss. You want it to taste good, or you want it to last?" he asks before he turns toward the well.

Settling down on a barstool that feels like it has a spring shoving deep up my ass, I growl, "I want it to last."

"DUDE, I think if you even put him in the car, you can be arrested."

"Ain't my problem. He can't sleep inside the bar."

"Fine," I slur. "Goin'."

"See? He can talk. You're fine, ain't ya, hoss?"

"Fine. Fine, fine, fine." Everything's always fine. Or it will be when I get to sleep and this nightmare ends.

"Come back anytime." The door slams behind me. I get my bearings for just a moment while I try to figure out where I am. I hiccup, and bile starts to rise.

"Food," I mumble. I squint. There's an all-night Krystal next door. I think? I'll just get a sack of burgers before I head home.

Ev's home. Tears begin to fall down my face. I sniffle as I engage my Jag and drive it from one parking lot to the next. I sit up straighter as I drive past a police officer. "Can't get caught driving by the po-po," I chuckle. "That'd be no bueno."

I wipe the tears of mixed laughter and pain from my eyes as I order. Realizing I used all my cash at the bar, I hand over my card to swipe at the window. Greedily, I begin chugging the drink when I realize I have to take a piss. "Hey, are your bathrooms open?" I ask the drive-thru cashier.

She shakes her head. "No, sir. You can try the Wawa down the road a ways."

I wave as I pull away from the window.

By the time I get to Wawa, I need to take a leak so badly, I leave the Jag running and race inside holding my crotch. All the urinals are in use, so I bust into a stall. My movements are so jerky, my phone—precariously pocketed at best—falls into the toilet. "Fuck," I yell out. Ah, the hell with it, I think. I don't have time to deal with a phone that's likely destroyed. I'll get a new one.

So, I drop my zipper long enough just to pee all over it, the seat, and the floor. The relief is so pervasive, I brace myself on the stall, not realizing I'm still peeing, this time on my shoes.

I tuck the most crucial shit away and walk out of the bathroom, hearing screeching behind me.

Jesus, how many men had to take a piss? And why were their damn urinals set so high? You'd have had to have arced your dick to land in those fucking things.

I almost collide with a guy coming out of the bathroom on the other side. Slapping him on the back, I think I'm whispering when I tell him, "Dude, you just came out of the women's room." Then I begin to laugh uproariously.

It's the last coherent memory I have. I don't remember him shoving me away. I don't remember leaving or getting back in my car.

But I do.

And in some alarming ways, it may have saved my life.

SIXTY-FIVE

EVANGELINE

"Y ou want to see what your 'help' has done?" I shiver as he gets closer. His anger is palpable. "You want to see what hope got him? Where faith led him? Then fine, let's go."

I hesitate, not because I don't want to be there for my father when he wakes up in a few hours, but because something is off with Monty. There's a subtle tremble to his body, and he reeks as if he hasn't showered in three days. "Do you want me to drive?" It's so late, and he looks like he's ready to collapse at the wheel.

"Just get in the damned car, Linnie."

My guilt about the transplant possibly failing carries me to the passenger-side door. I don't know who I'm dealing with right now. This isn't the man who touched my heart and my body with such care the other night. This is a man filled with so much undirected rage, I don't know what to do.

Other than being there.

Slamming into the car, he engages the engine and peels out of the driveway. I yelp as one of the larger pieces of gravel flies up and slams into the windshield, turning a small chip into a larger crack. "Monty, slow down!" I cry out.

"I'm trying to get us there as fast as I can. You don't know what they said. You won't get in there to see him. Are you going to run back to..." He's so busy snarling at me he doesn't slow down for the snakelike turns that run along the property line.

"Monty, please slow down," I beg. There's something else wrong; I know it. I can't pinpoint what it is.

"What did you do with my phone? It's your damn fault I went into the women's room." His words make no sense.

"What?" I ask carefully. I don't want to distract him. As it is, we're crossing the double yellow line too much for my liking.

"I hate the idea it was you who saved him. Happy? You're not a damn hero. You're someone who just invaded our lives and is going to leave. Why did you come at all?" His eyes come off the road to glare at me. As we pass under a lamppost, I see they're shot through with red as if he's been crying. My feet kick a sandwich bag at my feet. Well, that accounts for the stains on his clothes. But why does he smell like...

"Pull off and let me drive," I beg him. "Please."

"Why?" The car lists dangerously to the left. "I like fast. You like slow. Even fucking," His smile is predatory.

"I just want us to get there safely," I plead. I'm dying a thousand deaths inside as memories begin to flash through my mind of my mother coming in and Patrick sending me to my room.

"Safe?" His voice is full of derision. "Safe is an illusion created by people trying to sell you something."

The car swerves as Monty turns to look at me. My heart races in fear as we pick up speed.

"If I learned th'anything my life, it's that nothing is safe. No one can 'scape thiss living nightmare. Day after day." His words come out slurred. My heart sinks at the confirmation he's been drinking. But this is worse than the few drinks he's had dinner or even the occasional one in our room at night. This is my past nightmares come back to life.

Oh, God.

"Please, let me drive, sweetheart." I'm crying, sobbing, begging.

His only response is to slam his foot down harder on the accelerator.

"Monty, I promise we'll get through this." I want to reach for him, but I'm afraid my slightest touch will startle him.

"What have you done but speed up the end of his life?" I shrink back against the door when he screams at me. My skin feels like ice.

"Is that what you think?" My breath catches on a sob. I've forgotten about Monty's erratic driving in the wake of that devastating blow.

"Just let me concentrate, damnit. Can't think. Maybe..."

"Monty, look out!" I scream.

Through whatever haze he's in, my scream still penetrates. He jerks the wheel instinctively, but it's too late. We're already crashing through a picket fence. The windshield shatters and sprays shards all over the two of us. My hands lift to cover my face as the Jag tears through the rough spray of rhododendrons set a few feet back.

The last thing I consciously remember is the wet sliding its way along my cheek from my eye towards my mouth.

I don't know if it's blood or tears.

ACT 3 – THEN DON'T GIVE UP.

SIXTY-SIX

EVANGELINE

FEBRUARY

E ver since the night we were brought by ambulance to Loudoun County Hospital, I've calmly answered when asked who Monty is to me, "He's the man I love." I've endured pathetic looks from everyone. But they don't know what I do. Montague Parrish—the man inside—is utterly broken. His strength is an illusion, and he's been coping by using alcohol as a crutch. It's not right. Nothing of what happened is.

It wasn't when my mother did it either. Did it make me love her less? No.

Does it turn off my feelings for him? Of course not. This is the reason I refused to press charges and instead pushed for rehabilitation.

But if at the end of his treatment, he's unable to live without the bottle, I'm strong enough to walk away with a clear conscience.

But in the darkest of moments, it's hard not to let doubt creep in. Then I remember he didn't realize what he was saying, that it was the alcohol taking over. The man who yelled at me wasn't the man who held me so tenderly while I restored my sense of self. This is the man who made me realize I could rise even higher than the stars above

Broadway through love. He cradled me in the tub in my fear and told me his secrets in the rain. It's that Monty I remember when I put my hand to my heart, and it's the rhythm of his beating I feel.

I'm not a fool though. What he did negates my absolute commitment to him, to us, but it's hard to obliterate my love. But it's not me who has to fight for absolution, for forgiveness, for us. It's him.

I sit here waiting to feel the final blow of grief or to thank God for yet another miracle.

What everyone's forgetting is that down to his soul, Monty is a man built to protect the defenseless. It's going to destroy him even further when his faculties are restored enough to realize what happened. It's exhausting to keep reminding people we all succumb to demons when the foundations of our world have been shattered.

Leaning my head against the cold glass overlooking Central Park, I watch as people mill about on the street below. It's so easy to forget when you're surrounded by all the luxuries money buy can that you're just as susceptible to the powerlessness any person can feel. How many people wandering below are feeling this way but don't have the means to get help for those they love? Or themselves? One second, one minute at a time, I've been trying to heal, and the tendrils of strength are starting to reappear. But I've had one hell of a support system. How many people wander alone questioning if they'll have the courage to love again because they don't. I let out a tired sigh.

The question nags at me until the phone rings, distracting me from my introspection. Crossing over to the couch, I pick it up. A smile tightens the still-healing skin on my cheek. "Hey, Dad."

"Hello, beautiful. How are you doing today?"

"Shouldn't I be asking you that?" Due to his age, and the problems he had initially accepting my bone marrow, my father's still enjoying his hospital stay longer than anticipated.

"Damn hospital food. I told Char I want Coastal Flats the minute we set foot out of this place," he grumbles.

This surprises me not in the least. "You must be feeling better if you're thinking of your stomach," I tease gently.

"I'd feel better if you were here when I got out," he retorts.

"Dad..." His sigh of pleasure eases something deep inside of me, soothing a hurt that's been there longer than the night Monty slipped into alcoholic oblivion.

"That one word coming from your lips, Linnie. It makes me fight harder. I know intellectually it's impossible for me to will my cells to get better but..."

"Can I say something?"

"Anything," he affirms.

"You just explained why I haven't let him go," I tell my father quietly. "Why none of us should."

There's stillness on the other end of the line.

"It's impossible for me to will him to get better, but I have to believe that the strength of our combined faith in him might give him incentive." When he doesn't say anything, I keep going.

"Did I fail, did we fail, because we didn't notice his illness before it was too late? I knew about him having bad dreams, about the night-time drinking. Should I have said something? Pushed harder? Demanded he talk about something he wasn't ready to?"

Heavy breathing is followed by a growled "No."

"Mom earned her second chance. Despite everyone she hurt, she earned it," I tell him firmly. "She was an amazing mother. She raised a beautiful family after she gave up the bottle. She lived a glorious life."

"She never hurt my girl," he counters.

"She did. It's arguable about the ways, but she did." Silence greets my declaration. "And long ago, Patrick gave her a small measure of hope by not walking away. He knew how addicted she was, and he gave her a second, third, fourth, chance. He may not have been the best man to me at the end, but he taught us not to give up on people. I'm giving Monty one chance—one—to make the right choice. To choose love, to choose me. If he makes the wrong one, I will walk away with a clear conscience."

"It's easy to forget love can ruin lives."

"Just as it has the ability to change them," I concur sadly. "Which path we follow isn't always up to us. What is up to us is how we move forward on it."

"Where do you see your path leading you, my darling?" The rustle of the sheets tells me he's getting comfortable.

Blindly, I stare out at the skyline. "For now, to the stage. I need to lose myself for a while by becoming someone else. Sepi contacted me about a small role Off Broadway that's the most interesting thing I've read in ages."

His chuckle in my ear makes my eyebrows wing up. "Why are you laughing?"

"Because, the minute someone realizes that play is as amazing as you will make sure it is, I'm betting it will be moved to Broadway within six months. Tops."

"It'd be good if it did," I muse. "There's a lot of unknown talent in it."

"They won't be for long."

No, I guess not. "So, tell me about what they're saying about when you can go home? How are your favorite nurses? What does Dr. Spellman say?"

My father launches into a monologue about how things are in the hospital, grumbling about the tasteless food for at least ten minutes. I ask innocently, "So, you're not hoping to extend your stay?"

That sends him off on another diatribe about how he needs "a damn good night's sleep" and "some damn privacy."

About thirty minutes later, I hang up with some ease in my heart, knowing that no matter what cross I've had to bear, I gained something astounding out of this entire experience.

A man who gave me life whose life I helped save in return.

Maybe, just maybe, it will work out like that for Monty. And like my father, I won't give up at the first hurdle.

★

LATER THAT NIGHT, I'm smoothing cream gently over my face. Critically, I examine the remnants of the physical damage. After four weeks, and a lot of TLC, my bruises from the wreck have faded to a pale yellow; they're barely noticeable. Fortunately, there were no broken bones in my face from where the car crashed, just a lot of discoloration. The ER doctor recommended ice, sleeping with my head raised, plenty of rest, and using arnica cream three times a day, all of which I have done religiously.

But just because the bruises aren't visible doesn't mean my heart doesn't still ache as badly as when they were.

I have no idea if Monty is grateful for or resentful of the fact I concurred with his family that he goes to rehabilitation. By the time we were found, he technically would have escaped a jail sentence, but my father was willing to press charges if I was. I couldn't—no, *wouldn't*—stand by while the rest of his life was spent replaying his nightmares over and over when there was something I could do about it.

I had to get him help before the darkness that fell that night never lifted and it was too late.

For all of us.

Crawling into bed, I fluff the pillows as much as I can tolerate. I pick up one of my mother's journals, this one from long before she met Bristol's father, before she met mine. Flipping to where I left the bookmark, I continue reading. Her deepest fears are laid bare on these pages. The words are so dark, I'm sad but not surprised she often sought a bottle to take away the pain.

Much like Monty did when he felt he needed to carry the burdens of the Parrish family.

I read my mother's words aloud. "In the darkest moments, I wonder if it's easier to give up. It'd be so easy. The promises the stage offered are a damn lie. The glow of the lights are only bright from one side—if you're on it. Otherwise, it's so lonely. There's no such thing as friends because we're all enemies fighting to get on the boards."

Until that moment, I don't think I ever gave deeper thought to what Mom truly meant when she used to tell me to look beyond the stage lights. I always thought she was trying to tell me to be considerate of the patrons we performed for, but was she reminding me to consider the people less fortunate than we were who were still trying to break into the business? The actors, the technicians, the musicians? How many of them feel what she did at this very moment in time?

How many of them turn to the bottle or worse to get through the despair?

Placing the silk marker to hold my place, I put the journal back on the stand and turn out the lights. My dreams that night are a twisted mess. I'm standing in the middle of a performance of Monty, Mom, and me. There's no light. I spin around as hands grab me as I try to dance and sing, their voices discordant with the melody.

I wake up breathing hard, my hand pressed against my chest.

I'm scared, and I'm heartbroken. Nothing about what I'm feeling is right, but I know for sure I'm not alone.

SIXTY-SEVEN

MONTAGUE

T hirty days. I run my fingers over the smooth beard fully covering my face. I feel like a stranger's living in my body. A body that's been through worse hell in detox than when I was in training during the bitch of the summer heat of San Antonio. That long-ago agony seems like a cakewalk in comparison to nausea, anxiety, complete irrationality, and broken sleep I've endured. All I want to do is collapse against the nearest wall in fatigue and shame.

But it's nothing in comparison to what I imagine Linnie's feeling.

Dr. Riley—Victor—finally showed me the police report. That sent me careening into the hall to heave up the lunch I had eaten not an hour before. I have absolutely no recollection of even seeing Linnie after I went to the hospital that night. I read her statement she gave to the doctors, the words I'd hurled at her, the unusual way I was driving. The only thing that prevented me from being charged was that by the time we were found, my blood alcohol level was significantly under the legal limit and they couldn't pinpoint my exact blood alcohol level at the time of the crash. As the owner of the property, Ev could have pressed charges, but Linnie wouldn't let him.

Instead, she insisted I be given this chance, for myself. Only for myself.

After being discharged from the hospital, it was my mother who drove me to where I am now, a rehabilitation facility just outside Spotsylvania County. We didn't say a word between us on the two-hour drive. It wasn't until I signed the papers with a hand that shook so hard due to the lack of alcohol in my system after only three days that I opened my mouth to speak, and she laid her fingers across my lips. "I will always love you. No matter what happens. Please, please, use this time to get well." Standing on tiptoe, Mom cupped my cheek on one side, before kissing the other.

It was the last time someone I loved touched me.

Being in rehab isn't easy. I was stripped down physically, emotionally, and mentally. It wasn't for the therapists to break me, but a way for them to ensure me not self-sabotaging myself. They took my clothes off, had an onsite physician check all of the cavities of my body like I was a prisoner, while an orderly looked in all of my clothes—hems and all—for contraband. I wince remembering the cavalier way they tossed everything aside, letting me know they'd all be sent through scanners and laundry before they'd be returned to me. My harsh breathing reminds me of the invasion of privacy I invited by getting myself in that condition.

The humility of my situation didn't penetrate then. It hit when I was sobbing in the corner of my room, when alcohol began to leech out. I could smell the foulness of my own stench but was too afraid of moving to crawl to the shower. I was dependent on those same order-lies for wellness and care as they held my shaking body while I vomited out bile and pain. And they stayed close by while I showered off the first layer of my indignity.

Four weeks in, I still don't understand why charges weren't pressed but she'd instead insisted I come here. I'm not entirely certain if I would have been able to resist. But she was adamant. If I agreed to stay and get help, she wouldn't.

The images of her face so bruised from where the airbag

deployed haunt me. Her face was so swollen on one side, it was distorted. Her chiseled cheekbone was missing as puffiness helped redefine it. The blood from where her head smashed against the window sent me searching for the nearest trash can. But it was her eyes that haunt me. Hours before I had kissed them delicately as I pushed into her body, assuring her of my love. Now my last image of them had one swollen shut, but the other? The other was filled with such pain.

Linnie didn't have to worry about my wanting to be here. I'm doing everything I have to do to make sure I'd never be capable of being that man ever again.

I haven't been able to speak with any of my family, though I do know Ev is back at home with Mom. I don't remember a damn thing that night other than walking up to Ev's door. The rest of the night is a complete blank. I hurt so many people, but for what reason?

Then again, would I ever have admitted I had a problem if it wasn't for what happened?

Victor's had me writing letters to my family, a therapy of sorts. Even though I'm positive there's no way they could still love me the way I love them, it's another weight off my chest to know Ev's survived.

I pull on a pair of jeans and grab the first sweater I find. Slipping on socks and driving shoes, I grab my jacket and messenger bag, quickly checking to make sure my notebook and most recent letters are tucked inside.

As I walk from dormitory-style housing encased in an antebellum-style outbuilding to the main mansion that holds the offices and common areas, I spy a dark Suburban with tinted windows pull in. *Good luck,* I wish to whoever is about to enter the facility. *You're going to need it.*

Opening the back entrance, the enticing smell of bacon takes me back momentarily to the farm when Mom would cook up packages of it for us. A bittersweet nostalgia shifts through me as I head toward the dining room. Even though I haven't been super hungry since I got here, I might be able to eat a piece or two of that.

Because I know my Mom would want me to.

AN HOUR LATER, I knock on Victor's door. I'm about to push it open when I hear the distinct click of cups being set down. Shit, I'm interrupting. Frowning, I glance down at my watch. I'm on time, so he must be running over. I wonder why his assistant told me to go right in. Victor's door opens, and I start to apologize. "Hey, if you're in the middle of finishing something, I can wait. Carla just told me to come in."

Victor reassures me, "It's no problem at all. Come in and join us." Stepping back, he pulls the door open. And there they are: Mom and Ev.

"Hey, son," Ev calls out as he stands from the wingback chair he was sitting in. There's a face mask on the table in front of him.

My lips are trembling so hard. My eyes can't hold the tears back.

"Honey, it's okay," Mom soothes me. "Ev's fine to be here as long as he wears the mask in and out of the building."

I face her because it's easier. She gave birth to me. "But why? I don't understand why you're both here after what I did? He just called me 'son,'" I scrape out.

"Because that's what you are, damnit." Ev comes striding forward. His hands clasp my triceps, and he gives me a gentle shake. "Nothing changes that, Montague. You. Are. Loved."

The shaking of my head sends the tears flying to the left and right. I'm sure I should be worried that some of them land on Ev, but I'm in denial. "How could you? I saw what I did. I saw! I should be jailed for what I did, not..."

"Forgiven?" Ev accurately guesses.

I nod.

"Son, even if I didn't have all of your letters where you accepted every ounce of blame and never once asked for it, I would have forgiven you. Do you know why?" My letters? My head turns toward Victor, who shrugs. Ev continues. "Because you're not the only person who's made mistakes. You're not the only person who's broken under pressure."

"I'm the only one who's hurt your daughter," I remind him, bracing myself for the rejection. But other than a flash of pain in his eyes—Linnie's eyes—there's nothing.

"No, you don't even have that distinction. Her mother did, as well. It took her pointing that out for me to understand."

I shove the sleeve of my sweater under my nose as I sniffle, not caring that there are likely tissues a few feet away. "Understand what?"

"That being broken doesn't mean you can't be fixed." And with that, Ev grabs me into his once again strong arms while I sob. Soon, my mother is wrapping her arms around both of us and holding on fiercely.

"We love you, Monty," the man who raised me whispers in my ear.

And finally, at almost thirty-nine years old, I call Ev the one thing I never had the courage to in the most important sentence I can utter.

"I love you too, Dad. I always will."

And Mom is now the one crying the hardest out of all of us.

"YOU HAVEN'T ASKED," Ev—no, my dad—says mildly a few hours later. We've finished with our official session with Victor. Usually, after a family reunion, my parents would be permitted to eat with me in the dining room before they have to leave, but due to the medical complications because of my father's recent transplant, Victor arranged for a private meal for us in his office.

I was beginning to like Victor before. Now, I'm sure I do. Another mental wall is down as I know I can trust this person with my burdens.

I don't pretend to misunderstand him alluding to Linnie. "I don't have the right," I say, my appetite disappearing. Pushing the plate of pasta away, I lean my elbows on the table and press my forehead against my clasped hands. "What am I supposed to ask? Is she healing? I sure as hell hope so because if not, I want you to sell everything in my name to make sure she's getting the best medical care she can. Is she back in New York? Does she hate me? I bet I can answer that one already."

Dad wipes his lip with his napkin before saying, "Yes, yes, and no."

My brow lowers. "Huh?"

"Yes, she's healing quite well. If you had managed to come into contact with the stone wall instead of the split rail, I suspect you'd have had more damage. Once I was released, I went out to the accident site. It really could have been a lot worse."

"I should have been hit with a few boulders myself," I mutter. I feel a light slap on the back of my shoulder. My mother's narrow-eyed stare still makes me shake a little inside.

"Listen to your father," she demands. Then a beautiful smile crosses her face. "Do you know how many years I've wanted to say just that?"

He takes her hand and lifts it to his lips, just like I used to do with Linnie. The shaft of pain that shoots through me is worse than detox was. Focusing on me again, he says, "Yes, she's back in New York. She's working on an interesting play Off Broadway."

Instantly, I become incensed. "Why Off Broadway? Is it because of the time she took off? Are people so heartless up there they don't realize she saved your damn life? Is it because of her injuries? What the hell is wrong with them? She's Evangeline Brogan!" I'm shouting so loudly at the end, I don't realize my father is laughing. Hard.

"Calm down, Monty. Her agent had plenty of roles for her to

choose from. This was something that intrigued her. I have a side bet with her that it lasts a month before it ends up on the big stage."

"Oh." Feeling a bit foolish, I reach for my Shirley Temple with mint, something I began drinking because it made me feel closer to Linnie. "Is it going well?"

"She says it is. They're still practicing for opening night. It was written by a student from NYU's theater department," he says thoughtfully. "It's about the battle between Heracles and Hera."

My eyes pop out a bit at that. "It's not a musical?"

He shakes his head. "No, though she said she could practically hear music in her head. When Linnie called the other night, she said she's going to try to get the writer together with a composer she knows. She thinks they could be the next generation of Rodgers and Hammerstein."

"If anyone would know, she would," I murmur. A silence descends around the small card table that was brought in with our meal.

"And lastly, no."

I tip my head at him in confusion.

"Care to elaborate, old man? Or are you just telling me no to dessert? It's not half-bad around this place," I tell him, but my heart is thumping out of my chest. I think I know what he's saying, but I'm afraid to have him say it.

"Do you think if she hated you she'd be asking me every time we talk if I've heard any updates on your progress? She doesn't hate you, Monty."

Sitting back in my chair, I give him my truth.

"I appreciate knowing, but it doesn't change anything because I hate myself enough for both of us."

SIXTY-EIGHT

EVANGELINE

It's raining out. Even in the warmth of my home, chills race up and down my spine. My fingers trace the woven leather cover of the journal I just finished. And suddenly I hurl it across the room, taking out a vase of flowers left from the opening night of *Queen of the Stars*.

My mother's words are seared on my brain.

I'm married to a man I don't love with a daughter who will amount to nothing. And, God help me, to forget, I'm forced to repeat the same mistake over and over that caused her to be that way. The bottle is the only way I can endure this life.

I'm shaking so hard, my teeth are practically rattling.

"Blame your husband, blame me, for your fucking addiction? How dare you, you bitch?" I scream.

"Um, I take it this isn't practicing for the show?" I whirl around, and Bristol's holding Alex in her arms. He's fretting due to my outburst. My chest heaves as she makes her way closer. "Why don't you hold your nephew while I clean this mess up?"

"I'll do it," I bite off, starting to move past her toward my kitchen when she stops me.

"How about I rephrase that. Sit your ass down, hold your nephew, and I'll clean up." Shoving Alex into my arms, she turns me around and points me in the direction of my sectional.

Alex's blue eyes look up at me trustingly. I dip my face super close so he can get used to my features as I coo, "It's all right, sweetheart. Aunt Linnie is just having a little tantrum like you do when you're wet or hungry."

I get a gurgle in response that helps heal the fresh tear in my heart. Hearing the sound of the dustpan from across the room, I call out, "Do you think he's going to keep his blue eyes?"

"I don't know. I could get a kit, and we could just let him drool into it to find out?" Bristol teases me.

I burst into tears.

"Hey! What's wrong?" She drops the pan, and I hear the glass go flying again. "Linnie, talk to me." She starts to move toward us, but I shake my head.

Rubbing my tears against my shoulder while I still hold my nephew, I whisper, "Find the journal."

Turning left and right, she spots it. Snatching it up, she demands, "What am I looking for?"

"Last page." I wait for her response. When she comes over and wraps her arms around both of us, I let out a huge sigh. "I've been working off this premise he wants to get well, that it was all a mistake. What if..." I cry harder.

"Then as awful as it seems right now, you move on. You take the good you found—Everett and Char—and you move on."

"That seems impossible," I tell her honestly.

"Right now, I'm sure it does." She kisses my head and then her son's. "Now, let me get this cleaned up. How about coming to our place for dinner? Marco's taking a night off of work to spend time with this little guy. We're going to order in some Chinese."

Since I don't want to be alone with my thoughts, I agree. Soon enough, we're out the door and headed toward her building. But I'd be lying if I didn't wonder, as I rocked my nephew to sleep later, if Monty had the same attitude as my mother.

If the words that escaped his mouth that I thought was part of a drunken rampage were indeed *in vino veritas*—his genuine opinion of me.

SIXTY-NINE

MONTAGUE

I used to think that the world was made up of rules and order. It was simple; if you followed the rules, you'd have order.

Since I came to the rehab facility, I realize there are strict rules for a reason. They're not just for the protection and well-being of the patients, but for the staff who are trying to heal us. But it's so different than real life where, despite what people think, there are no rules, and there truly is no order. I understand now what I didn't before. Life is a nothing but series of chaotic patterns that causes a person to do something completely insane.

I can't help but think back to the conversation Linnie and I had when we left the Holocaust Museum. My answer was so resolute, almost without compassion. Even though I don't technically have a record, I'm one of the criminals now. I'm one of the statistics. And now? I'd have a different answer to give her.

Grief.

I can't say I don't crave the comfort the bottle offers me when my nightmares wake me up at night. The journal Victor gave me to write in is often a poor substitute for the oblivion I used to find at the bottom of a glass of Maker's Mark.

But it's an even more inferior substitute for the warmth of Linnie's body curled next to mine.

I would keep the shakes, the night terrors, and all my fear if I could somehow keep her, but I doubt that's an option. As I heal with one hand, I'm losing with the other.

Some of the other patients here believe there's a higher power guiding them through this healing process. That's for each person to decide. Once I would have believed in a miracle, but I wasted mine at the bottom of a bottle.

That's the grip I have on my sanity.

Closing the journal, I glance at the clock. 3:48 a.m. Why do the most uninhibited thoughts come out at the hours when I'm supposed to be sleeping, I think wearily. I have only a few hours to head back into bed to rest though it's doubtful I'll sleep. Dropping the notebook and pen on the chair I just evacuated, I make my way back over to the narrow bed and crawl in between the sheets Mom sent down after her and Dad's visit. They were—of course—thoroughly checked out for contraband before the gift was passed along. I let out a long sigh while my fingers pick at a loose stitch.

If I could give up sanity to bring Linnie peace, I would.

Closing my eyes, I think about her long dark hair as it would cascade on my chest. Turning a pillow sideways, I clutch it a little tighter. "I'm so sorry, my love," I whisper into the darkness.

My arms contract on the pillow one last time before I'm pulled back into sleep.

SEVENTY

MONTAGUE

"**I**'m glad you think you understand why I made the decisions I did, Victor," I lash out. "Because I sure as fuck don't. I ruined my entire fucking life because I lost the ability to carry the burden I needed to."

"Is that what you think, Monty?" my therapist asks me.

"Damn straight."

"What do you think was the most important decision you made in your relationship with Evangeline?" God, just hearing her name sends a shaft of searing pain through my chest.

"Driving home to the house, blaming her for things beyond her control, and demanding she get into a car with me," I say firmly.

Victor's shaking her head. "The most important decision you made was to become involved with her," he says, shocking me. "What happens after—everything that happens after—is life. A lot of it is perfect, but more often than not, it's either mediocre or downright crap. Finding your partner is finding the person who's willing to stick through those times with you."

"I don't remember anything," I admit quietly.

"That's not a surprise." I blink at him. "You had what's called an en bloc episode, Monty."

"What does that mean, exactly?"

"It's a fragmented alcohol-induced memory loss. Some episodes of significant drinking come back to you, that's called alcohol-induced amnesia. But with the amount you admitted to me you likely consumed, I'm not surprised you don't remember. Frankly, I'm surprised you managed to remain standing. I suspect your rage had something to do with that, and once it was expended, you went into a catatonic state."

"I hurt her." A lone tear trickles down my face and into the scruff of my beard. I reach up to scratch it away.

He nods. "There's no denying that. But I suspect, the physical pain from the accident was much less painful than your words."

"I want..." I take a deep breath. It's not about what I want. Not anymore. "How can I help?"

"For loved ones of alcoholics, if they've sustained physical injuries, those will heal well before any mental anguish." He hesitates before adding, "Our job is to get you to understand you need to walk that same path. For you, Monty. Otherwise, this will fail."

Thoughts of making love with Linnie the night before Dad's transplant in the oversized tub float in my mind. Then my mind flashes to being trapped in the rain on the GW Parkway after our visit to the NCIS building as she quietly told me taking on the pain about Tim McMann's death wasn't my fault. How her cheeks looked so rosy under the canopy of the oak tree the first time I kissed her. The way she talked about her mother being an alcoholic. She trusted me with her love, and all I did was add weight to her heart.

"What do you want to know?" I say determinedly.

"Let's start with this. Do you remember the first time you picked up a drink not because it was a social setting?"

And slowly, we begin talking.

It's a beginning. A different one than the way our other sessions have gone, but one I have to take if I want to get where I want to be.

Back to me. For me.

So maybe I can find my way back to her. If that's what she sees in the stars for us.

SEVENTY-ONE

EVANGELINE

One of the benefits of being in the cast of *Queen of the Stars* should be the schedule. I demanded—and received —a full three days off each week to relax. Since I just finished two shows to wind up my week, I'm anticipating the downtime. The cup of coffee I lift to my lips offers me much-needed caffeine since I haven't slept well recently, not since the night I finished reading that journal of Mom's a few weeks ago.

I'm afraid to start the next one.

Even the distraction of acting hasn't helped. The punishing dance classes I've returned to at the Broadway Dance Center have only brought me back to a perfect physical shape, not mental. My runs leave me with too much time to think. I've taken for granted my peace of mind. Funny, it wasn't Monty who broke it, but my mother.

And I'm afraid I'll never get it back.

My cell pings with a text. Reaching for it, I see it's Simon. *Coming up. You dressed?*

Assuming he's going to try to convince me to go to the park with Alex and him while Bristol is working, I type back, *In loungewear. Need me to get ready?*

There's no reply which tells me he's already in the elevator. Shrugging, I tell myself Simon can wait the mere minutes it will take me to put on something other than the yoga pants and droopy top I have on. Topping off my mug, I automatically reach for another one, calling out, "If you want me to go out, you're going to have to wait for me to change."

I hear a beloved voice behind me say, "Actually, we thought we could hang out here all day. Ev's been wearing that stupid mask for too long. He's trying to scrub the impressions of it off his face before you turn around."

My body starts to tremble. Placing the cup I'd just retrieved down on the counter before I drop it, I whirl around to find Char standing there. Her eyes—so like Monty's—are filled with tears. "I hope this is a happy surprise, sweetheart."

I run into her arms. Her eyes look tired but peaceful, something that was missing when I left eight weeks ago. "What are you doing here?" I bury my head into her shoulder.

"Stop hogging my girl, Char." His voice is rough behind us. We pull apart, and suddenly I'm swept into his arms.

"Dad. How? Why? Should you be here?"

"I should be anywhere my daughter is hurting." Pulling back slightly, I see the truth in his eyes, but I won't risk his health, not even for my happiness.

"But did the doctor's say it's okay? I mean..."

A stern look comes down on his face. "If you think, Evangeline, that I'd risk the gift you gave me by messing it up, we still have a great deal to learn about each other despite all our time together."

It's impressive that even at thirty-three, I feel scolded. "Yes, Dad."

"But to reassure you, money may not be able to buy health or peace of mind, but it can help when one needs a private jet and a private car. And that limits my exposure."

"Also, Bristol and Simon are having food brought in for us," Char adds. "We're not going anywhere for the next two days."

Happiness floods through my system. "You all did this for me?"

My father slips an arm around my shoulder. "Bristol called and told us you needed us. So, here we are."

Leaning into him, I lay my head on his chest. "I'm don't know what to say."

"I wish I could see them this visit," my father says with regret. I immediately understand. With his immune system so delicate, he can't be around Alex. "But next time, I should be in the clear."

I squeeze him hard. "That's good. Hey, if you didn't see them, how did you get in?"

Char laughs. "They made arrangements with your doorman."

I shake my head. Of course they did. "I'm such an idiot. Why are we just standing around? Do you guys want some coffee? Let me show you around."

"Sweetheart, you know we'll never turn down coffee," Char declares. I smile at my stepmother before I move out of my father's arms and quickly pour them each a mug.

"Follow me," I say eagerly, excited about something for the first time in weeks.

"FOR BEING RELATIVELY SMALL, those statues are damn impressive," my father remarks about my Tony awards. "They're heavy though." He throws me a smile. We're in my home office, the last place on the tour. Here's where I have all of my theater memorabilia up on the walls and spread across the shelves. I listen to all of my scripts in here to prepare for a performance. This room, more than any other, is the essence of the life I led before I met him.

If only Monty were here to see it with them. Shoving those thoughts aside, I reach for the statue he's holding and turn it over. On the back, it has my name, Best Actress, *The Dream Sequence*, 2014.

"When they call your name, it's surreal," I murmur. He passes the statue to Char before he takes my hand. She gasps. "And then you do that." We all laugh. "All the long hours, all the hard work and sweat, and then you're being honored the highest honor imaginable for a theater actor. It's such a rush."

He tugs me over to the sofa that's nestled under a pre-war window. "Then what happens?"

"You're caught up in a media frenzy that lasts for days, sometimes months, depending on the success of the show. And one day it ends. And you're fighting for another role trying to do it all over again."

"Do you think maybe that's what your mother was talking about?" Startled, I jump a bit. "Don't be so surprised, Linnie. Bristol's worried about you. She told Char about what your mother wrote and how you're handling it."

"I think your mother was going through a dark time, sweetheart." Char puts my Tony back on the shelf before coming to sit on the floor in front of me. "Add the alcohol to the mix..."

"Yeah..." I blow out a gust of air. "I guess I should try to let go of these feelings?"

"No, what we think is that you should be talking about them with your therapist," Char says firmly. "You're still going to see her, right?"

I squirm a bit.

"Damnit, Linnie," he bites out. "I thought you were still going."

"I was doing so much better after everything that I bailed on the last few appointments," I say weakly. "Besides, work started picking up. Anyway, this didn't have anything to do with the accident."

"They're all connected. If reading what Elle wrote set you back, what's reading something from Monty going to do?"

I open my mouth and then close it. He's right. I have no idea what would happen if I ever heard from Monty. But that hasn't happened, so the point is moot.

"Monty is dealing with his guilt, Linnie. We all have our own to deal with," Char shares. My head snaps to her. "When we saw him..."

I don't let her finish. "You...saw him?" My lips tremble. "How..."

"His guilt is killing him," Char says bluntly.

"He wants to talk to you more than he wants his next breath, but doesn't believe he's worthy," my father says grimly.

Is he? A small voice inside me wars with the huge heart that screams *YES!* I run my hands over my cheek where the glass left a small scar and realize the mark has faded. Will my anger toward my mother?. Rearing back, I stand and begin to pace.

In a small part of my heart, I dreamed of Monty getting well so we could move forward, be together. But ever since I read my mother's journal, the hesitation has been growing. Am I strong enough to handle life with Montague Parrish knowing what could come from it? Does he even want me? Am I a catalyst for this?

And why has he not contacted me?

"It's not that I don't want to hear what he has to say," I finally say. "I just don't know if I'm in a place to respond."

My words cause silence to hang in the room. "Then don't respond until you're ready. But I think for him to get what you fought for him to have out of that program, and for you to heal, you should read what he has to say." Compassionate green eyes rake over my face.

I nod. "And if I can't forget? What does that do to all of us?"

"Absolutely nothing. I'll always love both my children." My father stands and opens his arms. I move into them quickly as if I've been doing it for years instead of months. "I'll never force you to do or feel something you can't."

"Then maybe I should keep my appointment with my therapist this week. See what she has to say."

"Sounds like a good idea," Char murmurs. My head ducks down to see her resting her chin on her knees. "And as a mother, I think you should bring the journals with you. You're not betraying your mother by sharing your pain."

Char's words strike something deep inside me. That's precisely what I've been doing; suppressing my pain, hiding Mom's.

And isn't that what Monty did to put us in this predicament?

A full-body shudder racks my body. I'm held tighter. "I just can't believe it was all an act."

"Your mother?" he guesses.

I nod. "And Monty. I have to believe this pain will go away because I'm scared of the alternative."

"What's that?" He brushes hair away from my cheeks.

"That happiness has worse odds than you and I ever being a match."

Char pushes herself to her feet and wraps her arms around me from behind. Laying her head against my back, she whispers, "Happiness is going to find you again, Linnie. Whether that's with or without my son, well, that remains to be seen."

"At least my happy includes the two of you." I'm rewarded with a tight squeeze for my comment before Char moves away.

"That it does. Now, I heard something once about a deli sandwich the size of my head."

My eyes brighten before a V forms between my brows. "I don't think we can DoorDash Wolf's?" My stomach growls in protest.

"No, I'm going to phone a friend and have Simon go get it for us. He said he'd leave it outside the door once it's here. Just because I can't see him or Bristol doesn't mean the boy can't be put to use." He adds on, "Of course, I'm buying them dinner as well."

I nod solemnly. "Of course," I say before I laugh at the idea of my famous brother-in-law being used by my father as dinner delivery service.

"Come on, let's find a menu where you can tell me what to get," he tells me.

"As long as it doesn't have cilantro on it, I'll pretty much eat anything," I admit.

"Same here. See, Char. I'm not the only one who hates that crap," he calls over his shoulder.

Char laughs. "Genetic freaks," she teases.

Yeah, we are. But we're each other's genetic freak. And as I hug my dad to my side, I'm so grateful for it.

SEVENTY-TWO

MONTAGUE

MARCH

It's been sixty-three days since I've been here. I got a new letter from Mom today. She said she got to see Linnie perform on stage in this new Off Broadway show and is brilliant at it. I'm so fucking proud of her, I can hardly contain it. I can also barely stand the fact I'm not by her side watching it happen.

Nothing is holding this woman back except maybe the albatross of love.

I'm sitting outside of Victor's office waiting for our daily session when one of the framed quotations catches my eye. Standing, I move toward it slowly. "The way to right wrongs is to turn the light of truth upon them," I murmur.

"Ida B. Wells," Victor says behind me. "An investigative journalist and an early leader in the civil rights movement. She was also one of the founders of the NAACP."

I remain as still as a statue staring at the beauty and simplicity of her words. My hand slips into my pocket, fingering the letter I wrote in the middle of the night.

It's time to let her go. To be free to soar the way I know she did before she ever met me.

Turning, with tears burning in my eyes, I say, "Sometimes, the only way to right your wrongs is to just to own up to them and to let go." Pulling out the letter, I slap it into Victor's hands before I sidestep him and make my way into his office.

SEVENTY-THREE
EVANGELINE

"I wish you had told me about reading these, Linnie." My psychologist, Dr. Audrey Gilbride, strokes her hands over the leather-bound volumes on her lap.

"Would you have tried to stop me?"

"Stop is the wrong word. I would have tried to prepare you."

I get more comfortable on the oversized sofa in her office. "What do you mean?"

"Your mother had a disease. It would randomly manifest itself. Before she chose to stay sober, there were times when she was extra-ordinarily high functioning, much like what you experienced with Monty at the very end. It's how you recognized he needed help versus prosecution." Waiting for my slight acknowledgment, she continues. "But she persistently poisoned her body. Yes, you loved her, and you forged this incredible bond, but you forget about the woman who wrote these words—" Audrey lifts the volume that's been like a persistent point of a knife in my heart. "—isn't the woman who cried when you graduated from college. She isn't the woman who sang on stage with you. It's like comparing an infant to an adult in terms of understanding that it's two different people, but they live in the same body."

I don't respond right away. Instead, I turn and flop back on the couch so my head is facing the ceiling. There's a poster Audrey tacked up there that says, "If you think you've got problems, imagine dealing with our shit." And it's the faces of hundreds of adorable puppies. Every time I see it, I can't help but smile, which was her intent. "This is better than the poster at my gyno's office."

"What do they have?" she asks curiously.

"A poster that says, 'A kiss makes everything better' with a bunch of babies." Audrey's laugh bounces off all the walls of the room. "What would you suggest?"

"Parse out reading them," she says immediately. "Take a pulse of your mood. Texting your therapist when something like this bothers you."

I roll my head in her direction. "Oh, you mean being logical?"

"Crazy, I know." We both smile.

"Would you do me a favor?"

"Of course."

Reaching down, I pull out the next journal in the series. "Read this. Let me know if I should go on. Right now, if it's more of what I just dealt with, I...can't."

Audrey takes the volume from me and places it on top of the others. "I will. In the meantime, I have something for you. I've been briefed about it and, I've been waiting to give it to you." Standing, she walks over to her desk, where she places Mom's journals on the corner. She lifts a manila envelope with my name scribbled on the outside in an unfamiliar hand. Sitting up, I reach for it when she hands it to me.

"What's this?" I weigh the large envelope in my hand and hear a smaller weight shift back and forth.

"A letter." My face must be filled with confusion because Audrey continues. "From Monty."

Maybe it's just me, but the envelope seems to make a racket in the room as it shakes in my hand. "Do you know what's in this?" My voice is a harsh rasp.

Audrey shakes her head. "Dr. Riley read it; he's required to. In case there are threats they have to negate." Even if the idea of someone reading Monty's words to me initially shocks me, I understand that. "Once it cleared that check at his facility, I'm only briefed on the general contents so I can help you work through any issues."

I swallow to try to get moisture back in my mouth. Right now, my soul's so mentally exhausted, it comes out harsh when I ask, "Am I expected to write back?"

Her hand comes to lay on top of mine. "Only if you want to. If there's a message or anything you want to send, I can get that there as well."

"Should I read it here?"

"I think you should read it wherever you feel most comfortable."

An idea flashes into my mind. "Would it be impossible to have our session on FaceTime next week?"

"If you plan on actually attending it, it won't be a problem. Why?"

"Because I want to read it at my father's. I don't want to bring Monty to New York. Not just yet." And depending on what it says, maybe not ever.

Audrey's hand squeezes mine firmly. "Then, yes, I'm available for a session. Go see your father."

Standing, I hug her. "Thank you."

"My pleasure. And hopefully, by the time we talk next, I'll know more about how to handle those." She nods toward her desk where my mother's journals lie.

Slipping the envelope into my bag, I sling it over my shoulder. With a halfhearted smile, I duck out of Audrey's office.

★

THE MANILA ENVELOPE sits on the edge of my kitchen counter taunting me to open it all week. Every day I go to work, and every night it pulls at me. Just like Monty does in my dreams. But I was serious about what I said to Audrey. I'm not ready to invite Monty here, especially after what seeing the hateful side of my mother did to me.

I called Dad and Char to let them know I'd be arranging for my understudy to take the second show on Sunday and when I'd be arriving. As I step off the small private jet at Dulles Airport, I grab my weekender bag and walk through the VIP terminal briskly. When I see Char waiting for me just beyond security, I walk straight into her arms. "I could have rented a car," I murmur into her hair.

"Your father wouldn't hear of it. Now, come on, he's likely run out of his data plan by now." She reaches for my bag, but I hold it out of her reach.

"It's not heavy. But wait, Dad's here?"

She rolls her eyes. "Of course he is."

I tuck my arm beneath hers. "I'm glad I came here to do this."

"To do what?"

I shake my head. "I'll explain in the car."

We step out of the warmth of the VIP area, and there's Dad's Lexus. "Sit up front with him, Linnie," Char urges.

"You sure?'

"Positive, honey."

Walking up to the passenger side door, I open it to hear, "...you would think I'd have better reception than this. This is utterly ridiculous. We pay how much to have a hot spot in this car? I'm going to write to the provider tonight."

"You tell them, Dad," I tease. His head snaps up, and a broad smile crosses his face. God, even though I saw him two weeks ago, he looks better than before.

"Linnie, I swear you just keep getting more beautiful," he declares.

I laugh as I slide in. "I look like a wreck."

"You look perfect." Once I close the door, he leans over and gives me a one-armed hug. "Buckle up and let's head home."

Home. Now I understand why I came here to read Monty's letters. It wasn't because I wanted to keep Monty out of New York; it's because I want the cushion of home if the pain causes me to stumble and fall. What I don't understand is when did New York stop being home?

Relaxing back against my seat, I realize it was somewhere between meeting my father, trusting his wife, and falling in love with his stepson.

A smile touches my lips as my dad and Char catch me up on everything happening at the farm as we drive the thirty minutes to get there.

A FIRE CRACKLES in the room, sending a log rolling in the massive stone structure. "I tried my best not to take what she wrote personally," I get out.

"Be hard not to," Char sympathizes.

"But between everyone challenging my decision about Monty and then reading that, I began to doubt myself. If my mother would say things like that about me, what did Monty write?" I wonder aloud. I turn my head to take a sip of the spiced apple cider Char made when we got home.

"I couldn't do it alone this time. I knew if I read his letter, and it's bad, I needed to be around people who understood everything. I needed to be home." My father's fingers tighten around the hand he's holding.

"Every time you say you wanted to come home, it makes my heart flip in my chest," he admits.

Leaning my head against his shoulder, I tell him, "I didn't realize the farm had become home until you said it in the car."

He pulls back a little and puts a gentle kiss on top of my hair. "And let me say for the record, this is the last time you ask if you can come. We'll get you keys this weekend."

Char, who's sitting curled under a blanket across from us with her head resting on her fist, agrees. "First thing tomorrow."

A comfortable silence wraps around us before Dad breaks it. "You know we've heard from him, Linnie. And we've seen him too."

"I want to ask, but I think I should read his letter first," I tell him truthfully.

"That's fair." But I can't resist asking one thing. "Was he glad to see you?"

"That, my darling girl, is an understatement." Something I wasn't aware was coiled inside me relaxes. Pushing to his feet, my father holds out his hand. "Come on, it's late."

I push the blanket to the side. "Do you know how long it took me to get adjusted to New York hours after I left? I was practically asleep in the middle of the second act of *Queen of the Stars* when we first debuted."

Chuckles come from all around me. "And now?" Char asks, running a hand over my hair.

"Now, I go home and fall flat on my face. Maybe I'm just getting old," I grumble.

"Or you've been under a tremendous amount of stress," she counters. Leaning in, she kisses me on the cheek. "Blueberry-lemon crumble muffins for breakfast?"

"Sounds perfect."

"Then I'm off to bed. Night, you two." Char leans up and accepts a kiss from my father that makes me yearn for the days before his bone marrow transplant. The days when my blinders were still partially on.

"I'll be up soon," he calls out. She waves.

I watch as the process begins to extinguish the fire. First, there's prodding at the wood and embers with the fire poker. Then switching for a shovel, ash is scooped from the bottom of the fireplace and tossed on top. Soon, the fire's out. "We'll let that sit before I put on the baking soda," he declares, brushing his hands off on his pants.

We sit in silence for a few minutes before he says abruptly, "I heard a country song the other day that I thought reminded me of all of this. But then when I looked up the lyrics later, it didn't."

My heart pounding, I ask, "Why not?"

"Because you have never not once said Monty had to become a better man. You've said he was ill, that he needed help. But from the beginning, it's been you reminding the rest of us he's the best man there is." My father pulls me back down to the couch. "Before you ever came into my life, Monty did everything to make this easier on us. When you got hurt, I lost sight of that."

I reach out and take his hand. Is this the way my stepfather felt, this bleak sadness at being unable to help my mother? "He's getting the help now."

"Because you pushed for the right thing."

"I'm not the one who will have to fight every day to live life, Dad. That's on Monty," I remind him gently. "So who knows if the song you heard will be true after all or not."

He goes to open his mouth but instead closes it. "We'll see. Come on. Let me finish making sure this fire's out, and then we'll head up."

"Okay, Dad," I agree, ready to put myself to bed. "Is there anything I can do to help?"

He smiles. "No. Just talk with me while I finish up. Tell me more about Bristol, Simon, and Alex."

While I chatter with my father for a few more minutes about my sister, he douses the warm ashes with baking soda, using the shovel to mix them. After he scrapes them into a pail and puts them outside, and after I've shared Alex's new trick of blowing bubbles when people get close to kiss him, we hug each other before each heading up to sleep.

In my room, I lie awake for a while, clutching a pillow to my chest. It's hard not to wonder if I'll ever get back the dreams I had in this bed when Monty lay here next to me.

I guess tomorrow's letter opening will give me a better idea of that.

SEVENTY-FOUR

EVANGELINE

APRIL

My boots crunch on the gravel as I carry nothing but the yellow envelope toward the studio. Char asked me if I wanted any company, but I shook my head. The next part of this journey has to begin with Monty and me, or it won't happen at all.

The sounds of the horses being let out for some exercise stabilize my nerves as I approach the studio. I rest my head against the glass pane of the window. My heartbeat is racing. Why am I afraid?

"Because what lies behind those doors is a war," I whisper aloud. "And I don't know if I should be winning it or even if I should be playing it."

Realizing the truth gives me the strength to depress the handle. I drift over to the sound system even as I'm slipping off my jacket and dropping the envelope. Fiddling with a few buttons, I kick off my shoes. My body automatically flows into the routine I'd been dancing that night before he came into the door. Exaggerated pelvic thrusts leading into chaines turns as I'm hearing the accusations he flung at me. Adamant marching as I stomp out the crushing words. A full-body roll into a pas de bourrée. Repeat on the other side.

Double pirouette. A quick footstep combination ending in a ball change. I end with my one leg fully extended while raised on the other. My breath is coming in harsh gasps. And I'm shocked to realize that without having read a single word that no matter what, I may be a mess, but I will survive. I will walk out of this room stronger than when I walked in no matter what Monty may have to say.

I can do this.

Lowering my leg, I head over to the small bar. I grab a towel and dab at my face. I also open the minifridge, grateful it still has water in it. After lowering the music, I snatch up the envelope I dropped earlier before moving to the center of the room and sitting down.

It's time.

Using my nail, I tear open the back and upend the envelope. A single sealed envelope with the same unfamiliar writing as on the yellow greets me.

Before I pull it out, I take a deep breath.

Linnie,

There are words all over this place. That may not make a lot of sense, but in my repeated attempts to write this letter, to attempt to try to apologize for what I've been told I did, there are enormous piles of crumpled papers lining the floor of my room. I've stepped on all of them as I pace back and forth to find the right words. And I've come to the conclusion there might not be any other than I'm so damned sorry.

I don't know what happened because I have no memory of it. Nothing. There's nothing there. The last thing I remember was going to the hospital to see Ev and waking up in another with my mother's tears hitting my face. I don't know how I didn't manage to rip out the IVs to get to you; I was that fucking irrational at the thought of you being hurt.

But I was the one to hurt you.

Because of your strength, your honor, here is where I'm going to stay for a while. I have to because I can't stand to look in the mirror.

I'm an alcoholic, Linnie. Other than my therapist, you're the first person I'm saying the actual words to. Because you deserve to know them even if it's in writing—even if you never read this.

I have to tell you. It's tearing me up inside that I'm so weak. That I'm not the pillar of strength you need me to be. Not now. And maybe not ever.

I've also realized you can't hate me any more than I hate myself for what I did. And I know I'll never love another person the way I love you.

I take back what I wrote. I found some words I want you to have. Stay safe. Be happy. Don't let what I did to you hide the glory of your light from the world. And please, God. Get help. Then let me go. Live your life to its fullest. Don't let my illness leave you with any scars, mental or physical. I've already directed Mom and Dad to sell everything I own if the second is the case.

You were—are—the brightest star in my sky, Linnie. I wished for you, worshiped on you, and everything that was between us was real. My love for you was true. I'm just so sorry that with the dreams I wished for came your nightmares.

Monty

I wipe my eyes on the towel. I reread his letter twice, a third time.

I know what I want to say to Monty, but I don't want to write a letter. Pulling out my phone, I send a text to Bristol.

Can you research something for me? I wait for her to respond.

Of course. What do you need?

I need you to find a painting for me. Pressing Send, I wait for the response.

Little dots flash, then stop. Then they start again. *Just let me know all the info you can. I'll see what I can do.*

Just like that? Although I'm not surprised.

Always like that.

My fingers fly, giving her the information she needs.

A few hours later, I'm having dinner with Dad and Char when I get a text back. *I found it. It's yours if you want it.*

Taking a deep breath, I respond. *Here's what I want you to do with it.* Then I tell my sister the hoops I need her to jump through knowing she'll do it in a heartbeat.

Because that's what family does in a crisis: they hold you close when you're broken, and then they help put you back together. At least, that's what my family does.

God, I do live among the stars. I'm just damned lucky it has nothing to do with the wealth and everything to do with love.

SEVENTY-FIVE

MONTAGUE

MAY

"You got a delivery, Parrish," Jimmy calls out. He's just come from the hallway leading from the men's quarters. Likely Mom's baked something again and he's waiting for me to bring it out to share. I smile. My mother's baking has pretty much become legendary here at the center. Seventy days in and I swear everyone's loosening their belts a little bit.

I flick my hand out in a side wave as I travel down the same hall he just came down. Stopping at my door, I open it with my key. The illusion of privacy is only from patient to patient. There's nothing to prevent orderlies, therapists, or anyone I signed my rights away to from entering my room to inspect it. Mentally shrugging, I twist the knob. It's not like I have anything of value here anyway.

Entering the room with my head down, I flick on the lights, frowning because typically when someone's been in your room for whatever reason, it's a courtesy by the staff they leave the lights on. I lift my head to see if anything's out of place when every muscle of my body freezes.

Forgiveness. It's staring me right in the face. My breathing starts to accelerate to such a degree that I begin to wonder if I'm going to hyperventilate. Just like when I saw it for the first time in Gas Lamp, the painting's majestic colors begin to hypnotize me, sucking me into the swirl of emotions.

There's only one person who could have sent it to me.

One.

Taped to the easel it's resting on is a small white card. Forcing myself to move, I carefully remove the envelope so as not to disturb the painting. Stepping back, I get lost in the storm which seems to depict my life more than ever.

Trembling, I rip open the card, see the carefully scripted words, and fall to the floor. Suddenly the outrageously expensive painting becomes obsolete in comparison to the words on the tiny card in my hands.

Why would I forgive you for being in my dreams? The nightmare is you not having been there at all.

SEVENTY-SIX

EVANGELINE

JUNE

I sit in my dressing room alone, still dressed in a violet-and-gold ensemble from my battle onstage with Heracles, pain flowing through me. Being in *Queen of the Stars* has taught me so much about the battle people subject themselves to when their emotions are out of control. Look at the lengths Hera went to over her jealousy because of Zeus's infidelity?

How does someone recover from that kind of pain?

After all, if pain defeats gods, what does it do to mere men?

Pain breaks men.

Men like Monty.

Turing away from my mirror, I bow my head. Maybe I'm just coming to realize that not everyone is strong enough to be saved.

It's three months to the day that Monty entered rehab. I haven't heard another word from him since I received his letter and sent the painting to him in response. I don't know if my heart's suffering for a man I never really knew at all.

My phone flashes with an incoming call. Recognizing the number, I pick it up despite my overwhelming desire not to. "John

Thomas," I murmur. After all, this man could make or break the future of every man and woman beyond my door.

"Evangeline, I hope this isn't a bad time. Can your understudy take your place for the next few days? I want you in my studio to try out a few songs I've been working on for *Stars*. I think you'll like them."

And despite the bleeding in my heart for a faceless man, I answer the way I must.

"Absolutely."

John Thomas hangs up on me without a goodbye. At any other time, I'd be shouting for joy. Despite our long-standing business relationship, John Thomas didn't promise me anything. Nothing more than a chance. But that chance might save what's left of my soul after feeling nothing but empty for so long. Right now, I want the peace in knowing that trying was enough. With Monty, I may never have that answer, but for the cast and crew of *Stars*, I may have just pulled it off.

Pushing myself to stand, I know at the end of today, I'll keep breathing. I'll go on. Even if it's alone.

Quickly changing, I leave my costume and text Simon the news. The amount of bug-eyed emojis I get in response should make me laugh out loud at his over-the-top reaction. It doesn't. But it does make my lips curve up slightly as I wait for my Uber to come to pick me up from behind the stage door.

SEVENTY-SEVEN

EVANGELINE

JULY

"No!" I scream at Pasquale a few weeks later when he showed up at where the cast of *Stars* is rehearsing the revised script with John Thomas's musical score added. We're due to debut on Broadway in six weeks. Choreography is scheduled to come in starting tomorrow. "You're lying." My eyes flick over to Simon, who's standing alongside him. "Tell me it isn't true," I beg him.

"I'm sorry, love," my brother-in-law says as he approaches me. And it's a good thing he does because my knees give out as I start sobbing, crying harder than I remember doing since my mother died.

Veronica was found dead last night. The smell of her decomposing body alerted neighbors. When the police busted in the door with no response and authorization from her landlord, they found she pulled a bookcase down on top of herself. She died, and no one knew about it for days. Slapping a hand across my mouth, I lurch from Simon's arms over to stage left to let go of what's in my stomach.

"She was all alone," I weep. "She had no one there."

"Linnie," Pas says brokenly, but I hear it. The same guilt I'm feeling. She was shunned from the community she loved because of her behavior. *Because of me,* I think bitterly.

"She made her choices, Linnie," Simon reminds me. I whirl on him in a rage.

"I let her go because she was toxic, Simon. I hated what she did, but I loved her my whole life. That's why it hurt so bad that she lied to me." I curl into myself, sobbing. We're all three silent for a few moments, each remembering Veronica in our ways. Finally, I ask without lifting my head, "Does Bristol know yet?"

"No. I thought you should know first," Pasquale whispers.

"Okay...okay." I begin rocking myself back and forth. Bleary-eyed, I lift my head. "Call Sepi. Tell her to do what she can. Please? This is going to be...I don't even know how bad this is going to get. She didn't deserve this. No matter what happened between us, she didn't deserve this."

"She didn't deserve you," Simon mutters before he turns away to call our agent. I can hear him murmuring as Pasquale lowers himself to sit beside me.

"I don't even know if she had a will," I say with a bewildered air. "The only thing I can think of is maybe Mom browbeat her into it at some point."

"You won't be able to get in until after the police..." Pasquale's voice trails off.

"But you said...?" I'm so confused.

"Because her death wasn't by natural causes, they still have to perform an autopsy, Linnie. Until then, her home is considered a crime scene." Pas swallows hard. "There's time."

Tears fill my eyes again. "There's never enough time." There's no time to go back and tell Veronica I forgive her for the secrets. There's no time to save Monty. There's no time to find my heart from the hell it's just been sunk into. History can't be rewritten no matter how much we want it to be. With that in the forefront of my mind, I lean my head down on Pasquale's shoulder. "I'm sorry," I whisper.

He drops his on top of mine. "You have nothing to be sorry for, sweetheart. You never did. I should be apologizing to you. And Veronica should have as well."

I'm holding back the comment that wants to leap forth from my mouth about the dead not speaking when Simon ends his call with Sepi. "The news already reached her. She reached out to Courtney Jackson from The Fallen Curtain already for damage control. You're going to have to give her an exclusive," he warns me.

I nod, knowing there's no other way. "Hand me my phone?"

"You're not calling her now, are you?" Simon asks, appalled.

"No. I'm calling Eric Shea. I need to find out if he handled anything for Veronica," I say wearily.

Simon lets out an enormous sigh. "Right." Snagging my cell from where it's sitting on my dressing table, he hands it to me. Unlocking it, I quickly pull up my lawyer's direct line.

One ring. Two. Then he answers with a quiet "Ms. Brogan, I was expecting your call. I'm so sorry for your loss."

And I burst into tears all over again.

SEVEN DAYS LATER, I'm sitting on Bristol and Simon's couch holding an envelope in my hand like it might explode if I open it. I'm not entirely sure it won't.

It was handed to me by Eric Shea after the memorial service for Veronica earlier today. "Come see me when you're up to it, Ms. Brogan. We have quite a lot to discuss." He pressed warm fingers on top of my icy ones.

My name is scrawled on the outside of the envelope in Veronica's distinctive scrawl, handwriting I've seen on birthday and graduation cards. Each card from every bouquet from every show I'd been in since I was a little girl.

All except *Queen of the Stars*. A fiery burn pricks at the back of eyes when I remember the feeling of loss when there was no bouquet from Veronica and how I'd just squared my shoulders and performed.

"How could I have been so cold? How could I have just shut you out?" I murmur, my fingers tracing over my name.

"Because you needed to, Linnie. You're allowed to feel pain—then and now." Simon's voice startles me. I jump before turning slightly in his direction. "Bristol is trying to get Alex down," he explains. I merely nod.

Sighing, he drops down next to me on the couch. "I won't ask how you're holding up."

Tilting my head back, I stare unseeing up at the ceiling. "I'm breathing. That's more than I can say for Veronica." The bitter sob escapes before I can hold it in.

Simon tugs me against him. I let all my grief pour out. "I'm sorry," I gasp as rivers of tears pour out.

"How are you supposed to heal if this poison is still inside you?"

"I don't know that I'm supposed to anymore." Pushing away, I walk over to the window, leaving Veronica's letter lying on the couch.

"Why?"

"Because maybe it's love that's toxic. Maybe it's the booze," I fling out as I swipe my fingers under my eyes. "Or maybe it's me."

"And maybe you're simply saying something ridiculous because you've hit the point where you're ready to admit you're devastated by what happened to you, Evangeline." Simon shoves to his feet. "You are not wrong for wanting to be more important than that," Simon flings his arm out to the side to indicate the tea cart of liquor that he and Bristol occasionally indulge in.

"Yeah, I see how well that's worked out." I turn my back on him. Three seconds later, I hear a loud crash. Frightened, I jump backward as I turn.

Simon's chest is heaving. He's hurled the bottle of whatever the amber-colored liquid was against the wall. "You are!" he roars. "Whatever is in that piece of drivel that drunken madwoman wrote, whatever your mother wrote, whatever that man made you feel, you are worth more to us exactly as you are!"

"As much as I hate the fact Simon just woke up the baby—again —I agree with him." I jerk around to face Bristol who's holding an active Alex in her arms. My head bobs between the two of them. "You could have done what all of them did."

"What's that?" I manage to get out.

"Temporarily drown your life. Instead, you rose above it. So, no matter what that"—she nods at the letter—"says, you are still what you made yourself."

"Alone?" I question bitterly.

"Remarkable." Bristol hands Alex to Simon. Walking over, she picks up the letter. "Brave. And damnit, you've always been my damn idol." The last she says as she puts Veronica's message in my hands.

"And you and Mom were always mine," I whisper.

"I know."

"I don't know if I can do this. I don't know how much more pain I can take." That's an understatement.

"I'll be right here. Just like I was when all of this started," Bristol swears. Her hand reaches out to grip mine. We crush the envelope between us.

Leaning forward, I drop my forehead to hers. For long moments, I absorb her strength. After a while, I nod. Bristol steps back, leaving the envelope in my hands. Using a nail to unseal the back, I slide out the paper and unfold it. A card flutters to the floor. I look at the paper on both sides; it's blank. My brows lower in a V before I squat down to pick up the card.

You're not just the Queen of the Stars, darling. You're the only star in my world. Love, Veronica. PS - the carnations the first night were from me.

And in a flash, I remember the white carnations with no card that appeared in my dressing room. I kept meaning to ask someone about them but kept forgetting to write it down. Damn me. Damn my memory—damn time.

"I'm so sorry, Veronica," I weep. "I'm so sorry this happened to you." Bristol sits down next to me, holding on.

There's nothing else to say about a woman who pulled her death crashing down upon herself.

SEVENTY-EIGHT

EVANGELINE

Simon, Bristol, and I are sitting in our lawyer's office with mutual looks of astonishment on our faces. "She wanted us to do what?" Simon's the first one capable of speech.

"Ms. Solomone was explicit in her wishes." Eric glances down at his papers to review them one more time. "One hundred percent of the assets of her estate was to be donated to a charity as determined by Ms. Evangeline Brogan for individuals who are recovering from drug and alcohol addiction." A faint smile crosses his face. "She even sold her condominium to add to her assets.'

"That's why she was living in an apartment," Bristol says faintly. "I thought..."

"Exactly what you were supposed to think, Mrs. Houde. She didn't expect to go the way she did." His eyes are sad. "But she knew she was dying. She had been diagnosed with a somewhat advanced case of cirrhosis of the liver just after Mrs. Brogan passed away. She came in to see me not long after." He folds his hands together. "When you found out about your birth father, Ms. Brogan—"

Impatiently, I snap, "Evangeline. Christ, Eric, we've known each other for years. We were at the same college at the same time."

A smile briefly touches his lips. "I remember. If I get caught calling you that by my colleagues..."

"Then I'll handle it. I can't handle the 'Ms.' and 'Mrs.' formality crap right now. What did Veronica actually say?" My heart is thumping harder than any dance routine Veronica put it through.

"That you were rightfully angry with her. If she could have made better decisions, she would have. She should have listened to her angel that she was blessed with instead of the devil that ended up killing her. But maybe you could rewrite history in her honor."

I shove to my feet even as the first tear falls down my face.

"I have another letter for you to read, this one much lengthier than the one I gave to you the other day." Eric's voice holds great sorrow. "She explains her behavior in the last few months in great detail. She was trying to make this easier for you, Evangeline. She knew your feelings would be conflicted between getting to know your father and her...well, she liked to call it her transition."

"It wasn't her right," Bristol interjects quietly. I nod. That's all I can manage.

"Maybe not, but it was her decision." I close my eyes in pain because he's just communicating Veronica's wishes. She couldn't save herself, so in the end, she tried to save me.

In less than a year, I've watched people I love drown their demons and grief, and others pay the sins for doing so. And in the end, I'm left doing what I was doing exactly what I was doing at the beginning of it: searching for answers to questions I may never be able to solve. But there's one thing I can do. Tuning back into the conversation, I hear Eric say to Simon and Bristol "...took it upon myself to research some charities who would benefit from a donation of this sort."

"No." The word flies out of my mouth. "It's not enough. Not anymore. It doesn't honor her enough. Not Mom, not Veronica." *And not Monty*, I think silently.

"What are you thinking, Linnie?" Bristol crosses over to me. She reaches for my hand and grips it.

I grapple with putting what I'm thinking in perspective. "They needed help. Who was there for them? Your dad was there for Mom, but who was there for Veronica to stop her from going down this path?"

Bristol looks thoughtful. "Are you thinking about setting up a clinic? Therapy?"

I shake my head. "Not just therapy." Frustrated, I begin to pace back and forth. "Where were her mentors—not just Mom? Where was the support to guide her? It can't be just the two of them. Surely, this is happening more frequently than this."

"What do you want to do, ask everyone we know?" Simon jests, but I'm not in the mood.

"Yes! Why wouldn't we? These are our friends, our colleagues, who won't talk if we don't ask." I'm shouting, and I don't care.

Simon frowns at me thoughtfully. "What you're suggesting is going to be next to impossible."

"Then let's make it possible!" I cry out. "Because I can't go to sleep one more night knowing there's someone else out there we might have been able to help in our extended family, Simon. Can you?"

Slowly, he shakes his head back and forth. "No, I can't. Not anymore." Turning to Eric, he asks, "What do we need to do?"

Eric doesn't answer. Instead, he picks up his phone and punches a number. "Mr. Dalton? Yes, can you come downstairs please, sir? Ms. Brogan, Mr. and Mrs. Houde are in my office. We're going to need your assistance." He pauses briefly. "Thank you." Hanging up, he warns, "This isn't the kind of law Watson, Rubenstein, and Dalton does, Evangeline."

"Then tell us who we need to hire. We're doing this, Eric," Bristol warns him. Simon slips an arm around my sister and squeezes.

Tossing my hair over my shoulder, I stalk up to his desk and slap my hands down on it. "We're not just doing this; we're going to wake up the world by doing so."

"We're going to make history, Linnie," Simon says quietly. My head turns to face him just as Eric's boss walks in the room.

"No, they are. We're just their voice to do it."

SEVENTY-NINE

MONTAGUE

I'm determined to do the right thing even if that means ignoring the incredible overture made by the one person I want in my life more than any other in this world or the next.

My love for her hasn't abated; if anything, it's become stronger in the time I've spent away. And yes, in the darkness of the night I dream of her. If it weren't for Linnie, I wouldn't be standing here at a window admiring the view of the mountains.

I'd be in a cell.

But I'm ashamed of the man I was: the man who hurt her.

The man I've become is afraid to approach the woman I'll love for eternity. Because how do I begin to ask for forgiveness for the secrets, the lies? Even if the only person who should have been hurt was me? Even though I never meant harm to come to anyone else?

I can't because words won't heal what I carelessly shattered in the blackness of night.

She'll always be everything to me, and that's not enough.

And she survived loving me.

I want her to be happy. So, I pray for her happiness every time I see a star, all the stars.

Even the sun.

A FEW DAYS LATER, I'm packing to leave the facility when there's a knock at my door. Victor walks in with a manila envelope. "Are you sure this is what you want?"

I nod. In the last few months, I've embraced the urgency of having facilities of this nature, doctors of Victor's importance. "Who knows if it will work out?" I shrug.

"Well, if it doesn't, it's not because of what's in there." He hands me the envelope. "You're well prepared for what's outside these walls, Monty."

"Because of your help." Switching the envelope to my left hand, I hold out my right to shake his.

"Because of your determination to get well. You're an alcoholic, and you know what to do to counteract the triggers," Victor counters.

Catching sight of my Mom and Dad climbing out of Dad's SUV, I swallow hard. "Maybe."

"I have no doubts. I'm so certain, this came in the mail for you, and I think you should go." He reaches in his pocket for another envelope. After he hands it to me, I can see it's in Linnie's perfect penmanship.

Carefully pulling out the letter, I unfold it. "I'd like for you to join us," I read aloud. Flipping the message over and finding nothing else in the envelope, I scowl. "What's missing?"

Victor reaches back into his breast pocket for a ticket. Holding it up between two fingers, he hands it to me. "This."

And in my hand I read, *Broadway Against Drugs and Substance on Stage - A charity event benefit those who fought alone but whom we will fight for going forward — hosted by Evangeline Brogan and Simon Houde.*

It's dated for three days from now.

"Do you think I have a right to interfere with her life again?" I ask the man who brought me back from hell to the land of the living.

"I think you owe it to yourself to see her again if for no other reason than to close the chapter on your life." Making his way to the door, he spots *Forgiveness* wrapped up, ready to be transported to the farm. "If that's what you both choose."

No, I think as Victor leaves, I'd choose to live forever in a world that would allow me to orbit her in it in some way. The question is—I smile at my parents as they walk into my room—did this much time and distance between us with my ignoring her overtures cause her to wish I did?

EIGHTY

MONTAGUE

I nstead of a Playbill's usually vibrant appearance, the program is dark and somber much like my mood. I flip through it absent-mindedly, passing over the enormous sponsor list until I see her official headshot and bio. And other than it being a glammed-up image of the woman haunting my dreams the last six months, her official bio gives me no indication about where her mind is at.

My hand slips into the pocket of my jacket so I can pull out my cell to scroll through the photos reminding me our time together wasn't something I dreamed up when my fingers brush the encouragement coin in my pocket—the coin celebrating my sobriety.

I did it for the right reason: me. I'll earn the next one for the same reason. It isn't because of Linnie or my family I stayed in rehab; it's because after I got through detox, I hated the man facing me in the window's reflection. It wasn't just the destruction I caused to those around me, but the harm I was causing to myself that helped me scale the mountain to get to the other side. Don't get me wrong; I can still scent out a good brandy or whiskey at thirty paces. But the pain I was causing to myself and those I loved was a motivator to shove away the crutch the alcohol was giving me. But while I've tried to explain that in letter after letter to Linnie, I've never been able to send them. I truly meant to let her go, even though she gave me *Forgiveness*. That was, until the ticket arrived for tonight's event.

The lights overhead begin flicking on and off. "Distinguished guests, please take your seats. The show is about to start. As you are aware, this is a live broadcast. You have consented to be videotaped. In the event you need to leave your seat, we kindly ask you to wait until in between acts. A seat filler will take your place if your ticket has been marked with a special indicator." Reaching into my pocket, it's stamped with the words "SEAT FILLER REQUIRED."

The lights begin to dim. The theater goes black except for two spotlights aimed at either wing. I don't know where to look. My head is flying back and forth like it would at a tennis match. Nerves mix with excitement in my veins.

And then there she is.

She steps out in a similar outfit to the one she wore the first time she met her father. It has a little more pizzazz: the jacket and pants sparkle with a million lights, and the shoes are barely more than diamond straps, but it's Linnie. God, I'm so close to her. I want to race up onto the stage and scoop her into my arms. But more than the orchestra and stage lights that separate us, my behavior is the reason I haven't been with her every step of the way. My eyes close in pain as Linnie and Simon, now center stage, try to get everyone to take their seats. When they manage it, her voice rings out clear. "Welcome, everyone, to the first—"

"But sadly not the last." Simon slips an arm around her.

Her arm goes around him as naturally as if it was made to. "Tragic but true. It's unlikely the last event where Broadway comes together to present one show in support of our community. We have a problem."

Thunderous applause greets her words. When it begins to die down, she continues. "For those of you who may not recognize us without our costume du jour, my name is Evangeline Brogan. And I am a BADASS."

"I'm Simon Houde. I, too, am a BADASS. For those of you not aware, Linnie and I costarred together in the Broadway award-winning show *Miss Me*. And tonight, we are missing our colleagues and our friends who are not standing beside us."

"Across every Broadway show tonight, we've dimmed our lights because we lost not one, but two, of our own. We lost them as a direct result of drug and alcohol abuse. Over the years, there were attempts by many of us to put those individuals on a better path. Tragically, we failed. We're feeling that pain as individuals and as one community— one family. When their deaths occurred so close to one another, we were reminded this couldn't continue. We can't lose any more of our family this way. The brainchild for being a BADASS came shortly after the death of my godmother, celebrated choreographer, Veronica Solomone."

My lips part as Linnie's wounds begin to penetrate, but she forges on.

"As the cofounder of BADASS, or Broadway Against Drugs and Alcohol and Substances on Stage, and one of your hosts for tonight, it's my responsibility to help you understand the truth. We all often feel alone, vulnerable, and even isolated from the world around us. People feel stress, highs and lows. They consume the parts they are acting, shows being worked on, the life they are living. But when the low hits—and sometimes they hit hard—people are turning to the cushion of drugs and alcohol to stop the pain instead of more constructive outlets."

Simon takes over. "Tonight's benefit will not only help the families of those whose lights have gone out, but we'll help offer counseling for grief, dependency and depression free of charge." The audience breaks out in tremendous applause. They wait for it to die down before it continues.

"We call patrons of the arts our angels, but I have an actual angel looking down over me. She taught me to give back, to see beyond the stage lights. And she was a recovering alcoholic who was sober for more than thirty years. My mother, Brielle Brogan's, heart gave out last year. She abused alcohol in her early years to such a degree when it unknowingly damaged her heart. She was one of the lights I lost too soon. Way too soon." Linnie tips her head back and swallows. "I'd like to think she'd be proud of us becoming BADASSes," Linnie flashes a smile up at Simon, who has curled her into his side.

"I know she would." Directing his comments to the audience of thousands at Lincoln Center, Simon says, "You all donated handsomely to attend tonight. You are our angels funding something much greater than a single show. It is our promise to you that you'll receive a performance straight from our hearts—a show you will never forget."

"A show that will mix who we are with what we do," Linnie adds.

"If the spirit moves you, stand right up and sing along with us, but please keep the aisles clear for our amazing camera crews who are streaming this live," Simon warns.

"And to our audience who is watching from the comfort of your homes, there are not enough words to say thank you and bless you. This type of tragedy hits all of our communities. The fact you'd take your time to grieve and celebrate with us is something we'll never forget." Linnie blows a kiss to the nearest camera tracking her movements.

"We'll be back later. We promise." Simon bows. "But for now, please welcome to the stage members of the cast of *Miss Me* singing Delta Rae's 'Morning Comes.'" Linnie and Simon saunter offstage as the curtain opens to a dimly lit stage. The chords of the guitar strumming are soothing.

And then I listen to the words—really listen. The lyrics seem to have been ripped from my soul, tortured yearning overplayed with overripe jealousy. It's a song about someone who's been knocked down, but unlike the misery I buried myself in each time I chose to let the alcohol pass through my lips, they picked themselves up from their knees because a new day would come.

How often, I wonder, before that night when I blacked out and spewed such hate at the woman I love did Linnie wonder if I was going to fall? And was she prepared to catch me if I did? Almost as much as detox was, the thought is sobering. Settling back, I wait for the quartet to finish before leaping to my feet like the rest of patrons at the Koch Theater at Lincoln Center.

Simon strolls back out onstage. "Wasn't that brilliant? Now let's keep that energy going for the cast of *Book of Mormon*, who are a bunch of BADASSes themselves in this number for their Tony Award–winning show." Applause greets his departure.

I settle into my seat to enjoy the phenomenal efforts on stage to see Broadway unite as one. And to bide my time until I can brush my fingers against Linnie's face again.

If she'll let me.

I thought seeing Linnie come on and off the stage as emcee was enough until I could reach out and lay my hand to her gently at the reception to help repair the physical pain I caused. That was until the curtains parted without a word and she stood there in a short dress that glittered the second the lights hit it. Her long dark hair cascades around her shoulders in waves, begging me to slide it to the side and make her gasp as I feast on the delicate skin of her neck.

A lone guitar from the pit starts to play, and the blood rushes to my heart so fast, I fear I'm going to pass out.

Linnie begins to sing a rendition of Kelly Clarkson's "Sober" that shatters the last illusion I held I was going through my pain alone. Even though the song might give the impression it's about an alcoholic, it's not. It's about addiction in all its forms—including love. Linnie's voice sings about keeping her flowers as she rids herself of the destructive weeds, and I realize it's my choice to be one or the other for her. I can choose to have a drink, and she'll always love me, but she'll remove my toxicity from her life. Or I can stay firmly rooted in the steps I've taken to fix myself, and maybe we can see if what we had will take root.

Her voice soars to the heavens as she sings about how much harder it is now. *I agree, my love. It is harder now. I don't have a crutch anymore. I'm just this broken man who's crawling after a dream. And the only hope I have it's enough is the fact you sent me this ticket.*

Linnie's not done singing, but I don't think twice. I stand. I want her to know I'm waiting for her. Always.

When she turns from the other side of the stage, only someone who knows her every facial tick would catch her falter. But she makes her way over. Standing almost directly in front of me, she finishes singing the last few lines of the song, adapting them to her magnificent voice.

And soon, I'm not the only one standing.

But it's my eyes she holds while using her free hand to clasp her hand over her heart as she sings the last line of the song before she makes her way offstage to a standing ovation.

I know I'm clapping louder than anyone else there.

EIGHTY-ONE
MONTAGUE

Other than the time necessary for the network commercial breaks, the show hasn't stopped for hours. Either Linnie or Simon has come out to introduce every act, explaining how their lives have been impacted by drug or alcohol abuse.

Unfortunately, I'm less shocked than some of the other tuxedo-clad people sitting around me when Simon comes on stage to declare, "Tonight we entertained you because of the effects of how drugs and alcohol have affected Broadway and musical theater. But right now, I want to give you some statistics that affect everyone watching. According to the National Survey on Drug Use and Health performed in 2017, 19.7 million American adults—where an adult is considered twelve or older—are battling a substance abuse disorder." The room gets eerily silent.

"Seventy-four percent of adults suffering from a substance use disorder in 2017 also struggled with an alcohol use disorder. That same year, one out of every eight adults battled both a drug and alcohol disorder. 8.5 million Americans suffer from a mental health disorder and a substance abuse disorder concurrently." He takes a deep breath to keep going.

"The NSDUH also tells us the following: drug abuse and addiction cost Americans $740 billion annually in lost workplace activity, crime-related costs, and healthcare expenses. What if we can stop some of that now? By reaching out a hand to people who need some help?"

Linnie steps onto the stage. "Addiction isn't always something someone can control. I knew from an early age I'd have to be concerned. Addiction in all its forms is genetic; it accounts for 40 to 60 percent of the people at risk."

Simon says grimly, "Teenagers and people with mental health issues are more at risk for drug, alcohol, and other addictions than any other population in the nation. This includes our military veterans."

"And finally, emotional factors contribute to a risk of addiction. It starts with a tone from the top. This is where our children learn. When my mother put her sobriety ahead of anything, it's where I learned. I'm just grateful my sister never had to experience the same thing." Linnie's eyes drift out across the audience before they settle. I can only assume Bristol's here.

"At the end of tonight's broadcast, there will be information about how to get help. Please, if you or someone you love needs help, call those numbers. There are people who are in your area who care as much as we do." Simon's voice is heartfelt.

"And if it's you—if anything we've said or sung has got through—reach out. No one is going to turn away your hand."

"Linnie and I have one last number to sing tonight. We've asked the entire cast to join us. And we're going to ask some of you to join us up on stage. Take a look around." I and everyone on the floor of the theater turn around. Holy crap. The aisles have been cleared. Focusing forward, I see the orchestra drop and a stage move into place. Simon and Linnie clasp hands. "We're going to pull some of the people we love up on stage. These are people who helped bring this event together for us in our hearts. We're also going to ask you all to get on your feet." There's a muted roar of excitement as thousands of people start to get to their feet, myself included.

After the noise finishes, a lone banjo starts to play. Simon begins clapping and steps back. "Sing it, babe."

Linnie smiles before her lips begin to sing about being hurt, forgiveness, and hearts breaking free. She reaches the refrain where the two of them harmonize as they clasp their hands together and walk out to the new edge of the stage. Simon kisses her hand before he goes down a small set of stairs to walk over to Bristol. Grabbing her hand, he keeps singing with Linnie.

She's smiling and dancing around the stage for the people in the rafters until Simon's back on the stage before she starts her descent. It must be a dream when I feel her hand touch mine. "What?"

Pulling her mic away, she whispers, "Take my hand, Monty."

And as I touch her for the first time in six months, trying not to crush her delicate fingers in my larger ones, I follow blindly up the aisle while she sings with Simon. I can't see shit between the lights and my tears, so I stumble on the first step. Her head whips around in concern. I swipe at the wetness and shake my head. Her smile, dynamic before, trembles.

I don't know what to do other than absorb the moment in my soul. It's just Linnie and Simon facing each other harmonizing as if in a singing challenge. Then from behind me comes a voice—a gospel queen—singing on top of them. And someone else adds their voice. A four-part harmony that sends shivers through me to let me know I'm alive and blessed to be.

All because one woman stood by me.

The song ends. The applause rolls like thunder over the crowd. Even with their mics turned up, Linnie and Simon have to yell to be heard by the audience. The curtain closes for a brief minute, muffling the sound. But before I can say a word, it opens again. Simon yanks Linnie toward him to crush her close. I wait, uncertain of what I'm supposed to do.

After all, I'll stand by her through anything the way she stood by me.

"We're going to have to give them an encore," Simon yells to the entire crowd. There's a war whoop behind me.

Linnie nods excitedly. Her hair bounces around the gold dress she's been wearing since her solo number. "You guys ready?" she shouts.

The roar from the cast is her response. Giving a thumbs-up to someone to the side of the stage, she moves back into my space. Even though I've seen her eyes in Ev's face, I've missed them. *The happiness in them right now is the look I want to see in them when I take my last breath*, I decide. "This could take a while," she apologizes with a crooked twist of her lips.

"I'm here for as long as you want me by your side," I tell her honestly.

Something flashes behind her eyes. She holds out her hand. This time, I take it with no hesitation. Her fingers give mine a quick squeeze as the banjo starts up again. Linnie starts to sing. Simon joins her as they're both exposed to the audience. The spotlight smacks us all in the face as the curtain opens, and we quickly become blinded. She squeezes and tugs my hand. I move forward right beside her.

I don't care if anyone can see tears on my face more clearly.

They're a gift.

Just like the woman holding my hand singing.

AFTER WHAT SEEMS LIKE FOREVER, the curtain closes. I'm separated from Linnie as person after person sucks her into the vortex of the night's success. I panic a little when I lose track of her when suddenly she's hoisted high in the air by a strong set of arms. "She did it! She pulled it off! Let's hear it for our Linnie!"

Wolf whistles and cheers ratchet up a notch. Even as she blushes, her eyes are searching over the heads until they lock onto mine. Her face softens. Other than the few words, we haven't spoken. But something inside me relaxes when I see the look on her face.

That is until a hand clamps down on my shoulder. "Linnie looks beautiful, doesn't she?" Simon comes up behind me.

I nod. "And happy."

"You have no idea how long it's taken to get that way." His hand clenches harder. "Why don't we wait for her in my dressing room?" he offers. It's not a suggestion.

My heart thumps madly. It's my first test. "Have the fixings for a Shirley Temple in there?" I ask quietly. "It's my newest drink of choice."

The hand loosens a bit. A ghost of a smile flicks on his lips. "An homage?"

I shake my head. "Maybe at the beginning? Then I found when I drank regular soda I was searching for something else to be hidden in it. This way, I can see, smell, and taste exactly what I'm supposed to have."

"Which is?"

My eyes find Linnie through the multitude of people who are passing her around. "A chance. I don't deserve anything more than that, and I'll have to earn it every single day."

His hand, instead of clamping down again, relaxes completely. "Let's get you out of this chaos. I'll leave word for Linnie to meet all of us down in my dressing room."

Confused, I let Simon guide me out of the madness. "What did I say?"

"Something she's been telling me for a while. I guess I just needed to hear it from you."

Simon's greeted and congratulated the entire way to the space that's designated with a signed held up by duct tape as "Houde/Brogan." "Come on in." He opens the door.

I step across the threshold, and Bristol Houde is cradling a sleeping dark-haired baby to her chest. "Shh, Simon. I just got him down." She doesn't even look up.

"My love, we have company," Simon murmurs. Bristol's head snaps up. Her eyes dart to her husband before her face relaxes.

"Montague Parrish." Her voice sounds so much like Linnie's it's almost painful to hear the coolness I expected from one woman directed at me from the other.

"Bristol." I keep my distance from the small family.

After a few whispered words that I can't make out, Bristol's smile warms. "I saw you up on stage, Monty. How did that make you feel?"

"Petrified," I admit. Bristol laughs softly. Simon guffaws. As a result, their son jolts awake.

"Well then, since you're here, you can put him down again. The nanny's tried twice," Bristol says with a touch of bitterness to her husband.

"Because singing this little man to sleep is such a problem." Simon reaches over and takes the baby from his wife. She touches her free fingers to her lips.

"It is when you can't sing your way out of a bad karaoke bar. Did Linnie ever share that's one of the things they tested on our DNA tests?" Bristol's whiplash change of subject makes my head spin. "That and they check to see if we'll flush if we drink alcohol. Do you know if you do?"

Ah. Now I get it. "I think I learned to tolerate so much of it that I might have broken the test."

"And now?" She crosses her arms akimbo.

"I suspect the results would be more accurate, but I don't plan on finding out the traditional way. Maybe I'll take the test for my year sobriety."

Her lips curve. "I think that's a great idea."

A nervous laugh escapes me just as the door flies open, almost catching me in the back. And there she is, triumphant from the night of success. Her eyes are just as I remember them before I let the alcohol take my hand instead of the woman I love.

She's the only star I've ever genuinely wished upon. And now that alcohol isn't causing a haze over my memory, she's brighter than I remember, more vivid. What else was dulled about our relationship due to the bottle? And will I get a chance to find out?

Linnie breezes by me to be enveloped in Bristol's arms. Simon beams at both of them but doesn't stop crooning to the baby in his arms.

"I am so proud of you." Bristol buries her head against Linnie's shoulder.

"I sure as hell didn't do this alone," Linnie says.

"No, but it was your idea to do something more. It didn't have to be this," Bristol counters. "You took a stand. You believed. You opened your heart. You always do." Her eyes drift over her sister's shoulder to me. "And it looks like it might have paid off."

"Your instincts were right on." Simon's sitting; his hand gently rubbing his son's head as he cradles him. "If we can help prevent one more family from being hurt the way ours was..."

"Then it was worth it," Linnie concludes as she pulls away from her sister. Slowly, she turns. I hold my breath as she walks toward me and holds out her hand just like she did when she was singing. Like I'm in a trance, I lift mine toward hers. "How many days has it been since you've last had a drink?" she calmly asks me as our fingers touch. That spark, the one that pulled us together from the very first moment, ignites.

"One hundred eighty-three days, twelve hours, and—" I look away to check my watch. "—sixteen minutes. But that's just from the time I woke up in the hospital. I don't count the time I was blacked out before that. That's how long it's been since I woke up and realized my life was over."

"That's not when your life was over, Monty. That's when your life started again."

Shuddering, my voice cracks when I get out, "You're right."

"Are you planning on drinking tomorrow?" No quarter given, but I don't deserve any after what she's been through.

I shake my head. "No. Nor the day after that." I'm firm in my declaration.

"Then let's celebrate tonight, and we'll just...see." As she turns to talk with her sister and brother-in-law again, I know I didn't imagine the way her pulse fluttered in her neck.

Maybe it's just left overexcitement from tonight.

Or maybe I'm being granted one final wish upon a star.

EIGHTY-TWO

MONTAGUE

It's hours later. I've been on the outskirts watching Linnie celebrate with the rest of the cast. Euphoria and exhaustion are warring for equal time on her beautiful face. Tonight wasn't just about putting on a charity show; it was about exposing her soul for the world to see. She's pushed herself beyond her limits and can't say no. She's thinner than she was, more drawn. She's lost a part of herself and hasn't had a chance to recharge to be who needs to be.

It's my turn to try to be a hero if only for a little while.

Stepping up behind her, I gently lay my hand at the small of her back. She jumps but not noticeably. "Didn't you mention something about Simon and Bristol's?" I say, being deliberately vague.

The look she shoots me is laced with gratitude. "Yes. I'm sorry, everyone, but I have to go. We're late."

There's a flurry of well wishes before I'm able to guide her down a crowded hallway back to the dressing room we were in hours before. Once we're inside, her head bows. Her hair cascades forward, exposing the smooth nape of her neck. I swallow hard. "What do you want to do?" I ask quietly.

"I just want to go home."

"Do you want me to call you a car?" It's the last thing I want to do, but I can see the trembling exhaustion beginning to set in.

"No." I remain silent by the door, uncertain whether I should stay or go until she takes the decision out of my hands. "Will you walk me back? I'd like to talk."

"Of course. I'll step outside." I fumble for the knob behind me.

"Thank you. I'll be just a moment." She comes closer until mere inches separate us. And then she quietly closes the door in my face.

I fear that's only the beginning of what's going to happen on the way back to her condo.

SHE'S CHANGED into an oversized cardigan, leggings, and ballet flats. After the heels she's been wearing all night, I imagine they feel like heaven on her feet. She's struggling to shrug on a long black coat while holding on to an enormous purse. "Let me," I offer quietly.

She stills before turning her back to me. I hold the collar of the coat while she slips in one arm and then another. "Would you mind holding this?" She hands me the oversized leather bag.

I take it and it almost pulls my wrist to the floor. "Jesus, what do you have in here? Anvils?"

Linnie's lips tip up, revealing a flash of her dimples. "Shoes, makeup, you know—all the things I don't want to leave here overnight."

"How about I carry this while you navigate?"

"It's not that heavy," she protests. I take a chance and lay my hand on her shoulder. Even through layers of coats and clothes, I feel her stiffen.

"You're running on empty, Linnie. I can help with this." I hold her gaze for a moment before she acquiesces.

"Okay." Taking a deep breath, she nods toward the right. "Let's head out the back. If we try to go the way we came, we'll be here till dawn."

"Whatever you say." We begin walking. After a few more well wishes, we're left alone on a dimly lit staircase heading down a flight. To break the awkward silence hovering between us, I tell her, "I'm sorry to hear about your godmother."

She pauses on the stairs. Then she begins running. It takes everything in me not to slip and fall while I'm in dress shoes as I chase after her. "Linnie, wait!" I call out.

Through the dimness, there's a glimpse of light as I hear Linnie slam the door open with all her might. She rushes through it. I'm seconds behind her. New York glory is lighting the street behind us for what's going to be our confrontation. I can feel it.

Slowly, I let her bag slide from my shoulder down my arm until it lands at my feet while I wait for her to speak.

I don't have long.

"I thought I could do this." Tears are beginning to form in her gem-colored eyes. "But it's eating me up inside. I needed to know there was hope, but I didn't even have that. You threw me—us—away and yet you're here. Don't get me wrong, I'm thrilled you're on a good path, but why? Why are you here after all this time? I was waiting for you to reach out to me the way you did Dad and Char, and you let me go!"

"Then why did you invite me to come?" I ask her quietly.

"To show you I did as you asked. I moved on." I want to wrap my arms around her, but I have no right. "Then you stood during 'Sober,' and there was no way for me to ignore you. Damn you, Monty!" she hurls at me.

Yes, damn me. Damn me to hell and back for sentencing the woman I love to live the same hell I was right alongside me. I can't change what was, what happened. I can only admit I was wrong.

"I deserve to know why." Standing tall and proud, she faces me. "I understood your problem. I fought to get you help. And still..."

My heart clenches thinking about how different my life could have been if it hadn't been for her strength and will.

Both of which the world saw tonight.

"I'm sorry, Linnie. There isn't a thing I can say to make the thoughts in your head easier." I close my eyes and take a deep breath. "If there's a slim chance you're able to forgive me, please understand this. I was afraid I wasn't going to be able to make it. At the time I wrote that letter, I was terrified I wasn't going to be able to recover."

"Monty." She steps forward and lays her delicate hand against my chest. I want to shake it off as penance, but I can't. I'm not that noble.

"I was trying to protect you the only way I knew how. There's no way to rehearse for life, Linnie. The things I was discovering inside about myself made me feel like less of a man. How could that person be enough to support all the beautiful things you need, including the strength that lives inside you? I was supposed to be the hero, and here you were saving me. What do you call that?"

"Love," she says bluntly. Her nails dig in slightly against the dress shirt I'm wearing. If she could draw my blood, I think she would.

I know I'd let her.

"Some days, I thought I'd die without seeing your face. When it was time for me to leave, I was so scared." A garbage truck rolls by, its noxious fumes permeating the air. Part of me can't believe we're having this conversation in the middle of a New York city street, but at least we're having it, which is more than I ever hoped for.

"Why?"

"Because a few days before the first time Mom and Dad were due to pick me up, a man was brought into the center who still reeked of alcohol. I could almost taste it on him. I felt like a damn vampire. I turned to my therapist and asked if I could stay longer. He said he had high hopes for me if I recognized I still wasn't ready."

Linnie's face softens. "You're calling him Dad?"

My brow puckers. "He didn't tell you?" She shakes her head. "Is...is it a problem?" I ask cautiously.

"I think it's about damn time." We share a mutual smile before hers fades.

"There were days where I felt like I was suffocating. There were days when I felt like my life was falling apart. And days where every muscle and cavity ached. And that was just detox. But two things were scarier."

"What's that?" Her thumb is moving back and forth across my chest.

"Fear of having come so far and failing."

"Then you find a way to try again," she tells me firmly. There's the Linnie I know and love. An eternal optimist. I reach up and capture her hand against my chest. "Then there's the second."

Her breathing spikes as her eyes meet mine.

"What I did to myself I found a way to forgive with your help. But I don't know how to ask you to forgive me," I manage to croak out. "What happened could have..."

"Yes. It could. But we have time for you to figure out what you want to say to me, don't we?" God, I could spend my life kneeling at her feet and never humble myself enough to be worthy of what she's offering. Her face isn't bitter, though it has a right to be. It isn't loving, like I'd die for it to be.

It's understanding. It's more than I expected and more than I deserve.

I can work with that.

I almost ruined it all. Not just the us that we were, but the individuals we are. All because I wouldn't admit I couldn't carry the burdens I was shouldering alone. Fortunately, somewhere along the way, the wishes I made on the stars were answered. I was sent miracles. Science took care of my Dad; it took something a hell of a lot stronger to cure me.

Faith.

Slowly, carefully, I lift my hand to her cheek. Perhaps the shaft of pain I'll feel when I do will be my final penance before my reward— her love entrusted back into my care.

"So, I thought I'd visit the city for a while. Maybe get to see the city from a whole new perspective. Any suggestions on where I should go first?"

Her eyes are full of wary curiosity under the streetlamp. "How long do you plan on staying?"

My fingers dance along her cheek. It's oddly personal not to have kissed her. I want her to know down to the marrow she gave so freely that once my lips land on hers that there's no chance alcohol will ever pass through them again. "Until I can convince a close match to become a perfect one," I say gruffly.

She averts her eyes. "I can't make any promises."

"I don't expect you to," I admit painfully, albeit truthfully.

She backs away. My heart aches at the loss of contact, at the remembered feel of her lips on mine. Something I have no right to mourn, but I do. "No more lies, Linnie. I promise."

"We can't start again," she whispers, and my heart stops dead in my chest. At that moment, I know what Tim McCann felt like when he pulled the trigger.

Desperate.

Agonized.

Hopeless.

But I keep listening. I owe her the right to say and do what she wants. Even if it's walking away. So, I nod. My eyes drift shut.

"All I can do is take each moment with you one step at a time." I feel my heart start to beat again in my chest. "If you can't handle that, then walk away now, Monty. We'll have each other through our family, and well, that will have to be enough."

Some might push harder for a more definitive resolution. Me? I had only just over six months—none of it spent with her, although a great deal of it was spent thinking about her—to back my case.

"I'm not going anywhere." And slowly, oh so slowly, I'm blessed by her smile which has both dimples popping out. This isn't her performance smile; it's the one she deserves for those closest to her heart.

"Then how about we meet at Wolf's Deli for lunch?" she recommends shyly. "I'll show you where to get the best pastrami sandwiches in New York."

"That sounds..." Like more than I deserve. "Perfect."

"I'll see you there at noon tomorrow?" Quickly, Linnie texts my phone with the address. It's the first message she's sent me since before the accident.

"I'll meet you there." Reaching up, I brush a lock of hair off her face the wind blew in. "You must be exhausted."

"That doesn't begin to cover it."

"Then let's get you home."

"It's two blocks this way." She points her arm out, and we begin walking in companionable silence.

As we approach her entrance, her doorman leaps up to open the door. "Thank you." Turning her head over her shoulder, she calls out, "Until tomorrow?"

"I'll be counting the hours." I assure her of nothing more than the truth.

She starts to walk through the door, but then she hesitates. I'm stock-still, my heart pounding in my chest as her head drops forward. Turning, she faces me. "To hell with it." Dropping a bag heavy enough to take out a mugger on her doorman's foot, she runs at me. I brace for impact.

One arm wraps around my neck. The other cups my chin. "I want to taste you with nothing between us but air." Tugging at my cheek, her lips meet mine.

The kiss isn't long, but my head spins over it. My arms band around her waist to hold her in place as she drinks from my lips, knowing all she'll taste is me and my love for her.

Slowly, I let her go. She steps back and puts her fingers over her smiling lips. "So, that's what hope tastes like," she murmurs. "Thanks for walking me home."

"Night, Linnie." My voice sounds rough even to my own ears.

"Night, Monty." As she races past her doorman, she scoops up her bag and offers a quick apology. He shakes his head but smiles. Though it's me he outright laughs at when she disappears from my sight, and I jump up and pump my fist in the air.

I haven't won the war for her heart; I haven't even won a battle.

But I'm in the fight.

As long as there's breath in my body, I'll keep fighting for another chance at my heart's perfect match.

EPILOGUE

MONTAGUE - FOUR YEARS LATER

"Jesus, you mean to tell me they can't manage to figure out a better way to do this than spitting? I've been at this for ten minutes!" I yell as I try to come up with enough saliva to fill a small plastic test tube.

"Keep at it, Parrish! I had to do it times two," Linnie calls back, absolutely no sympathy in her voice. She says something I can't quite understand before her laughter rings out in the penthouse. "No, Bris. I don't have the same cravings you do. Fortunately for Monty, all I want is lo mein, and that's easily delivered." There's another pause before Linnie yells, "Simon said to tell you that you suck, my love."

"Tell him it's not my fault his woman has a sweet tooth." Then, knowing it will just aggravate him, I yell back, "It's likely all the cilantro. Poor kid needs something to counterbalance that garbage." Then I spit again.

Linnie's laughter can be heard from the other room where she's making plans with Bristol to go shopping for decorating our nursery. She has in mind a rainbow theme regardless if we have a boy or a girl.

I lied.

It wasn't until my fiancée walked into the room waving a stick telling me she was pregnant this week that I ended up doing my DNA test. It didn't matter if I ever found out whether I flushed when I drank alcohol since it's been almost four years and seven months since I've had a drink. I count the days not only because I've been sober that whole time, but because the orbit of my world righted itself.

Linnie doesn't hold me to my sobriety. It's my choice. Deciding every day to be sober is entirely on me just as it was on her mother and every other person who walks the same road we do. None of what happened was her fault, so why should my recovery be her responsibility? Because she loves me? That makes me damned lucky. What it doesn't do is make her a fucking martyr or a nursemaid.

That long-ago night of the first BADASS benefit, I was already texting my father—our father. My texts were so long, I switched to voice texts because my fingers couldn't keep up the pace. Giving up trying to walk and text at the same time, I stood on the corner of Fifth Avenue and just babbled into my phone for an hour. People must have thought I was crazy. I didn't care.

Maybe Van Gogh needed all the stars to dream, to hope, but I just needed one.

Linnie and I spent the next few days together exploring her New York. She showed me the city the tourists overlook: tiny neighborhoods, hidden markets, and above all, the best place to get a slice of pizza. "On your next trip, I'll show you more," she promised me. I grabbed at her words with one hand as the other was filled with the best pizza I've ever had. She laughed as I was already searching for flights on my phone before we left our cramped table at John's in the West Village.

I still recall the last time I kissed her for the first time. I hadn't instigated anything between us on any of my visits on her days off during *Stars*. But we had just come back from a long run through Central Park two months after the benefit. I almost tripped over my feet when I realized where I was.

"What's wrong? Are you okay?" She jogged back to where I was frozen in place.

"It was here where it all began." I reached out and tugged her into my arms. "I was standing right here the first time you ran by—when I felt what stardust felt like."

Linnie was a complete mess. Her hair was flying out of her long braid in every direction. And she'd never looked more beautiful when I cupped her chin and lowered my lips to hers, murmuring, "Nothing between us but air."

Long moments later, we were only broken apart when another runner bumped into us. Her eyes shining, she pulled back and touched her fingers to her lips. Trapping our taste against her lips, she whispered, "And that's what hope tastes like. It's perfect."

When we weren't together, we talked on the phone every day. Whether it was the big things or the little things, we just wanted a touchpoint with each other. At first, Linnie admitted, "I don't want you to think you can't talk to me about your day. You're not alone even if I'm not there."

The truth is, I wanted her to know she could lean on me as well. If we were going to work for the rest of our lives, then she needed to know I was here to shoulder her burdens and not fall apart the way I did before.

The last night Linnie morphed into Hera, we woke up in each other's arms. It coincided with my tenth month of sobriety. When we woke in each other's arms and celebrated, we closed that chapter of her life and focused on our future. One where I'd made a decision to move to New York full time.

My eyes drifting to where I can just see her curled up on the couch, I think about the quiet ceremony we have planned on the farm with Mom, Dad, Bristol, Simon, and Marco once this semester of school is done. We've been engaged for years, but Linnie isn't in any rush. "The right moment takes time. We have plenty of that." She's right.

Just like I knew it was the perfect time to slip the ruby on her finger on the anniversary of my sixteenth month of sobriety. When I did, I whispered, "Life has taken us on one hell of a road. But because of you, I got help. Because of me, I'll stay healthy. Because of us, we'll make sure we give our love the time and care it needs. Just like those trees on Skyline. For years they've stood there sprouting the red leaves the first time I kissed you. I can still see the way they illuminated your face when our lips met under the trees that were this color."

Her eyes, just as bright in our bed because of the tears overflowing them, blinked rapidly. "Yes."

"You have to let me ask the question first, my love."

"Then ask before I figure out a way to see if that ring fits you," she blubbered.

"Evangeline Katherine Brogan." She'd long since had Todd dropped from her name legally. "Will you do me the honor of becoming the other part of my heart for eternity?" I slipped the ring on the third finger of her left hand. "And becoming my wife?"

"I already gave you my answer." Then she drove her fingers in my hair and sealed our engagement with a kiss.

SALIVA'S DRYING UP in my mouth as I spit into the tube again. "What a way to celebrate our future child." I curse as spit lands on the lip of the not-so-very helpful mouthpiece and ends up on my hand. I try to scoop it up to throw it into the tube.

"Eww!" Linnie strolls into our kitchen. "You can't do that. You might skew the results!"

"Jesus, it's not like we're looking for any deep dark secrets with this, right?" I demand.

Linnie taps her long nails against her lips. "True, but we should know about any paternal DNA issues before this little one makes an appearance." She pats her still-flat stomach. We only found out this week she's pregnant, and I don't think I've had a full night sleep since.

On the other hand, my bride-to-be is calm about the whole thing. She wanted to wait until she's done with her current show before she announces her pregnancy, so we're waiting before her publicist makes the announcement. While her pregnancy was a complete surprise, the timing couldn't have been better for her professionally as there's nothing on the immediate horizon she wants to act in.

We've jetted between New York and Virginia for the last few years while Linnie continued to saunter up and down the Great White Way. As for me, I decided to go back to school while Linnie was working. It felt crazy, and frankly scary as hell, at my age to walk into a classroom. And I finally walked across a graduation stage where not only my parents but Linnie and her family could watch when I got my master's degree a few months ago. Seeing the look of pride on their faces made every hour of hard work worth it.

Linnie slides her arms around my waist. Her fingers trail over the waistband of my boxers, and saliva pools in my mouth. I quickly spit before I swallow it out of agony. "What are you doing?"

Pressing a kiss to my back, I can feel her lips in a smile. "Giving you the incentive to finish."

Yeah, that'll do it. I finish with the tube, cap it off, and put it back in the counter as Linnie's fingertips trail up the inside of my thighs. "Hmm. I think your next paper should be on Pavlovian responses. You seem to have the same reaction every time I do this." Her nails leave a trail of fire in their wake.

Spinning around, I catch her lips in a hard and fast kiss. "Think that would be more interesting than evaluating the progressiveness between PTSD and alcoholism?"

"Pretty certain you'd have a more captive audience." She cups my sac loosely.

"You seem to have a pretty good handle on that topic," I growl as I bend down to nibble at her neck. My hands slide beneath her rear. I give a tug, and she boosts herself up. Turning, I plant her on the counter so I have better leverage to kiss her senseless.

"I MUST BE insane for trying to do this at my age." I fling my laptop to the side. I don't give a shit if the thing breaks, as it bounces off the couch. Pulling off my reading glasses, I toss them onto the end table in frustration.

"Monty, you've come so far." Linnie plops down next to me with a pint of cookies and cream ice cream and two spoons. "This is just the first class in your PhD. Relax before you have a coronary."

"This teacher is insane. I swear Dr. Lee is going to cause me to violate HIPAA laws to record what he says. He talks as fast as you do pirouettes." I pinch my fingers in the corner of my eyes.

Linnie laughs ruefully. "That's not as fast as it used to be."

"I don't think I got even half of the notes down, and I know I was typing as fast as I can."

Spooning up a large bite of ice cream, she offers it to me. I sigh before taking the spoon. "You'll get it, Monty. I know you will. You're determined to work with those people," Linnie declares with pride.

Leaning down, I touch my forehead to hers. "I know. I was feeling sorry for myself."

She snorts. Grabbing my hand, she places it on her flat stomach. "Feel sorry for me. I'm the one who's going to be huge with your child while all the nubile Columbia undergrads drool over my smart, sexy man."

I roll my eyes.

"What you want to do, why you want to do it...I don't care if it takes you ten years, Monty."

"I do, babe." And that's the truth. When I realized I wanted to work at a rehabilitation center like the one that helped bring me back from the depths of an unceasing black hole to my life, I voraciously attacked classes. And during breaks, Linnie and I manage to make it down to the farm, though more often than not, it's Mom and Dad coming up to visit. After all, Columbia's Clinical Psychology program waits for no man. We'll be tied to New York for at least the next three years. I groan aloud when I realize I'll be forty-four at the earliest before I am truly able to help the people who, like me, need someone that can see beyond what they are doing to why they are doing it. Someone who isn't going to give up. Someone who maybe can help them find a path to sobriety.

"Dr. Parrish," she purrs. God, when she says it like that, my cock gets rock hard.

"Not helping," I grit out. There's no way I'm going to be able to prep for my clinical walk-through with Dr. Lee tomorrow if my fiancée keeps distracting me.

"Fine," she huffs, moving away. Damn, she took the ice cream with her. My lips set into a frown. Just as I'm about to reach for my laptop, I hear her whisper in a dreamy voice, "Dr. and Mrs. Parrish."

Done. I'm completely done. Hoping my brain remembers medical shorthand as well as it remembered military orders when I'd have no sleep, I dive for Linnie, tackling her against the soft cushions. Ripping the ice cream from her hand, I place it on the floor.

Her beautiful green eyes are sparkling up at me, innocently. "Was it something I said?"

"Yes."

"What was that?"

Leaning down so my nose touches hers, I whisper, "You said my life started again that night. You were right. But you were wrong. It started the day you decided to take a chance on meeting your close match."

Her lips graze mine when she reminds me, "And I not only found the other half of my blood, but I found the other half of my heart. Not bad for $195. Including New York sales tax, of course."

Even as my body shakes with laughter, my lips capture hers in a fierce kiss of agreement.

Einstein, when he was asked about God, said that he saw a

pattern but that he couldn't imagine what that pattern led to. Everything has a pattern. For both of us, what appeared to be chaos took both of our lives down the path toward a simple DNA test to find out answers.

Neither of us could have imagined how it would change our lives. In our case, for the better.

THE END

WHERE TO GET HELP

Every three minutes, someone is diagnosed with a blood cancer. Every hour, more than six people die from it. Seventy percent of patients do not have a fully matched donor in their family. People are in a race against time to find a genetic match through an unrelated donor or through cord blood.

I've stood by and helplessly watched, prayed, and collapsed in relief when a perfect match was found for someone I love. But a perfect match is a near improbability. Today, family genetics have beautiful twists in them, remarkable parents are adopting children, and when tragedy strikes those we love who might have been a match, we have to be able to turn somewhere for help.

Be the Match, operated by the National Marrow Donor Program, manages the largest and most diverse bone marrow registry in the world. It is a remarkable organization to look into supporting whether through a donation, a fundraiser, or by becoming a donor yourself.

Because sometimes, close is good enough. It can save a life.

ALSO BY TRACEY JERALD

Midas Series

Perfect Proposal

Perfect Assumption (Coming April 2021)

Perfect Composition (Coming Summer 2021)

Perfect Order (Coming Fall 2021)

Amaryllis Series

FREE - AN AMARYLLIS PREQUEL

(NEWSLETTER SUBSCRIBERS ONLY)

FREE TO DREAM

FREE TO RUN

FREE TO REJOICE

FREE TO BREATHE

FREE TO BELIEVE

FREE TO LIVE

FREE TO WISH: AN AMARYLLIS SERIES SHORT STORY - 1,001 DARK
NIGHTS SHORT STORY ANTHOLOGY WINNER

FREE TO DANCE (COMING SPRING 2021)

Glacier Adventure Series

RETURN BY AIR

RETURN BY LAND

RETURN BY SEA

Sandalones

Close Match

Ripple Effect

Lady Boss Press Releases

Challenged by You

ACKNOWLEDGEMENTS

First, last, always, and forever, to my husband, Nathan. You are the heart that beats within me. Thank you for loving me the way you do every single day.

To my son, who keeps growing taller and stronger. You don't know how proud you make me just by being you. I love you beyond infinity.

Mom, you are such an inspiration to me. If I can be as spectacular as you, then I've reached the best life goal. Keep dancing circles around everyone!

Jen, let me guess? You're reading the back first again, right? You know I'd fly anywhere to meet you. I love you, always.

Meows, gah! You were living inside my head during this book remembering our times together in NoVA? I love you all so much.

To Jennifer Wolfel, never be anyone different to me. XOXO.

To Sandra Depukat from One Love Editing. It is such a blessing to work with you; someone who is brilliant but is passionate about the story. I love you!

To Holly Malgeri. My twin, it is a blessing to have you in my life every day. To have you work on my books in an honor. Thank you for being a part of this crazy ride with me.

To my cover designer, Madhat Studios, I am blown away on how you managed to bring Linnie and Monty to life. Love you! Now, let's have some Girl Scout cookies!

To my team at Foreword PR, there is so much you do that people barely see. You deserve pages of accolades. Thank you for the big things, the little things, the everyday things, and the crazy things you handle for me.

Linda Russell, you are brilliance, a superstar, and a book boyfriend hoarder! You inspire so much from me, including your own mini-series when I send you emails. Yeah, you're just that amazing. All joking aside, this doesn't work without you in my life and my heart. I love you hard! Now, find me a plot of land.

For my Facebook group — Tracey's Tribe. I'm sending my love to you always. A special shout out to Susan Henn who had no idea that I was researching this book when she and I debated the merits of which DNA test I should take. Also, thank you to Dawn Hurst for so closely checking the "results" when she read for me.

To all of the bloggers who read and take the time to review my books, thank you from the bottom of my heart.

To my readers. Your words mean everything to me. Thank you for your support and for choosing to read my words.

And finally, to the incredible talent of Delta Rae and Rush. The heart and soul of these diverse musicians persistently inspire me through my own life's journey.

ABOUT THE AUTHOR

Tracey Jerald knew she was meant to be a writer when she would re-write the ending of books in her head when she was a young girl growing up in southern Connecticut. It wasn't long before she was typing alternate endings and extended epilogues "just for fun".

After college in Florida, where she obtained a degree in Criminal Justice, Tracey traded the world of law and order for IT. Her work for a world-wide internet startup transferred her to Northern Virginia where she met her husband in what many call their own happily ever after. They have one son.

When she's not busy with her family or writing, Tracey can be found in her home in north Florida drinking coffee, reading, training for a runDisney event, or feeding her addiction to HGTV.